D0016781

The Worlds of Clifford Simak

By Clifford Simak

SIMON AND SCHUSTER, NEW YORK

Published by Simon and Schuster, Inc.
Rockefeller Center, 630 Fifth Avenue
New York 20, N. Y.

Acknowledgment is hereby made to the following magazines in which these stories first appeared: GALAXY MAGAZINE—*Dusty Zebra, Honorable Opponent, Carbon Copy, Founding Father, Idiot's Crusade, Operation Stinky, Jackpot, Green Thumb, Lulu.* ASTOUNDING SCIENCE FICTION—*The Big Front Yard, Neighbor.* INFINITY SCIENCE FICTION—*Death Scene.*

MANUFACTURED IN THE UNITED STATES OF AMERICA

Contents

THE WORLDS OF CLIFFORD SIMAK

1. Dusty Zebra

IF YOU'RE HUMAN, you can't keep a thing around the house. You're always losing things and never finding them and you go charging through the place, yelling, cross-examining, blaming.

That's the way it is in all families.

Just one warning—don't try to figure out where all those things have gone or who might have taken them. If you have any notion of investigating, forget it. You'll be happier!

I'll tell you how it was with me.

I'd bought the sheet of stamps on my way home from the office so I could mail out the checks for the monthly bills. But I'd just sat down to write the checks when Marge and Lewis Shaw dropped over. I don't care much for Lewis and he barely tolerates me. But Marge and Helen are good friends, and they got to talking, and the Shaws stayed all evening.

Lewis told me about the work he was doing at his research laboratory out at the edge of town. I tried to switch him off to something else, but he kept right on. I suppose he's so interested in his work that he figures everyone else must be. But I don't know a thing about electronics and I can't tell a microgauge from a microscope.

It was a fairly dismal evening and the worst of it was that I couldn't say so. Helen would have jumped all over me for being antisocial.

So, the next evening after dinner, I went into the den to write the checks and, of course, the stamps were gone.

I had left the sheet on top of the desk and now the desk was bare except for one of the Bildo-Blocks that young Bill had outgrown several years before, but which still turn up every now and then in the most unlikely places.

I looked around the room. Just in case they might have blown off the desk, I got down on my hands and knees and searched under everything. There was no sign of the stamps.

I went into the living room, where Helen was curled up in a chair, watching television.

"I haven't seen them, Joe," she said. "They must be where you left them."

It was exactly the kind of answer I should have expected.

"Bill might know," I said.

"He's scarcely been in the house all day. When he does show up, you've got to speak to him."

"What's the matter now?"

"It's this trading business. He traded off that new belt we got him for a pair of spurs."

"I can't see anything wrong in that. When I was a kid . . ."

"It's not just the belt," she said. "He's traded everything. And the worst of it is that he always seems to get the best of it."

"The kid's smart."

"If you take that attitude, Joe . . ."

"It's not *my* attitude," I said. "It's the attitude of the whole business world. When Bill grows up . . ."

"When he grows up, he'll be in prison. Why, the way he trades, you'd swear he was training to be a con man!"

"All right, I'll talk to him."

I went back into the den because the atmosphere wasn't exactly as friendly as it might have been and, anyhow, I had to send out those checks, stamps or no stamps.

I got the pile of bills and the checkbook and the fountain pen out of the drawer. I reached out and picked up the Bildo-Block to put it to one side, so I'd have a good, clear space to work on. But the moment I picked it up, I knew that this thing was no Bildo-Block.

It was the right size and weight and was black and felt like plastic, except that it was slicker than any plastic I had ever felt. It felt as if it had oil on it, only it didn't.

I set it down in front of me and pulled the desk lamp closer. But there wasn't much to see. It still looked like one of the Bildo-Blocks.

Turning it around, I tried to make out what it was. On the second turn, I saw the faint oblong depression along one side of it—a very shallow depression, almost like a scratch.

I looked at it a little closer and could see that the depression was machined and that within it was a faint red line. I could have sworn the red line flickered just a little. I held it there, studying it, and could detect no further flicker. Either the red had faded or I had been seeing things to start with, for after a few seconds I couldn't be sure there was any line at all.

I figured it must have been something Bill had picked up or traded for. The kid is more than half pack-rat, but there's nothing wrong with that, nor with the trading, either, for all that Helen says. It's just the first signs of good business sense.

I put the block over to one side of the desk and went on with the checks. The next day, during lunch hour, I bought some more stamps so I could mail them. And off and on, all day, I wondered what could have happened to that sheet of stamps.

I didn't think at all about the block that had the oily feel. Possibly I would have forgotten it entirely, except that when I got home, the fountain pen was missing.

I went into the den to get the pen and there the pen was, lying on top of the desk where I'd left it the night before. Not that I remembered leaving it there. But when I saw it there, I remembered having forgotten to put it back into the drawer.

I picked it up. It wasn't any pen. It felt like a cylinder of cork, but much too heavy to be any kind of cork. Except that it was heavier and smaller, it felt something–somehow–like a fly rod.

Thinking of how a fly rod felt, I gave my hand a twitch, the way you do to cast a line, and suddenly it seemed to be, in fact, a fly rod. It apparently had been telescoped and now it came untelescoped and lengthened out into what might have been a rod. But the funny thing about it was that it went out only about four feet and then disappeared into thin air.

Instinctively, I brought it up and back to free the tip from wherever it might be. I felt the slack take up against a sudden weight and I knew I had something on the other end of it. Just like a fish feels, only it wasn't fighting.

Then, as quickly as it happened, it unhappened. I felt the tension snap off and the weight at the other end was gone and the rod had telescoped again and I held in my hand the thing that looked like a fountain pen.

I laid it down carefully on the desk, being very certain to make no more casting motions, and it wasn't until then that I saw my hand was shaking.

I sat down, goggling at the thing that looked like the missing fountain pen and the other thing that looked like a Bildo-Block.

And it was then, while I was looking at the two of them, that I saw, out of the corner of my eye, the little white dot in the center of the desk.

It was on the exact spot where the bogus pen had lain and more than likely, I imagined, the exact spot where I'd found the Bildo-Block the night before. It was about a quarter of an inch in diameter and it looked like ivory.

I put out my thumb and rubbed it vigorously, but the dot would not rub off. I closed my eyes so the dot would have a chance to go away, and then opened them again, real quick, to surprise it if it hadn't. It still was there.

I bent over the desk to examine it. I could see it was inlaid in the wood, and an excellent job of inlaying, too. I couldn't find even the faintest line of division between the wood and the dot.

It hadn't been there before; I was sure of that. If it had been, I would have noticed it. What's more, Helen would have noticed it, for she's hell on dirt and forever after things with a dusting cloth. And to cinch the fact that it had not been there before, no one I ever heard of sold desks with single inlaid ivory dots.

And no one sold a thing that looked like a fountain pen but could become a fly rod, the business end of which disappeared and hooked a thing you couldn't even see—and which, the next time, might bring in whatever it had caught instead of losing it.

Helen called to me from the living room. "Joe."

"Yeah. What is it?"

"Did you talk to Bill?"

"Bill? About what?"

"About the trading."

"No. I guess I forgot."

"Well, you'll have to. He's at it again. He traded Jimmy out of that new bicycle. Gave him a lot of junk. I made him give back the bicycle."

"I'll have a talk with him," I promised again.

But I'm afraid I wasn't paying as close attention to the ethics of the situation as I should have been.

You couldn't keep a thing around the house. You were always losing this or that. You knew just where you'd put it and you were sure it was there and then, when you went to look for it, it had disappeared.

It was happening everywhere—things being lost and never turning up.

But other things weren't left in their places—at least not that you heard about.

Although maybe there had been times when things had been left that a man might pick up and examine and not know what they were and puzzle over, then toss in a corner somewhere and forget.

Maybe, I thought, the junkyards of the world were loaded with outlandish blocks and crazy fishing rods.

I got up and went into the living room, where Helen had turned on the television set.

She must have seen that something had me upset, because she asked, "What's the matter now?"

"I can't find the fountain pen."

She laughed at me. "Honestly, Joe, you're the limit. You're always losing things."

That night, I lay awake after Helen went to sleep and all I could think about was the dot upon the desk. A dot, perhaps, that said: *Put it right here, pardner, and we will make a swap.*

And, thinking of it, I wondered what would happen if someone moved the desk.

I lay there for a long time, trying not to worry, trying to tell myself it didn't matter, that I was insane to think what I was thinking.

But I couldn't get it out of my mind.

So I finally got up and sneaked out of the bedroom and, feeling like a thief in my own house, headed for the den.

I closed the door, turned on the desk lamp and took a quick look to see if the dot was still there.

It was.

I opened the desk drawer and hunted for a pencil and couldn't find one, but I finally found one of Bill's crayons. I got down on my knees and carefully marked the floor around the desk legs, so that, if the desk were moved, I could put it back again.

Then, pretending I had no particular purpose for doing it, I laid the crayon precisely on the dot.

In the morning, I sneaked a look into the den and the crayon was still there. I went to work a little easier in my mind, for by then I'd managed to convince myself that it was all imagination.

But that evening, after dinner, I went back into the den and the crayon was gone.

In its place was a triangular contraption with what appeared to be lenses set in each angle, and with a framework of some sort of metal, holding in place what apparently was a suction cup in the center of the triangle.

While I was looking at it, Helen came to the door. "Marge and I are going to see a movie," she said. "Why don't you go over and have a beer with Lewis?"

"With that stuffed shirt?"

"What's the matter with Lewis?"

"Nothing, I guess." I didn't feel up to a family row right then.

"What's that you've got?" she asked.

"I don't know. Just something I found."

"Well, don't *you* start bringing home all sorts of junk, the way Bill does. One of you is enough to clutter up the house."

I sat there, looking at the triangle, and the only thing I could figure out was that it might be a pair of glasses. The suction cup in the center might hold it on the wearer's face and, while that might seem a funny way to wear a pair of glasses, it made sense when you thought about it. But if that were true, it meant that the wearer had three eyes, set in a triangle in his face.

I sat around for quite a while after Helen left, doing a lot of thinking. And what I was thinking was that even if I didn't care too much about Lewis, he was the only man I knew who might be able to help me out.

So I put the bogus fountain pen and the three-eyed glasses in the drawer and put the counterfeit Bildo-Block in my pocket and went across the street.

Lewis had a bunch of blueprints spread out on the kitchen table, and he started to explain them to me. I did the best I could to act as if I understood them. Actually, I didn't know head nor tail of it.

Finally, I was able to get a word in edgewise and I pulled the block out of my pocket and put it on the table.

"What is that?" I asked.

I expected him to say right off it was just a child's block. But he didn't. There must have been something about it to tip him off that it wasn't just a simple block. That comes, of course, of having a technical education.

Lewis picked the block up and turned it around in his fingers. "What's it made of?" he asked me, sounding excited.

I shook my head. "I don't know what it is or what it's made of or anything about it. I just found it."

"This is something I've never seen before." Then he spotted the depression in one side of it and I could see I had him hooked. "Let me take it down to the shop. We'll see what we can learn."

I knew what he was after, of course. If the block was something new, he wanted a chance to go over it—but that didn't bother me any. I had a hunch he wouldn't find out too much about it.

We had a couple more beers and I went home. I hunted up an old pair of spectacles and put them on the desk right over the dot.

I was listening to the news when Helen came in. She said she was glad I'd spent the evening with Lewis, that I should try to get to know him better and that, once I got to know him better, I might like him. She said, since she and Marge were such good friends, it was a shame Lewis and I didn't hit it off.

"Maybe we will," I said and let it go at that.

The next afternoon, Lewis called me at the office.

"Where'd you get that thing?" he asked.

"Found it," I said.

"Have any idea what it is?"

"Nope," I told him cheerfully. "That's why I gave it to you."

"It's powered in some way and it's meant to measure something. That depression in the side must be a gauge. Color seems to be used as an indicator. At any rate, the color line in the depression keeps changing all the time. Not much, but enough so you can say there's some change."

"Next thing is to find out what it's measuring."

"Joe, do you know where you can get another of them?"

"No, I don't."

"It's this way," he said. "We'd like to get into this one, to see what makes it tick, but we can't find any way to open it. We could break into it, probably, but we're afraid to do that. We might damage it. Or it might explode. If we had another . . ."

"Sorry, Lewis. I don't know where to get another."

He had to let it go at that.

I went home that evening grinning to myself, thinking about Lewis. The guy was fit to be tied. He wouldn't sleep until he found out what the thing was, now that he'd started on it. It probably would keep him out of my hair for a week or so.

I went into the den. The glasses still were on the desk. I stood there for a moment, looking at them, wondering what was wrong. Then I saw that the lenses had a pinkish shade.

I picked them up, noticing that the lenses had been replaced by the kind in the triangular pair I had found there the night before.

Just then, Helen came into the room and I could tell, even before she spoke, that she had been waiting for me.

"Joe Adams," she demanded, "what have you been up to?"

"Not a thing," I told her.

"Marge says you got Lewis all upset."

"It doesn't take a lot to upset him."

"There's something going on," she insisted, "and I want to know what it is."

I knew I was licked. "I've been trading."

"Trading! After all I've said about Bill!"

"But this is different."

"Trading is trading," she said flatly.

Bill came in the front door, but he must have heard his mother say "trading," for he ducked out again. I yelled for him to come back.

"I want both of you to sit down and listen to me," I said. "You can ask questions and offer suggestions and give me hell after I'm through."

So we sat down, all three of us, and had a family powwow.

It took quite a bit to make Helen believe what I had to tell, but I pointed out the dot in the desk and showed them the triangular glasses and the pair of glasses that had been refitted with the pink lenses and sent back to me. By that time, she was ready to admit there was something going on. Even so, she was fairly well burned up at me for marking up the floor around the desk legs.

I didn't show either her or Bill the pen that was a fishing rod, for I was scared of that. Flourish it around a bit and there was no telling what would happen.

Bill was interested and excited, of course. This was trading, which was right down his alley.

I cautioned both of them not to say a word about it. Bill wouldn't, for he was hell on secrets and special codes. But bright and early in the morning, Helen would probably swear Marge to secrecy, then tell her all about it and there wasn't a thing that I could do or say to stop her.

Bill wanted to put the pink-lensed spectacles on right away, to see how they were different from any other kind. I wouldn't let him. I wanted to put those specs on myself, but I was afraid to, if you want to know the truth.

When Helen went out to the kitchen to get dinner, Bill and I held a strategy session. For a ten-year-old, Bill had a lot of good ideas. We agreed that we ought to get some system into the trading, because, as Bill pointed out, the idea of swapping sight unseen was a risky sort of business. A fellow ought to have some say in what he was getting in return.

But to arrive at an understanding with whoever we were trading with meant that we'd have to set up some sort of communication system. And how do you communicate with someone you don't know the first thing about, except that perhaps it has three eyes?

Then Bill hit upon what seemed a right idea. What we needed, he said, was a catalogue. If you were going to trade with someone, the logical first step would be to let them know what you had to trade.

To be worth anything in such a circumstance, it would have to be an illustrated catalogue. And even then it might be worthless, for how could we be sure that the Trader on the other side of the desk would know what a picture was? Maybe he'd never seen a picture before. Maybe he saw differently–not so much physically, although that was possible, too, but from a different viewpoint and with totally alien concepts.

But it was the only thing we had to go on, so we settled down to work up a catalogue. Bill thought we should draw one, but neither of us was any good at drawing. I suggested illustrations from magazines. But that wasn't too hot an idea, either, for pictures of items in the magazine ads are usually all prettied up, designed to catch the eye.

Then Bill had a top-notch idea. "You know that kid dictionary Aunt Ethel gave me? Why don't we send that to them? It's got a lot of pictures and not much reading in it, and that's important. The reading might confuse them."

So we went into his room and started looking through all the junk he had, searching for the dictionary. But we ran across one of the old ABC books he'd had when he was just a toddler and decided it was even better than the dictionary. It had good clear pictures and almost no reading at all. You know the kind of book I mean—A for apple, B for ball and so forth.

We took the book into the den and put it on the desk, centering it on the dot, then went out to dinner.

In the morning the book had disappeared and that was a little odd. Up until then, nothing had disappeared from the desk until late in the day.

Early that afternoon, Lewis called me up. "I'm coming down to see you, Joe. Is there a bar handy where the two of us can be alone?"

I told him there was one only a block from me and said I'd meet him there.

I got a few things cleared away, then left the office, figuring I'd go over to the bar and have a quick one before Lewis showed up.

I don't know how he did it, but he was there ahead of me, back in a corner booth. He must have broken every traffic regulation on the books.

He had a couple of drinks waiting for us and was all huddled over, like a conspirator. He was a bit out of breath, as he had every right to be.

"Marge told me," he said.

"I suspected she would."

"There could be a mint in it, Joe!"

"That's what I thought, too. That's why I'm willing to give you ten per cent . . ."

"Now look here," squawked Lewis. "You can't pull a deal like that. I wouldn't touch it for less than fifty."

"I'm letting you in on it," I said, "because you're a neighbor. I don't know beans about this technical business. I'm getting stuff I don't understand and I need some help to find out what it is, but I can always go to someone else . . ."

It took us three drinks to get the details settled—35 per cent for him, 65 for me.

"Now that that's settled," I said, "suppose you tell me what you found."

"Found?"

"That block I gave you. You wouldn't have torn down here and had the drinks all set up and waiting if you hadn't found something."

"Well, as a matter of fact . . ."

"Now just a minute," I warned him. "We're going to put this in the contract—any failure to provide full and complete analysis . . ."

"What contract?"

"We're going to have a contract drawn up, so either of us can sue the other within an inch of his life for breaking it."

Which is a hell of a way to start out a business venture, but it's the only way to handle a slippery little skate like Lewis.

So he told me what he'd found. "It's an emotion gauge. That's awkward terminology, I know, but it's the best I can thing of."

"What does it do?"

"It tells how happy you are or how sad or how much you hate someone."

"Oh, great," I said, disappointed. "What good is a thing like that? I don't need a gauge to tell me if I'm sore or glad or anything."

He waxed practically eloquent. "Don't you see what an instrument like that would mean to psychiatrists? It would tell more about patients than they'd ever be willing to tell about themselves. It could be used in mental institutions and it might be important in gauging reactions for the entertainment business, politics, law-enforcement and Lord knows what else."

"No kidding! Then let's start marketing!"

"The only thing is . . ."

"Yes?"

"We can't manufacture them," he said frustratedly. "We haven't got the materials and we don't know how they're made. You'll have to trade for them."

"I can't. Not right away, that is. First I've got to be able to make the Traders understand what I want, and then I'll have to find out what they're willing to trade them for."

"You have some other stuff?"

"A few things."

"You better turn them over to me."

"Some that could be dangerous. Anyhow, it all belongs to me. I'll give you what I want, when I want and . . ."

We were off again.

We finally wound up by adjourning to an attorney's office. We wrote up a contract that is probably one of the legal curiosities of all time.

I'm convinced the attorney thought, and still thinks, both of us are crazy, but that's the least of my worries now.

The contract said I was to turn over to Lewis, for his determination of its technical and merchandisable nature, at least 90 per cent of certain items, the source of which I alone controlled, and with the further understanding that said source was to remain at all times under my exclusive control. The other 10 per cent might, without prejudice, be withheld from his examination, with the party of the first part having sole authority to make determination of which items should constitute the withheld 10 per cent.

Upon the 90 per cent of the items supplied him, the party of the second part was to make a detailed analysis, in writing, accompanied by such explanatory material as was necessary to the complete understanding of the party of the first part, within no more than three months after receipt, at the end of which time the items reverted solely to the ownership of the party of the first part. Except that such period of examination and determination might be extended, under a mutual agreement made in writing, for any stated time.

Under no circumstances should the party of the second part conceal from the party of the first part any findings he might have made upon any of the items covered by the agreement, and that such concealment, should it occur, should be considered sufficient cause for action for the recovery of damages. That under certain conditions where some of the items might be found to be manufacturable, they could be manufactured under the terms of clauses A, B and C, section XII of this agreement.

Provisions for a sales organization to market any of said items shall be set up and made a part of this agreement. That any proceeds from such sales shall be divided as follows: 65 per cent to the party of the first part (me, in case you've gotten lost, which is understandable), and 35 per cent to the party of the second part (Lewis); costs to be apportioned accordingly.

There were a lot more details, of course, but that gives you an idea.

We got home from the attorney's office, without either of us knifing the other, and found Marge over at my place. Lewis went in with me to have a look at the desk.

Apparently the Trader had received the ABC book all right and had been able to understand why it was sent, for there, lying on the desk, was a picture cut out of the book. Well, not cut out, exactly—it looked more as though it had been burned out.

The picture on the desk was Z for zebra.

Lewis stared worriedly at it. "Now we're really in a fix."

"Yeah," I admitted. "I don't know what the market price is, but they can't be cheap."

"Figure it out—expedition, safari, cages, ship, rail, fodder, keeper. You think we can switch him to something else?"

"I don't see how. He's put in his order."

Bill came wandering in and wanted to know what was up. When I glumly told him, he said cheerfully, "Aw, that's the whole trick in trading, Pop. If you got a bum jackknife you want to trade, you unload it on somebody who doesn't know what a good knife is like."

Lewis didn't get it, but I did. "That's right! He doesn't know a zebra is an animal, or, if he does, how big it is!"

"Sure," Bill said confidently. "All he saw was a picture."

It was five o'clock then, but the three of us went uptown and shopped. Bill found a cheap bracelet charm about the size of the drawing in the book. When it comes to junk like that, my kid knows just where it's sold and how much it costs. I considered making him a junior partner in charge of such emergencies, with about 10 per cent share or so—out of Lewis's 35 per cent, of course—but I was sure Lewis wouldn't hold still for that. I decided instead to give Bill a dollar a week allowance, said compensation to commence immediately upon our showing a profit.

Well, we had Z for zebra—provided the Trader was satisfied with a little piece of costume jewelry. It was lucky, I thought, that it hadn't been Z for zephyr.

The rest of the alphabet was easy, yet I couldn't help but kick myself over all the time we were wasting. Of all the unworthy catalogues we might have sent, that ABC book was the worst. But until the Trader had run through the whole list, I was afraid to send another for fear of confusing him.

So I sent him an apple and a ball and a small doll for a girl and toy cat and toy dog, and so on, and then I lay awake nights wondering what the Trader would make of them. I could picture him trying to learn the use of a rubber doll or cat.

I'd given Lewis the two pairs of glasses, but had held back the fountain-pen fishing rod, for I was still scared of that one. He had turned over the emotion gauge to a psychiatrist to try out in his practice as a sort of field test.

Marge and Helen, knowing that Lewis and I had entered into some kind of partnership, were practically inseparable now. Helen kept telling me how glad she was that I had finally recognized what a sterling fellow Lewis was. I suppose Lewis heard the same thing about me from Marge.

Bill went around practically busting to do some bragging. But Bill is a great little businessman and he kept his mouth shut. I told him about the allowance, of course.

Lewis was all for trying to ask the Trader for a few more of the emotion gauges. He had a draftsman at the plant draw up a picture of the gauge and he wanted me to send it through to indicate that we were interested in it.

But I told him not to try to rush things. While the emotion gauge might be a good deal, we should sample what the Trader had to offer before we made up our minds.

The Trader, apparently certain now that someone was co-operating with him, had dropped his once-a-day trade schedule and was open for business around the clock. After he had run through the list in the ABC book, he sent back a couple of blank pages from the book with very crude drawings on them—drawings that looked as if they had been made with crumbly charcoal. Lewis drew a series of pictures, showing how a pencil worked, and we sent the Trader a ream of paper and a gross of sharpened pencils, then sat back to wait.

We waited a week and were getting sort of edgy, when back came the entire ream of paper, with each sheet covered on both sides with all kinds of drawings. So we sent him a mail-order catalogue, figuring that would hold him for a while, and settled down to try to puzzle out the drawings he had made.

There wasn't a single thing that made any sense at all—not even to Lewis. He'd study some of the drawings, then pace up and down the room, pulling his hair and twitching his ears. Then he'd study the drawings some more.

To me, it all looked plain Rube Goldbergish.

Finally, we figured we might as well forget about the catalogue idea, for the time being at least, and we started feeding all sorts of stuff through the desk—scissors, dishes, shoes, jackknives, mucilage, cigars, paper clips, erasers, spoons—almost anything that was handy. It wasn't the scientific way, I know, but we didn't have the time to get very methodical about it and, until we had a chance to work out a more sensible program, we figured we might as well try the shotgun method.

And the Trader started shooting things back at us. We'd sit for hours and feed stuff through to him and then he'd shoot stuff back at us and we had the damnedest pile of junk heaped all over the place you ever laid eyes on.

We rigged up a movie camera and took a lot of film of the spot on the desk where the exchange was going on. We spent a lot of time viewing that film, slowing it down and even stopping it, but it didn't tell us anything at all. When the stuff disappeared or appeared, it just disappeared or appeared. One frame it would be there, the next frame it would be gone.

Lewis canceled all his other work and used the lab for nothing but trying to puzzle out the gadgets that we got. Most of them we couldn't crack at all. I imagine they were useful in some way, but we never managed to learn how.

There was the perfume bottle, for example. That is what we called it, anyhow. But there was a suspicion in our minds that the perfume was simply a secondary effect, that the so-called bottle was designed for some other purpose entirely.

Lewis and his boys were studying it down at the lab, trying to make out some rhyme or reason for it, and somehow they turned it on. They worked for three days, the last two in gas masks, trying to turn it off again. When the smell got so bad that people began calling the police, we took the contraption out into the country and buried it. Within a few days, all the vegetation in the area was dead. All the rest of the summer, the boys from the agricultural department at the university ran around, practically frothing at the mouth, trying to find the cause.

There was the thing that might have been a clock of some sort, although it might just as easily have been something else. If it was a clock, the Trader had a time system that would drive you nuts, for it would measure the minutes or hours or whatever they were like lightning for a while, then barely move for an entire day.

And there was the one you'd point at something and press a certain spot on it–not a button or a knob or anything as crass and mechanical as that, just a certain spot–and there'd be just a big blank spot in the landscape. But when you stopped pressing, the landscape would come back again, unchanged. We filed it away in the darkest corner of the laboratory safe, with a big red tag on it marked: *Dangerous! Don't Monkey with This!*

But most of the items we just drew blanks on. And it kept coming all the time. I piled the garage full of it and started dumping it in the basement. Some of it I was scared of and hauled out to the dump.

In the meantime, Lewis was having trouble with the emotion gauge. "It works," he said. "The psychiatrist I gave it to to try out is enthusiastic about it. But it seems almost impossible to get it on the market."

"If it works," I objected, handing him a can of beer, "it ought to sell."

"In any other field, it might, but you don't handle merchandise that way in the medical field. Before you can put something on the market, you have to have it nailed down with blueprints and theory and field tests and such. And we can't. We don't know *how* it works. We don't know *why* it works. Until we do, no reputable medical supply house will take it on, no approved medical journal will advertise it, no practitioner will use it."

"Then I guess it's out." I felt fairly blue about it, because it was the only thing we had that we knew how to use.

Lewis nodded and drank his beer and was glummer than ever.

Looking back on it, it's funny how we found the gadget that made us all the money. Actually, it wasn't Lewis but Helen who found it.

Helen is a good housewife. She's always going after things with the vacuum and the dustcloth and she washes the woodwork so often and so furiously that we have to paint it every year.

One night, we were sitting in the living room, watching television.

"Joe," she asked me, "did you dust the den?"

"Dust the den? What would I want to do that for?"

"Well, someone did. Maybe it was Bill."

"Bill wouldn't be caught dead with a dustcloth in his mitt."

"I can't understand it, Joe," she said. "I went in there to dust it and it was absolutely clean. Everything just shone."

Sgt. Friday was trying to get the facts out of someone and his sidekick was complaining about some relatives that had come to visit and I didn't pay much attention at the time.

But the next day, I got to thinking about it and I couldn't get it off my mind. I certainly hadn't dusted the den and it was a cinch Bill hadn't, yet someone had if Helen was ready to admit it was clean.

So, that evening, I went out into the street with a pail and shoveled up a pailful of dirt and brought it in the house.

Helen caught me as I was coming in the door. "What do you think you're doing with that?"

"Experimenting," I told her.

"Do it in the garage."

"It isn't possible," I argued. "I have to find out who's been dusting the den."

I knew that, if my hunch failed, I'd have a lot to answer for when she followed me and stood in the doorway, ready to pounce.

There was a bunch of junk from the Trader standing on the desk and a lot more of it in one corner. I cleared off the desk and that was when Bill came in.

"What you doing, Dad?" he asked.

"Your father's gone insane," Helen explained quietly.

They stood there, watching me, while I took a handful of dirt and sprinkled it on the desk top.

It stayed there for just an instant–and then it was gone. The top of the desk was spotless.

"Bill," I said, "take one of those gadgets out to the garage."

"Which one?"

"It doesn't matter."

So he took one and I spread another handful of dirt and, in a second, it was gone.

Bill was back by that time and I sent him out with another gadget.

We kept on like that for quite a while and Bill was beginning to get disgusted with me. But finally I sprinkled the dirt and it stayed.

"Bill," I said, "you remember the last thing you took out?"

"Sure."

"Well, go out and bring it back again."

He got it and, as soon as he reached the door of the den, the dirt disappeared.

"Well, that's it," I said.

"That's what?" asked Helen.

I pointed to the contraption Bill had in his hand. "That. Throw away your vacuum cleaner. Burn up the dustcloth. Heave out the mop. Just have one of those in the house and . . ."

She threw herself into my arms.

"Oh, *Joe!*"

We danced a jig, the two of us.

Then I sat around for a while, kicking myself for tying up with Lewis, wondering if maybe there wasn't some way I could break the contract now that I had found something without any help from him. But I remembered all those clauses we had written in. It wouldn't have been any use, anyhow, for Helen was already across the street, telling Marge about it.

2

So I phoned Lewis at the lab and he came tearing over.

We ran field tests.

The living room was spotless from Bill just having walked through it, carrying the gadget, and the garage, where he had taken it momentarily, was spick-and-span. While we didn't check it, I imagine that an area paralleling the path he had taken from the front door to the garage was the only place outdoors that didn't have a speck of dust upon it.

We took the gadget down in the basement and cleaned that up. We sneaked over to a neighbor's back yard, where we knew there was a lot of cement dust, held the gadget over it and in an instant there wasn't any cement dust. There were just a few pebbles left and the pebbles, I suppose, you couldn't rightly classify as dust.

We didn't need to know any more.

Back at the house, I broke open a bottle of Scotch I'd been saving, while Lewis sat down at the kitchen table and drew a sketch of the gadget.

We had a drink, then went into the den and put the drawing on the desk. The drawing disappeared and we waited. In a few minutes, another one of the gadgets appeared. We waited for a while and nothing happened.

"We've got to let him know we want a lot of them," I said.

"There's no way we can," said Lewis. "We don't know his mathematical symbols, he doesn't know ours, and there's no sure-fire way to teach him. He doesn't know a single word of our language and we don't know a word of his."

We went back to the kitchen and had another drink.

Lewis sat down and drew a row of the gadgets across a sheet of paper, then sketched in representations of others behind them so that, when you looked at it, you could see that there were hundreds of them.

We sent that through.

Fourteen gadgets came back—the exact number Lewis had sketched in the first row.

Apparently the Trader had no idea of perspective. The lines that Lewis had drawn to represent the other gadgets behind the first row didn't mean a thing to him.

We went back to the kitchen and had a few more drinks.

"We'll need thousands of the things," said Lewis, holding his head in his hands. "I can't sit here day and night, drawing them."

"You may have to do that," I said, enjoying myself.

"There *must* be another way."

"Why not draw a bunch of them, then mimeograph the drawing?" I suggested. "We could send the mimeographed sheets through to him in bundles."

I hated to say it, because I was still enamored of the idea of sticking Lewis somewhere off in a corner, sentenced to a lifetime of drawing the same thing over and over.

"That might work," said Lewis, brightening annoyingly. "It's just simple enough . . ."

"Practical is the word," I snapped. "If it were simple, you'd have thought of it."

"I leave things like that to detail men."

"You'd better!"

It took a while and a whole bottle before we calmed down.

Next day, we bought a mimeograph machine and Lewis drew a stencil with twenty-five of the gadgets on it. We ran through a hundred sheets and sent them through the desk.

It worked—we were busy for several hours, getting those gadgets out of the way as they poured through to us.

I'm afraid we never stopped to think about what the Trader might want in return for the dust-collectors. We were so excited that we forgot, for the moment, that this was a commercial proposition and not just something gratis.

But the next afternoon, back came the mimeographed sheets we'd sent through and, on the reverse side of each of them, the Trader had drawn twenty-five representations of the zebra bracelet charm.

And there we were, faced with the necessity of getting together pronto, twenty-five hundred of those silly zebras.

I tore down to the store where I'd gotten the bracelet, but all they had in stock were two dozen of the things. They said they didn't think they could order any more. The number, they said, had been discontinued.

The name of the company that made them was stamped on the inside of the bracelet and, as soon as I got home, I put in a long distance call.

I finally got hold of the production manager. "You know those bracelets you put out?"

"We put out millions of 'em. Which one are you talking about?"

"The one with the zebra on it."

He thought a moment. "Yeah, we did. Quite a while ago. We don't make them any more. In this business . . . ."

"I need at least twenty-five hundred of them."

"Twenty-five hundred bracelets?"

"No, just the zebras."

"Look, is this a gag?"

"It's no gag, mister," I said. "I need those zebras. I'm willing to pay for them."

"We haven't any in stock."

"Couldn't you make them?"

"Not just twenty-five hundred of them. Wouldn't be worth it to put through a special order for so few. If it was fifty thousand, say, we might consider it."

"All right, then," I said. "How much for fifty thousand?"

He named a price and we haggled some, but I was in no position to do much bargaining. We finally agreed on a price I knew was way too high, considering the fact that the entire bracelet, with the zebra and a lot of other junk, had only retailed at 39 cents.

"And hold the order open," I told him. "We might want more of them."

"Okay," he said. "Just one thing—would you mind telling me what you want with fifty thousand zebras?"

"Yes, I would," I said and hung up.

I suppose he thought I was off my rocker, but who cared what he thought?

It took ten days to get that shipment of fifty thousand zebras and I sweated out every minute of it. Then there was the job of getting them under cover when it came and, in case you don't know, fifty thousand zebras, even when they're only bracelet charms, take up room.

But first I took out twenty-five hundred and sent them through the desk.

For the ten days since we'd gotten the dust-collectors, we'd sent nothing through and there had been no sign from the Trader that he might be getting impatient. I wouldn't have blamed him a bit if he'd done something, like sending through his equivalent of a bomb, to express his dissatisfaction at our slow delivery. I've often wondered what he thought of the long delay—if he hadn't suspected we were reneging on the bargain.

All this time, I had been smoking too much and gnawing my

fingernails and I'd figured that Lewis was just as busy seeing what could be done about marketing the dusters.

But when I mentioned it to him he just looked blank. "You know, Joe, I've been doing a lot of worrying."

"We haven't a thing to worry about now," I said, "except getting these things sold."

"But the dust must go somewhere," he fretted.

"The dust?"

"Sure, the dust these things collect. Remember we picked up an entire pile of cement dust? What I want to know is where it all went. The gadget itself isn't big enough to hold it. It isn't big enough to hold even a week's collection of dust from the average house. That's what worries me—where does it go?"

"I don't care where. It goes, doesn't it?"

"That's the pragmatic view," he said scornfully.

It turned out that Lewis hadn't done a thing about marketing, so I got busy.

But I ran into the same trouble we'd had trying to sell the emotion gauge.

The dust collector wasn't patented and it didn't have a brand name. There was no fancy label stuck on it and it didn't bear a manufacturer's imprint. And when anybody asked me how it worked, I couldn't answer.

One wholesaler did make me a ridiculous offer. I laughed in his face and walked out.

That night, Lewis and I sat around the kitchen table, drinking beer, and neither of us too happy. I could see a lot of trouble ahead in getting the gadgets sold. Lewis, it seemed, was still worrying about what happened to the dust.

He had taken one of the dust-collectors apart and the only thing he could find out about it was that there was some feeble force-field operating inside of it—feeble yet strong enough to play hell with the electrical circuits and fancy metering machinery he has at the lab. As soon as he found out what was happening, he slapped the cover back on as quick as he could and then everything was all right. The cover was a shield against the force-field.

"That dust must be getting thrown into another dimension," he told me, looking like a hound dog that had lost a coon track.

"Maybe not. It could be winding up in one of those dust clouds way out in space."

He shook his head.

"You can't tell me," I said, "that the Trader is crazy enough to sell us a gadget that will throw dust back into his face."

"You miss the point entirely. The Trader is operating from another dimension. He *must* be. And if there are two dimensions, his and ours, there may be others. The Trader must have used these dust-collectors himself—not for the same purpose we intend, perhaps, but they get rid of something that he doesn't want around. So, necessarily, they'd have to be rigged to get rid of it in a dimension other than his."

We sat there drinking beer and I started turning over that business about different dimensions in my head. I couldn't grasp the concept. Maybe Lewis was right about me being a pragmatist. If you can't see it or touch it or even guess what it would be like, how can you believe there might be another dimension? I couldn't.

So I started to talk about marketing the dust-collector and before Lewis went home that night, we'd decided that the only thing left to do was sell it door to door. We even agreed to charge $12.50 for it. The zebras figured out to four cents each and we would pay our salesmen ten per cent commission, which would leave us a profit of $11.21 apiece.

I put an ad in the paper for salesmen and the next day we had several applicants. We started them out on a trial run.

Those gadgets sold like hot cakes and we knew we were in!

I quit my job and settled down to handling the sales end, while Lewis went back to the lab and started going through the pile of junk we had gotten from the Trader.

There are a lot of headaches running a sales campaign. You have to map out territories for your salesmen, get clearance from Better Business Bureaus, bail out your men if they're thrown in the clink for running afoul of some obscure village ordinance. There are more worrisome angles to it than you can ever imagine.

But in a couple of months' time, things were running pretty smoothly. We had the state well covered and were branching out into others. I had ordered another fifty thousand zebras and told them to expect re-orders—and the desk top was a busy place. It got to a point, finally, where I had to hire three men full time, paying them plenty not to talk, to man that desk top twenty-four hours a day. We'd send through zebras for eight hours, then take away dust gadgets for eight hours, then feed through zebras for another eight.

If the Trader had any qualms about what was happening, he gave no sign of it. He seemed perfectly happy to send us dust-collectors so long as we sent him zebras.

The neighbors were curious and somewhat upset at first, but finally they got used to it. If I could have moved to some other location, I would have, for the house was more an office than a home and we had practically no family life at all. But if we wanted to stay in business, we had to stay right where we were because it was the only place we had contact with the Trader.

The money kept rolling in and I turned the management of it over to Helen and Marge. The income tax boys gave us a rough time when we didn't show any manufacturing expenses, but since we weren't inclined to argue over what we had to pay, they couldn't do anything about it.

Lewis was wearing himself down to a nubbin at the lab, but he wasn't finding anything that we could use.

But he still did some worrying now and then about where all that dust was going. And he was right, probably for the first time in his life.

One afternoon, a couple of years after we'd started selling the dust-collectors, I had been uptown to attend to some banking difficulties that Helen and Marge had gotten all bollixed up. I'd no more than pulled into the driveway when Helen came busting out of the house. She was covered with dust, her face streaked with it, and she was the maddest-looking woman I have ever seen.

"You've got to do something about it, Joe!" she shrieked.

"About what?"

"The dust! It's pouring into the house!"

"Where is it pouring from?"

"From *everywhere!*"

I could see she'd opened all the windows and there was dust pouring out of them, almost like a smoke cloud. I got out of the car and took a quick look up and down the street. Every house in the block had its windows open and there was dust coming out of all of them and the neighborhood was boiling with angry, screaming women.

"Where's Bill?" I asked.

"Out back."

I ran around the house and called him and he came running.

Marge had come across the street and, if anything, she was about six degrees sorer about all the dust than Helen was.

"Get in the car," I said.

"Where are we going?" Marge demanded.

"Out to pick up Lewis."

I must have sounded like nothing to trifle with, for they piled in and I got out of there as fast as the car would take us.

The homes and factories and stores that had bought the gadget were gushing so much dust, visibility wouldn't be worth a damn before long.

I had to wade through about two feet of dust on the laboratory floor to get to Lewis's office and hold a handkerchief over my nose to keep from suffocating.

Inside the car we got our faces wiped off and most of the dust hacked out of our throats. I could see then that Lewis was about three shades paler than usual, although, to tell the truth, he always was a pasty-looking creature.

"It's the creatures from that third dimension," he said anxiously. "The place where we were sending all the dust. They got sick and tired of having it pour in on them and they got it figured out and now they're firing the dust right back at us."

"Now calm down. We're just jumping at the conclusion that this was caused by our gadget."

"I checked, Joe. It was. The dust is coming out in jets from every single place where we sent it through. No place else."

"Then all we have to do is fire it back at them."

He shook his head. "Not a chance. The gadget works one way now —from them to us." He coughed and looked wildly at me. "Think of it! A couple of million of those gadgets, picking up dust from a couple of million homes, stores and factories—some of them operating for two whole years! Joe, what are we going to do?"

"We're going to hole up somewhere till this—well, blows over."

Being of a nasty legal turn of mind, he probably foresaw even then the countless lawsuits that would avalanche on us. Personally, I was more scared of being mobbed by angry women.

But that's all past history. We hid out till people had quieted down and then began trying to settle the suits out of court. We had a lot of money and were able to pay off most of them. The judgments against us still outstanding don't amount to more than a few hundred thousand. We could wipe that out pretty quickly if we'd just hit on something else as profitable as the cleaning gadget.

Lewis is working hard at it, but he isn't having any luck. And the Trader is gone now. As soon as we dared come home, I went into the house and had a look at the desk. The inlaid dot was gone. I tried putting something where it had been, but nothing happened.

What scared the Trader off? I'd give a lot to know. Meanwhile, there are some commercial prospects.

The rose-tinted glasses, for instance, that we call the Happiness Lenses. Put them on and you're happy as a clam. Almost every person on the face of the Earth would like a pair of them, so they could forget their troubles for a while. They would probably play hob with the liquor business.

The trouble is that we don't know how to make them and, now that the Trader's gone, we can't swap for them.

But there's one thing that keeps worrying me. I know I shouldn't let it bother me, but I can't keep it out of mind.

Just what did the Trader do with those couple of million zebras we sent him?

2. Honorable Opponent

THE FIVERS were late.

Perhaps they had misunderstood.

Or this might be another of their tricks.

Or maybe they never had intended to stick to their agreement.

"Captain," asked General Lyman Flood, "what time have we got now?"

Captain Gist looked up from the chessboard. "Thirty-seven oh eight, galactic, sir."

Then he went back to the board again. Sergeant Conrad had pinned his knight and he didn't like it.

"Thirteen hours late!" the general fumed.

"They may not have got it straight, sir."

"We spelled it out to them. We took them by the hand and we went over it time and time again so they'd have it clear in mind. They couldn't possibly misunderstand."

But they very possibly could, he knew.

The Fivers misunderstood almost everything. They had been confused about the armistice—as if they'd never heard of an armistice before. They had been obtuse about the prisoner exchange. Even the matter of setting a simple time had involved excruciating explanation—as if they had never heard of the measurement of time and were completely innocent of basic mathematics.

"Or maybe they broke down," the captain offered.

The general snorted. "They don't break down. Those ships of theirs are marvels. They'd live through anything. They whipped us, didn't they?"

"Yes, sir," said the captain.

"How many of them, Captain, do you estimate we destroyed?"

"Not more than a dozen, sir."

"They're tough," the general said.

He went back across the tent and sat down in a chair.

The captain had been wrong. The right number was eleven. And of those, only one had been confirmed destroyed. The others had been no better than put out of action.

And the way it figured out, the margin had been more than ten to one in favor of the Fivers. Earth, the general admitted to himself, had never taken such a beating. Whole squadrons had been wiped out; others had come fleeing back to Base with their numbers cut in half.

They came fleeing back to Base and there were no cripples. They had returned without a scratch upon them. And the ships that had been lost had not been visibly destroyed—they had simply been wiped out, leaving not a molecule of wreckage.

How do you beat a thing like that, he asked himself. How do you fight a weapon that cancels out a ship in its entirety?

Back on Earth and on hundreds of other planets in the Galactic Confederacy, thousands of researchers were working day and night in a crash-priority program to find an answer to the weapon—or at least to find the weapon.

But the chance of success ran thin, the general knew, for there was not a single clue to the nature of it. Which was understandable, since every victim of the weapon had been lost irretrievably.

Perhaps some of the human prisoners would be able to provide a clue. If there had been no such hope, he knew, Earth never would have gone to all the trouble to make this prisoner exchange.

He watched the captain and the sergeant hunched above the chessboard, with the captive Fiver looking on.

He called the captive over.

The captive came like a trundling roly-poly.

And once again, watching him, the general had that strange, disturbing sense of outrage.

For the Fiver was a droll grotesque that held no hint of the martial spirit. He was round and jolly in every feature, expression and gesture, dressed in a ribald clash of colors, as though designed and clad deliberately to offend any military man.

"Your friends are late," the general told him.

"You wait," the Fiver said and his words were more like whistling than talk. One had to listen closely to make out what he said.

The general held himself in check.

No use in arguing.

No point blowing up.

He wondered if he—or the human race—would ever understand the Fivers.

Not that anyone really wanted to, of course. Just to get them combed out of Earth's hair would be enough.

"You wait," the Fiver whistled. "They come in middle time from now."

And when in hell, the general wondered, would be middle time from now?

The Fiver glided back to watch the game.

The general walked outside.

The tiny planet looked colder and more desolate and forbidding than it ever had before. Each time he looked at it, the general thought, the scene was more depressing than he had remembered it.

Lifeless, worthless, of no strategic or economic value, it had qualified quite admirably as neutral territory to carry out the prisoner exchange. Neutral mostly because it wasn't worth the trouble for anyone to grab it.

The distant star that was its sun was a dim glow in the sky. The black and naked rock crept out to a near horizon. The icy air was like a knife inside the general's nostrils.

There were no hills or valleys. There was absolutely nothing—just the smooth flatness of the rock stretching on all sides, for all the world like a great space field.

It had been the Fivers, the general remembered, who had suggested this particular planet and that in itself was enough to make it suspect. But Earth, at that point in the negotiations, had been in no position to do much haggling.

He stood with his shoulders hunched and he felt the cold breath of apprehension blowing down his neck. With each passing hour, it seemed, the place felt more and more like some gigantic trap.

But he must be wrong, he argued. There was absolutely nothing in the Fivers' attitude to make him feel like that. They had, in fact, been almost magnanimous. They could have laid down their terms—almost any terms—and the Confederacy would have had no choice but to acquiesce. For Earth must buy time, no matter what the price. Earth had to be ready next time–five years or ten or whatever it might be.

But the Fivers had made no demands, which was unthinkable.

Except, the general told himself, one could never know what they might be thinking or what they might be planning.

The exchange camp huddled in the dimness–a few tents, a portable power plant, the poised and waiting ship and, beside it, the little scouter the captive Fiver had been piloting.

The scouter in itself was a good example of the gulf which separated the Fivers and the humans. It had taken three full days of bickering before the Fivers had been able to make clear their point that the scouter as well as its pilot must be returned to them.

No ship in all the Galaxy had ever gotten so thorough a study as that tiny craft. But the facts that it had yielded had been few indeed. And the captive Fiver, despite the best efforts of the experts in Psych, had furnished even fewer.

The area was quiet and almost deserted. Two sentries strode briskly up and down. Everyone else was under cover, killing time, waiting for the Fivers.

The general walked quickly across the area to the medic tent. He stooped and went inside.

Four men were sitting at a table, drearily playing cards. One of them put down his hand and rose.

"Any word, General?"

The general shook his head. "They should be coming soon, Doc. Everything all set?"

"We've been ready for some time," said the psychiatrist. "We'll bring the boys in here and check them over as soon as they arrive. We've got the stuff all set. It won't take long."

"That's fine. I want to get off this rock as quickly as I can. I don't like the feel of it."

"There's just one thing . . ."

"What's that?"

"If we only knew how many they are handing back."

The general shook his head. "We never could find out. They're not so hot on figures. And you'd think, wouldn't you, that math would be universal?"

"Well," said Doc resignedly, "we'll do the best we can."

"There can't be many," the general said. "We're only giving back one Fiver and one ship. How many humans do you figure a ship is worth to them?"

"I wouldn't know. You really think they'll come?"

"It's hard to be certain that they understood. When it comes to sheer stupidity–"

"Not so stupid," Doc replied, quietly. "We couldn't learn their language, so they learned ours."

"I know," the general said impatiently. "I realize all that. But that armistice business–it took days for them to get what we were driving at. And the time reckoning system still more days. Good Lord, man, you could do better using sign language with a Stone Age savage!"

"You should," said Doc. "The savage would be human."

"But these Fivers are intelligent. Their technology, in many ways, has us beaten seven ways from Sunday. They fought us to a standstill."

"They licked us."

"All right, then, they licked us. And why not? They had this weapon that we didn't have. They were closer to their bases. They had no logistics problem to compare with ours. They licked us, but I ask you, did they have the sense to know it? Did they take advantage of it? They could have wiped us out. They could have laid down peace terms that would have crippled us for centuries. Instead, they let us go. Now how does that make sense?"

"You're dealing with an alien race," said Doc.

"We've dealt with other aliens. And we always understood them. Mostly, we got along with them."

"We dealt with them on a commercial basis," Doc reminded him. "Whatever trouble we might have had with them came after a basic minimum of understanding had been achieved. The Fivers are the first that ever came out shooting."

"I can't figure it," the general said. "We weren't even heading for them. We might have passed them by. They couldn't have known who we were. Point is, they didn't care. They just came piling out and opened up on us. And it's been the same with everyone else who came within their reach. They take on every comer. There's never a time when they aren't fighting someone–sometimes two or three at once."

"They have a defensive complex," said Doc. "Want to be left alone. All they aim to do is keep others off their planets. As you say they could have wiped us out."

"Maybe they get hurt real easy. Don't forget we gave them a bloody nose or two–not as much as they busted us, but we hurt them some. I figure they'll come out again, soon as they can cut it."

He drew a deep breath. "Next time, we have to be ready for them. Next time, they may not stop. We have to dope them out."

It was tough work, he thought, to fight an enemy about which one knew next to nothing. And a weapon about which one knew absolutely nothing.

There were theories in plenty, but the best no more than educated guesses.

The weapon might operate in time–hurling its targets back into unimagined chaos. Or it might be dimensional. Or it might collapse the atoms in upon themselves, reducing a spaceship to the most deadly massive dustmote the universe had known.

One thing for certain–it was not disintegration, for there was no flash and there was no heat. The ship just disappeared and that was the end of it–the end and all of it.

"There's another thing that bothers me," said Doc. "Those other races that fought the Fivers before they jumped on us. When we tried to contact them, when we tried to get some help from them, they wouldn't bother with us. They wouldn't tell us anything."

"This is a new sector of space for us," the general said. "We are strangers here."

"It stands to reason," argued Doc, "they should jump at the chance to gang up on the Fivers."

"We can't depend on alliances. We stand alone. It is up to us."

He bent to leave the tent.

"We'll get right on it," said Doc, "soon as the men show up. We'll have a preliminary report within an hour, if they're in any shape at all."

"That's fine," the general said and ducked out of the tent.

It was a bad situation, blind and terrifying if one didn't manage to keep a good grip on himself.

The captive humans might bring back some information, but even so, you couldn't buy it blind, for there might be a gimmick in it–as there was a gimmick in what the captive Fiver knew.

This time, he told himself, the psych boys might have managed to outsmart themselves.

It had been a clever trick, all right–taking the captive Fiver on that trip and showing him so proudly all the barren, no-good planets, pretending they were the showplaces of the Confederacy.

Clever–if the Fiver had been human. For no human would have

fought a skirmish, let alone a war, for the kind of planets he'd been shown.

But the Fiver wasn't human. And there was no way of knowing what kind of planet a Fiver might take a fancy to.

And there always was the chance that those crummy planets had given him the hunch that Earth would be easy prey.

The whole situation didn't track, the general thought. There was a basic wrongness to it. Even allowing for all the differences which might exist between the Fiver and the human cultures, the wrongness still persisted.

And there was something wrong right here.

He heard the sound and wheeled to stare into the sky.

The ship was close and coming in too fast.

But even as he held his breath, it slowed and steadied and came to ground in a perfect landing not more than a quarter of a mile from where the Earth ship stood.

The general broke into a run toward it, then remembered and slowed to a stiff military walk.

Men were tumbling out of tents and forming into lines. An order rang across the area and the lines moved with perfect drill precision.

The general allowed himself a smile. Those boys of his were good. You never caught them napping. If the Fivers had expected to sneak in and catch the camp confused and thus gain a bit of face, it was a horse on them.

The marching men swung briskly down the field. An ambulance moved out from beneath its tarp and followed. The drums began to roll and the bugles sounded clear and crisp in the harsh, cold air.

It was men like these, the general told himself with pride, who held the expanding Confederacy intact. It was men like these who kept the peace across many cubic light-years. It was men like these who some day, God willing, would roll back the Fiver threat.

There were few wars now. Space was too big for it. There were too many ways to skirt around the edge of war for it to come anything but seldom. But something like the Fiver threat could not be ignored. Some day, soon or late, either Earth or Fiver must go down to complete defeat. The Confederacy could never feel secure with the Fivers on its flank.

Feet pounded behind him and the general turned. It was Captain Gist, buttoning his tunic as he ran. He fell in beside the general.

"So they finally came, sir."

"Fourteen hours late," the general said. "Let us, for the moment, try to look our best. You missed a button, Captain."

"Sorry, sir," the captain said, fastening the button.

"Right, then. Get those shoulders back. Smartly, if you will. Right, left, hup, hup!"

Out of the corner of his eye, he saw that Sergeant Conrad had his squad moving out with precision, escorting the captive Fiver most correctly forward, with all the dignity and smartness that anyone might wish.

The men were drawn up now in two parallel lines, flanking the ship. The port was swinging open and the ramp was rumbling out and the general noted with some satisfaction that he and Captain Gist would arrive at the foot of the ramp about the time it touched the ground. The timing was dramatic and superb, almost as if he himself had planned it down to the last detail.

The ramp snapped into position and three Fivers came sedately waddling down it.

A seedy-looking trio, the general thought. Not a proper uniform nor a medal among the lot of them.

The general seized the diplomatic initiative as soon as they reached the ground.

"We welcome you," he told them, speaking loudly and slowly and as distinctly as he could so they would understand.

They lined up and stood looking at him and he felt a bit uncomfortable because there was that round jolly expression in their faces. Evidently they didn't have the kind of faces that could assume any other expression. But they kept on looking at him.

The general plunged ahead. "It is a matter of great gratification to Earth to carry out in good faith our obligations as agreed upon in the armistice proceedings. It marks what we sincerely hope will be the beginning of an era . . ."

"Most nice," one of the Fivers said. Whether he meant the general's little speech or the entire situation or was simply trying to be gracious was not at once apparent.

Undaunted, the general was ready to go on, but the spokesman Fiver raised a short round arm to halt him.

"Prisoners arrive briefly," he whistled.

"You mean you didn't bring them?"

"They come again," the Fiver said with a glorious disregard for preciseness of expression.

He continued beaming at the general and he made a motion with the arm that might have been a shrug.

"Shenanigans," the captain said, close to the general's ear.

"We talk," the Fiver said.

"They're up to something," warned the captain. "It calls for Situation Red, sir."

"I agree," the general told the captain. "Set it up quietly." He said to the Fiver delegation: "If you gentlemen will come with me, I can offer you refreshments."

He had a feeling that they were smiling at him, mocking him, but one could never tell. Those jolly expressions were always the same. No matter what the situation.

"Most happy," said the Fiver spokesman. "These refresh—"

"Drink," the general said and made a motion to supplement the word.

"Drink is good," the Fiver answered. "Drink is friend?"

"That is right," the general said.

He started for the tent, walking slowly so the Fivers could keep up.

He noted with some satisfaction that the captain had carried on most rapidly, indeed. Sergeant Conrad was marching his squad back across the area, with the captive Fiver shambling in the center. The tarps were coming off the guns and the last of the crew was clambering up the ladder of the ship.

The captain caught up with them just short of the tent.

"Everything all set, sir," Sergeant Conrad reported in a whisper.

"Fine," the general said.

They reached the tent and went inside. The general opened a refrigerating unit and took out a gallon jug.

"This," he explained, "is a drink we made for your compatriot. He found it very tasty."

He set out glasses and sipping straws and uncorked the jug, wishing he could somehow hold his nose, for the drink smelled like something that had been dead too long. He didn't even like to guess what might have gone into it. The chemists back on Earth had whomped it up for the captive Fiver, who had consumed gallon after gallon of it with disconcerting gusto.

The general filled the glasses and the Fivers picked them up in their tentacles and stuck the straws into their drawstring mouths. They drank and rolled their eyes in appreciation.

The general took the glass of liquor the captain handed him and gulped half of it in haste. The tent was getting just a little thick. What things a man goes through, he thought, to serve his planets and his peoples.

He watched the Fivers drinking and wondered what they might have up their sleeves.

Talk, the spokesman had told him, and that might mean almost anything. It might mean a reopening of negotiations or it might be nothing but a stall.

And if it was negotiation, Earth was across the barrel. For there was nothing he could do but negotiate. Earth's fleet was crippled and the Fivers had the weapon and a renewal of the war was unthinkable. Earth needed five years at the minimum and ten years would be still better.

And if it was attack, if this planet was a trap, there was only one thing he could do—stand and fight as best he could, a thoroughly suicidal course.

Either way, Earth lost, the general realized.

The Fivers put down their glasses and he filled them up again.

"You do well," one of the Fivers said. "You got the paper and the marker?"

"Marker?" the general asked.

"He means a pencil," said the captain.

"Oh, yes. Right here." The general reached for a pad of paper and a pencil and laid them on the desk.

One of the Fivers set down his glass and, picking up the pencil, started to make a laborious drawing. He looked for all the world like a five-year-old printing his first alphabet.

They waited while the Fiver drew. Finally he was finished. He laid the pencil down and pointed to the wiggly lines.

"Us," he said.

He pointed to the sawtooth lines.

"You," he told the general.

The general bent above the paper, trying to make out what the Fiver had put down.

"Sir," the captain said, "it looks like a battle diagram."

"Is," said the Fiver proudly.

He picked the pencil up.

"Look," he said.

He drew directional lines and made a funny kind of symbol for the points of contact and made crosses for the sections where the battle lines were broken. When he was done, the Earth fleet had been shattered and sliced into three segments and was in headlong flight.

"That," the general said, with the husk of anger rising in his throat, "was the engagement in Sector 17. Half of our Fifth Squadron was wiped out that day."

"Small error," said the Fiver and made a deprecatory gesture.

He ripped the sheet of paper off the pad and tossed it on the floor. He laboriously drew the diagram again.

"Attend," he said.

The Fiver drew the directional lines again, but this time he changed them slightly. Now the Earth line pivoted and broke and became two parallel lines that flanked the Fiver drive and turned and blunted it and scattered it in space.

The Fiver laid the pencil down.

"Small matter," he informed the general and the captain. "You good. You make one thin mistake."

Holding himself sternly in hand, the general filled the glasses once again.

What are they getting at, he thought. Why don't they come flat out and say it?

"So best," one of the Fivers said, lifting his glass to let them know that he meant the drink.

"More?" asked the Fiver tactician, picking up the pencil.

"Please," said the general, seething.

He walked to the tent flap and looked outside. The men were at the guns. Thin wisps of vapor curled from the ship's launching tubes; in just a little while, it would be set to go, should the need arise. The camp was quiet and tense.

He went back to the desk and watched as the Fiver went on gaily with his lesson on how to win a battle. He filled page after page with diagrams and occasionally he was generous–he sometimes showed how the Fivers lost when they might have won with slightly different tactics.

"Interesting!" he piped enthusiastically.

"I find it so," the general said. "There is just one question."

"Ask," the Fiver invited.

"If we should go to war again, how can you be sure we won't use all of this against you?"

"But fine," the Fiver enthused warmly. "Exactly as we want."

"You fight fine," another Fiver said. "But just too slightly hard. Next time, you able to do much better."

"Hard!" the general raged.

"Too roughly, sir. No need to make the ship go poof."

Outside the tent, a gun cut loose and then another one and above the hammering of the guns came the full-throated, ground-shaking roar of many ship motors.

The general leaped for the entrance, went through it at a run, not bothering with the flap. His cap fell off and he staggered out, thrown slightly off his balance. He jerked up his head and saw them coming in, squadron after squadron, painting the darkness with the flare of tubes.

"Stop firing!" he shouted. "You crazy fools, stop firing!"

But there was no need of shouting, for the guns had fallen silent.

The ships came down toward the camp in perfect flight formation. They swept across it and the thunder of their motors seemed to lift it for a moment and give it a mighty shake. Then they were climbing, rank on serried rank, still with drill precision—climbing and jockeying into position for regulation landing.

The general stood like a frozen man, with the wind ruffling his iron-gray hair, with a lump, half pride, half thankfulness, rising in his throat.

Something touched his elbow.

"Prisoners," said the Fiver. "I told you bye and bye."

The general tried to speak, but the lump was there to stop him. He swallowed it and tried once again.

"We didn't understand," he said.

"You did not have a taker," said the Fiver. "That why fight so rough."

"We couldn't help it," the general told him. "We didn't know. We never fought this way before."

"We give you takers," said the Fiver. "Next time, we play it right. You do much better with the takers. It easier for us."

No wonder, the general thought, they didn't know about an armistice. No wonder they were confused about the negotiations and the prisoner exchange. Negotiations are not customarily needed to hand back the pieces one had won in a game.

And no wonder those other races had viewed with scorn and loathing Earth's proposal to gang up on the Fivers.

"An unsporting thing to do," the general said aloud. "They could have told us. Or maybe they were so used to it."

And now he understood why the Fivers had picked this planet. There had to be a place where all the ships could land.

He stood and watched the landing ships mushing down upon the rock in clouds of pinkish flame. He tried to count them, but he became confused, although he knew every ship Earth had lost would be accounted for.

"We give you takers," said the Fiver. "We teach you how to use. They easy operate. They never hurt people or ships."

And there was more to it, the general told himself, than just a silly game–though maybe not so silly, once one understood the history and the cultural background and the philosophic concepts that were tied into it. And this much one could say for it: It was better than fighting actual wars.

But with the takers, there would be an end of war. What little war was left would be ended once for all. No longer would an enemy need to be defeated; he could be simply taken. No longer would there be years of guerrilla fighting on newly settled planets; the aborigines could be picked up and deposited in cultural reservations and the dangerous fauna shunted into zoos.

"We fight again?" the Fiver asked with some anxiety.

"Certainly," said the general. "Any time you say. Are we really as good as you claim?"

"You not so hot," the Fiver admitted with disarming candor. "But you the best we ever find. Play plenty, you get better."

The general grinned. Just like the sergeant and the captain and their eternal chess, he thought.

He turned and tapped the Fiver on the shoulder.

"Let's get back," he said. "There's still some drinking in that jug. We mustn't let it go to waste."

3. *Carbon Copy*

THE MAN WHO CAME into Homer Jackson's office was wearing his left shoe on his right foot and his right shoe on his left.

He gave Homer quite a start.

The man was tall and had a gangling look about him, but he was smartly dressed—except for his shoes. And his shoes were all right, too; it was just the way he wore them.

"Am I addressing Mr. Homer Jackson?" he asked with a formality to which Homer was entirely unaccustomed.

"That's me," said Homer.

He squirmed a bit uncomfortably in his chair. He hoped this wasn't one of Gabby Wilson's jokes.

Gabby had an office just down the hall and loved to pester Homer plenty. When Gabby cooked up a joke, he did a massive job on it; he left out not a single detail. And some of Gabby's jokes got pretty rough.

But the man seemed to be dead serious and perhaps a little anxious.

"Mr. Homer Jackson, the suburban realtor?" he persisted.

"That's right," said Homer.

"Specializing in lake properties and country acreages?"

"I'm your man." Homer began to feel uncomfortable. This man was spreading it on a trifle thick and Homer thought he could see Gabby's hand in it.

"I'd like to talk with you. I have a matter of small business."

"Fire away," said Homer, motioning toward a chair.

The man sat down carefully, bolt upright in the chair.

"My name is Oscar Steen," he said. "We're building a development on what is known as the Saunders place. We call it Happy Acres."

Homer nodded. "I'm acquainted with the place. It's the last good holding on the lake. You were fortunate to get it."

"Thank you, Mr. Jackson. We think that it is nice."

"How are you getting on?"

"We have just finished it. But now comes the most important part. We must get people onto the property."

"Well," said Homer, "things are a little tough right now. Money has tightened up and the interest rates are higher and Washington is no help and besides that–"

"We wondered if you'd be interested in handling it for us."

Homer choked a little, but recovered quickly. "Well, now, I don't know. Those houses may be hard to sell. You'd have to get a solid figure for them and the prices will run high. That stone wall you put around the place and those fancy gates and all, I would suspect you have high-class houses. You have gone and made it into an exclusive section. There'll be only a certain class of buyer who might be interested."

"Mr. Jackson," said Steen, "we have a new approach. You won't have to sell them. We're only leasing them."

"Renting them, you mean."

"No, sir, leasing them."

"Well, it all comes out to the same thing in the end. You'll have to get a lot for them."

"Five thousand."

"Five thousand is an awful lot of money. At least, out here it is. Five thousand a year comes to over four hundred a month and–"

"Not for a year," corrected Steen. "For ninety-nine."

"For what!"

"Ninety-nine. We're leasing at five thousand dollars for ninety-nine full years."

"But, man, you can't do that! Why, that's absolutely crazy! Taxes would eat up–"

"We're not so interested in making money on the houses as we are in creating business for our shopping center."

"You mean you have a shopping center in there, too?"

Steen allowed himself a smile. "Mr. Jackson, we obtain the property and then we build the wall to have some privacy so there can be no snoopers."

"Yes, I know," said Homer. "It's smart to do it that way. Good publicity. Whets the public's interest. Gives you a chance to have a big unveiling. But that twelve-foot wall–"

"Fourteen, Mr. Jackson."

"All right, then, fourteen. And it's built of solid stone. I know–I watched them put it up. And no one builds walls of solid stone any more. They just use stone facing. The way you built that wall set you back a hunk–"

"Mr. Jackson, please. We know what we are doing. In this shopping center, we sell everything from peanuts to Cadillacs. But we need customers. So we build houses for our customers. We desire to create a good stable population of rather well-to-do families."

Jumping to his feet in exasperation, Homer paced up and down the office.

"But, Mr. Steen, you can't possibly build up enough business at your shopping center by relying solely on the people in your development. For instance, how many houses have you?"

"Fifty."

"Fifty families are a mere drop in the bucket for a shopping center. Even if every one of those fifty families bought all their needs from you–and you can't be sure they will–but if they did, you'd still have little volume. And you won't pick up any outside trade–not behind that wall, you won't."

He stopped his pacing and went back to his chair.

"I don't know why I'm upset about it," he told Steen. "It's no skin off my nose. Yes, I'll handle the development, but I can't handle leasing at my usual five per cent."

"Oh, I forgot to tell you," said Steen. "You keep the entire five thousand."

Homer gasped like a fish hauled suddenly from water.

"On one condition," added Steen. "One has to be so careful. We have a bank, you see. Part of the shopping center service."

"A bank," Homer said feebly.

"Chartered under the state banking regulations."

"And what has a bank to do with me?"

"You'll take ten per cent," said Steen. "The rest will be credited to your account in the Happy Acres Bank. Every time you lease a unit, you get five hundred cash; forty-five hundred goes into your bank account."

"I don't quite see–"

"There are advantages."

"Yes, I know," Homer said. "It builds up your business. You're out to make that shopping center go."

"That might be one factor. Another is that we can't have you getting rich in front of all your friends and neighbors. There'd be too much talk about it and we don't want that kind of publicity. And there are tax advantages as well."

"Tax advantages?"

"Mr. Jackson, if you lease all fifty houses, you will have earned a quarter million dollars. Have you figured what the income tax might be on a quarter million dollars?"

"It would be quite a lot."

"It would be a crying shame," said Steen. "The bank could be a help."

"I don't quite see how."

"You leave that to us. Leave everything to us. You just lease the houses."

"Mr. Steen, I've been an honest man for years in an occupation where there's opportunity—"

"Honesty, Mr. Jackson. Of course we know you're honest. That's why we came to you. Have you got your car here?"

"It's parked outside."

"Fine. Mine is at the station getting serviced. Let's drive out and look the houses over."

The houses were all that anyone could wish. They were planned with practical imagination and built with loving care. There was, Homer admitted to himself, more honest workmanship in them than he had seen for many years in this era of mass-production building. They had that quiet sense of quality material, of prideful craftsmanship, of solidity, of dignity and tradition that was seldom found any more.

They were well located, all fifty of them, in the wooded hills that stretched back from the lake, and the contractor had not indulged in the ruthless slashing out of trees. Set in natural surroundings with decent amounts of space around them, they stood, each one of them, in comparative privacy.

In the spring, there would be wild flowers, and in the autumn, the woods would flame with color and there would be birds and squirrels and rabbits. And there was a stretch of white sand beach, the last left on the whole lake.

Homer began mentally to write the ad he'd put in the Sunday

paper and found that he looked forward with some anticipation to setting down the words. This was one he could pull out all the stops on, use all the purple prose he wanted.

"I like it, Mr. Steen," he said. "I think they won't be too hard to move."

"That is good," Steen replied. "We are prepared to give you an exclusive contract for a period of ten years. Renewable, of course."

"But why ten years? I can get this tract handled in a year or two, if it goes at all."

"You are mistaken. The business, I can assure you, will be continuing."

They stood on the brick walk in front of one of the houses and looked toward the lake. There were two white sails on the water, far toward the other shore, and a rowboat bobbed in the middle distance, with the black smudge of a hunched fisherman squatted in the stern.

Homer shook his head in some bewilderment. "I don't understand."

"There'll be some subletting," Steen told him smoothly. "When fifty families are involved, there are always some who move."

"But that's another story. Subletting–"

Steen pulled a paper from his pocket and handed it to Homer. "Your contract. You'll want to look it over. Look it over closely. You're a cautious man and that's the kind we want."

Homer drove along the winding, wooded road back to the shopping center with Steen.

The center was a lovely place. It stretched along the entire south side of the property, backed by the fourteen-foot wall, and was a shining place of brand-new paint and gleaming glass and metal.

Homer stopped the car to look at it.

"You've got everything," he said.

"I think we have," said Steen proudly. "We've even got our own telephone exchange."

"Isn't that unusual?"

"Not at all. What we have set up here amounts to a model village, a model living space. We have our own water system and our sewage plant. Why not a telephone exchange?"

Homer let it pass. There was no sense arguing. It all was just this side of crazy, anyhow. No matter how fouled up it was, Steen seemed satisfied.

Maybe, Homer told himself, he knows what he is doing.

But Homer doubted it.

"One thing more," said Steen. "It is just a minor matter, but you should know about it. We have a car agency, you see. Many agencies, in fact. We can supply almost any make of car—"

"But how did you do—"

"We know our way around. Any make of car a person would want. And anyone who leases must buy a car from us."

"Mister," Homer said, "I've heard a lot of fast ones in the auto business, but this one beats them all. If you think I'll sell cars for you—"

"There's nothing wrong with it," said Steen. "We have some good connections. Any car one wants at a fair and honest price. And we are prepared to give good value on their trade-ins, too. It would never do to have old rattle-traps in a high-class development like this."

"And what else? I think you better tell me how many other tie-in deals you have."

"Not a single one. The automobile is all."

Homer put the car in gear and drove slowly toward the gate.

The uniformed gateman saw them coming and swung the gates wide open. He waved to them cheerily as they went past his kiosk.

"I wouldn't touch it with a ten-foot pole," Homer told his wife, Elaine, "if there weren't so much money in it. But things have been kind of slow with this higher interest rate and all and this deal would give me a chance—"

"If it's Mr. Steen wearing his shoes on the wrong feet," Elaine said, "I don't think you need to worry. You remember Uncle Eb?"

"Sure. He was the one who wore his vest inside out."

"Pure stubbornness, that's what it was with Uncle Eb. He put it on inside out one day and someone laughed at him. So Uncle Eb said that was the way to wear a vest. And that's the way he wore it to his dying day."

"Well, sure," said Homer, "that might be it, of course. But wearing a vest inside out wouldn't hurt your chest. Shoes on the wrong feet would hurt something terrible."

"This poor Mr. Steen might be a cripple of some sort. Maybe he was born that way."

"I never heard of anyone born with his right and left feet switched."

"It's queer, naturally," Elaine persisted, "but what difference does it make? If you lease all those houses, we can go to Europe like we've always planned. As far as I'm concerned, he can go barefoot if he wants."

"Yeah, I suppose so."

"And we need a car," Elaine said, beginning on her catalogue. "And drapes for the living room. And I haven't had a new dress in ages. And it's shameful to be using our old silver. We should have replaced it years ago. It's the old stuff Ethel gave us when we were married–"

"All right," said Homer. "If I lease the houses, if the deal holds up, if I don't get in jail–we'll go to Europe."

He knew when he was licked.

He read the contract carefully. It was all right. It said, in black and white, that he got the whole five thousand.

Maybe, he told himself, he should have a lawyer see it. Al Congdon could tell him in a minute if it was ironclad. But he shrank from showing it. There seemed something sinful, almost shameful, about his getting all that money.

He checked on the Happy Acres Bank. A charter had been issued and all regulations had been met.

He checked on building permits and they were in order, too.

So what was a man to do?

Especially when he had a wife who had yearned loudly for ten years to go to Europe.

Homer sat down and wrote an ad for the real estate section of the Sunday paper. On second thought he dismissed the purple prose that he had planned to use. He employed the low-key technique. The ad wasn't long. It didn't cost too much. It read:

$4.16!!!!!

WOULD YOU PAY ONLY $4.16
a month to live in a house
that would sell for $35,000
to $50,000?

If so, call or see
JACKSON REAL ESTATE
Specializing in Lake Property
and Country Acreages

The first prospect was a man named H. F. Morgan. He came into the office early Sunday morning. He was belligerent. He slammed the folded want ad section down on Homer's desk. He had ringed Homer's ad with a big red-pencil mark.

"This isn't true!" yelled Morgan. "What kind of come-on is this?"

"It's substantially true," Homer answered quietly. "That's what it figures out to."

"You mean I just pay $4.16 a month?"

"Well," hedged Homer, "it's not quite as simple as all that. You lease it for ninety-nine years."

"What would I want with a house for ninety-nine years? I won't live that long."

"Actually, it's better than owning a house. You can live there a lifetime, just as if you owned the place, and there are no taxes and no maintenance. And if you have children, they can go on living there."

"You mean this is on the level?"

Homer emphatically nodded. "Absolutely."

"What's wrong with this house of yours?"

"There's nothing wrong with it. It's a new house among other new houses in an exclusive neighborhood. You have a shopping center just up the road that's as good as any city—"

"You say it's new?"

"Right. There are fifty houses. You can pick out the one you want. But I wouldn't take too long to decide, because these will go like hot cakes."

"I got my car outside."

"All right," said Homer, reaching for his hat. "I'll take my car and show you the way. The houses are unlocked. Look at them and choose the one you want."

Out on the street, Homer got into his car and sat down on something angular. He cursed because it hurt. He lifted himself and reached down and picked up the thing he'd sat on.

It was nothing he had ever seen before and he tossed it to the other side of the seat. It was, he thought, something like one of those clip-together plastic blocks that were made for children, but how it had gotten in his car, he could not imagine.

He wheeled out into the street and signaled for the Morgan car to follow.

There were Mrs. Morgan and Jack, a hell-raising eight-year-old, and Judy, a winsome five-year-old, and Butch, the Boxer pup. All of them, Homer saw, were taken by surprise at the sight of Happy Acres. He could tell by the way Mrs. Morgan clasped her hands together and by the way suspicion darkened Morgan's face. One could almost hear him thinking that no one was crazy enough to offer a deal like this.

Jack and Butch, the pup, went running in the woods and Judy danced gaily on the lawn and, Homer told himself, he had them neatly hooked.

Homer spent a busy day. His phone was jammed with calls. House-hunting families, suspicious, half-derisive, descended on the office.

He did the best he could. He'd never had a crowd like this before. He directed the house-hunting families out to Happy Acres. He patiently explained to callers that it was no hoax, that there were houses to be had. He urged all of them to hurry and make up their minds.

"They won't last long," he told them, intoning unctuously that most ancient of all real estate selling gimmicks.

After church, Elaine came down to the office to help him with the phone while he talked to the prospects who dropped in.

Late in the afternoon, he drove out to Happy Acres. The place was an utter madhouse. It looked like a homecoming or a state fair or a monster picnic. People were wandering around, walking through the houses. One had three windows broken. The floors were all tracked up. Water faucets had been left running. Someone had turned on a hose and washed out a flowerbed.

He tried to talk with some of them, but he made no headway. He went back to the office and waited for the rush to start.

There wasn't any rush.

A few phone calls came in and he assured the callers it was on the level. But they were still hard to convince.

He went home beat.

He hadn't leased a house.

Morgan was the first one who came back. He came back alone, early Monday morning. He was still suspicious.

"Look," he said, "I'm an architect. I know what houses cost. What's the catch?"

"The catch is that you pay five thousand cash for a ninety-nine-year lease."

"But that's no catch. That's like buying it. The normal house when it stands a hundred years, has long since lost its value."

"There's another catch," said Homer. "The builder won't lease to you unless you buy a new car from him."

"That's illegal!" shouted Morgan.

"I wouldn't know. Nobody's forcing you to take the offer."

"Let's forget about the car for the moment," Morgan urged. "What I want to know is, how can the builder put up a place like that for five thousand dollars? I know for a fact that he can't."

"So do I. But if he wants to lose a lot of money, who are we to stop him?"

Morgan pounded on the desk. "What's the gimmick, Jackson?"

"The builder wears his shoes on the wrong feet, if that means anything to you."

Morgan stared at him. "I think you're crazy, too. What would that have to do with it?"

"I don't know," said Homer. "I just mentioned it, thinking it might help you."

"Well, it doesn't."

Homer sighed. "It's got me puzzled, too."

Morgan picked up his hat and jammed it on his head. "I'll be seeing you," he said. It sounded like a threat.

"I'll be right here," said Homer as Morgan went slamming out the door.

Homer went down to the drugstore for a cup of coffee.

When he got back, a second visitor was waiting for him. The man sat stiffly in a chair and tapped nervous fingers on his briefcase, held primly in his lap. He looked as if he'd eaten something sour.

"Mr. Jackson," he said, "I represent the County Realtors Association."

"Not interested," said Homer. "I've gotten along for years without joining that outfit. I can get along a few years more."

"I'm not here to solicit membership. I am here about that ad of yours in the paper yesterday."

"Good ad, I thought. It brought in a lot of business."

"It's exactly the kind of advertising that our association frowns upon. It is, if you will pardon the expression, nothing but a come-on."

"Mr.—by the way, what is your name?"

"Snyder," said the man.

"Mr. Snyder, if you happen to be in the market for a place out in this area at the ridiculously low cost of $4.16 a month, I shall be glad to show you any one of fifty houses. If you have a moment, I can drive you out."

The man's mouth snapped together like a trap. "You know what I mean, Jackson. This is fraudulent advertising and you know it is. It is misrepresentation. We mean to show it is."

Homer pitched his hat on top of the filing cabinet and sat down in his chair.

"Snyder," he said, "you're cluttering up the place. You've done your duty—you've warned me. Now get out of here."

It wasn't exactly what he had meant to say and he was surprised at himself for saying it. But now that it was said, there was no way of recalling it and he rather liked the feel of strength and independence that it gave him.

"There is no use flying off the handle," said Snyder. "We could talk this over."

"You came in and made your threat," Homer retorted. "There's nothing to talk over. You said you were going to get me, so come ahead and get me."

Snyder got to his feet savagely. "You'll regret this, Jackson."

"Maybe so," admitted Homer. "Sure you don't need a house?"

"Not from you," said Snyder, and went stalking out.

Must have hurt their weekend sales, Homer told himself, watching Snyder go stumping down the street.

He sat quietly, thinking. He'd known there would be trouble, but there had been no way he could have passed up the deal. Not with Elaine set on that trip to Europe.

And now he was committed. He could not back out even if he wished. And he wasn't sure that he wanted to. There could be a lot of money in it.

The car deal he didn't like, but there was nothing he could do about it. And by handling it right, he might keep in the clear. Maybe, he thought, he should go out and talk to Steen about it.

Gabby Wilson, his insurance-selling neighbor down the hall, came in and flopped into a chair. Gabby was a loudmouth.

"Howsa boy?" he yelled. "Hear you got that Happy Acres deal. How's about cutting in your old pal on the insurance end?"

"Go chase yourself," invited Homer irritably.

"Heard a good story the other day. It seems this wrecking outfit got a job to tear down a building. And the straw boss got his orders wrong and tore down another building." Gabby slapped his knee and roared with laughter. "Can you imagine the look on that contractor's face when he heard the news?"

"It cost him a lot of money," Homer said. "He had a right to be good and sore."

"You don't think it's funny?"

"No, I don't."

"How you getting on with this Happy Acres gang?"

"Fine, so far," said Homer.

"Cheap outfit," Gabby told him. "I been checking round. They got some two-bit contractor from out in the sticks somewhere to do the job for them. Didn't even buy their material from the dealers here. The contractor brought his own crew with him. The developers didn't spend a nickel locally."

"Unpatriotic of them."

"Not smart, either. Houses probably will fall down in a year or two."

"I don't care particularly. Just so I get them leased."

"Do anything so far?"

"Got some interest in them. Here comes a prospect now."

It was Morgan. He had parked in front and was getting out of a new and shiny car, agleam with chrome.

Gabby beat a swift retreat.

Morgan came into the office. He sat down down in a chair and pulled out his checkbook.

"I bought the car," he said. "How do you want this check made out?"

Six weeks later, Homer dropped in at the shopping center office. Steen was sitting with his feet up on the desk. He was wearing black shoes instead of the brown ones he had worn before. They still were on the wrong feet.

"Howdy, Mr. Jackson," he said easily.

Homer sat down in a chair. "I finally got rid of them. All the fifty houses are leased."

"That's fine." Steen reached into a drawer, took out a small book and tossed it across the desk to Homer. "Here. This belongs to you."

Homer picked it up. It was a bank book. He opened it and saw a neat row of $4,500 entries marching down the page.

"You made yourself a mint," said Steen.

"I wish I had fifty more," Homer told him. "Or two hundred more. This thing is catching on. I could lease them in a week. I've got a waiting list longer than my arm."

"Well, why don't you go ahead and lease them?"

"I can't lease them a second time."

"Funny thing," said Steen. "There's no one living in those houses. They all are standing empty."

"But that can't be!" objected Homer. "There might be a few still empty—a few that the people haven't occupied yet. But most of them have moved in. They're living in those houses."

"That's not the way it looks to me."

"What's happened to those people then? Where have they—"

"Mr. Jackson!"

"Yes?"

"You haven't trusted me. You didn't trust me from the start. I don't know why. You thought the deal was queer. You were scared of it. But I've played fair with you. You'll have to admit I have."

Homer stroked the bank book. "More than fair."

"I know what I am doing, Mr. Jackson. I'm not anybody's fool. I have the angles figured out. String along with me. I need a man like you."

"You mean lease all those houses a *second* time!" Homer asked uneasily.

"A second time," said Steen. "And a third. And a fourth. Lease them as often as you like. Keep right on leasing them. No one will mind at all."

"But the people will mind—the people that I lease those houses to," Homer pointed out.

"Mr. Jackson, let me handle this. Don't you worry about a solitary thing. You just keep those houses moving."

"But it isn't right."

"Mr. Jackson, in some six weeks' time, you've made a quarter million dollars. I suppose that's what's wrong with you. I suppose you figure that's enough—"

"Well, no. With income tax and all—"

"Forget the income tax. I told you that this bank of ours had tax advantages."

"I don't get it," Homer said. "This is no way to do business."

"But it is," said Steen. "I challenge you to find a better way to do business. There's no end to it. You can become a multi-millionaire—"

"In jail."

"I've told you we weren't doing wrong. If you don't want to handle it—"

"Let me think it over," Homer pleaded. "Give me a day or two."

"Noon tomorrow," said Steen decisively. "If you don't tell me you are willing to go ahead by noon tomorrow, I'll look for someone else."

Homer got up. He thrust the bank book in his pocket. "I'll be in to see you."

Steen put his feet back on the desk. "Fine. I'll be expecting you."

Out on the concourse, Homer walked along the gleaming shop fronts. And the shops, he saw, were no more than half-staffed and entirely innocent of buyers. He went into a drugstore to buy a cigar and was waited on by a girl of just slightly more than high-school age. He failed to recognize her.

"You live around here?" he asked.

"No, sir. In the city."

He went into a hardware store and into a grocery supermarket. He saw no one he knew. And that was queer. He'd lived in the area for almost thirteen years and thought he knew everyone.

He recalled what Gabby had said about the contractor from somewhere out of town. Maybe, for some zany reason, Steen had a policy against employing local people. Still, he'd employed Homer.

It was a crazy setup, Homer told himself. None of it made sense—and least of all, the leasing of the houses a second time around.

Perhaps he should get out of it. He'd made a fair amount of money. Right now, most likely, he could get out slick and clean. If he stayed, there might be trouble.

He lighted up the cigar and went back to his car. Wheeling out of the parking lot, he headed for the road that led into the housing development.

He drove slowly, looking closely at each house. All of them seemed empty. The windows stared blindly without drapes or curtains. The lawns had not been cut for weeks. There was no sign of anyone—and there should be children and pets playing. Almost everyone he'd leased to had had children and dogs and cats. The place should be jumping, he told himself, and instead it was silent and deserted.

He stopped the car and went into a house. It was bare and empty. There was sawdust in the corners and wood shavings here and there. There were no scuff marks on the floor, no handprints on the wall. The windows had not been washed; the trade-mark paper still was sticking to them.

He went out puzzled.

He inspected two more houses. They were the same.

Steen had been right, then. Steen, with his shoes on the wrong feet, and with something else—with his different way of talking now. Six weeks ago, when Steen had come into Homer's office, he had been stiff and formal, awkward, yet striving for preciseness. And now he was easy in his manner, now he put his feet up on the desk, now he talked slangily.

There was no one living in the houses, Homer admitted to himself. No one had ever lived in them. He had leased all fifty of them and no one had moved in.

And it had a fishy smell—it had a terribly fishy smell.

On his way out, he stopped at Steen's office. The place was locked up.

The old gateman opened the gate and waved at him from the window of his kiosk.

Back in his own office, Homer took out of a drawer the list of leases he had drawn. He phoned Morgan, the first name on the lease.

"That number has been changed," the operator told him.

She gave him the new number and he dialed it.

"Happy Acres," said a singsong operator-voice.

"Huh?"

"Happy Acres," the voice sang. "Whom did you wish, sir?"

"The Morgan residence."

He waited and it was Morgan who answered.

"Homer Jackson. Just checking. How do you like the house? Are you getting on okay?"

"Perfectly," Morgan told him happily. "I've been meaning to come in and thank you for putting me onto this."

"Everything is really all right?"

"Couldn't be better. I hardly ever go into my office now. I stay out here and work in the amusement room. I go fishing and I take walks. The wife and kids are just as pleased as I am." Morgan lowered his voice. "How do you guys manage this? I've tried to figure it out and I can't."

"It's a secret," Homer replied, thinking on his feet. "The answer to the housing problem."

"Not that I care," Morgan said. "Just curious, you know. I'll be dropping in one day. I'll bring you something."

"Glad to see you," said Homer.

He called the Happy Acres number and asked for another family. He went halfway through the list. He talked mostly to the women, although some of the men were home. They were not only happy, but enthusiastic. They asked him jokingly how he got away with it.

When he finished, he was glassy-eyed.

He went down to the drugstore for a cup of coffee.

When he returned, he'd made up his mind.

He took out his waiting list and began making calls.

"There just happens to be a vacancy in Happy Acres if you are interested."

They were.

He reminded them about the cars. They said they'd take care of that matter first thing in the morning.

By suppertime, he'd leased twenty of the houses by making twenty phone calls.

"There's something wrong," Homer said to his wife. "But there's money in it."

"It's just that you don't understand," said Elaine. "There may be a perfectly good reason why Mr. Steen can't explain it all to you."

"But it means we have to give up our trip to Europe. And after we had got our passports and all."

"We can go to Europe later. You'll never get a chance like this again."

"It worries me," said Homer.

"Oh, you're always worried over things that never happen. Mr. Steen is satisfied and the people you have leased to are, so why are you worrying?"

"But where *are* these people? They aren't living in the houses and yet they talk as if they were. And some of them asked me how I got away with it or words to that effect. They asked it as if they admired me for being slick in some kind of shady deal, and if it turns out that I *am* smart, I'd like to know just how I managed—"

"Forget it," Elaine said. "You aren't smart and you never were. If I didn't keep behind you, pushing all the time—"

"Yes, dear," said Homer. He'd heard it all before.

"And quit your worrying."

He tried to, but he couldn't.

The next morning, he drove to Happy Acres and parked across the road from the gate. From seven o'clock until nine, he counted forty-three cars coming out of the development. Some of the people in them he recognized as those he had leased the houses to. Many of them waved to him.

At 9:30, he drove in through the gate and went slowly down the road.

The houses still were empty.

When he got back to the office, there were people waiting for him. The block was clogged with cars that gleamed with newness.

He did a rushing business. No one, it turned out, was interested in seeing the houses. Most of them had seen them earlier. All they wanted was a lease. He filled out the forms as rapidly as he could and raked in the checks and cash.

Some other people showed up. Word had got around, they said, that there were vacancies in the Happy Acres tract. Yes, he said, there were. Just a few of them. He reminded them about the cars.

The last man in line, however, did not want to lease a house.

"My name is Fowler," he said. "I represent the Contractors and Builders Association. Maybe you can help me."

"I've got another house, if that is what you want," said Homer.

"I don't need a house. I have one, thanks."

"Pay you to sell it and get in on this deal. The newest thing in housing. A completely new concept."

Fowler shook his head. "All I want to know is, how do I get hold of Steen?"

"No trouble at all," said Homer. "You just go out to Happy Acres. He has an office there."

"I've been out there a dozen times. He is never in. Usually the office is locked."

"I never have any trouble finding him, although I don't see him often. I'm too busy handling the property."

"Can you tell me how he does it, Mr. Jackson?"

"How he does what? How he is always out?"

"No. How he can sell a house for five thousand dollars."

"He doesn't sell. He leases."

"Don't pull that one on me. It's the same as selling. And he can't build for anywhere near that kind of money. He's losing a good twenty thousand or more on every house out there."

"If a man wants to lose his money–"

"Mr. Jackson," said Fowler, "that is not the point at all. The point is that it's unfair competition."

"Not if he leases," Homer pointed out. "If he sold, it might be."

"If this keeps on, it'll put every contractor in the area out of business."

"That," said Homer, "would be no more than simple justice in a lot of cases. They throw up a shack with plenty of glitter and charge a fancy price and–"

"Nevertheless, Mr. Jackson, none of them intend to be put out of business."

"And you're going to sue," guessed Homer.

"We certainly intend to."

"Don't look at me. I only lease the places."

"We intend to get out an injunction against your leasing them."

"You make the second one," Homer informed him, annoyed.

"The second what?"

"The real estate boys sent a guy like you out here several weeks ago. He made a lot of threats and nothing's happened yet. He was bluffing, just like you."

"Let me set your mind at rest," said Fowler. "I'm not doing any bluffing."

He got up from his chair and stalked stiffly out.

Homer looked at his watch. It was long past lunchtime. He went down to the drugstore for a sandwich and a cup of coffee. The place was empty and he had the counter to himself.

He sat hunched over the lunch and thought about it, trying to get all the queer goings-on straightened out into some sort of logic. But the only thing he could think about was that Steen wore his shoes on the wrong feet.

Wearily, still worried, Homer went back to the office. There were people waiting, with their new cars parked outside. He leased houses right and left.

Apparently the word was spreading. The house-seekers drifted in all afternoon. He leased four more houses before it was time to close.

It was funny, he thought, very, very funny how the word had got around. He hadn't advertised in the last three weeks and they still were coming in.

Just as he was getting ready to lock up, Morgan strode in breezily. He had a package underneath his arm.

"Here you are, pal," he said. "I told you I'd bring you something. Caught them just an hour or two ago."

The package was beginning to get soggy. Homer took it gingerly.

"Thanks very much," he said in a doubtful voice.

"Think nothing of it. I'll bring you more in a week or two."

As soon as Morgan left, Homer closed the blinds and unwrapped the package warily.

Inside were brook trout—trout fresh-caught, with the ferns in which they had been wrapped not even wilting yet.

And there was no trout stream closer than a couple of hundred miles!

Homer stood and shivered. For there was no point in pretending ignorance, no point in repeating smugly to himself that it was all right. Even at five thousand a deal, there still was something wrong–very badly wrong.

He had to face it. They were beginning to close in on him. Fowler had sounded as if he might mean business and the Real Estate Association undoubtedly was lying in ambush, waiting for him to make one little slip. And when he made that slip, they'd snap the trap shut.

To protect himself, he had to know what was going on. He could no longer go at it blind.

Knowing, he might be able to go on. He might know when to quit. And that time, he told himself, might have been as early as this afternoon.

He stood there, with the fish and ferns lying in the wet wrapping paper on the desk, and envisioned a long street of houses, and behind that long street of houses, another identical street of houses, and behind the second street, another–street after street, each behind the other, each exactly like the other, fading out of sight on a flat and level plain.

And that was the way it must be–except there was no second street of houses. There was just the one, standing lone and empty, and yet, somehow, with people living in them.

Lease them a second time, Steen had said, and a third time and a fourth. Don't you worry about a thing. Let me handle it. Leave the worry all to me. You just keep on leasing houses.

And Homer leased one house and the people moved, not into the house he'd leased them, but into the second identical house immediately behind it, and he leased the first house yet again and the people moved into the third, also identical, also directly behind the first and second house, and that was how it was.

Except it was just a childish thing he had dreamed up to offer an explanation–any explanation–for a thing he couldn't understand. A fairy tale.

He tried to get the idea back on the track again, tried to rationalize it, but it was too weird.

A man could trust his sense, couldn't he? He could believe what he could see. And there were only fifty houses–empty houses, despite the fact that people lived in them. He could trust his ears and he had talked to people who were enthusiastic about living in those empty houses.

It was crazy, Homer argued with himself. All those other folks were crazy—Steen and all the people living in the houses.

He wrapped up the fish and retied the package clumsily. No matter where they came from, no matter what lunacy might prevail, those trout surely would taste good. And that, the taste of fresh-caught trout, was one of the few true, solid things left in the entire world.

There was a creaking sound and Homer jumped in panic, whirling swiftly from the desk.

The door was being opened! He'd forgotten to lock the door!

The man who came in wore no uniform, but there was no doubt that he was a cop or detective.

"My name is Hankins," he said. He showed his badge to Homer.

Homer shut his mouth tight to keep his teeth from chattering.

"I think you may be able to do something for me," Hankins said.

"Surely," Homer chattered. "Anything you say."

"You know a man named Dahl?"

"I don't think I do."

"Would you search your records?"

"My records?" Homer echoed wildly.

"Mr. Jackson, you're a businessman. Surely you keep records—the names of persons to whom you sell property and other things like that."

"Yes," said Homer, all in a rush. "Yes, I keep that sort of record. Of course. Sure."

With shaking hands, he pulled out a desk drawer and brought out the folder he'd set up on Happy Acres. He looked through it, fumbling at the papers.

"I think I may have it," he said. "Dahl, did you say the name was?"

"John H. Dahl," said Hankins.

"Three weeks ago, I leased a house in Happy Acres to a John H. Dahl. Do you think he might be the one?"

"Tall, dark man. Forty-three years old. Acts nervous."

Homer shook his head. "I don't remember him. There have been so many people."

"Have you one there for Benny August?"

Homer searched again. "B. J. August. The day after Mr. Dahl."

"And perhaps a man named Drake? More than likely signs himself Hanson Drake."

Drake was also there.

Hankins seemed well pleased. "Now how do I get to this Happy Acres place?"

With a sinking feeling, Homer told him how.

He gathered up his fish and walked outside with Hankins. He stood and watched the officer drive away. He wouldn't want to be around, he suspected, when Hankins returned from Happy Acres. He hoped with all his heart that Hankins wouldn't look him up.

He locked up the office and went down to the drugstore to buy a paper before going home.

He unfolded it and the headlines leaped at him:

THREE HUNTED IN
STOCK SWINDLE

Three photographs on column cuts were ranged underneath the headline. He read the names in turn. Dahl. August. Drake.

He folded the paper tightly and thrust it beneath his arm and he felt the sweat begin to trickle.

Hankins would never find his men, he knew. No one would ever find them. In Happy Acres, they'd be safe. It was, he began to see, a ready-made hideout for all kinds of hunted men.

He wondered how many of the others he had leased the houses to might be hunted, too. No wonder, he thought, the word had spread so quickly. No wonder his office had been filled all day with people who'd already bought the cars.

And what was it all about? How did it work? Who had figured it all out?

And why did he, Homer Jackson, have to be the one who'd get sucked into it?

Elaine took a searching look at him as he came in the door.

"You've been worrying," she scolded.

Homer lied most nobly. "Not worrying. Just a little tired."

"Scared to death" would have been closer to the truth.

At 9 o'clock next morning, he drove to Happy Acres. He was inside the door before he saw that Steen was busy. The man who had been talking to Steen swung swiftly from the desk.

"Oh, it's you," he said.

Homer saw that the man was Hankins.

Steen smiled wearily. "Mr. Hankins seems to think that we're obstructing justice."

"I can't imagine," Homer said, "why he should think that."

Hankins was on the edge of rage. "Where are these people? What have you done with them?"

Steen said: "I've told you, Mr. Hankins, that we only lease the property. We cannot undertake to go surety for anybody who may lease from us."

"You've hidden them!"

"How could we hide them, Mr. Hankins? *Where* could we hide them? The entire development is open to you. You can search it to your heart's content."

"I don't know what is going on," said Hankins savagely, "but I'm going to find out. And once I do, both of you had better have your explanations ready."

"I think," Steen commented, "that Mr. Hankins' determination and deep sense of duty are very splendid things. Don't you, Mr. Jackson?"

"I do, indeed," said Homer, at loss as to what to say.

"You'll be saying that out of the other side of your mouth before I'm through with you," Hankins promised them.

He went storming out the door.

"What a nasty man," Steen remarked, unconcerned.

"I'm getting out," said Homer. "I've got a pocket full of checks and cash. As soon as I turn them over, I am pulling out. You can find someone else to do your dirty work."

"Now I am sorry to hear that. And just when you were doing well. There's a lot of money to be made."

"It's too risky."

"I grant you that it may appear a little risky, but actually it's not. Men like Hankins will raise a lot of dust, but what can they really do? We are completely in the clear."

"We're leasing the same houses over and over again."

"Why, certainly," said Steen. "How else would you expect me to build up the kind of clientele I need to give me business volume in this shopping center? You yourself have told me that fifty families were by no means enough. And you were right, of course. But you lease the houses ten times and you have five hundred families, which is not bad. Lease each one a hundred times and you have five thousand–And incidentally, Mr. Jackson, by the time you lease each of them a hundred times, you will have made yourself twenty-five million dollars, which is not a bad amount for a few years' work.

"Because," Steen concluded, "you see, despite what you may have thought of me, I'm squarely on the level. I gave you the straight goods. I told you I was not interested in money from the houses, but merely from the shopping center."

Homer tried to pretend that he was unimpressed. He kept on emptying checks and wads of money from his pockets. Steen reached out for the checks and began endorsing them. He stacked the money neatly.

"I wish you would reconsider, Mr. Jackson," he urged. "I have need of a man like you. You've worked out so satisfactorily, I hate to see you go."

"Come clean with me," said Homer, "and I might stay. Tell me all there is to tell—how it all works and what all the angles are and what you plan to do."

Steen laid a cautionary finger across his lips. "Hush! You don't know what you're asking."

"You mean you see no trouble coming?"

"Some annoyance, perhaps. Not real trouble."

"They could throw the book at us if they could prove we were hiding people wanted by the law."

Steen sighed deeply. "Mr. Jackson, how many fugitives have you sheltered in the last six weeks?"

"Not a one," said Homer.

"Neither have I." Steen spread his arms wide. "So we have nothing to fear. We've done no wrong. At least," he amended, "none that they can prove."

He picked up the money and the checks and handed them to Homer. "Here," he said. "You might as well take it to the bank. It's your money."

Homer took the money and the checks and stood with them in his hand, thinking about what Steen had said about not doing any wrong. Maybe Steen was right. Maybe Homer was getting scared when there was no need to be.

What could they be charged with?

Fraudulent advertising? There had been no specific claims that had not been performed.

For tying in the auto sales? Just possibly, although he had not made an auto sale a condition of transaction; he had merely mentioned that it would be very nice if they bought a car from Happy Acres Auto Sales.

For selling at less than cost? Probably not, for it would be a fine point of law to prove a lease a sale. And selling or leasing below cost in any case was no crime.

For leasing the same house more than once? Certainly not until it could be proved that someone had suffered damage and it was most unlikely that it could be proved.

For doing away with people? But those people could be reached by telephone, could drive out through the gate. And they were well and happy and enthusiastic.

"Perhaps," Steen said gently, "you have changed your mind. Perhaps you'll stay with us."

"Perhaps I will," said Homer.

He walked down the concourse to the bank. It was an impressive place. The foyer was resplendent in coppery metal and with brightly polished mirrors. There were birds in hanging cages and some of the birds were singing.

There were no customers, but the bank was spick-and-span. An alert vice-president sat behind his polished desk without a thing to do. An equally alert teller waited shiny-faced behind the wicket window.

Homer walked to the window and shoved through the money and the checks. He took his passbook from his pocket and handed it across.

The teller looked at it and said, "I'm sorry, Mr. Jackson, but you have no account with us."

"No account!" cried Homer. "I have a quarter of a million!"

His heart went plunk into his boots, and if he'd had Steen there, he'd have broken him to bits.

"No," said the teller calmly, "you've made an error. That is all."

"Error!" gasped Homer, hanging onto the window to keep from keeling over.

"An understandable error," the teller said sympathetically. "One that any one could make. Your account is not with us, but with the Second Bank."

"Second Bank," wheezed Homer. "What are you talking about? This is the only bank there is."

"Look, it says *Second Bank* right here." He showed Homer the passbook. It did say *Second Happy Acres State Bank*.

"Well, now," said Homer, "that's better. Will you tell me how I get to this Second Bank?"

"Gladly, sir. Right over there. Just go through that door."

He handed back the passbook and the money.

"That door, you say?" inquired Homer.

"Yes. The one beside the drinking fountain."

Homer clutched the passbook and the money tightly in his hand and headed for the door. He opened it and stepped inside and got it shut behind him before he realized that he was in a closet.

It was just a tiny place, not much bigger than a man, and it was as black as the inside of a cat.

Sweat started out on Homer and he searched frantically for the doorknob and finally found it.

He pushed the door open and stumbled out. He strode wrathfully back across the foyer to the teller's window. He rapped angrily on the ledge and the teller turned around.

"What kind of trick is this?" yelled Homer. "What do you think you're pulling? What is going on here? That is nothing but a closet."

"I'm sorry, sir," the teller said. "My fault. I forgot to give you this."

He reached into his cash drawer and handed Homer a small object. It looked for all the world like the replica of a bizarre radiator ornament.

Juggling the object in his hand, Homer asked, "What has this got to do with it?"

"Everything," the teller said. "It will get you to the Second Bank. Don't lose it. You'll need it to get back."

"You mean I just hold it in my hand?"

"That is all you do, sir," the teller assured him.

Homer went back to the door, still unconvinced. It was all a lot of mumbo-jumbo, he told himself. These guys were just the same as Gabby Wilson—full of smart pranks. And if that teller was making a fool of him, he promised himself, he'd mop up the floor with him.

He opened the door and stepped into the closet, only it was no closet. It was another bank.

The metal still was coppery and the mirrors were a-glitter and the birds were singing, but there were customers. There were three tellers instead of the single one in the first bank and the bland, smooth vice-president at his shiny desk was industriously at work.

Homer stood quietly just outside the door through which he'd come from the other bank. The customers seemed not to have noticed him, but as he looked them over, he was startled to discover that there were many whose faces were familiar.

Here, then, were the people who had leased the houses, going about their business in the Second Bank.

He put the miniature radiator ornament in his pocket and headed for the window that seemed to be least busy. He waited in line while the man ahead of him finished making a deposit.

Homer could only see the back of the man's head, but the head seemed to be familiar. He stood there raking through the memories of the people he had met in the last six weeks.

Then the man turned around and Homer saw that it was Dahl. It was the same face he had seen staring at him from the front page of the paper only the night before.

"Hello, Mr. Jackson," said Dahl. "Long time no see."

Homer gulped. "Good day, Mr. Dahl. How do you like the house?"

"Just great, Mr. Jackson. It's so quiet and peaceful here, I can't tear myself away from it."

I bet you can't, thought Homer.

"Glad to hear you say so," he said aloud, and stepped up to the window.

The teller glanced at the passbook. "Good to see you, Mr. Jackson. The president, I think, would like to see you, too. Would you care to step around after I finish your deposit?"

Homer left the teller's window, feeling a little chilly at the prospect of seeing the president, wondering what the president might want and what new trouble it portended.

A hearty voice told him to come in when he knocked on the door.

The president was a beefy gentleman and extremely pleasant.

"I've been hoping you'd come in," he said. "I don't know if you realize it or not, but you're our biggest depositor."

He shook Homer's hand most cordially and motioned him to a chair. He gave him a cigar and Homer, a good judge of tobacco, figured it for at least a fifty-center.

The president, puffing a little, sat down behind his desk.

"This is a good setup here," said Homer, to get the conversation started.

"Oh, yes," the president said. "Most splendid. It's just a test, though, you know."

"No, I hadn't known that."

"Yes, surely. To see if it will work. If it does, we will embark on much bigger projects—ones that will prove even more economically feasible. One never knows, of course, how an idea will catch on. You can run all the preliminary observations and make innumerable surveys and still never know until you try it out."

"That's true," said Homer, wondering what in the world the president was talking about.

"Once we get it all worked out," the president said, "we can turn it over to the natives."

"I see. You're not a native here?"

"Of course not. I am from the city."

And that, thought Homer, was a funny thing to say. He watched the man closely, but there was nothing in his face to indicate that he had misspoken–no flush of embarrassment, no sign of flurry.

"I'm especially glad to have a chance to see you," Homer told him. "As a matter of fact, I had been thinking of switching my account and–"

The president's face took on a look of horror. "But why? Certainly you've been told about the tax advantages."

"I think that the matter got some mention. But, I must confess, I don't understand."

"Why, Mr. Jackson, it is simple. No mystery at all. So far as the authorities of your country are concerned–"

"My country?"

"Well, of course. I think it might logically be argued, even in a court of law, that this place we're in is no longer the United States of America. But even if it should be part of your great nation–I doubt that such a contention would hold up if put to the decision–why, even so, our records are not available to the agents of your country. Don't tell me you fail to see the implications of a situation such as that."

"The income tax," Homer said.

"Correct," said the president, smiling very blandly.

"That is interesting. Interesting, indeed." Homer rose and held out his hand to the president. "I'll be in again."

"Thank you," said the president. "Drop in any time you wish."

On the street outside the bank, the sun was shining brightly. The shopping center stretched along the mall and there were people here and there, walking on the concourse or shopping in the stores. A few cars were parked in the lot and the world of this Second Bank looked exactly like the First Bank's world, and if a man had not known the difference–

Good Lord, thought Homer, what *was* the difference? What had really happened? He'd walked through the door and there was the other bank. He'd walked through a door and found the missing people —the people who had not been living in the empty houses of the First Bank's world.

Because that other world where the houses still stood empty was no more than a show window? It might simply be a street lined with demonstration homes. And here was that second street of houses he'd dreamed up the other night. And beyond this second street, would there be another street and another and another?

He stumbled along the concourse, shaken, now that he realized there really was that second street of houses. It was an idea that was hard to take in stride. He didn't take it in his stride. His mind balked and shied away from it and he told himself it wasn't true. But it was true and there was no way to rationalize it, to make it go away.

There *was* a second street!

He walked along and saw that he was near the gate. The gate, he saw, was the same as ever, with its expanse of massive iron. But there was no gateman.

And a car was coming up the road, heading directly for the gate, and it was moving fast, as if the driver did not see the gate.

Homer shouted and the car kept on. He started to run, waving his arms, but the driver paid not the least attention.

The crazy fool, thought Homer. He'll hit the gate and—

And the car hit the gate, slammed into it, but there was no sound, no crash, no screech of rending metal. There was simply nothing.

The gate was there, undented. And there was no car. The car had disappeared.

Homer stalked the gate.

Ten feet away, he stopped.

The road came up to the gate; beyond it was no road. Beyond the gate was wilderness. The road came up and ended and the wilderness began.

Cautiously, Homer walked out into the road and peered through the gate.

Just a few feet away, a giant oak towered into the air and behind it was the forest, wild and hoary and primeval, and in the forest was the happy sound, the abandoned sound of water running in a brook.

Fish, thought Homer. Maybe that brook is where the trout came from.

He moved toward the gate for a closer look and reached out his hands to grasp the ironwork. Even as he did, the forest went away and the gate as well as he stood in the old familiar entrance to Happy Acres, with the gate wide open, with the state highway running along the wall and the road from the development running out to meet it.

"Good morning, sir," said the gateman. "Maybe you ought to move over to one side. A car is apt to hit you."

"Huh?" Homer asked blankly.

"A car. This is a road, you know."

Homer turned around and brushed past the gateman. He hustled down the concourse, aiming for Steen's office.

But the office was locked. Homer shook the door. He rapped wildly on the glass. He pounded on the frame. Absolutely nothing happened.

Turning from the door, he stared out across the development with incredulous eyes–the vacant concourse, the empty houses among the trees, the faint patches of shining lake peeking through the clearings.

He jammed his hands into his pockets and his fingers touched the little radiator ornament. He took it out and looked at it. He'd seen it before–not the little replica, but the ornament itself.

He had seen it, he remembered, on the new cars parked outside his office by the people seeking leases. He had seen it on the car that had crashed the gate and disappeared.

He walked slowly to the parking lot and drove home.

"I don't think I'll go back to the office today," he told Elaine. "I don't feel so good."

"You've been working too hard," she told him accusingly. "You look all worn out."

"That's a fact," he admitted.

"After lunch, you lie down. And see that you get some sleep."

"Yes, dear," he said.

So it began to fall into a pattern, he thought, lying on his bed and staring at the ceiling. Finally it was clear enough so a man could begin to make some head and tail of it.

It was unbelievable, but there was no choice–one could not disbelieve in it. It was there to see. And if one looked at it any other way, it made no sense at all.

Someone–Steen, perhaps, or maybe someone else for whom Steen was serving as a front–had found out how to build one house, yet have many houses, houses stretching back street after street from the first house, all shadows of the first house, but substantial just the same –substantial enough for families to live in.

Dimensional extensions of that first house. Or houses stretching into time. Or something else as weird.

But however they might do it, it was a swell idea. For you could build one house and sell it, or lease it, time and time again. Except that one was crazy to get hold of an idea that was as good as that and then let someone else make all the money from the leasing of the houses.

And there was no question that Steen was crazy. That idea he had about the shopping center was completely batty–although, stop to think of it, if one had five thousand houses and leased each of them ten times and had a monopoly on all the shops and stores–why, it would pay off tremendously.

And the bank president's slant on sovereignty had certain angles, too, that should not be overlooked.

A new idea in housing, Steen had told him. It was all of that. It was a new idea that would apply to many things–to industry and farming and mining and a lot of other ventures. A man could make one car and there would be many others. A man could build a manufacturing plant and he would have many plants.

It was like a carbon copy, Homer thought–an economic carbon copy. And a man apparently could make as many carbons as he wished. Possibly, he speculated, once you knew the principle, there was no limit to the carbons. Possibly the ghostly parade of Happy Acres houses stretched limitless, forever and forever. There might be no end to them.

He fell asleep and dreamed of going down a line of ghostly houses, counting them frantically as he ran along, hoping that he'd soon get to the end of them, for he couldn't quit until he did get to the end. But they always stretched ahead of him, as far as he could see, and he could find no end to them.

He woke, damp with perspiration, his tongue a dry and bitter wad inside a flannel mouth. He crept out of bed and went to the bathroom. He held his head under a cold faucet. It helped, but not much.

Downstairs, he found a note that Elaine had propped against the radio on the breakfast table: *Gone to play bridge at Mabel's. Sandwiches in refrigerator.*

It was dark outside. He'd slept the daylight hours away. A wasted day, he berated himself–a completely wasted day. He hadn't done a dollar's worth of work.

He found some milk and drank it, but left the sandwiches where they were.

He might as well go to the office and get a little work done, compensate in part for the wasted day. Elaine wouldn't return until almost midnight and there was no sense in staying home alone.

He got his hat and went out to where he'd parked the car in the driveway. He got into it and sat down on something angular and hard. He hoisted himself wrathfully and searched the seat with a groping hand to find the thing he'd sat on.

His fingers closed about it and then he remembered. He'd sat on it on that day Morgan had showed up in answer to the ad. It had been rolling around ever since, unnoticed in the seat.

It was smooth to the touch and warm—warmer than it should be—as if there were a busy little motor humming away inside it.

And suddenly it winked.

He caught his breath and it flashed again.

Exactly like a signal.

Instinct told him to get rid of it, to heave it out the window, but a voice suddenly spoke out of it—a thick, harsh voice that mouthed a sort of chant he could not recognize.

"What the hell?" chattered Homer, fearful now. "What's going on?"

The chanting voice ceased and a heavy silence fell, so thick and frightening that Homer imagined he could feel it closing in on him.

The voice spoke again. This time, it was one word, slow and labored, as if the thick, harsh tongue drove itself to create a new and alien sound.

The silence fell again and there was a sense of waiting. Homer huddled in the seat, cold with fear.

For now he could guess where the cube had come from. Steen had ridden in the car with him and it had fallen from his pocket.

The voice took up again: "Urrr—urr—urrth—mum!"

Homer almost screamed.

Rustling, panting sounds whispered from the cube.

Earthman? Homer wondered wildly. Was that what it had tried to say?

And if that was right, if the cube in fact had been lost by Steen, then it meant that Steen was not a man at all.

He thought of Steen and the way he wore his shoes and suddenly it became understandable why he might wear his shoes that way. Perhaps, where Steen came from, there was no left or right, maybe not even shoes. No man could expect an alien, a being from some distant star, to get the hang of all Earth's customs—not right away, at least. He recalled the first day Steen had come into the office and the precise way he had talked and how stiffly he'd sat down in the chair. And that other day, six weeks later, when Steen had talked slangily and had sat slouched in his chair, with his feet planted on the desk.

Learning, Homer thought. Learning all the time. Getting to know his way around, getting the feel of things, like a gawky country youth learning city ways.

But it sure was a funny thing that he'd never learned about the shoes.

The cube went on gurgling and panting and the thick voice muttered and spat out alien words. One could sense the tenseness and confusion at the other end.

Homer sat cold and rigid, with horror seeping into him drop by splashing drop, while the cube blurted over and over a single phrase that meant not a thing to him.

Then, abruptly, the cube went dead. It lay within his hand, cooling, silent, just a thing that looked and felt like a clip-together plastic block for children.

From far off, he heard the roar of a car as it left the curb and sped off in the night. From someone's backyard, a cat meowed for attention. Nearby, a bird cheeped sleepily.

Homer opened the glove compartment and tossed the cube in among the rags and scraper and the dog-eared road map and the other odds and ends.

He felt the terror and the loathing and the wild agony begin to drain out of his bones and he sat quietly in the car, trying to readjust his mind to this new situation—that Steen must be an alien.

He dipped his hand into his pocket and found the replica of the radiator ornament. And that was the key, he knew—not only the key to the many streets of homes, but the key to Steen and the alien world.

They hadn't meant for him to keep the ornament, of course. If he had returned the way he'd entered the world of the Second Bank, the teller more than likely would have demanded that he give it back. But he'd returned another way, an unexpected way, and it still was in his pocket.

And the radiator ornament, of course, was the reason that Steen had insisted that anyone who leased a house must also buy a car. For the ornament was a key that bridged one world and another. Although, thought Homer, it was rather drastic to insist that a man should buy a car simply so he'd have the correct radiator ornament.

But that might be the way, he told himself, that an alien mind would work.

He was calmer now. The fear still lingered, but pushed back, buried just a little.

Exactly how is a man supposed to act, he asked himself, when he learns there are aliens in the land? Run screeching through the streets, rouse all the citizens, alert the law, go baying on the trail? Or does he continue about his business?

Might he not, he wondered, take advantage of his knowledge, turn it to his own benefit?

He was the only human being on all of Earth who knew.

Steen might not like it known that he was an alien. Perhaps it would be worth a lot to Steen not to have it known.

Homer sat and thought about it. The more he thought, the more reasonable it seemed that Steen might be ready to lay plenty on the line to keep the fact a secret.

Not that I don't have it coming to me, Homer told himself. Not that he hasn't caused me a heap of worry and trouble.

He put his hand into his pocket. The miniature ornament was there. There was no need to wait. Now was as good as any time.

He turned the ignition key and the motor came to life. He backed out of the driveway and took the road to Happy Acres.

The development was dark and quiet. Even the usual advertising signs were turned off in the shop fronts.

He parked in front of Steen's office and got out. Opening the trunk, he found the jack handle in the dark.

He stood staring toward the gate. There was no sign of the gateman. But that was a chance he'd have to take. If the old fool tried to interfere, he could handle him.

For a moment, in front of the door to Steen's office, he hesitated, trying to reassure himself. Certainly there would be another closet, some way to get to those other worlds, inside the office.

He struck savagely at the glass in the door with the jack handle. The glass splintered and rained down, with crashing, tinkling sounds.

Homer waited, tense, listening, watching. Nothing stirred. The old gateman, if he was around, apparently had not heard the crash.

Carefully, Homer reached through the broken glass and manipulated the night lock. The door swung easily open. He walked inside and closed the door behind him.

In the empty office, Homer paused until his eyes became accustomed to the deeper darkness. He moved forward, groping with his hands, and found the desk. He could make out the dim bulk of a filing case. There should be a door somewhere. Perhaps not a door into the street, but a door into a hideout—some room where Steen could disappear to eat and rest and sleep; some place that might have a touch of his alien home about it.

Homer moved from the desk to the filing cabinet and felt along the wall. Almost immediately, he found a door.

He took a firmer grip on the jack handle and twisted on the knob. He walked through the door and there was the room, lighted a garish green by a lantern suspended from the ceiling.

There was sound and the sense of movement. Homer's hair stood straight on end and he felt his skin trying very hard to roll up his back. The hairy monster reached out a paw and grabbed him by the shoulder just as Homer swung around to dive back through the door.

The monster's paw was heavy and very strong. It was hairy and it tickled. Homer opened his mouth to scream, but his tongue dried up and his throat closed and he couldn't make a sound. The jack handle slipped from his numb fingers and clattered to the floor.

For a long moment, he stood there in the grip of the hairy monster and he supposed it had a face, but he could not see the face, for the hair grew all over it and drooped down where its face should be. The monster was a large one, with massive chest and shoulders that tapered down to a slim, athletic waist. Frightened as he was, Homer still could not keep from thinking that it looked a lot like an English sheepdog with a wrestler's body.

And all the while, there was something rolling on the floor and moaning.

Then the hairy monster said, in halting, stumbling syllables: "You Mister Jackson, you are not?"

Homer made a croaking sound.

"I apologize," the monster told him. "I very poor at your words. I work on your planet survey, but not so good with words."

He motioned at the thing moaning and rolling on the floor. "That was good with words."

The hairy hand dropped from Homer's shoulder.

"That," it said, gesturing at the floor again, "your Mister Steen."

"What is wrong with him?" Homer blurted out. "Is he sick or something?"

"He die himself," the monster said.

"You mean he's dying and you're just standing there—"

"No, no. He—how do you word it right?—he unlive himself."

"You mean he's killing himself? Committing suicide?"

"Yes," the monster said. "He does it very well. Do you not agree?"

"But you can't—"

"He take great pride in it. He make spectacular. He just starting now. He work up to grand finale. You must stay and watch. It be something to remember."

"No, thank you," Homer said faintly.

Homer turned to go, but the monster put out a hairy paw and stopped him.

"You must not be afraid of us. I stay half myself, all right? Could change entirely into human, but much trouble. Good enough this way?"

"It's all right," said Homer.

"We owe you debt," the monster said. "This Mister Steen of yours got things all scrambled up."

"I'll say he did," said Homer feelingly.

"He just a stumblebum. Bungler. He likewise is a joker."

"Joker?"

"Clown? Wise guy? You know—he made the joke. Sometimes very sly joke, but stupid just the same."

The monster leaned forward to peer into Homer's face.

"Your planet, it has its jokers, too?"

"Yes, indeed," Homer said. "There's one down the hall from me. His name is Gabby Wilson."

"So you understand then. A joker not too bad if that is all he is. But take a joker who makes mistakes and that is most bad. You have name for it. Smart aleck?"

"That's the name," said Homer.

"We make projects for the planets, for very many planets. We try to make each project fit the planet. The kind that will help the planet, the kind it needs the most."

"Like foreign aid," Homer supplied.

"So this bungler," said the monster, his voice rising in forthright and honest wrath, "this smart aleck, this nincompoop, this Mister Steen of yours, what do you think he does? He came to Earth as project manager—and he brings *wrong plan!* He is like that other times, going off not cocked. But this, it is too much. Final straw."

"You mean this Happy Acres business was never meant for Earth, but for some other planet?"

The monster draped his arm around Homer's shoulder in a gesture of understanding and affection. "That exactly what he do. No need of Happy Acres here. You still have room enough for all your people. No need to double up."

"But, sir," said Homer earnestly, "it is a swell idea. It has possibilities."

"Other things you need much worse, my friend. We have better plan for you."

Homer couldn't decide whether he liked the way the monster talked about the better plan.

"What other plan?" he asked.

"That is topmost secret. To make project big success, it must be done so that the natives think they the ones who do it. And that," the monster said, gesturing toward the floor, "is where this silly obscenity failed in second place. He let you find out what was going on."

"But there were all the other people, too," Homer protested. "All the people in the shops. The bank president and the gateman and—"

"All of them is us," the monster explained. "Them the crew that came with Mister Steen."

"But they were so human-looking! They looked exactly like us!"

"They play it straight. This ape, he ham it up."

"But they dressed like us and they wore shoes—"

"The shoes was more joke," the monster said furiously. "Your Mister Steen, he know how to make himself a human like the rest of them. But he wear his shoes wrong to get you humans—your humans'—there is a word for it."

"Goat?"

"That is it! He wear them wrong to get your humans' goat. And he make outrageous deal with you and he watch you worry and he rejoice greatly and think himself superior and smart because he that kind of clown. That, I tell you, is no way to treat anyone. That is no true-blue friendship. But your Mister Steen, he was plain jerk. Let us go and watch him suffer."

"No," said Homer, horrified.

"You no like this dying?"

"It's inhuman."

"Of course, inhuman. We not humans, us. It is a way we have, a social law. He make himself a fool. He make bonehead blunder. He must dead himself. He must do it good. Great honor, do it good. He bungle everything in life, he must not bungle dying. He forever heel if he do."

Homer shivered, listening to the anguish of the alien on the floor, sick at stomach and giddy in the green flood of alien light.

"Now it is to end," said the alien. "We wipe out project. It was nonsensical mistake. We will take it all away."

"You can't mean that!" argued Homer. "We need it. We could make use of it. Just show us the principle."

"No," the monster said.

"But if you wipe out the project, there'll be all these people—"

"Sorry."

"They'll murder me! I was the one who leased the houses to them—"

"Too bad," the monster said.

"And all that money in the bank! A quarter of a million dollars, more than a quarter of a million dollars! It will be wiped out!"

"You have human money in bank?"

"I did. I suppose *that's* too bad, too."

"We can pay you off. Mister Steen make a lot of money. He store it over there."

He pointed to the far wall. "You see that pile of bags? You take all that you can carry."

"Money?" Homer asked.

"Good money."

"All I can carry?" insisted Homer, nailing it down tight. "And you will let me leave?"

"We do you wrong," the monster said. "This fix it just a little?"

"I'll tell the world," said Homer, with enthusiasm.

Steen was becoming noisier. He had changed into his alien form and now he rolled upon the floor, knotted up and writhing.

Homer walked wide around him to get to the farther wall. He lifted down the bags and they were fairly heavy. He could take two at least, he figured. He hoisted two on his back, then piled on the third. He barely made it back across the room.

The monster watched him with some admiration. "You like money, huh?"

"You bet," Homer panted. "Everyone likes money."

He set the bags down by the door.

"You sure you not stay and watch? It get good directly. It be amusing, maybe even interesting."

Homer held down a rising shudder. "No, thank you very much."

The monster helped him get the bags on his shoulder. "I hold the door for you."

"Thank you," said Homer. "Good day to you and thanks for everything."

"Good-by, my friend," the monster said.

He held the door and Homer walked on through.

He came back into the office he'd left an hour before, the glass in the door shattered and his car still parked outside.

Homer hurried.

In less than five minutes, he went roaring out the gate, with the bags of money locked inside the trunk.

There was little time, he realized. What he did had to be done fast. For when the monster wiped out Happy Acres, there would be a battalion of families marooned there in the woods and they'd come boiling out with a single thought in mind—to get their hands on Homer Jackson.

He tried to imagine what it might be like, and then tried to stop thinking what it might be like, but couldn't.

There would be a lot of people there without any houses. They'd wake up in the wild, wet woods, with their furniture and belongings scattered all about them. And all those bright new cars would be in among the trees. And the people would be plenty sore.

Not that he blamed them much.

He was sore himself.

That lousy Steen, he said. Like that contractor Gabby told about—the one who went out on a wrecking job and demolished the wrong house.

The dashboard clock said slightly after midnight. Elaine would be home by now and they could start right out.

Homer turned into the driveway and braked to a halt. There was a light in the kitchen window. He ran up the walk and burst into the house.

"Oh, *there* you are," said Elaine. "I wondered where you were. What's wrong with you?"

"We're getting out of here," Homer babbled.

"Have you gone stark crazy? Getting out!"

"Now for once," said Homer, "don't give me an argument. We're getting out of here. Tonight. I've got three sacks of money out there in the car–"

"Money! How did you get three sacks–"

"It's legal," Homer pleaded. "There's nothing wrong with it. I didn't rob a bank. There's no time to explain. Let us just get going."

She got icy calm. "Where are we going, Homer?"

"We can decide that later. Maybe Mexico."

"You're ill," she scolded. "You've been working too hard lately. And worrying about that Happy Acres deal–"

It was too much for Homer. He turned toward the door.

"Homer! Where are you going, Homer!"

"I'll show you the money," he gritted. "I'll show you I really have it."

"Wait for me," she cried, but he didn't wait. She ran down the walk behind him.

He opened the car trunk. "There it is. We'll carry it up to the house. You can take off your shoes and walk in it. Then maybe you'll believe me."

"No, Homer, no!"

"Here, help me with these sacks," he said.

Inside the house, he opened the sacks. Neatly bundled sheafs of bills spilled out on the floor.

Elaine knelt and picked up a package.

"Why, it's real!" she cried happily.

"Of course it is," said Homer.

"And, Homer, these are twenty-thousand-dollar bills!"

She dropped the package that she held and picked up another and another and another.

"And so are these!" she screamed. "There are millions and millions here!"

Homer was pawing desperately through the heap of money. Sweat was running down his face.

"Are they all twenty-thousand-dollar bills?" she asked hopefully.

"Yes," said Homer in a beaten voice.

"But what is wrong?"

"That dirty, lowdown, bungling Steen," he said bitterly.

"But what is wrong?" she cried again.

"They aren't worth a dime," said Homer. "There are no such things as twenty-thousand-dollar bills. The Treasury never issued any!"

4. Founding Father

WINSTON-KIRBY WALKED HOME across the moor just before the twilight hour and it was then, he felt, that the land was at its best. The sun was sinking into a crimson froth of clouds and the first gray-silver light began to run across the swales. There were moments when it seemed all eternity grew quiet and watched with held breath.

It had been a good day and it would be a good home-coming, for the others would be waiting for him with the dinner table set and the fireplace blazing and the drinks set close at hand. It was a pity, he thought, that they would not go walking with him, although, in this particular instance, he was rather glad they hadn't. Once in a while, it was a good thing for a man to be alone. For almost a hundred years, aboard the ship, there had been no chance to be alone.

But that was over now and they could settle down, just the six of them, to lead the kind of life they'd planned. After only a few short weeks, the planet was beginning to seem like home; in the years to come, it would become in truth a home such as Earth had never been.

Once again he felt the twinge of recurring wonder at how they'd ever got away with it. That Earth should allow six of its immortals to slip through its clutches seemed unbelievable. Earth had real and urgent need for all of its immortals, and that not one, but six, of them should be allowed to slip away, to live lives of their own, was beyond all logic. And yet that was exactly what had happened.

There was something queer about it, Winston-Kirby told himself. On the century-long flight from Earth, they'd often talked about it and wondered how it had come about. Cranford-Adams, he recalled, had been convinced that it was some subtle trap, but after a hundred years there was no evidence of any trap and it had begun to seem Cranford-Adams must be wrong.

Winston-Kirby topped the gentle rise that he had been climbing and, in the gathering dusk, he saw the manor house–exactly the kind of house he had dreamed about for years, precisely the kind of house to be built in such a setting–except that the robots had built it much too large. But that, he consoled himself, was what one had to expect of robots. Efficient, certainly, and very well intentioned and obedient and nice to have around, but sometimes pretty stupid.

He stood on the hilltop and gazed down upon the house. How many times had he and his companions, at the dinner table, planned the kind of house they would build? How often had they speculated upon the accuracy of the specifications given for this planet they had chosen from the Exploratory Files, fearful that it might not be in every actuality the way it was described?

But here, finally, it was–something out of Hardy, something from the Baskervilles–the long imagining come to comfortable reality.

There was the manor house, with the light shining from its windows, and the dark bulk of the outbuildings built to house the livestock, which had been brought in the ship as frozen embryos and soon would be emerging from the incubators. And there the level land that in a few more months would be fields and gardens, and to the north the spaceship stood after years of roving. As he watched, the first bright star sprang out just beyond the spaceship's nose, and the spaceship and the star looked for all the world like a symbolic Christmas candle.

He walked down the hill, with the first night wind blowing in his face and the ancient smell of heather in the air, and was happy and exultant.

It was sinful, he thought, to be so joyful, but there was reason for it. The voyage had been happy and the planet-strike successful and here he was, the undisputed proprietor of an entire planet upon which, in the fullness of time, he would found a family and a dynasty. And he had all the time there was. There was no need to hurry. He had all of eternity if he needed it.

And, best of all, he had good companions.

They would be waiting for him when he stepped through the door. There would be laughter and a quick drink, then a leisurely dinner, and, later, brandy before the blazing fire. And there'd be talk–good talk, sober and intimate and friendly.

It had been the talk, he told himself, more than anything else, which had gotten them sanely through the century of space flight. That and their mutual love and appreciation of the finer points of the human culture—understanding of the arts, love of good literature, interest in philosophy. It was not often that six persons could live intimately for a hundred years without a single spat, without a touch of cabin fever.

Inside the manor house, they would be waiting for him in the fire- and candlelight, with the drinks all mixed and the talk already started, and the room would be warm with good fellowship and perfect understanding.

Cranford-Adams would be sitting in the big chair before the fire, staring at the flames and thinking, for he was the thinker of the group. And Allyn-Burbage would be standing, with one elbow on the mantel, a glass clutched in his hand and in his eyes the twinkle of good humor. Cosette-Middleton would be talking with him and laughing, for she was the gay one, with her elfin spirit and her golden hair. Anna-Quinze more than likely would be reading, curled up in a chair, and Mary-Foyle would be simply waiting, glad to be alive, glad to be with friends.

These, he thought, were the long companions of the trip, so full of understanding, so tolerant and gracious that a century had not dulled the beauty of their friendship.

Winston-Kirby hurried, a thing he almost never did, at the thought of those five who were waiting for him, anxious to be with them, to tell them of his walk across the moor, to discuss with them still again some details of their plans.

He turned into the walk. The wind was becoming cold, as it always did with the fall of darkness, and he raised the collar of his jacket for the poor protection it afforded.

He reached the door and stood for an instant in the chill, to savor the never-failing satisfaction of the massive timbering and the stout, strong squareness of the house. A place built to stand through the centuries, he thought, a place of dynasty with a sense of foreverness.

He pressed the latch and thrust his weight against the door and it came slowly open. A blast of warm air rushed out to greet him. He stepped into the entry hall and closed the door behind him. As he took off his cap and jacket and found a place to hang them, he stamped and scuffed his feet a little to let the others know that he had returned.

But there were no greetings for him, no sound of happy laughter. There was only silence from the inner room.

He turned about so swiftly that his hand trailed across his jacket and dislodged it from the hook. It fell to the floor with a smooth rustle of fabric and lay there, a little mound of cloth.

His legs suddenly were cold and heavy, and when he tried to hurry, the best he could do was shuffle, and he felt the chill edge of fear.

He reached the entrance to the room and stopped, shocked into immobility. His hands went out and grasped the door jamb on either side of him.

There was no one in the room. And not only that—the room itself was different. It was not simply the companions who were gone. Gone, as well, were the rich furnishings of the room, gone the comfort and the pride.

There were no rugs upon the floor, no hangings at the windows, no paintings on the wall. The fireplace was a naked thing of rough and jagged stone. The furniture—the little there was—was primitive, barely knocked together. A small trestle table stood before the fireplace, with a three-legged stool pulled up to a place that was set for one.

Winston-Kirby tried to call. The first time, the words gurgled in his throat and he could not get them out. He tried again and made it: "Job! Job, where are you?"

Job came running from somewhere in the house. "What's the trouble, sir?"

"Where are the others? Where have they gone? They should be waiting for me."

Job shook his head, just slightly, a quick move right and left. "Mister Kirby, sir, they were never here."

"Never here! But they were here when I left this morning. They knew I'd be coming back."

"You fail to understand, sir. There were never any others. There were just you and I and the other robots. And the embryos, of course."

Winston-Kirby let go of the door and walked a few feet forward. "Job," he said, "you're joking." But he knew something was wrong—robots never joke.

"We let you keep them as long as we could," said Job. "We hated to have to take them from you, sir. But we needed the equipment for the incubators."

"But this room! The rugs, the furniture, the—"

"That was all part of it, sir. Part of the dimensino."

Winston-Kirby walked slowly across the room, used one foot to hook the three-legged stool out from the table. He sat down heavily.

"The dimensino?" he asked.

"Surely you remember."

He frowned to indicate he didn't. But it was coming back to him, some of it, slowly and reluctantly, emerging vaguely after all the years of forgetfulness.

He fought against the remembering and the knowledge. He tried to push it back into that dark corner of his mind from which it came. It was sacrilege and treason—it was madness.

"The human embryos," Job told him, "came through very well. Of the thousand of them, all but three are viable."

Winston-Kirby shook his head, as if to clear away the mist that befogged his brain.

"We have the incubators all set up in the outbuildings, sir," said Job. "We waited as long as we could before we took the dimensino equipment. We let you have it until the very last. It might have been easier, sir, if we could have done it gradually, but there is no provision for that. You either have dimensino or you haven't got it."

"Of course," said Winston-Kirby, mumbling just a little. "It was considerate of you. I thank you very much."

He stood up unsteadily and rubbed his hand across his eyes.

"It's not possible," he said. "It simply can't *be* possible. I lived for a hundred years with them. They were as real as I am. They were flesh and blood, I tell you. They were . . . ."

The room still was bare and empty, a mocking emptiness, an alien mockery.

"It is possible," said Job gently. "It is just the way it should be. Everything has gone according to the book. You are here, still sane, thanks to the dimensino. The embryos came through better than expected. The equipment is intact. In eight months or so, the children will be coming from the incubators. By that time, we will have gardens and a crop on the way. The livestock embryos will also have emerged and the colony will be largely self-sustaining."

Winston-Kirby strode to the table, picked up the plate that was laid at the single place. It was lightweight plastic.

"Tell me," he said. "Have we any china? Have we any glassware or silver?"

Job looked as near to startled as a robot ever could. "Of course not, sir. We had no room for more than just the bare essentials this trip.

The china and the silver and all the rest of it will have to wait until much later."

"And I have been eating ship rations?"

"Naturally," said Job. "There was so little room and so much we had to take . . ."

Winston-Kirby stood with the plate in his hand, tapping it gently on the table, remembering those other dinners—aboard the ship and since the ship had landed—the steaming soup in its satiny tureen, the pink and juicy prime ribs, the huge potatoes baked to a mealy turn, the crisp green lettuce, the shine of polished silver, the soft sheen of good china, the—

"Job," he said.

"Sir?"

"It was all delusion, then?"

"I am afraid it was. I am sorry, sir."

"And you robots?"

"All of us are fine, sir. It was different with us. We can face reality."

"And humans can't?"

"Sometimes it is better if they can be protected from it."

"But not now?"

"Not any more," said Job. "It must be faced now, sir."

Winston-Kirby laid the plate down on the table and turned back to the robot. "I think I'll go up to my room and change to other clothes. I presume dinner will be ready soon. Ship rations, doubtless?"

"A special treat tonight," Job told him. "Hezekiah found some lichens and I've made a pot of soup."

"Splendid!" Winston-Kirby said, trying not to gag.

He climbed the stairs to the door at the head of the stairs.

As he was about to go into the room, another robot came tramping down the hall.

"Good evening, sir," it said.

"And who are you?"

"I'm Solomon," said the robot. "I'm fixing up the nurseries."

"Soundproofing them, I hope."

"Oh, nothing like that. We haven't the material or time."

"Well, carry on," said Winston-Kirby, and went into the room.

It was not his room at all. It was small and plain. There was a bunk instead of the great four-poster he had been sleeping in and there were no rugs, no full-length mirror, no easy chairs.

Delusion, he had said, not really believing it.

But here there was no delusion.

The room was cold with a dread reality—a reality, he knew, that had been long delayed. In the loneliness of this tiny room, he came face to face with it and felt the sick sense of loss. It was a reckoning that had been extended into the future as far as it might be—and extended not alone as a matter of mercy, of mere consideration, but because of a cold, hard necessity, a practical concession to human vulnerability.

For no man, no matter how well adjusted, no matter if immortal, could survive intact, in mind and body, a trip such as he had made. To survive a century under space conditions, there must be delusion and companionship to provide security and purpose from day to day. And that companionship must be more than human. For mere human companionship, however ideal, would give rise to countless irritations, would breed deadly cabin fever.

Dimensino companionship was the answer, then, providing an illusion of companionship flexible to every mood and need of the human subject. Providing, as well, a background to that companionship—a wish-fulfillment way of life that nailed down security such as humans under normal circumstances never could have known.

He sat down on the bunk and began to unlace his heavy walking shoes.

The practical human race, he thought—practical to the point of fooling itself to reach destination, practical to the point of fabricating the dimensino equipment to specifications which could be utilized, upon arrival, in the incubators.

But willing to gamble when there was a need to gamble. Ready to bet that a man could survive a century in space if he were sufficiently insulated against reality—insulated by seeming flesh and blood which, in sober fact, existed only by the courtesy of the human mind assisted by intricate electronics.

For no ship before had ever gone so far on a colonizing mission. No man had ever existed for even half as long under the influence of dimensino.

But there were few planets where Man might plant a colony under natural conditions, without extensive and expensive installations and precautions. The nearer of these planets had been colonized and the survey had shown that this one which he finally had reached was especially attractive.

So Earth and Man had bet. Especially one man, Winston-Kirby

told himself with pride, but the pride was bitter in his mouth. The odds, he recalled, had been five to three against him.

And yet, even in his bitterness, he recognized the significance of what he had done. It was another breakthrough, another triumph for the busy little brain that was hammering at the door of all eternity.

It meant that the Galaxy was open, that Earth could remain the center of an expanding empire, that dimensino and immortal could travel to the very edge of space, that the seed of Man would be scattered wide and far, traveling as frozen embryos through the cold, black distances which hurt the mind to think of.

He went to the small chest of drawers and found a change of clothing, laid it on the bunk and began to take off his hiking outfit.

Everything was going according to the book, Job had said.

The house was bigger than he had wanted it, but the robots had been right—a big building would be needed to house a thousand babies. The incubators were set up and the nurseries were being readied and another far Earth colony was getting under way.

And colonies were important, he remembered, reaching back into that day, a hundred years before, when he and many others had laid their plans—including the plan whereby he could delude himself and thus preserve his sanity. For with more and more of the immortal mutations occurring, the day was not too distant when the human race would require all the room that it could grab.

And it was the mutant immortals who were the key persons in the colonizing programs—going out as founding fathers to supervise the beginning of each colony, staying on as long as needed, to act as a sort of elder statesman until that day when the colony could stand on its own feet.

There would be busy years ahead, he knew, serving as father, proctor, judge, sage and administrator, a sort of glorified Old Man of a brand-new tribe.

He pulled on his trousers, scuffed his feet into his shoes, rose to tuck in his shirttail. And he turned, by force of habit, to the full-length mirror.

And the glass was there!

He stood astounded, gaping foolishly at the image of himself. And behind him, in the glass, he saw the great four-poster and the easy chairs.

He swung around and the bed and chairs were gone. There were just the bunk and the chest of drawers in the small, mean room.

Slowly he sat down on the edge of the bunk, clasping his hands so they wouldn't shake.

It wasn't true! It couldn't be! The dimensino was gone.

And yet it was with him still, lurking in his brain, just around the corner if he would only try.

He tried and it was easy. The room changed as he remembered it—with the full-length mirror and the massive bed upon which he sat, the thick rugs, the gleaming liquor cabinet and the tasteful drapes.

He tried to make it go away, barely remembering back in some deep, black closet of his mind that he must make it go.

But it wouldn't go away.

He tried and tried again, and it still was there, and he felt the will to make it go, slipping from his consciousness.

"No!" he cried in terror, and the terror did it.

He sat in the small, bare room.

He found that he was breathing hard, as if he'd climbed a high, steep hill. His hands were fists and his teeth were clenched and he felt the sweat trickling down his ribs.

It would be easy, he thought, so easy and so pleasant to slip back to the old security, to the warm, deep friendship, to the lack of pressing purpose.

But he must not do it, for here was a job to do. Distasteful as it seemed now, as cold, as barren, it still was something he must do. For it was more than just one more colony. It was the breakthrough, the sure and certain knowledge, the proved knowledge, that Man no longer was chained by time or distance.

And yet there was this danger to be recognized; it was not something on which one might shut one's mind. It must be reported in every clinical detail so that, back on Earth, it might be studied and the inherent menace somehow remedied or removed.

Side effect, he wondered, or simply a matter of learning? For the dimensino was no more than an aid to the human mind—an aid to a very curious end, the production of controlled hallucinations operating on the wish-fulfillment level.

After a hundred years, perhaps, the human mind had learned the technique well, so well that there was no longer need of the dimensino.

It was something he should have realized, he insisted to himself. He had gone on long walks and, during all those hours alone, the delusion had not faded. It had taken the sudden shock of silence and emptiness, where he had expected laughter and warm greeting, to penetrate the haze of delusion in which he'd walked for years. And even now it lurked, a conditioned state of mind, to ambush him at every hidden thicket.

How long would it be before the ability would start to wear away? What might be done to wipe it out entirely? How does one unlearn a thing he's spent a century in learning? Exactly how dangerous was it—was there necessity of a conscious thought, an absolute command or could a man slip into it simply as an involuntary retreat from drear reality?

He must warn the robots. He must talk it over with them. Some sort of emergency measure must be set up to protect him against the wish or urge, some manner of drastic action be devised to rescue him, should he slip back into the old delusion.

Although, he thought, it would be so fine to walk out of the room and down the stairs and find the others waiting for him, with the drinks all ready and the talk well started. . . .

"Cut it out!" he screamed.

Wipe it from his mind—that was what he must do. He must not even think of it. He must work so hard that he would have no time to think, become so tired from work that he'd fall into bed and go to sleep at once and have no chance to dream.

He ran through his mind all that must be done—the watching of the incubators, preparing the ground for gardens and for crops, servicing the atomic generators, getting in timbers against the need of building, exploring and mapping and surveying the adjacent territory, overhauling the ship for the one-robot return flight to Earth.

He filled his mind with it. He tagged items for further thought and action. He planned the days and months and years ahead. And at last he was satisfied.

He had it under control.

He tied his shoes and finished buttoning his shirt. Then, with a resolute tread, he opened the door and walked out on the landing.

A hum of talk floating up the stairway stopped him in his tracks.

Fear washed over him. Then the fear evaporated. Gladness burst within him and he took a quick step forward.

At the top of the stairs, he halted and reached out a hand to grasp the banister.

Alarm bells were ringing in his brain and the gladness fell away. There was nothing left but sorrow, a terrible, awful grieving.

He could see one corner of the room below and he could see that it was carpeted. He could see the drapes and paintings and one ornate golden chair.

With a moan, he turned and fled to his room. He slammed the door and stood with his back against it.

The room was the way it should be, bare and plain and cold.

Thank God, he thought. Thank God!

A shout came up the stairway.

"Winston, what's wrong with you? Winston, hurry up!"

And another voice: "Winston, we're celebrating. We have a suckling pig."

And still another voice: "With an apple in its mouth."

He didn't answer.

They'll go away, he thought. They have to go away.

And even as he thought it, half of him—more than half—longed in sudden agony to open up the door and go down the stairs and know once again the old security and the ancient friendship.

He found that he had both his hands behind his back and that they were clutching the doorknob as if they were frozen there.

He heard steps on the stairway, the sound of many happy, friendly voices, coming up to get him.

5. *Idiot's Crusade*

FOR A LONG TIME I was the village idiot, but not any longer—although they call me "dummy" still and even worse than that.

I'm a genius now, but I won't let them know.

Not ever.

If they found out, they'd be on their guard against me.

No one has suspected me and no one will. My shuffle is the same and my gaze as vacant and my mumblings just as vague as they ever were. At times, it has been hard to remember to keep the shuffle and the gaze and mumblings as they were before, times when it was hard not to overdo them. But it's important not to arouse suspicion.

It all started the morning I went fishing.

I told Ma I was going fishing while we were eating breakfast and she didn't object. She knows I like fishing. When I fish, I don't get into trouble.

"All right, Jim," she said. "Some fish will taste real good."

"I know where to get them," I told her. "That hole in the creek just past Alf Adams' place."

"Now don't you get into any fracas with Alf," Ma warned me. "Just because you don't like him—"

"He was mean to me. He worked me harder than he should have. And he cheated me out of my pay. And he laughs at me."

I shouldn't have said that, because it hurts Ma when I say someone laughs at me.

"You mustn't pay attention to what people do," said Ma, speaking kind and gentle. "Remember what Preacher Martin said last Sunday. He said—"

"I know what he said, but I still don't like being laughed at. People shouldn't laugh at me."

"No," Ma agreed, looking sad. "They shouldn't."

I went on eating my breakfast, thinking that Preacher Martin was a great one to be talking about humility and patience, knowing the kind of man he was and how he was carrying on with Jennie Smith, the organist. He was a great one to talk about anything at all.

After breakfast, I went out to the woodshed to get my fishing tackle and Bounce came across the street to help me. After Ma, Bounce is the best friend I have. He can't talk to me, of course—not actually, that is—but neither does he laugh at me.

I talked to him while I was digging worms and asked him if he wanted to go fishing with me. I could see he did, so I went across the street to tell Mrs. Lawson that Bounce was going along. He belonged to her, but he spent most of his time with me.

We started out, me carrying my cane pole and all my fishing stuff and Bounce walking at my heels, as if I were someone he was proud to be seen walking with.

We went past the bank, where Banker Patton was sitting in the big front window, working at his desk and looking like the most important man in all of Mapleton, which he was. I went by slow so I could hate him good.

Ma and me wouldn't be living in the old tumbledown house we're living in if Banker Patton hadn't foreclosed on our home after Pa died.

We went out past Alf Adams' place, which is the first farm out of town, and I hated him some, too, but not as hard as Banker Patton. All Alf had done was work me harder than he should have, then cheat me out of my pay.

Alf was a big, blustery man and a good enough farmer, I guess—at least he made it pay. He had a big new barn and it's just like him not to paint it red, the way any proper barn is painted, but white with red trim. Who ever heard of paint trim on a barn?

Just beyond Alf's place, Bounce and I turned off the road and went down across the pasture, heading for the big hole in the creek.

Alf's prize Hereford bull was way off in another corner of the pasture with the rest of the stock. When he saw us, he started coming for us, not mean or belligerent, but just investigating and ready for a fight if one was offered him. I wasn't afraid of him, because I'd made friends with him that summer I had worked for Alf. I used to pet him and scratch behind his ears. Alf said I was a crazy fool and someday the bull would kill me.

"You can never trust a bull," Alf said.

When the bull was near enough to see who it was, he knew we meant no harm, so he went back across the pasture again.

We got to the hole and I started fishing, while Bounce went up the stream to do some investigating. I caught a few fish, but they weren't very big and they weren't biting very often and I got disinterested. I like to fish, but to keep my interest up, I have to catch some.

So I got to daydreaming. I began wondering if you marked off a certain area of ground—a hundred feet square, say—and went over it real careful, how many different kinds of plants you'd find. I looked over a patch of ground next to where I was sitting and I could see just ordinary pasture grass and some dandelions and some dock and a couple of violets, and a buttercup which didn't have any flowers as yet.

Suddenly, when I was looking at the dandelion, I realized I could see *all* that dandelion, not just the part that showed above the ground!

I don't know how long I'd been seeing it that way before realizing it. And I'm not certain that "seeing" is the right word. Maybe "know" would be better. I *knew* how that dandelion's big taproot went down into the ground and how the little feathery roots grew out of it, and I knew where all the roots were, how they were taking water and chemicals out of the ground, how reserve food was stored in the root and how the dandelion used the sunlight to convert its food into a form it could use. And the funniest thing about it was that I had never known any of it before.

I looked at the other plants and I could see all of them the same way. I wondered if something had gone wrong with my eyes and if I would have to go around looking into things instead of at them, so I tried to make the new seeing go away and it did.

Then I tried to see the dandelion root again and I saw it, just the way I had before.

I sat there, wondering why I had never been able to see that way before and why I was able to now. And while I was wondering, I looked into the pool and tried to see down into the pool and I could, just as plain as day. I could see clear to the bottom of it and into all the corners of it, and there were lunkers lying in there, bigger than any fish that ever had been taken from the creek.

I saw that my bait was nowhere near any of the fish, so I moved it over until it was just in front of the nose of one of the biggest ones. But the fish didn't seem to see it, or if he did, he wasn't hungry, for he just lay there, fanning the water with his fins and making his gills work.

I moved the bait down until it bumped his nose, but he still didn't pay any attention to it.

So I made the fish hungry.

Don't ask me how I did it. I can't tell you. I all at once knew I could and just how to do it. So I made him hungry and he went for that bait like Bounce grabbing a bone.

He pulled the cork clear under and I heaved on the pole and hoisted him out. I took him off the hook and put him on the stringer, along with the four or five little ones I'd caught.

Then I picked out another big fish and lowered my bait down to him and made him hungry.

In the next hour and a half, I just about cleaned out all the big fish. There were some little ones left, but I didn't bother with them. I had the stringer almost full and I couldn't carry it in my hand, for then the fish would have dragged along the ground. I had to sling it over my shoulder and those fish felt awfully wet.

I called Bounce and we went back to town.

Everyone I met stopped and had a look at my fish and wanted to know where I'd got them and what I'd caught them on and if there were any left or had I taken them all. When I told them I'd taken all there was, they laughed fit to kill.

I was just turning off Main Street on my way home when Banker Patton stepped out of the barber shop. He smelled nice from the bottles of stuff that Jake, the barber, uses on his customers.

He saw me with my fish and stopped in front of me. He looked at me and looked at the fish and he rubbed his fat hands together. Then he said, like he was talking to a child, "Why, Jimmy, where did you get all those fish?" He sounded a little bit, too, like I might not have a right to them and probably had used some lowdown trick to get them.

"Out in the hole on Alf's place," I told him.

All at once, without even trying to do it, I saw him the same way I had seen the dandelion—his stomach and intestines and something that must have been his liver—and up above them all, surrounded by a doughy mass of pink, a pulsating thing that I knew must be his heart.

I guess that's the first time anybody ever *really* hated someone else's guts.

I shot out my hands—well, not my hands, for one was clutching the cane pole and the other was busy with the fish—but it felt almost exactly as if I'd put them out and grabbed his heart and squeezed it hard.

He gasped once, then sighed and wilted, like all the starch had gone out of him, and I had to jump out of the way so he wouldn't bump into me when he fell.

He never moved after he hit the ground.

Jake came running out of his barber shop.

"What happened to him?" he asked me.

"He just fell over," I said.

Jake looked at him. "It's a heart attack. I'd know it anywhere. I'll run for Doc."

He took off up the street for Doc Mason while other people came hurrying out of the places along the street.

There was Ben from the cheese factory and Mike from the pool hall and a couple of farmers who were in the general store.

I got out of there and went on home and Ma was pleased with the fish.

"They'll taste real good," she said, looking at them. "How did you come to catch that many, Jim?"

"They were biting good," I said.

"Well, you hurry up and clean them. We'll have to eat some right away and I'll take some over to Preacher Martin's and I'll rub salt in the others and put them in the cellar where it's good and cool. They'll keep for several days."

Just then, Mrs. Lawson ran across the street and told Ma about Banker Patton.

"He was talking to Jim when it happened," she told Ma.

Ma said to me, "Why didn't you tell me, Jim?"

"I never got around to it," I said. "I was showing you these fish."

So the two of them went on talking about Banker Patton and I went out to the woodshed and cleaned the fish. Bounce sat alongside me and watched me do it and I swear he was as happy over those fish as I was, just like he might have had a hand in catching them.

"It was a nice day, Bounce," I said and Bounce said he'd thought so, too. He recalled running up and down the stream and how he'd chased a frog and the good smell there was when he stuck his nose down to the ground and sniffed.

Now I don't want you to think I'm trying to make you believe

Bounce actually talked, because he didn't. But it was just as if he'd said those very words.

People all the time are laughing at me and making cracks about me and trying to bait me because I'm the village idiot, but there are times when the village idiot has it over all of them. They would have been scared they were going crazy if a dog talked to them, but I didn't think it was strange at all. I just thought how much nicer it was now that Bounce could talk and how I wouldn't have to guess at what he wanted to say. I never thought it was queer at all, because I always figured Bounce could talk if he only tried, being a smart dog.

So Bounce and I sat there and talked while I cleaned the fish. When I came out of the woodshed, Mrs. Lawson had gone home and Ma was in the kitchen, getting a skillet ready to cook some of the fish.

"Jim, you . . ." she hesitated, then went on, "Jim, you didn't have anything to do with what happened to Banker Patton, did you? You didn't push him or hit him or anything?"

"I never even touched him," I said and that was true. I certainly hadn't touched him.

In the afternoon, I went out and worked in the garden. Ma does some housework now and then and that brings in some money, but we couldn't get along if it wasn't for the garden. I used to work some, but since the fight I had with Alf over him not paying me, she don't let me work for anyone. She says if I take care of the garden and catch some fish, I'm helping out enough.

Working in the garden, I found a different use for my new way of seeing. There were worms in the cabbages and I could see every one of them and I killed them all by squeezing them, the way I'd squeezed Banker Patton. I found a cloudy sort of stuff on some of the tomato plants and I suppose it was some kind of virus, because it was so small I could hardly see it at first. So I magnified it and could see it fine, and I made it go away. I didn't squeeze it like I did the worms. I just made it go away.

It was fun working in the garden, when you could look down into the ground and see how the parsnips and radishes were coming and could kill the cutworms you found there, and know just how the soil was and if everything was all right.

We'd had fish for lunch and we had fish again for supper, and after supper I went for a walk.

Before I knew it, I was walking by Banker Patton's place and, going past, I felt the grief inside the house.

I stood out on the sidewalk and let the grief come into me. I suppose that outside any house in town, I could have felt just as easily whatever was going on inside, but I hadn't known I could and I hadn't tried. It was only because the grief in the Patton house was so deep and strong that I noticed it.

The banker's oldest daughter was upstairs in her room and I could feel her crying. The other daughter was sitting with her mother in the living room and neither of them was crying, but they seemed lost and lonely. There were other people in the house, but they weren't very sad. Some neighbors, probably, who'd come in to keep the family company.

I felt sorry for the three of them and I wanted to help them. Not that I'd done anything wrong in killing Banker Patton, but I felt sorry for those women, because, after all, it wasn't their fault the way Banker Patton was, so I stood there, wishing I could help them.

And all at once I felt that perhaps I could and I tried first with the daughter who was upstairs in her room. I reached out to her and I told her happy thoughts. It wasn't easy to start with, but pretty soon I got the hang of it and it wasn't hard to make her happy. Then I made the other two happy and went on my way, feeling better about what I'd done to the family.

I listened in on the houses I passed. Most of them were happy, or at least contented, though I found a couple that were sad. Automatically, I reached out my mind and gave them happiness. It wasn't that I felt I should do something good for any particular person. To tell the truth, I don't remember which houses I made happy. I just thought if I was able to do a thing like that, I should do it. It wasn't right for someone to have that kind of power and refuse to use it.

Ma was sitting up for me when I got home. She was looking kind of worried, the way she always does when I disappear for a long time and she don't know where I am.

I went up to my room and got into bed and lay awake for a long time, wondering how come I could do all the things I could and how, suddenly, today I was able to do them when I'd never been able to before. But finally I went to sleep.

The situation is not ideal, of course, but a good deal better than I had any reason to expect. It is not likely that one should find on every alien planet a host so made to order for our purpose as is this one of mine.

It has accepted me without recognizing me, has made no attempt to deny itself to me or to reject me. It is of an order of intelligence which has enabled it, quickly and efficiently, to make use of those most-readily manipulated of my abilities and this has aided me greatly in my observations. It is fairly mobile and consorts freely with its kind, which are other distinct advantages.

I reckon myself fortunate, indeed, to have found so satisfactory a host so soon upon arrival.

When I got up and had breakfast, I went outside and found Bounce waiting for me. He said he wanted to go and chase some rabbits and I agreed to go along. He said since we could talk now, we ought to make a good team. I could stand up on a stump or a pile of rocks or even climb a tree, so I could overlook the ground and see the rabbit and yell out to him which way it was going, and he could intercept it.

We went up the road toward Alf's place, but turned off down across the pasture, heading for some cut-over land on the hill across the creek.

When we were off the road, I turned around to give Alf a good hating and while I was standing there, hating him, a thought came into my mind. I didn't know if I could do it, but it seemed to be a good idea, so I tried.

I moved my seeing up to Alf's barn and went right through and came out in the middle of the haymow, with hay packed all around me. But all the time, you understand, I was standing out there in the pasture with Bounce, on our way to chase some rabbits.

I'd like to explain what I did next and how I did it, but mostly what worries me is how I knew enough to do it–I mean enough about chemical reaction and stuff like that. I did something to the hay and something to the oxygen and I started a fire up there in the center of the haymow. When I saw it was started good, I got out of there and was in myself again and Bounce and I went on across the creek and up the hill.

I kept looking back over my shoulder, wondering if the fire might not have gone out, but all at once there was a little trickle of smoke coming out of the haymow opening up under the gable's end.

We'd got up into the cut-over land by that time and I sat down on a stump and enjoyed myself. The fire had a good start before it busted out and there wasn't a thing that could be done to save the barn. It went up with a roar and made the prettiest column of smoke you've ever seen.

On the way home, I stopped at the general store. Alf was there and he seemed much too happy to have just lost his barn.

But it wasn't long until I understood why he was so happy.

"I had her insured," he told Bert Jones, the storekeeper, "plumb up to the hilt. Anyhow, it was too big a barn, a lot bigger than I needed. When I built it, I figured I was going to go into milking heavier than I've done and would need the space."

Bert chuckled. "Handy fire for you, Alf."

"Best thing that ever happened to me. I can build another barn and have some cash left over."

I was pretty sore about bungling it, but I thought of a way to get even.

After lunch, I went up the road again and out into Alf's pasture and hunted up the bull. He was glad to see me, although he did a little pawing and some bellowing just to show off.

I had wondered all the way out if I could talk to the bull the way I talked to Bounce and I was afraid that maybe I couldn't, for Bounce was bound to be smarter than a bull.

I was right, of course. It was awful hard to make that bull understand anything.

I made the mistake of scratching behind his ears while I tried to talk to him and he almost went to sleep. I could feel just how good the scratching felt to him. So I hauled off and kicked him in the ribs to wake him up, so he would pay attention. He did pay a little closer attention and even did a little answering, but not much. A bull is awful dumb.

But I felt fairly sure I'd got my idea across, for he started acting sore and feisty and I'm afraid that I overdid it just a mite. I made it to the fence ahead of him and went over without even touching it. The bull stopped at the fence and stood there, pawing and raising Cain, and I got out of there as fast as I could go.

I went home fairly pleased with myself for thinking up as smart a thing as that. I wasn't surprised in the least to hear that evening that Alf had been killed by his bull.

It wasn't a pretty way to die, of course, but Alf had it coming to him, the way he beat me out of my summer wages.

I was sitting in the pool hall when the news was brought in by someone and they all talked about it. Some said Alf had always claimed you couldn't trust no bull, and someone else said he'd often said I was the only one who'd ever gotten along with this particular bull and he was scared all the time I was there for fear the bull would kill me.

They saw me sitting there and they asked me about it and I acted dumb and all of them laughed at me, but I didn't mind their laughing. I knew something they didn't know. Imagine how surprised they'd be if they ever learned the truth!

They won't, of course.

I'm too smart for that.

When I went home, I got a tablet and a pencil and started to write down the names of all my enemies—everyone who had ever laughed at me or done mean things to me or said mean things about me.

The list was pretty long. It included almost everyone in town.

I sat there thinking and I decided maybe I shouldn't kill everyone in town. Not that I couldn't, for I could have, just as slick as anything. But thinking about Alf and Banker Patton, I could see there wasn't any lasting satisfaction in killing people you hate. And I could see as plain as day that if you killed a lot of people, it could leave you pretty lonesome.

I read down through the list of names I'd made and I gave a couple of them the benefit of a doubt and scratched them out. I read those that were left over and I had to admit that every one of them was bad. I decided that if I didn't kill them, I'd have to do something else about them, for I couldn't let them go on being bad.

I thought about it a long time and I remembered some of the things I'd heard Preacher Martin say, although, as I've mentioned before, he's a great one to be saying them. I decided I'd have to lay aside my hate and return good for evil.

I am puzzled and disturbed, although that, perhaps, is the normal reaction when one attaches oneself to an alien being. This is a treacherous and unprincipled species and, as such, an incalculably important one to study.

I am continually amazed at the facility with which my host has acquired the use of my talents, continually appalled by the use he makes of them. I am more than puzzled by his own conviction that he is less intelligent than his fellows; his actions during my acquaintance with him do not bear this out. I wonder if it may not be a racial trait, a sort of cult-attitude of inferiority, that it may be ill-mannered to think of oneself in any other way.

But I half suspect that he may have sensed me in some way without my knowing it and may be employing this strange concept as a device to force me from his mind. Under such a circumstance, it would not be prime ethics for me to remain with him—but he has proved to be such an excellent seat of observation that I am loath to leave him.

The fact is, I don't know. I could, of course, seize control of his mind and thus learn the truth of this and other matters which are perplexing me. But I fear that, in doing so, I would destroy his effectiveness as a free agent and thus impair his observational value. I have decided to wait before using such a drastic measure.

I ate breakfast in a hurry, being anxious to get started. Ma asked me what I was going to do and I said just walk around a bit.

First off, I went to the parsonage and sat down outside the hedge between it and the church. Pretty soon, Preacher Martin came out and began to walk up and down in what he called his garden, pretending he was sunk in holy thought, although I always suspected it was just an act to impress old ladies who might see him.

I put out my mind real easy and finally I got it locked with his so neatly, it seemed that it was me, not him, who was walking up and down. It was a queer feeling, I can tell you, for all the time I knew good and well that I was sitting there back of the hedge.

He wasn't thinking any holy thoughts at all. He was going over in his mind all the arguments he intended to use to hit up the church board for a raise in salary. He was doing some minor cussing out of some of the members of the board for being tight-fisted skinflints and that I agreed with, because they surely were.

Taking it easy, just sort of stealing in on his thoughts, I made him think about Jennie Smith, the organist, and the way he was carrying on with her, and I made him ashamed of himself for doing it.

He tried to push me away, though he didn't know it was me; he just thought it was his own mind bringing up the matter. But I wouldn't let him push the thought away. I piled it on real heavy.

I made him think how the people in the church trusted him and looked to him for spiritual leadership, and I made him remember back to when he was a younger man, just out of seminary, and looked on his lifetime work as a great crusade. I made him think of how he'd betrayed all the things he'd believed in then, and I got him down so low, he was almost bawling. Then I made him tell himself that owning up was the only way he could absolve himself. Once he'd done that, he could start life over again and be a credit to himself and his church.

I went away, figuring I'd done a fair job of work on him, but knowing that I'd have to check up on him every now and then.

At the general store, I sat around and watched Bert Jones sweep out the place. While he was talking to me, I sneaked into his mind and recalled to him all the times he'd paid way less than market prices for the eggs the farmers brought in, and the habit of sneaking in extra items on the bills he sent out to his charge customers, and how he'd cheated on his income tax. I scared him plenty on the income tax and I kept working at him until he'd about decided to make it right with everyone he'd cheated.

I didn't finish the job airtight, but I knew I could come back any time I wanted to and, in a little while, I'd make an honest man of Bert.

Over at the barber shop, I watched Jake cut a head of hair. I wasn't too interested in the man Jake was working on—he lived four or five miles out of town—and at the moment, I figured that I'd better confine my work to the people in the village.

Before I left, I had Jake plenty worried about the gambling he'd been doing in the back room at the pool hall and had him almost ready to make a clean breast of it to his wife.

I went over to the pool hall. Mike was sitting back of the counter with his hat on, reading the baseball scores in the morning paper. I got a day-old paper and pretended to read it. Mike laughed and asked me when I'd learned to read, so I laid it on good and thick.

When I left, I knew, just as soon as I was out the door, he'd go down into the basement and dump all the moonshine down the drain, and before too long, I'd get him to close up the back room.

Over at the cheese factory, I didn't have much chance to work on Ben. The farmers were bringing in their milk and he was too busy for me to really get into his mind. But I did manage to make him think of what would happen if Jake ever caught him with Jake's wife. And I knew when I could catch him alone, I could do a top-notch job on him, for I saw he scared easy.

And that's the way it went.

It was tough work and at times I felt it was just too much of a job. But then I'd sit down and remind myself that it was my duty to keep on—that for some reason this power had been given me and that it was up to me to use it for all it was worth. And furthermore, I was not to use it for myself, for any selfish ends, but for the good of other people.

I don't think I missed a person in the village.

Remember how we wondered if there might not be unseen flaws in this plan of ours? We went over it most carefully and could find none, yet all of us feared that some might show up in actual practice. Now I can report there is one. It is this:

Accurate, impersonal observation is impossible, for as soon as one introduces one's self into a host, his abilities become available to the host and at once become a factor which upsets the norm.

As a result of this, I am getting a distorted picture of the culture of this planet. Reluctant to intervene before, I am now convinced that I must move to take command of the situation.

Bert, now that he's turned honest, is the happiest man you ever saw. Even losing all the customers who got sore at him when he explained why he paid them back some money doesn't bother him. I don't know how Ben is getting along–he disappeared right after Jake took the shotgun to him. But, then, everyone agrees Ben was overdoing it when he went to Jake and told him he was sorry for what had been going on. Jake's wife is gone, too, and some folks say she followed Ben.

To tell the truth, I am well satisfied with the way everything's turned out. Everyone is honest and no one is fooling around with anyone else and there ain't a lick of gambling or drinking going on in town. Mapleton probably is the most moral village in the United States.

I feel that perhaps it turned out the way it did because I started out by conquering my own evil thoughts and, instead of killing all the folks I hated, set out to do them good.

I'm a little puzzled when I walk through the streets at night because I don't pick up near as many happy thoughts as I used to. In fact, there are times when it keeps me busy almost all night long, getting them cheered up. You'd think honest folks would be happy folks. I imagine it's because, now they're good instead of bad, they're not so given to giddy pleasures, but are more concerned with the solid, worth-while side of life.

I'm a little worried about myself. While I did a lot of good, I may have done it for a selfish reason. I did it, perhaps partly, to make up for killing Alf and Banker Patton. And I did it not for just people, but for people I know. That doesn't seem right. Why should only people I know benefit?

Help! Can you hear me? I'm trapped! I can neither control my host nor can I escape from him. Do not under any circumstances let anyone else try to use another member of this race as a host!

Help!

Can you hear me?

Help!

I've sat up all night, thinking, and now the way is clear.

Having reached my decision, I feel important and humble, both at once. I know I'm a chosen instrument for good and must not let anything stop me. I know the village was no more than a proving ground, a place for me to learn what I could really do. Knowing now, I'm determined to use the power to its utmost for the good of all humanity.

Ma's been saving up a little money for a long time for a decent burial.

I know just where she hides it.

It's all she's got.

But it's enough to get me to the U.N.

6. The Big Front Yard

HIRAM TAINE CAME AWAKE and sat up in his bed.

Towser was barking and scratching at the floor.

"Shut up," Taine told the dog.

Towser cocked quizzical ears at him and then resumed the barking and scratching at the floor.

Taine rubbed his eyes. He ran a hand through his rat's-nest head of hair. He considered lying down again and pulling up the covers. But not with Towser barking.

"What's the matter with you, anyhow?" he asked Towser, with not a little wrath.

"Whuff," said Towser, industriously proceeding with his scratching at the floor.

"If you want out," said Taine, "all you got to do is open the screen door. You know how it is done. You do it all the time."

Towser quit his barking and sat down heavily, watching his master getting out of bed.

Taine put on his shirt and pulled on his trousers, but didn't bother with his shoes.

Towser ambled over to a corner, put his nose down to the baseboard and snuffled moistly.

"You got a mouse?" asked Taine.

"Whuff," said Towser, most emphatically.

"I can't ever remember you making such a row about a mouse," Taine said, slightly puzzled. "You must be off your rocker."

It was a beautiful summer morning. Sunlight was pouring through the open window.

Good day for fishing, Taine told himself, then remembered that there'd be no fishing, for he had to go out and look up that old four-poster maple bed that he had heard about up Woodman way. More than likely, he thought, they'd want twice as much as it was worth. It was getting so, he told himself, that a man couldn't make an honest dollar. Everyone was getting smart about antiques.

He got up off the bed and headed for the living room.

"Come on," he said to Towser.

Towser came along, pausing now and then to snuffle into corners and to whuffle at the floor.

"You got it bad," said Taine.

Maybe it's a rat, he thought. The house was getting old.

He opened the screen door and Towser went outside.

"Leave that woodchuck be today," Taine advised him. "It's a losing battle. You'll never dig him out."

Towser went around the corner of the house.

Taine noticed that something had happened to the sign that hung on the post beside the driveway. One of the chains had become unhooked and the sign was dangling.

He padded out across the driveway slab and the grass, still wet with dew, to fix the sign. There was nothing wrong with it—just the unhooked chain. Might have been the wind, he thought, or some passing urchin. Although probably not an urchin. He got along with kids. They never bothered him, like they did some others in the village. Banker Stevens, for example. They were always pestering Stevens.

He stood back a way to be sure the sign was straight.

It read, in big letters:

HANDY MAN

And under that, in smaller lettering:

I fix anything

And under that:

ANTIQUES FOR SALE

What have you got to trade?

Maybe, he told himself, he'd ought to have two signs, one for his fix-it shop and one for antiques and trading. Some day, when he had the time, he thought, he'd paint a couple of new ones. One for each side of the driveway. It would look neat that way.

He turned around and looked across the road at Turner's Woods. It was a pretty sight, he thought. A sizable piece of woods like that right at the edge of town. It was a place for birds and rabbits and woodchucks and squirrels and it was full of forts built through generations by the boys of Willow Bend.

Some day, of course, some smart operator would buy it up and start a housing development or something equally objectionable and when that happened a big slice of his own boyhood would be cut out of his life.

Towser came around the corner of the house. He was sidling along, sniffing at the lowest row of siding and his ears were cocked with interest.

"That dog is nuts," said Taine and went inside.

He went into the kitchen, his bare feet slapping on the floor.

He filled the teakettle, set it on the stove and turned the burner on underneath the kettle.

He turned on the radio, forgetting that it was out of kilter.

When it didn't make a sound, he remembered and, disgusted, snapped it off. That was the way it went, he thought. He fixed other people's stuff, but never got around to fixing any of his own.

He went into the bedroom and put on his shoes. He threw the bed together.

Back in the kitchen the stove had failed to work again. The burner beneath the kettle still was cold.

Taine hauled off and kicked the stove. He lifted the kettle and held his palm above the burner. In a few seconds he could detect some heat.

"Worked again," he told himself.

Some day, he knew, kicking the stove would fail to work. When that happened, he'd have to get to work on it. Probably wasn't more than a loose connection.

He put the kettle back onto the stove.

There was a clatter out in front and Taine went out to see what was going on.

Beasly, the Hortons' yardboy-chauffeur-gardener, et cetera, was backing a rickety old truck up the driveway. Beside him sat Abbie Horton, the wife of H. Henry Horton, the village's most important citizen. In the back of the truck, lashed on with ropes and half-protected by a garish red and purple quilt, stood a mammoth television set. Taine recognized it from of old. It was a good ten years out of date and still, by any standard, it was the most expensive set ever to grace any home in Willow Bend.

Abbie hopped out of the truck. She was an energetic, bustling, bossy woman.

"Good morning, Hiram," she said. "Can you fix this set again?"

"Never saw anything that I couldn't fix," said Taine, but nevertheless he eyed the set with something like dismay. It was not the first time he had tangled with it and he knew what was ahead.

"It might cost you more than it's worth," he warned her. "What you really need is a new one. This set is getting old and–"

"That's just what Henry said," Abbie told him, tartly. "Henry wants to get one of the color sets. But I won't part with this one. It's not just TV, you know. It's a combination with radio and a record player and the wood and style are just right for the other furniture, and, besides–"

"Yes, I know," said Taine, who'd heard it all before.

Poor old Henry, he thought. What a life the man must lead. Up at that computer plant all day long, shooting off his face and bossing everyone, then coming home to a life of petty tyranny.

"Beasly," said Abbie, in her best drill-sergeant voice, "you get right up there and get that thing untied."

"Yes'm," Beasly said. He was a gangling, loose-jointed man who didn't look too bright.

"And see you be careful with it. I don't want it all scratched up."

"Yes'm," said Beasly.

"I'll help," Taine offered.

The two climbed into the truck and began unlashing the old monstrosity.

"It's heavy," Abbie warned. "You two be careful of it."

"Yes'm," said Beasly.

It was heavy and it was an awkward thing to boot, but Beasly and Taine horsed it around to the back of the house and up the stoop and through the back door and down the basement stairs, with Abbie following eagle-eyed behind them, alert to the slightest scratch.

The basement was Taine's combination workshop and display room for antiques. One end of it was filled with benches and with tools and machinery and boxes full of odds and ends and piles of just plain junk were scattered everywhere. The other end housed a collection of rickety chairs, sagging bedposts, ancient highboys, equally ancient lowboys, old coal scuttles painted gold, heavy iron fireplace screens and a lot of other stuff that he had collected from far and wide for as little as he could possibly pay for it.

He and Beasly set the TV down carefully on the floor. Abbie watched them narrowly from the stairs.

"Why, Hiram," she said, excited, "you put a ceiling in the basement. It looks a whole lot better."

"Huh?" asked Taine.

"The ceiling. I said you put in a ceiling."

Taine jerked his head up and what she said was true. There was a ceiling there, but he'd never put it in.

He gulped a little and lowered his head, then jerked it quickly up and had another look. The ceiling was still there.

"It's not that block stuff," said Abbie with open admiration. "You can't see any joints at all. How did you manage it?"

Taine gulped again and got back his voice. "Something I thought up," he told her weakly.

"You'll have to come over and do it to our basement. Our basement is a sight. Beasly put the ceiling in the amusement room, but Beasly is all thumbs."

"Yes'm," Beasly said contritely.

"When I get the time," Taine promised, ready to promise anything to get them out of there.

"You'd have a lot more time," Abbie told him acidly, "if you weren't gadding around all over the country buying up that broken-down old furniture that you call antiques. Maybe you can fool the city folks when they come driving out here, but you can't fool me."

"I make a lot of money out of some of it," Taine told her calmly.

"And lose your shirt on the rest of it," she said.

"I got some old china that is just the kind of stuff you are looking for," said Taine. "Picked it up just a day or two ago. Made a good buy on it. I can let you have it cheap."

"I'm not interested," she said and clamped her mouth tight shut.

She turned around and went back up the stairs.

"She's on the prod today," Beasly said to Taine. "It will be a bad day. It always is when she starts early in the morning."

"Don't pay attention to her," Taine advised.

"I try not to, but it ain't possible. You sure you don't need a man? I'd work for you cheap."

"Sorry, Beasly. Tell you what—come over some night soon and we'll play some checkers."

"I'll do that, Hiram. You're the only one who ever asks me over. All the others ever do is laugh at me or shout."

Abbie's voice came bellowing down the stairs. "Beasly, are you coming? Don't go standing there all day. I have rugs to beat."

"Yes'm," said Beasly, starting up the stairs.

At the truck, Abbie turned on Taine with determination: "You'll get that set fixed right away? I'm lost without it."

"Immediately," said Taine.

He stood and watched them off, then looked around for Towser, but the dog had disappeared. More than likely he was at that woodchuck hole again, in the woods across the road. Gone off, thought Taine, without his breakfast, too.

The teakettle was boiling furiously when Taine got back to the kitchen. He put coffee in the maker and poured in the water. Then he went downstairs.

The ceiling was still there.

He turned on all the lights and walked around the basement, staring up at it.

It was a dazzling white material and it appeared to be translucent—up to a point, that is. One could see into it, but he could not see through it. And there were no signs of seams. It was fitted neatly and tightly around the water pipes and the ceiling lights.

Taine stood on a chair and rapped his knuckles against it sharply. It gave out a bell-like sound, almost exactly as if he'd rapped a fingernail against a thinly-blown goblet.

He got down off the chair and stood there, shaking his head. The whole thing was beyond him. He had spent part of the evening repairing Banker Stevens' lawn mower and there'd been no ceiling then.

He rummaged in a box and found a drill. He dug out one of the smaller bits and fitted it in the drill. He plugged in the cord and climbed on the chair again and tried the bit against the ceiling. The whirling steel slid wildly back and forth. It didn't make a scratch. He switched off the drill and looked closely at the ceiling. There was not a mark upon it. He tried again, pressing against the drill with all his strength. The bit went *ping* and the broken end flew across the basement and hit the wall.

Taine stepped down off the chair. He found another bit and fitted it in the drill and went slowly up the stairs, trying to think. But he was too confused to think. That ceiling should not be up there, but there it was. And unless he were stark, staring crazy and forgetful as well, he had not put it there.

In the living room, he folded back one corner of the worn and faded carpeting and plugged in the drill. He knelt and started drilling in the floor. The bit went smoothly through the old oak flooring, then stopped. He put on more pressure and the drill spun without getting any bite.

And there wasn't supposed to be anything underneath that wood! Nothing to stop a drill. Once through the flooring, it should have dropped into the space between the joists.

Taine disengaged the drill and laid it to one side.

He went into the kitchen and the coffee now was ready. But before he poured it, he pawed through a cabinet drawer and found a pencil flashlight. Back in the living room he shone the light into the hole that the drill had made.

There was something shiny at the bottom of the hole.

He went back to the kitchen and found some day-old doughnuts and poured a cup of coffee. He sat at the kitchen table, eating doughnuts and wondering what to do.

There didn't appear, for the moment at least, much that he could do. He could putter around all day trying to figure out what had happened to his basement and probably not be any wiser than he was right now.

His money-making Yankee soul rebelled against such a horrid waste of time.

There was, he told himself, that maple four-poster that he should be getting to before some unprincipled city antique dealer should run afoul of it. A piece like that, he figured, if a man had any luck at all, should sell at a right good price. He might turn a handsome profit on it if he only worked it right.

Maybe, he thought, he could turn a trade on it. There was the table model TV set that he had traded a pair of ice skates for last winter. Those folks out Woodman way might conceivably be happy to trade the bed for a reconditioned TV set, almost like brand new. After all, they probably weren't using the bed and, he hoped fervently, had no idea of the value of it.

He ate the doughnuts hurriedly and gulped down an extra cup of coffee. He fixed a plate of scraps for Towser and set it outside the door. Then he went down into the basement and got the table TV set and put it in the pickup truck. As an afterthought, he added a reconditioned shotgun which would be perfectly all right if a man were careful not to use these far-reaching, powerful shells, and a few other odds and ends that might come in handy on a trade.

He got back late, for it had been a busy and quite satisfactory day. Not only did he have the four-poster loaded on the truck, but he had as well a rocking chair, a fire screen, a bundle of ancient magazines, an old-fashioned barrel churn, a walnut highboy and a Governor Winthrop on which some half-baked, slap-happy decorator had applied a coat of apple-green paint. The television set, the shotgun and five dollars had gone into the trade. And what was better yet, he'd managed it so well that the Woodman family probably was dying of laughter at this very moment about how they'd taken him.

He felt a little ashamed of it—they'd been such friendly people. They had treated him so kindly and had him stay for dinner and had sat and talked with him and shown him about the farm and even asked him to stop by if he went through that way again.

He'd wasted the entire day, he thought, and he rather hated that, but maybe it had been worth it to build up his reputation out that way as the sort of character who had softening of the head and didn't know the value of a dollar. That way, maybe some other day, he could do some more business in the neighborhood.

He heard the television set as he opened the back door, sounding loud and clear, and he went clattering down the basement stairs in something close to a panic. For now that he'd traded off the table model, Abbie's set was the only one downstairs and Abbie's set was broken.

It was Abbie's set, all right. It stood just where he and Beasly had put it down that morning and there was nothing wrong with it—nothing wrong at all. It was even televising color.

Televising color!

He stopped at the bottom of the stairs and leaned against the railing for support.

The set kept right on televising color.

Taine stalked the set and walked around behind it.

The back of the cabinet was off, leaning against a bench that stood behind the set, and he could see the innards of it glowing cheerily.

He squatted on the basement floor and squinted at the lighted innards and they seemed a good deal different from the way that they should be. He'd repaired the set many times before and he thought he had a good idea of what the working parts would look like. And now they all seemed different, although just how he couldn't tell.

A heavy step sounded on the stairs and a hearty voice came booming down to him.

"Well, Hiram, I see you got it fixed."

Taine jackknifed upright and stood there slightly frozen and completely speechless.

Henry Horton stood foursquarely and happily on the stairs, looking very pleased.

"I told Abbie that you wouldn't have it done, but she said for me to come over anyway–Hey, Hiram, it's in color! How did you do it, man?"

Taine grinned sickly. "I just got fiddling around," he said.

Henry came down the rest of the stairs with a stately step and stood before the set, with his hands behind his back, staring at it fixedly in his best executive manner.

He slowly shook his head. "I never would have thought," he said, "that it was possible."

"Abbie mentioned that you wanted color."

"Well, sure. Of course I did. But not on this old set. I never would have expected to get color on this set. How did you do it, Hiram?"

Taine told the solemn truth. "I can't rightly say," he said.

Henry found a nail keg standing in front of one of the benches and rolled it out in front of the old-fashioned set. He sat down warily and relaxed into solid comfort.

"That's the way it goes," he said. "There are men like you, but not very many of them. Just Yankee tinkerers. You keep messing around with things, trying one thing here and another there and before you know it you come up with something."

He sat on the nail keg, staring at the set.

"It's sure a pretty thing," he said. "It's better than the color they have in Minneapolis. I dropped in at a couple of the places the last time I was there and looked at the color sets. And I tell you honest, Hiram, there wasn't one of them that was as good as this."

Taine wiped his brow with his shirt sleeve. Somehow or other, the basement seemed to be getting warm. He was fine sweat all over.

Henry found a big cigar in one of his pockets and held it out to Taine.

"No, thanks. I never smoke."

"Perhaps you're wise," said Henry. "It's a nasty habit."

He stuck the cigar into his mouth and rolled it east to west.

"Each man to his own," he proclaimed, expansively. "When it comes to a thing like this, you're the man to do it. You seem to think in mechanical contraptions and electronic circuits. Me, I don't know a thing about it. Even in the computer game, I still don't know a thing about it; I hire men who do. I can't even saw a board or drive a nail. But I can organize. You remember, Hiram, how everybody snickered when I started up the plant?"

"Well, I guess some of them did, at that."

"You're darn tooting they did. They went around for weeks with their hands up to their faces to hide smart-aleck grins. They said, what does Henry think he's doing, starting up a computer factory out here in the sticks; he doesn't think he can compete with those big companies in the east, does he? And they didn't stop their grinning until I sold a couple of dozen units and had orders for a year or two ahead."

He fished a lighter from his pocket and lit the cigar carefully, never taking his eyes off the television set.

"You got something there," he said, judiciously, "that may be worth a mint of money. Some simple adaptation that will fit on any set. If you can get color on this old wreck, you can get color on any set that's made."

He chuckled moistly around the mouthful of cigar. "If RCA knew what was happening here this minute, they'd go out and cut their throats."

"But I don't know what I did," protested Taine.

"Well, that's all right," said Henry, happily. "I'll take this set up to the plant tomorrow and turn loose some of the boys on it. They'll find out what you have here before they're through with it."

He took the cigar out of his mouth and studied it intently, then popped it back in again.

"As I was saying, Hiram, that's the difference in us. You can do the stuff, but you miss the possibilities. I can't do a thing, but I can organize it once the thing is done. Before we get through with this, you'll be wading in twenty-dollar bills clear up to your knees."

"But I don't have—"

"Don't worry. Just leave it all to me. I've got the plant and whatever money we may need. We'll figure out a split."

"That's fine of you," said Taine mechanically.

"Not at all," Henry insisted, grandly. "It's just my aggressive, grasping sense of profit. I should be ashamed of myself, cutting in on this."

He sat on the keg, smoking and watching the TV perform in exquisite color.

"You know, Hiram," he said, "I've often thought of this, but never got around to doing anything about it. I've got an old computer up at the plant that we will have to junk because it's taking up room that we really need. It's one of our early models, a sort of experimental job that went completely sour. It sure is a screwy thing. No one's ever been able to make much out of it. We tried some approaches that probably were wrong—or maybe they were right, but we didn't know enough to make them quite come off. It's been standing in a corner all these years and I should have junked it long ago. But I sort of hate to do it. I wonder if you might not like it—just to tinker with."

"Well, I don't know," said Taine.

Henry assumed an expansive air. "No obligation, mind you. You may not be able to do a thing with it—I'd frankly be surprised if you could, but there's no harm in trying. Maybe you'll decide to tear it down for the salvage you can get. There are several thousand dollars worth of equipment in it. Probably you could use most of it one way or another."

"It might be interesting," conceded Taine, but not too enthusiastically.

"Good," said Henry, with an enthusiasm that made up for Taine's lack of it. "I'll have the boys cart it over tomorrow. It's a heavy thing. I'll send along plenty of help to get it unloaded and down into the basement and set up."

Henry stood up carefully and brushed cigar ashes off his lap.

"I'll have the boys pick up the TV set at the same time," he said. "I'll have to tell Abbie you haven't got it fixed yet. If I ever let it get into the house, the way it's working now, she'd hold onto it."

Henry climbed the stairs heavily and Taine saw him out the door into the summer night.

Taine stood in the shadow, watching Henry's shadowed figure go across the Widow Taylor's yard to the next street behind his house. He took a deep breath of the fresh night air and shook his head to try to clear his buzzing brain, but the buzzing went right on.

Too much had happened, he told himself. Too much for any single day—first the ceiling and now the TV set. Once he had a good night's sleep he might be in some sort of shape to try to wrestle with it.

Towser came around the corner of the house and limped slowly up the steps to stand beside his master. He was mud up to his ears.

"You had a day of it, I see," said Taine. "And, just like I told you, you didn't get the woodchuck."

"Woof," said Towser, sadly.

"You're just like a lot of the rest of us," Taine told him, severely. "Like me and Henry Horton and all the rest of us. You're chasing something and you think you know what you're chasing, but you really don't. And what's even worse, you have no faint idea of why you're chasing it."

Towser thumped a tired tail upon the stoop.

Taine opened the door and stood to one side to let Towser in, then went in himself.

He went through the refrigerator and found part of a roast, a slice or two of luncheon meat, a dried-out slab of cheese and half a bowl of cooked spaghetti. He made a pot of coffee and shared the food with Towser.

Then Taine went back downstairs and shut off the television set. He found a trouble lamp and plugged it in and poked the light into the innards of the set.

He squatted on the floor, holding the lamp, trying to puzzle out what had been done to the set. It was different, of course, but it was a little hard to figure out in just what ways it was different. Someone had tinkered with the tubes and had them twisted out of shape and there were little white cubes of metal tucked here and there in what seemed to be an entirely haphazard and illogical manner—although, Taine admitted to himself, there probably was no haphazardness. And the circuit, he saw, had been rewired and a good deal of wiring had been added.

But the most puzzling thing about it was that the whole thing seemed to be just jury-rigged—as if someone had done no more than a hurried, patch-up job to get the set back in working order on an emergency and temporary basis.

Someone, he thought!

And who had that someone been?

He hunched around and peered into the dark corners of the basement and he felt innumerable and many-legged imaginary insects running on his body.

Someone had taken the back off the cabinet and leaned it against the bench and had left the screws which held the back laid neatly in a row upon the floor. Then they had jury-rigged the set and jury-rigged it far better than it had ever been before.

If this was a jury-job, he wondered, just what kind of job would it have been if they had had the time to do it up in style?

They hadn't had the time, of course. Maybe they had been scared off when he had come home–scared off even before they could get the back on the set again.

He stood up and moved stiffly away.

First the ceiling in the morning–and now, in the evening, Abbie's television set.

And the ceiling, come to think of it, was not a ceiling only. Another liner, if that was the proper term for it, of the same material as the ceiling, had been laid beneath the floor, forming a sort of boxed-in area between the joists. He had struck that liner when he had tried to drill into the floor.

And what, he asked himself, if all the house were like that, too?

There was just one answer to it all: *There was something in the house with him!*

Towser had heard that *something* or smelled it or in some other manner sensed it and had dug frantically at the floor in an attempt to dig it out, as if it were a woodchuck.

Except that this, whatever it might be, certainly was no woodchuck.

He put away the trouble light and went upstairs.

Towser was curled up on a rug in the living room beside the easy chair and beat his tail in polite decorum in greeting to his master.

Taine stood and stared down at the dog. Towser looked back at him with satisfied and sleepy eyes, then heaved a doggish sigh and settled down to sleep.

Whatever Towser might have heard or smelled or sensed this morning, it was quite evident that as of this moment he was aware of it no longer.

Then Taine remembered something else.

He had filled the kettle to make water for the coffee and had set it on the stove. He had turned on the burner and it had worked the first time.

He hadn't had to kick the stove to get the burner going.

He woke in the morning and someone was holding down his feet and he sat up quickly to see what was going on.

But there was nothing to be alarmed about; it was only Towser who had crawled into bed with him and now lay sprawled across his feet.

Towser whined softly and his back legs twitched as he chased dream rabbits.

Taine eased his feet from beneath the dog and sat up, reaching for his clothes. It was early, but he remembered suddenly that he had left all of the furniture he had picked up the day before out there in the truck and should be getting it downstairs where he could start reconditioning it.

Towser went on sleeping.

Taine stumbled to the kitchen and looked out of the window and there, squatted on the back stoop, was Beasly, the Horton man-of-all-work.

Taine went to the back door to see what was going on.

"I quit them, Hiram," Beasly told him. "She kept on pecking at me every minute of the day and I couldn't do a thing to please her, so I up and quit."

"Well, come on in," said Taine. "I suppose you'd like a bite to eat and a cup of coffee."

"I was kind of wondering if I could stay here, Hiram. Just for my keep until I can find something else."

"Let's have breakfast first," said Taine, "then we can talk about it."

He didn't like it, he told himself. He didn't like it at all. In another hour or so Abbie would show up and start stirring up a ruckus about how he'd lured Beasly off. Because, no matter how dumb Beasly might be, he did a lot of work and took a lot of nagging and there wasn't anyone else in town who would work for Abbie Horton.

"Your ma used to give me cookies all the time," said Beasly. "Your ma was a real good woman, Hiram."

"Yes, she was," said Taine.

"My ma used to say that you folks were quality, not like the rest in town, no matter what kind of airs they were always putting on. She said your family was among the first settlers. Is that really true, Hiram?"

"Well, not exactly first settlers, I guess, but this house has stood here for almost a hundred years. My father used to say there never was a night during all those years that there wasn't at least one Taine beneath its roof. Things like that, it seems, meant a lot to father."

"It must be nice," said Beasly, wistfully, "to have a feeling like that. You must be proud of this house, Hiram."

"Not really proud; more like belonging. I can't imagine living in any other house."

Taine turned on the burner and filled the kettle. Carrying the kettle back, he kicked the stove. But there wasn't any need to kick it; the burner was already beginning to take on a rosy glow.

Twice in a row, Taine thought. This thing is getting better!

"Gee, Hiram," said Beasly, "this is a dandy radio."

"It's no good," said Taine. "It's broke. Haven't had the time to fix it."

"I don't think so, Hiram. I just turned it on. It's beginning to warm up."

"It's beginning to–Hey, let me see!" yelled Taine.

Beasly told the truth. A faint hum was coming from the tubes.

A voice came in, gaining in volume as the set warmed up.

It was speaking gibberish.

"What kind of talk is that?" asked Beasly.

"I don't know," said Taine, close to panic now.

First the television set, then the stove and now the radio!

He spun the tuning knob and the pointer crawled slowly across the dial face instead of spinning across as he remembered it, and station after station sputtered and went past.

He tuned in the next station that came up and it was strange lingo, too–and he knew by then exactly what he had.

Instead of a $39.50 job, he had here on the kitchen table an all-band receiver like they advertised in the fancy magazines.

He straightened up and said to Beasly: "See if you can get someone speaking English. I'll get on with the eggs."

He turned on the second burner and got out the frying pan. He put it on the stove and found eggs and bacon in the refrigerator.

Beasly got a station that had band music playing.

"How's that?" he asked.

"That's fine," said Taine.

Towser came out from the bedroom, stretching and yawning. He went to the door and showed he wanted out.

Taine let him out.

"If I were you," he told the dog, "I'd lay off that woodchuck. You'll have all the woods dug up."

"He ain't digging after any woodchuck, Hiram."

"Well, a rabbit, then."

"Not a rabbit, either. I snuck off yesterday when I was supposed to be beating rugs. That's what Abbie got so sore about."

Taine grunted, breaking eggs into the skillet.

"I snuck away and went over to where Towser was. I talked with him and he told me it wasn't a woodchuck or a rabbit. He said it was something else. I pitched in and helped him dig. Looks to me like he found an old tank of some sort buried out there in the woods."

"Towser wouldn't dig up any tank," protested Taine. "He wouldn't care about anything except a rabbit or a woodchuck."

"He was working hard," insisted Beasly. "He seemed to be excited."

"Maybe the woodchuck just dug his hole under this old tank or whatever it might be."

"Maybe so," Beasly agreed. He fiddled with the radio some more. He got a disk jockey who was pretty terrible.

Taine shoveled eggs and bacon onto plates and brought them to the table. He poured big cups of coffee and began buttering the toast.

"Dive in," he said to Beasly.

"This is good of you, Hiram, to take me in like this. I won't stay no longer than it takes to find a job."

"Well, I didn't exactly say–"

"There are times," said Beasly, "when I get to thinking I haven't got a friend and then I remember your ma, how nice she was to me and all–"

"Oh, all right," said Taine.

He knew when he was licked.

He brought the toast and a jar of jam to the table and sat down, beginning to eat.

"Maybe you got something I could help you with," suggested Beasly, using the back of his hand to wipe egg off his chin.

"I have a load of furniture out in the driveway. I could use a man to help me get it down into the basement."

"I'll be glad to do that," said Beasly. "I am good and strong. I don't mind work at all. I just don't like people jawing at me."

They finished breakfast and then carried the furniture down into the basement. They had some trouble with the Governor Winthrop, for it was an unwieldy thing to handle.

When they finally horsed it down, Taine stood off and looked at it. The man, he told himself, who slapped paint onto that beautiful cherrywood had a lot to answer for.

He said to Beasly: "We have to get the paint off that thing there.

And we must do it carefully. Use paint remover and a rag wrapped around a spatula and just sort of roll it off. Would you like to try it?"

"Sure, I would. Say, Hiram, what will we have for lunch?"

"I don't know," said Taine. "We'll throw something together. Don't tell me you're hungry."

"Well, it was sort of hard work, getting all that stuff down here."

"There are cookies in the jar on the kitchen shelf," said Taine. "Go and help yourself."

When Beasly went upstairs, Taine walked slowly around the basement. The ceiling, he saw, was still intact. Nothing else seemed to be disturbed.

Maybe that television set and the stove and radio, he thought, was just their way of paying rent to me. And if that were the case, he told himself, whoever they might be, he'd be more than willing to let them stay right on.

He looked around some more and could find nothing wrong.

He went upstairs and called to Beasly in the kitchen.

"Come on out to the garage, where I keep the paint. We'll hunt up some remover and show you how to use it."

Beasly, a supply of cookies clutched in his hand, trotted willingly behind him.

As they rounded the corner of the house they could hear Towser's muffled barking. Listening to him, it seemed to Taine that he was getting hoarse.

Three days, he thought–or was it four?

"If we don't do something about it," he said, "that fool dog is going to get himself wore out."

He went into the garage and came back with two shovels and a pick.

"Come on," he said to Beasly. "We have to put a stop to this before we have any peace."

Towser had done himself a noble job of excavation. He was almost completely out of sight. Only the end of his considerably bedraggled tail showed out of the hole he had clawed in the forest floor.

Beasly had been right about the tanklike thing. One edge of it showed out of one side of the hole.

Towser backed out of the hole and sat down heavily, his whiskers dripping clay, his tongue hanging out of the side of his mouth.

"He says that it's about time that we showed up," said Beasly.

Taine walked around the hole and knelt down. He reached down a hand to brush the dirt off the projecting edge of Beasly's tank. The clay was stubborn and hard to wipe away, but from the feel of it the tank was heavy metal.

Taine picked up a shovel and rapped it against the tank. The tank gave out a clang.

They got to work, shoveling away a foot or so of topsoil that lay above the object. It was hard work and the thing was bigger than they had thought and it took some time to get it uncovered, even roughly.

"I'm hungry," Beasly complained.

Taine glanced at his watch. It was almost one o'clock.

"Run on back to the house," he said to Beasly. "You'll find something in the refrigerator and there's milk to drink."

"How about you, Hiram? Ain't you ever hungry?"

"You could bring me back a sandwich and see if you can find a trowel."

"What you want a trowel for?"

"I want to scrape the dirt off this thing and see what it is."

He squatted down beside the thing they had unearthed and watched Beasly disappear into the woods.

"Towser," he said, "this is the strangest animal you ever put to ground."

A man, he told himself, might better joke about it—if to do no more than keep his fear away.

Beasly wasn't scared, of course. Beasly didn't have the sense to be scared of a thing like this.

Twelve feet wide by twenty long and oval shaped. About the size, he thought, of a good-size living room. And there never had been a tank of that shape or size in all of Willow Bend.

He fished his jackknife out of his pocket and started to scratch away the dirt at one point on the surface of the thing. He got a square inch free of dirt and it was no metal such as he had ever seen. It looked for all the world like glass.

He kept on scraping at the dirt until he had a clean place as big as an outstretched hand.

It wasn't any metal. He'd almost swear to that. It looked like cloudy glass—like the milk-glass goblets and bowls he was always on the lookout for. There were a lot of people who were plain nuts about it and they'd pay fancy prices for it.

He closed the knife and put it back into his pocket and squatted, looking at the oval shape that Towser had discovered.

And the conviction grew: Whatever it was that had come to live with him undoubtedly had arrived in this same contraption. From space or time, he thought, and was astonished that he thought it, for he'd never thought such a thing before.

He picked up his shovel and began to dig again, digging down this time, following the curving side of this alien thing that lay within the earth.

And as he dug, he wondered. What should he say about this—or should he say anything? Maybe the smartest course would be to cover it again and never breathe a word about it to a living soul.

Beasly would talk about it, naturally. But no one in the village would pay attention to anything that Beasly said. Everyone in Willow Bend knew Beasly was cracked.

Beasly finally came back. He carried three inexpertly-made sandwiches wrapped in an old newspaper and a quart bottle almost full of milk.

"You certainly took your time," said Taine, slightly irritated.

"I got interested," Beasly explained.

"Interested in what?"

"Well, there were three big trucks and they were lugging a lot of heavy stuff down into the basement. Two or three big cabinets and a lot of other junk. And you know Abbie's television set? Well, they took the set away. I told them that they shouldn't, but they took it anyway."

"I forgot," said Taine. "Henry said he'd send the computer over and I plumb forgot."

Taine ate the sandwiches, sharing them with Towser, who was very grateful in a muddy way.

Finished, Taine rose and picked up his shovel.

"Let's get to work," he said.

"But you got all that stuff down in the basement."

"That can wait," said Taine. "This job we have to finish."

It was getting dusk by the time they finished.

Taine leaned wearily on his shovel.

Twelve feet by twenty across the top and ten feet deep—and all of it, every bit of it, made of the milk-glass stuff that sounded like a bell when you whacked it with a shovel.

They'd have to be small, he thought, if there were many of them, to live in a space that size, especially if they had to stay there very long. And that fitted in, of course, for if they weren't small they couldn't now be living in the space between the basement joists.

If they were really living there, thought Taine. If it wasn't all just a lot of supposition.

Maybe, he thought, even if they had been living in the house, they might be there no longer—for Towser had smelled or heard or somehow sensed them in the morning, but by that very night he'd paid them no attention.

Taine slung his shovel across his shoulder and hoisted the pick.

"Come on," he said, "let's go. We've put in a long, hard day."

They tramped out through the brush and reached the road. Fireflies were flickering off and on in the woody darkness and the street lamps were swaying in the summer breeze. The stars were hard and bright.

Maybe they still were in the house, thought Taine. Maybe when they found out that Towser had objected to them, they had fixed it so he'd be aware of them no longer.

They probably were highly adaptive. It stood to good reason they would have to be. It hadn't taken them too long, he told himself grimly, to adapt to a human house.

He and Beasly went up the gravel driveway in the dark to put the tools away in the garage and there was something funny going on, for there was no garage.

There was no garage and there was no front on the house and the driveway was cut off abruptly and there was nothing but the curving wall of what apparently had been the end of the garage.

They came up to the curving wall and stopped, squinting unbelieving in the summer dark.

There was no garage, no porch, no front of the house at all. It was as if someone had taken the opposite corners of the front of the house and bent them together until they touched, folding the entire front of the building inside the curvature of the bent-together corners.

Taine now had a curved-front house. Although it was, actually, not as simple as all that, for the curvature was not in proportion to what actually would have happened in case of such a feat. The curve was long and graceful and somehow not quite apparent. It was as if the front of the house had been eliminated and an illusion of the rest of the house had been summoned to mask the disappearance.

Taine dropped the shovel and the pick and they clattered on the driveway gravel. He put his hand up to his face and wiped it across his eyes, as if to clear his eyes of something that could not possibly be there.

And when he took the hand away it had not changed a bit.

There was no front to the house.

Then he was running around the house, hardly knowing he was running, and there was a fear inside of him at what had happened to the house.

But the back of the house was all right. It was exactly as it had always been.

He clattered up the stoop with Beasly and Towser running close behind him. He pushed open the door and burst into the entry and scrambled up the stairs into the kitchen and went across the kitchen in three strides to see what had happened to the front of the house.

At the door between the kitchen and the living room he stopped and his hands went out to grasp the door jamb as he stared in disbelief at the windows of the living room.

It was night outside. There could be no doubt of that. He had seen the fireflies flickering in the brush and weeds and the street lamps had been lit and the stars were out.

But a flood of sunlight was pouring through the windows of the living room and out beyond the windows lay a land that was not Willow Bend.

"Beasly," he gasped, "look out there in front!"

Beasly looked.

"What place is that?" he asked.

"That's what I'd like to know."

Towser had found his dish and was pushing it around the kitchen floor with his nose, by way of telling Taine that it was time to eat.

Taine went across the living room and opened the front door. The garage, he saw, was there. The pickup stood with its nose against the open garage door and the car was safe inside.

There was nothing wrong with the front of the house at all.

But if the front of the house was all right, that was all that was.

For the driveway was chopped off just a few feet beyond the tail end of the pickup and there was no yard or woods or road. There was just a desert—a flat, far-reaching desert, level as a floor, with occasional boulder piles and haphazard clumps of vegetation and all of the ground covered with sand and pebbles. A big blinding sun hung just above a horizon that seemed much too far away and a funny thing about it was that the sun was in the north, where no proper sun should be. It had a peculiar whiteness, too.

Beasly stepped out on the porch and Taine saw that he was shivering like a frightened dog.

"Maybe," Taine told him, kindly, "you'd better go back in and start making us some supper."

"But, Hiram—"

"It's all right," said Taine. "It's bound to be all right."

"If you say so, Hiram."

He went in and the screen door banged behind him and in a minute Taine heard him in the kitchen.

He didn't blame Beasly for shivering, he admitted to himself. It was a sort of shock to step out of your front door into an unknown land. A man might eventually get used to it, of course, but it would take some doing.

He stepped down off the porch and walked around the truck and around the garage corner and when he rounded the corner he was half prepared to walk back into familiar Willow Bend—for when he had gone in the back door the village had been there.

There was no Willow Bend. There was more of the desert, a great deal more of it.

He walked around the house and there was no back to the house. The back of the house now was just the same as the front had been before—the same smooth curve pulling the sides of the house together.

He walked on around the house to the front again and there was desert all the way. And the front was still all right. It hadn't changed at all. The truck was there on the chopped-off driveway and the garage was open and the car inside.

Taine walked out a way into the desert and hunkered down and scooped up a handful of the pebbles and the pebbles were just pebbles.

He squatted there and let the pebbles trickle through his fingers.

In Willow Bend there was a back door and there wasn't any front. Here, wherever here might be, there was a front door, but there wasn't any back.

He stood up and tossed the rest of the pebbles away and wiped his dusty hands upon his breeches.

Out of the corner of his eye he caught a sense of movement on the porch and there they were.

A line of tiny animals, if animals they were, came marching down the steps, one behind another. They were four inches high or so and they went on all four feet, although it was plain to see that their front feet were really hands, not feet. They had ratlike faces that were vaguely human, with noses long and pointed. They looked as if they might have scales instead of hide, for their bodies glistened with a rippling motion as they walked. And all of them had tails that looked very much like the coiled-wire tails one finds on certain toys and the tails stuck straight up above them, quivering as they walked.

They came down the steps in single file, in perfect military order, with half a foot or so of spacing between each one of them.

They came down the steps and walked out into the desert in a straight, undeviating line as if they knew exactly where they might be bound. There was something deadly purposeful about them and yet they didn't hurry.

Taine counted sixteen of them and he watched them go out into the desert until they were almost lost to sight.

There go the ones, he thought, who came to live with me. They are the ones who fixed up the ceiling and who repaired Abbie's television set and jiggered up the stove and radio. And more than likely, too, they were the ones who had come to Earth in the strange milk-glass contraption out there in the woods.

And if they had come to Earth in that deal out in the woods, then what sort of place was this?

He climbed the porch and opened the screen door and saw the neat, six-inch circle his departing guests had achieved in the screen to get out of the house. He made a mental note that some day, when he had the time, he would have to fix it.

He went in and slammed the door behind him.

"Beasly," he shouted.

There was no answer.

Towser crawled from beneath the love seat and apologized.

"It's all right, pal," said Taine. "That outfit scared me, too."

He went into the kitchen. The dim ceiling light shone on the overturned coffee pot, the broken cup in the center of the floor, the upset bowl of eggs. One broken egg was a white and yellow gob on the linoleum.

He stepped down on the landing and saw that the screen door in the back was wrecked beyond repair. Its rusty mesh was broken—exploded might have been a better word—and a part of the frame was smashed.

Taine looked at it in wondering admiration.

"The poor fool," he said. "He went straight through it without opening it at all."

He snapped on the light and went down the basement stairs. Halfway down he stopped in utter wonderment.

To his left was a wall—a wall of the same sort of material as had been used to put in the ceiling.

He stooped and saw that the wall ran clear across the basement, floor to ceiling, shutting off the workshop area.

And inside the workshop, what?

For one thing, he remembered, the computer that Henry had sent over just this morning. Three trucks, Beasly had said—three truckloads of equipment delivered straight into their paws!

Taine sat down weakly on the steps.

They must have thought, he told himself, that he was co-operating! Maybe they had figured that he knew what they were about and so went along with them. Or perhaps they thought he was paying them for fixing up the TV set and the stove and radio.

But to tackle first things first, why had they repaired the TV set and the stove and radio? As a sort of rental payment? As a friendly gesture? Or as a sort of practice run to find out what they could about this world's technology? To find, perhaps, how their technology could be adapted to the materials and conditions on this planet they had found?

Taine raised a hand and rapped with his knuckles on the wall beside the stairs and the smooth white surface gave out a pinging sound.

He laid his ear against the wall and listened closely and it seemed to him he could hear a low-key humming, but if so it was so faint he could not be absolutely sure.

Banker Stevens' lawn mower was in there, behind the wall, and a lot of other stuff waiting for repair. They'd take the hide right off him, he thought, especially Banker Stevens. Stevens was a tight man.

Beasly must have been half-crazed with fear, he thought. When he had seen those things coming up out of the basement, he'd gone clean off his rocker. He'd gone straight through the door without even bothering to try to open it and now he was down in the village yapping to anyone who'd stop to listen to him.

No one ordinarily would pay Beasly much attention, but if he yapped long enough and wild enough, they'd probably do some checking. They'd come storming up here and they'd give the place a going over and they'd stand goggle-eyed at what they found in front and pretty soon some of them would have worked their way around to sort of running things.

And it was none of their business, Taine stubbornly told himself, his ever-present business sense rising to the fore. There was a lot of real estate lying around out there in his front yard and the only way anyone could get to it was by going through his house. That being the case, it stood to reason that all that land out there was his. Maybe it wasn't any good at all. There might be nothing there. But before he had other people overrunning it, he'd better check and see.

He went up the stairs and out into the garage.

The sun was still just above the northern horizon and there was nothing moving.

He found a hammer and some nails and a few short lengths of plank in the garage and took them in the house.

Towser, he saw, had taken advantage of the situation and was sleeping in the gold-upholstered chair. Taine didn't bother him.

Taine locked the back door and nailed some planks across it. He locked the kitchen and the bedroom windows and nailed planks across them, too.

That would hold the villagers for a while, he told himself, when they came tearing up here to see what was going on.

He got his deer rifle, a box of cartridges, a pair of binoculars and an old canteen out of a closet. He filled the canteen at the kitchen tap and stuffed a sack with food for him and Towser to eat along the way, for there was no time to wait and eat.

Then he went into the living room and dumped Towser out of the gold-upholstered chair.

"Come on, Tows," he said. "We'll go and look things over."

He checked the gasoline in the pickup and the tank was almost full.

He and the dog got in and he put the rifle within easy reach. Then he backed the truck and swung it around and headed out, north, across the desert.

It was easy traveling. The desert was as level as a floor. At times it got a little rough, but no worse than a lot of the back roads he traveled hunting down antiques.

The scenery didn't change. Here and there were low hills, but the desert itself kept on mostly level, unraveling itself into that far-off horizon. Taine kept on driving north, straight into the sun. He hit some sandy stretches, but the sand was firm and hard and he had no trouble.

Half an hour out he caught up with the band of things—all sixteen of them—that had left the house. They were still traveling in line at their steady pace.

Slowing down the truck, Taine traveled parallel with them for a time, but there was no profit in it; they kept on traveling their course, looking neither right or left.

Speeding up, Taine left them behind.

The sun stayed in the north, unmoving, and that certainly was queer. Perhaps, Taine told himself, this world spun on its axis far more slowly than the Earth and the day was longer. From the way the sun appeared to be standing still, perhaps a good deal longer.

Hunched above the wheel, staring out into the endless stretch of desert, the strangeness of it struck him for the first time with its full impact.

This was another world—there could be no doubt of that—another planet circling another star, and where it was in actual space no one on Earth could have the least idea. And yet, through some machination of those sixteen things walking straight in line, it also was lying just outside the front door of his house.

Ahead of him a somewhat larger hill loomed out of the flatness of the desert. As he drew nearer to it, he made out a row of shining objects lined upon its crest. After a time he stopped the truck and got out with the binoculars.

Through the glasses, he saw that the shining things were the same sort of milk-glass contraptions as had been in the woods. He counted eight of them, shining in the sun, perched upon some sort of rock-gray cradles. And there were other cradles empty.

He took the binoculars from his eyes and stood there for a moment, considering the advisability of climbing the hill and investigating closely. But he shook his head. There'd be time for that later on. He'd better keep on moving. This was not a real exploring foray, but a quick reconnaissance.

He climbed into the truck and drove on, keeping watch upon the gas gauge. When it came close to half full he'd have to turn around and go back home again.

Ahead of him he saw a faint whiteness above the dim horizon line and he watched it narrowly. At times it faded away and then came in again, but whatever it might be was so far off he could make nothing of it.

He glanced down at the gas gauge and it was close to the halfway mark. He stopped the pickup and got out with the binoculars.

As he moved around to the front of the machine he was puzzled at how slow and tired his legs were and then remembered–he should have been in bed many hours ago. He looked at his watch and it was two o'clock and that meant, back on Earth, two o'clock in the morning. He had been awake for more than twenty hours and much of that time he had been engaged in the back-breaking work of digging out the strange thing in the woods.

He put up the binoculars and the elusive white line that he had been seeing turned out to be a range of mountains. The great, blue, craggy mass towered up above the desert with the gleam of snow on its peaks and ridges. They were a long way off, for even the powerful glasses brought them in as little more than a misty blueness.

He swept the glasses slowly back and forth and the mountains extended for a long distance above the horizon line.

He brought the glasses down off the mountains and examined the desert that stretched ahead of him. There was more of the same that he had been seeing–the same floorlike levelness, the same occasional mounds, the self-same scraggy vegetation.

And a house!

His hands trembled and he lowered the glasses, then put them up to his face again and had another look. It was a house, all right. A funny-looking house standing at the foot of one of the hillocks, still shadowed by the hillock so that one could not pick it out with the naked eye.

It seemed to be a small house. Its roof was like a blunted cone and it lay tight against the ground, as if it hugged or crouched against the ground. There was an oval opening that probably was a door, but there was no sign of windows.

He took the binoculars down again and stared at the hillock. Four or five miles away, he thought. The gas would stretch that far and even if it didn't he could walk the last few miles into Willow Bend.

It was queer, he thought, that a house should be all alone out here. In all the miles he'd traveled in the desert he'd seen no sign of life beyond the sixteen little ratlike things that marched in single file, no sign of artificial structure other than the eight milk-glass contraptions resting in their cradles.

He climbed into the pickup and put it into gear. Ten minutes later he drew up in front of the house, which still lay within the shadow of the hillock.

He got out of the pickup and hauled his rifle after him. Towser leaped to the ground and stood with his hackles up, a deep growl in his throat.

"What's the matter, boy?" asked Taine.

Towser growled again.

The house stood silent. It seemed to be deserted.

The walls were built, Taine saw, of rude, rough masonry crudely set together, with a crumbling, mudlike substance used in lieu of mortar. The roof originally had been of sod and that was queer, indeed, for there was nothing that came close to sod upon this expanse of desert. But now, although one could see the lines where the sod strips had been fitted together, it was nothing more than earth baked hard by the desert sun.

The house itself was featureless, entirely devoid of any ornament, with no attempt at all to soften the harsh utility of it as a simple shelter. It was the sort of thing that a shepherd people might have put together. It had the look of age about it; the stone had flaked and crumbled in the weather.

Rifle slung beneath his arm, Taine paced toward it. He reached the door and glanced inside and there was darkness and no movement.

He glanced back for Towser and saw that the dog had crawled beneath the truck and was peering out and growling.

"You stick around," said Taine. "Don't go running off."

With the rifle thrust before him, Taine stepped through the door into the darkness. He stood for a long moment to allow his eyes to become accustomed to the gloom.

Finally he could make out the room in which he stood. It was plain and rough, with a rude stone bench along one wall and queer unfunctional niches hollowed in another. One rickety piece of wooden furniture stood in a corner, but Taine could not make out what its use might be.

An old and deserted place, he thought, abandoned long ago. Perhaps a shepherd people might have lived here in some long-gone age, when the desert had been a rich and grassy plain.

There was a door into another room and as he stepped through it he heard the faint, far-off booming sound and something else as well —the sound of pouring rain! From the open door that led out through the back he caught a whiff of salty breeze and he stood there frozen in the center of that second room.

Another one!

Another house that led to another world!

He walked slowly forward, drawn toward the outer door, and he stepped out into a cloudy, darkling day with the rain streaming down from wildly racing clouds. Half a mile away, across a field of jumbled, broken, iron-gray boulders, lay a pounding sea that raged upon the coast, throwing great spumes of angry spray high into the air.

He walked out from the door and looked up at the sky, and the rain drops pounded at his face with a stinging fury. There was a chill and a dampness in the air and the place was eldritch—a world jerked straight from some ancient Gothic tale of goblin and of sprite.

He glanced around and there was nothing he could see, for the rain blotted out the world beyond this stretch of coast, but behind the rain he could sense or seemed to sense a presence that sent shivers down his spine. Gulping in fright, Taine turned around and stumbled back again through the door into the house.

One world away, he thought, was far enough; two worlds away was more than one could take. He trembled at the sense of utter loneliness that tumbled in his skull and suddenly this long-forsaken house became unbearable and he dashed out of it.

Outside the sun was bright and there was welcome warmth. His clothes were damp from rain and little beads of moisture lay on the rifle barrel.

He looked around for Towser and there was no sign of the dog. He was not underneath the pickup; he was nowhere in sight.

Taine called and there was no answer. His voice sounded lone and hollow in the emptiness and silence.

He walked around the house, looking for the dog, and there was no back door to the house. The rough rock walls of the sides of the house pulled in with that funny curvature and there was no back to the house at all.

But Taine was not interested; he had known how it would be. Right now he was looking for his dog and he felt the panic rising in him. Somehow it felt a long way from home.

He spent three hours at it. He went back into the house and Towser was not there. He went into the other world again and searched among the tumbled rocks and Towser was not there. He went back to the desert and walked around the hillock and then he climbed to the crest of it and used the binoculars and saw nothing but the lifeless desert, stretching far in all directions.

Dead-beat with weariness, stumbling, half asleep even as he walked, he went back to the pickup.

He leaned against it and tried to pull his wits together.

Continuing as he was would be a useless effort. He had to get some sleep. He had to go back to Willow Bend and fill the tank and get some extra gasoline so that he could range farther afield in his search for Towser.

He couldn't leave the dog out here—that was unthinkable. But he had to plan, he had to act intelligently. He would be doing Towser no good by stumbling around in his present shape.

He pulled himself into the truck and headed back for Willow Bend, following the occasional faint impressions that his tires had made in the sandy places, fighting a half-dead drowsiness that tried to seal his eyes shut.

Passing the higher hill on which the milk-glass things had stood, he stopped to walk around a bit so he wouldn't fall asleep behind the wheel. And now, he saw, there were only seven of the things resting in their cradles.

But that meant nothing to him now. All that meant anything was to hold off the fatigue that was closing down upon him, to cling to the wheel and wear off the miles, to get back to Willow Bend and get some sleep and then come back again to look for Towser.

Slightly more than halfway home he saw the other car and watched it in numb befuddlement, for this truck that he was driving and the car at home in his garage were the only two vehicles this side of his house.

He pulled the pickup to a halt and tumbled out of it.

The car drew up and Henry Horton and Beasly and a man who wore a star leaped quickly out of it.

"Thank God we found you, man!" cried Henry, striding over to him.

"I wasn't lost," protested Taine. "I was coming back."

"He's all beat out," said the man who wore the star.

"This is Sheriff Hanson," Henry said. "We were following your tracks."

"I lost Towser," Taine mumbled. "I had to go and leave him. Just leave me be and go and hunt for Towser. I can make it home."

He reached out and grabbed the edge of the pickup's door to hold himself erect.

"You broke down the door," he said to Henry. "You broke into my house and you took my car–"

"We had to do it, Hiram. We were afraid that something might have happened to you. The way that Beasly told it, it stood your hair on end."

"You better get him in the car," the sheriff said. "I'll drive the pickup back."

"But I have to hunt for Towser!"

"You can't do anything until you've had some rest."

Henry grabbed him by the arm and led him to the car and Beasly held the rear door open.

"You got any idea what this place is?" Henry whispered conspiratorily.

"I don't positively know," Taine mumbled. "Might be some other–"

Henry chuckled. "Well, I guess it doesn't really matter. Whatever it may be, it's put us on the map. We're in all the newscasts and the papers are plastering us in headlines and the town is swarming with reporters and cameramen and there are big officials coming. Yes, sir, I tell you, Hiram, this will be the making of us–"

Taine heard no more. He was fast asleep before he hit the seat.

He came awake and lay quietly in the bed and he saw the shades were drawn and the room was cool and peaceful.

It was good, he thought, to wake in a room you knew–in a room that one had known for his entire life, in a house that had been the Taine house for almost a hundred years.

Then memory clouted him and he sat bolt upright.

And now he heard it–the insistent murmur from outside the window.

He vaulted from the bed and pulled one shade aside. Peering out, he saw the cordon of troops that held back the crowd that overflowed his back yard and the back yards back of that.

He let the shade drop back and started hunting for his shoes, for he was fully dressed. Probably Henry and Beasly, he told himself, had dumped him into bed and pulled off his shoes and let it go at that. But he couldn't remember a single thing of it. He must have gone dead to the world the minute Henry had bundled him into the back seat of the car.

He found the shoes on the floor at the end of the bed and sat down upon the bed to pull them on.

And his mind was racing on what he had to do.

He'd have to get some gasoline somehow and fill up the truck and stash an extra can or two into the back and he'd have to take some food and water and perhaps his sleeping bag. For he wasn't coming back until he'd found his dog.

He got on his shoes and tied them, then went out into the living room. There was no one there, but there were voices in the kitchen.

He looked out the window and the desert lay outside, unchanged. The sun, he noticed, had climbed higher in the sky, but out in his front yard it was still forenoon.

He looked at his watch and it was six o'clock and from the way the shadows had been falling when he'd peered out of the bedroom window, he knew that it was 6:00 P.M. He realized with a guilty start that he must have slept almost around the clock. He had not meant to sleep that long. He hadn't meant to leave Towser out there that long.

He headed for the kitchen and there were three persons there—Abbie and Henry Horton and a man in military garb.

"There you are," cried Abbie merrily. "We were wondering when you would wake up."

"You have some coffee cooking, Abbie?"

"Yes, a whole pot full of it. And I'll cook up something else for you."

"Just some toast," said Taine. "I haven't got much time. I have to hunt for Towser."

"Hiram," said Henry, "this is Colonel Ryan. National guard. He has his boys outside."

"Yes, I saw them through the window."

"Necessary," said Henry. "Absolutely necessary. The sheriff couldn't handle it. The people came rushing in and they'd have torn the place apart. So I called the governor."

"Taine," the colonel said, "sit down. I want to talk with you."

"Certainly," said Taine, taking a chair. "Sorry to be in such a rush, but I lost my dog out there."

"This business," said the colonel, smugly, "is vastly more important than any dog could be."

"Well, colonel, that just goes to show that you don't know Towser. He's the best dog I ever had and I've had a lot of them. Raised him from a pup and he's been a good friend all these years—"

"All right," the colonel said, "so he is a friend. But still I have to talk with you."

"You just sit and talk," Abbie said to Taine. "I'll fix up some cakes and Henry brought over some of that sausage that we get out on the farm."

The back door opened and Beasly staggered in to the accompaniment of a terrific metallic banging. He was carrying three empty five-gallon gas cans in one hand and two in the other hand and they were bumping and banging together as he moved.

"Say," yelled Taine, "what's going on here?"

"Now, just take it easy," Henry said. "You have no idea the problems that we have. We wanted to get a big gas tank moved through here, but we couldn't do it. We tried to rip out the back of the kitchen to get it through, but we couldn't–"

"You did what!"

"We tried to rip out the back of the kitchen," Henry told him calmly. "You can't get one of those big storage tanks through an ordinary door. But when we tried, we found that the entire house is boarded up inside with the same kind of material that you used down in the basement. You hit it with an ax and it blunts the steel–"

"But, Henry, this is my house and there isn't anyone who has the right to start tearing it apart."

"Fat chance," the colonel said. "What I would like to know, Taine, what is that stuff that we couldn't break through?"

"Now you take it easy, Hiram," cautioned Henry. "We have a big new world waiting for us out there–"

"It isn't waiting for you or anyone," yelled Taine.

"And we have to explore it and to explore it we need a stockpile of gasoline. So since we can't have a storage tank, we're getting together as many gas cans as possible and then we'll run a hose through here–"

"But, Henry–"

"I wish," said Henry sternly, "that you'd quit interrupting me and let me have my say. You can't even imagine the logistics that we face. We're bottlenecked by the size of a regulation door. We have to get supplies out there and we have to get transport. Cars and trucks won't be so bad. We can disassemble them and lug them through piecemeal, but a plane will be a problem."

"You listen to me, Henry. There isn't anyone going to haul a plane through here. This house has been in my family for almost a hundred years and I own it and I have a right to it and you can't come in high-handed and start hauling stuff through it."

"But," said Henry plaintively, "we need a plane real bad. You can cover so much more ground when you have a plane."

Beasly went banging through the kitchen with his cans and out into the living room.

The colonel sighed. "I had hoped, Mr. Taine, that you would understand how the matter stood. To me it seems very plain that it's your patriotic duty to co-operate with us in this. The government, of course, could exercise the right of eminent domain and start condemnation action, but it would rather not do that. I'm speaking unofficially, of course, but I think it's safe to say the government would much prefer to arrive at an amicable agreement."

"I doubt," Taine said, bluffing, not knowing anything about it, "that the right of eminent domain would be applicable. As I understand it, it applies to buildings and to roads—"

"This is a road," the colonel told him flatly. "A road right through your house to another world."

"First," Taine declared, "the government would have to show it was in the public interest and that refusal of the owner to relinquish title amounted to an interference in government procedure and—"

"I think," the colonel said, "that the government can prove it is in the public interest."

"I think," Taine said angrily, "I better get a lawyer."

"If you really mean that," Henry offered, ever helpful, "and you want to get a good one—and I presume you do—I would be pleased to recommend a firm that I am sure would represent your interests most ably and be, at the same time, fairly reasonable in cost."

The colonel stood up, seething. "You'll have a lot to answer, Taine. There'll be a lot of things the government will want to know. First of all, they'll want to know just how you engineered this. Are you ready to tell that?"

"No," said Taine, "I don't believe I am."

And he thought with some alarm: They think that I'm the one who did it and they'll be down on me like a pack of wolves to find just how I did it. He had visions of the FBI and the state department and the Pentagon and, even sitting down, he felt shaky in the knees.

The colonel turned around and marched stiffly from the kitchen. He went out the back and slammed the door behind him.

Henry looked at Taine speculatively.

"Do you really mean it?" he demanded. "Do you intend to stand up to them?"

"I'm getting sore," said Taine. "They can't come in here and take over without even asking me. I don't care what anyone may think, this is my house. I was born here and I've lived here all my life and I like the place and–"

"Sure," said Henry. "I know just how you feel."

"I suppose it's childish of me, but I wouldn't mind so much if they showed a willingness to sit down and talk about what they meant to do once they'd taken over. But there seems no disposition to even ask me what I think about it. And I tell you, Henry, this is different than it seems. This isn't a place where we can walk in and take over, no matter what Washington may think. There's something out there and we better watch our step–"

"I was thinking," Henry interrupted, "as I was sitting here, that your attitude is most commendable and deserving of support. It has occurred to me that it would be most unneighborly of me to go on sitting here and leave you in the fight alone. We could hire ourselves a fine array of legal talent and we could fight the case and in the meantime we could form a land and development company and that way we could make sure that this new world of yours is used the way it should be used.

"It stands to reason, Hiram, that I am the one to stand beside you, shoulder to shoulder, in this business since we're already partners in this TV deal."

"What's that about TV?" shrilled Abbie, slapping a plate of cakes down in front of Taine.

"Now, Abbie," Henry said patiently, "I have explained to you already that your TV set is back of that partition down in the basement and there isn't any telling when we can get it out."

"Yes, I know," said Abbie, bringing a platter of sausages and pouring a cup of coffee.

Beasly came in from the living room and went bumbling out the back.

"After all," said Henry, pressing his advantage, "I would suppose I had some hand in it. I doubt you could have done much without the computer I sent over."

And there it was again, thought Taine. Even Henry thought he'd been the one who did it.

"But didn't Beasly tell you?"

"Beasly said a lot, but you know how Beasly is."

And that was it, of course. To the villagers it would be no more than another Beasly story—another whopper that Beasly had dreamed up. There was no one who believed a word that Beasly said.

Taine picked up the cup and drank his coffee, gaining time to shape an answer and there wasn't any answer. If he told the truth, it would sound far less believable than any lie he'd tell.

"You can tell me, Hiram. After all, we're partners."

He's playing me for a fool, thought Taine. Henry thinks he can play anyone he wants for a fool and sucker.

"You wouldn't believe me if I told you, Henry."

"Well," Henry said, resignedly, getting to his feet, "I guess that part of it can wait."

Beasly came tramping and banging through the kitchen with another load of cans.

"I'll have to have some gasoline," said Taine, "if I'm going out for Towser."

"I'll take care of that right away," Henry promised smoothly. "I'll send Ernie over with his tank wagon and we can run a hose through here and fill up those cans. And I'll see if I can find someone who'll go along with you."

"That's not necessary. I can go alone."

"If we had a radio transmitter, then you could keep in touch."

"But we haven't any. And, Henry, I can't wait. Towser's out there somewhere—"

"Sure, I know how much you thought of him. You go out and look for him if you think you have to and I'll get started on this other business. I'll get some lawyers lined up and we'll draw up some sort of corporate papers for our land development—"

"And, Hiram," Abbie said, "will you do something for me, please?"

"Why, certainly," said Taine.

"Would you speak to Beasly. It's senseless the way he's acting. There wasn't any call for him to up and leave us. I might have been a little sharp with him, but he's so simple-minded he's infuriating. He ran off and spent half a day helping Towser at digging out that woodchuck and—"

"I'll speak to him," said Taine.

"Thanks, Hiram. He'll listen to you. You're the only one he'll listen to. And I wish you could have fixed my TV set before all this came about. I'm just lost without it. It leaves a hole in the living room. It matched my other furniture, you know."

"Yes, I know," said Taine.

"Coming, Abbie?" Henry asked, standing at the door.

He lifted a hand in a confidential farewell to Taine. "I'll see you later, Hiram. I'll get it all fixed up."

I just bet you will, thought Taine.

He went back to the table, after they were gone, and sat down heavily in a chair.

The front door slammed and Beasly came panting in, excited.

"Towser's back!" he yelled. "He's coming back and he's driving in the biggest woodchuck you ever clapped your eyes on."

Taine leaped to his feet.

"Woodchuck! That's an alien planet. It hasn't any woodchucks."

"You come and see," yelled Beasly.

He turned and raced back out again, with Taine following close behind.

It certainly looked considerably like a woodchuck–a sort of man-size woodchuck. More like a woodchuck out of a children's book, perhaps, for it was walking on its hind legs and trying to look dignified even while it kept a weather eye on Towser.

Towser was back a hundred feet or so, keeping a wary distance from the massive chuck. He had the pose of a good sheep-herding dog, walking in a crouch, alert to head off any break that the chuck might make.

The chuck came up close to the house and stopped. Then it did an about-face so that it looked back across the desert and it hunkered down.

It swung its massive head to gaze at Beasly and Taine and in the limpid brown eyes Taine saw more than the eyes of an animal.

Taine walked swiftly out and picked up the dog in his arms and hugged him tight against him. Towser twisted his head around and slapped a sloppy tongue across his master's face.

Taine stood with the dog in his arms and looked at the man-size chuck and felt a great relief and an utter thankfulness.

Everything was all right now, he thought. Towser had come back.

He headed for the house and out into the kitchen.

He put Towser down and got a dish and filled it at the tap. He placed it on the floor and Towser lapped at it thirstily, slopping water all over the linoleum.

"Take it easy, there," warned Taine. "You don't want to overdo it."

He hunted in the refrigerator and found some scraps and put them in Towser's dish.

Towser wagged his tail with doggish happiness.

"By rights," said Taine, "I ought to take a rope to you, running off like that."

Beasly came ambling in.

"That chuck is a friendly cuss," he announced. "He's waiting for someone."

"That's nice," said Taine, paying no attention.

He glanced at the clock.

"It's seven-thirty," he said. "We can catch the news. You want to get it, Beasly?"

"Sure. I know right where to get it. That fellow from New York."

"That's the one," said Taine.

He walked into the living room and looked out the window. The man-size chuck had not moved. He was sitting with his back to the house, looking back the way he'd come.

Waiting for someone, Beasly had said, and it looked as if he might be, but probably it was all just in Beasly's head.

And if he were waiting for someone, Taine wondered, who might that someone be? *What* might that someone be? Certainly by now the word had spread out there that there was a door into another world. And how many doors, he wondered, had been opened through the ages?

Henry had said that there was a big new world out there waiting for Earthmen to move in. And that wasn't it at all. It was the other way around.

The voice of the news commentator came blasting from the radio in the middle of a sentence:

". . . finally got into the act. Radio Moscow said this evening that the Soviet delegate will make representations in the U.N. tomorrow for the internationalization of this other world and the gateway to it.

"From that gateway itself, the home of a man named Hiram Taine, there is no news. Complete security had been clamped down and a cordon of troops form a solid wall around the house, holding back the crowds. Attempts to telephone the residence are blocked by a curt voice which says that no calls are being accepted for that number. And Taine himself has not stepped from the house."

Taine walked back into the kitchen and sat down.

"He's talking about you," Beasly said importantly.

"Rumor circulated this morning that Taine, a quiet village repairman and dealer in antiques, and until yesterday a relative unknown, had finally returned from a trip which he made out into this new and unknown land. But what he found, if anything, no one yet can say. Nor is there any further information about this other place beyond the fact that it is a desert and, to the moment, lifeless.

"A small flurry of excitement was occasioned late yesterday by the finding of some strange object in the woods across the road from the residence, but this area likewise was swiftly cordoned off and to the moment Colonel Ryan, who commands the troops, will say nothing of what actually was found.

"Mystery man of the entire situation is one Henry Horton, who seems to be the only unofficial person to have entry to the Taine house. Horton, questioned earlier today, had little to say, but managed to suggest an air of great conspiracy. He hinted he and Taine were partners in some mysterious venture and left hanging in midair the half impression that he and Taine had collaborated in opening the new world.

"Horton, it is interesting to note, operates a small computer plant and it is understood on good authority that only recently he delivered a computer to Taine, or at least some sort of machine to which considerable mystery is attached. One story is that this particular machine had been in the process of development for six or seven years.

"Some of the answers to the matter of how all this did happen and what actually did happen must wait upon the findings of a team of scientists who left Washington this evening after an all-day conference at the White House, which was attended by representatives from the military, the state department, the security division and the special weapons section.

"Throughout the world the impact of what happened yesterday at Willow Bend can only be compared to the sensation of the news, almost twenty years ago, of the dropping of the first atomic bomb. There is some tendency among many observers to believe that the implications of Willow Bend, in fact, may be even more earth-shaking than were those of Hiroshima.

"Washington insists, as is only natural, that this matter is of internal concern only and that it intends to handle the situation as it best affects the national welfare.

"But abroad there is a rising storm of insistence that this is not a matter of national policy concerning one nation, but that it necessarily must be a matter of world-wide concern.

"There is an unconfirmed report that a U.N. observer will arrive in Willow Bend almost momentarily. France, Britain, Bolivia, Mexico and India have already requested permission of Washington to send observers to the scene and other nations undoubtedly plan to file similar requests.

"The world sits on edge tonight, waiting for the word from Willow Bend and–"

Taine reached out and clicked the radio to silence.

"From the sound of it," said Beasly, "we're going to be overrun by a batch of foreigners."

Yes, thought Taine, there might be a batch of foreigners, but not exactly in the sense that Beasly meant. The use of the word, he told himself, so far as any human was concerned, must be outdated now. No man of Earth ever again could be called a foreigner with alien life next door–literally next door. What were the people of the stone house?

And perhaps not the alien life of one planet only, but the alien life of many. For he himself had found another door into yet another planet and there might be many more such doors and what would these other worlds be like, and what was the purpose of the doors?

Someone, *something,* had found a way of going to another planet short of spanning light-years of lonely space–a simpler and a shorter way than flying through the gulfs of space. And once the way was open, then the way stayed open and it was as easy as walking from one room to another.

But one thing–one ridiculous thing–kept puzzling him and that was the spinning and the movement of the connected planets, of all the planets that must be linked together. You could not, he argued, establish solid, factual links between two objects that move independently of one another.

And yet, a couple of days ago, he would have contended just as stolidly that the whole idea on the face of it was fantastic and impossible. Still it had been done. And once one impossibility was accomplished, what logical man could say with sincerity that the second could not be?

The doorbell rang and he got up to answer it.

It was Ernie, the oil man.

"Henry said you wanted some gas and I came to tell you I can't get it until morning."

"That's all right," said Taine. "I don't need it now."

And swiftly slammed the door.

He leaned against it, thinking: I'll have to face them sometime. I can't keep the door locked against the world. Sometime, soon or late, the Earth and I will have to have this out.

And it was foolish, he thought, for him to think like this, but that was the way it was.

He had something here that the Earth demanded; something that Earth wanted or thought it wanted. And yet, in the last analysis, it was his responsibility. It had happened on his land, it had happened in his house; unwittingly, perhaps, he'd even aided and abetted it.

And the land and house are mine, he fiercely told himself, and that world out there was an extension of his yard. No matter how far or where it went, an extension of his yard.

Beasly had left the kitchen and Taine walked into the living room. Towser was curled up and snoring gently in the gold-upholstered chair.

Taine decided he would let him stay there. After all, he thought, Towser had won the right to sleep anywhere he wished.

He walked past the chair to the window and the desert stretched to its far horizon and there before the window sat the man-size woodchuck and Beasly side by side, with their backs turned to the window and staring out across the desert.

Somehow it seemed natural that the chuck and Beasly should be sitting there together—the two of them, it appeared to Taine, might have a lot in common.

And it was a good beginning—that a man and an alien creature from this other world should sit down companionably together.

He tried to envision the setup of these linked worlds, of which Earth now was a part, and the possibilities that lay inherent in the fact of linkage rolled thunder through his brain.

There would be contact between the Earth and these other worlds and what would come of it?

And come to think of it, the contact had been made already, but so naturally, so undramatically, that it failed to register as a great, important meeting. For Beasly and the chuck out there were contact and if it all should go like that, there was absolutely nothing for one to worry over.

This was no haphazard business, he reminded himself. It had been planned and executed with the smoothness of long practice. This was not the first world to be opened and it would not be the last.

The little ratlike things had spanned space—how many light-years of space one could not even guess—in the vehicle which he had unearthed out in the woods. They then had buried it, perhaps as a child might hide a dish by shoving it into a pile of sand. Then they had come to this very house and had set up the apparatus that had made this house a tunnel between one world and another. And once that had been done, the need of crossing space had been canceled out forever. There need be but one crossing and that one crossing would serve to link the planets.

And once the job was done the little ratlike things had left, but not before they had made certain that this gateway to their planet would stand against no matter what assault. They had sheathed the house inside the studdings with a wonder-material that would resist an ax and that, undoubtedly, would resist much more than a simple ax.

And they had marched in drill-order single file out to the hill where eight more of the space machines had rested in their cradles. And now there were only seven there, in their cradles on the hill, and the ratlike things were gone and, perhaps, in time to come, they'd land on another planet and another doorway would be opened, a link to yet another world.

But more, Taine thought, than the linking of mere worlds. It would be, as well, the linking of the peoples of those worlds.

The little ratlike creatures were the explorers and the pioneers who sought out other Earthlike planets and the creature waiting with Beasly just outside the window must also serve its purpose and perhaps in time to come there would be a purpose which man would also serve.

He turned away from the window and looked around the room and the room was exactly as it had been ever since he could remember it. With all the change outside, with all that was happening outside, the room remained unchanged.

This is the reality, thought Taine, this is all the reality there is. Whatever else may happen, this is where I stand—this room with its fireplace blackened by many winter fires, the bookshelves with the old thumbed volumes, the easy chair, the ancient worn carpet—worn by beloved and unforgotten feet through the many years.

And this also, he knew, was the lull before the storm.

In just a little while the brass would start arriving—the team of scientists, the governmental functionaries, the military, the observers from the other countries, the officials from the U.N.

And against all these, he realized, he stood weaponless and shorn of his strength. No matter what a man might say or think, he could not stand off the world.

This was the last day that this would be the Taine house. After almost a hundred years, it would have another destiny.

And for the first time in all those years there'd be no Taine asleep beneath its roof.

He stood looking at the fireplace and the shelves of books and he sensed the old, pale ghosts walking in the room and he lifted a hesitant hand as if to wave farewell, not only to the ghosts but to the room as well. But before he got it up, he dropped it to his side.

What was the use, he thought.

He went out to the porch and sat down on the steps.

Beasly heard him and turned around.

"He's nice," he said to Taine, patting the chuck upon the back. "He's exactly like a great big teddy bear."

"Yes, I see," said Taine.

"And best of all, I can talk with him."

"Yes, I know," said Taine, remembering that Beasly could talk with Towser, too.

He wondered what it would be like to live in the simple world of Beasly. At times, he decided, it would be comfortable.

The ratlike things had come in the spaceship, but why had they come to Willow Bend, why had they picked this house, the only house in all the village where they would have found the equipment that they needed to build their apparatus so easily and so quickly? For there was no doubt that they had cannibalized the computer to get the equipment they needed. In that, at least, Henry had been right. Thinking back on it, Henry, after all, had played quite a part in it.

Could they have foreseen that on this particular week in this particular house the probability of quickly and easily doing what they had come to do had stood very high?

Did they, with all their other talents and technology, have clairvoyance as well?

"There's someone coming," Beasly said.

"I don't see a thing."

"Neither do I," said Beasly, "but Chuck told me that he saw them."

"Told you!"

"I told you we been talking. There, I can see them, too."

They were far off, but they were coming fast–three dots that rode rapidly up out of the desert.

He sat and watched them come and he thought of going in to get the rifle, but he didn't stir from his seat upon the steps. The rifle would do no good, he told himself. It would be a senseless thing to get it; more than that, a senseless attitude. The least that man could do, he thought, was to meet these creatures of another world with clean and empty hands.

They were closer now and it seemed to him that they were sitting in invisible easy chairs that traveled very fast.

He saw that they were humanoid, to a degree at least, and there were only three of them.

They came in with a rush and stopped very suddenly a hundred feet or so from where he sat upon the steps.

He didn't move or say a word–there was nothing he could say. It was too ridiculous.

They were, perhaps, a little smaller than himself, and black as the ace of spades, and they wore skin-tight shorts and vests that were somewhat oversize and both the shorts and vests were the blue of April skies.

But that was not the worst of it.

They sat on saddles, with horns in front and stirrups and a sort of a bedroll tied on the back, but they had no horses.

The saddles floated in the air, with the stirrups about three feet above the ground and the aliens sat easily in the saddles and stared at him and he stared back at them.

Finally he got up and moved forward a step or two and when he did that the three swung from the saddles and moved forward, too, while the saddles hung there in the air, exactly as they'd left them.

Taine walked forward and the three walked forward until they were no more than six feet apart.

"They say hello to you," said Beasly. "They say welcome to you."

"Well, all right, then, tell them–Say, how do you know all this!"

"Chuck tells me what they say and I tell you. You tell me and I tell him and he tells them. That's the way it works. That is what he's here for."

"Well, I'll be–" said Taine. "So you can really talk to him."

"I told you that I could," stormed Beasly. "I told you that I could talk to Towser, too, but you thought that I was crazy."

"Telepathy!" said Taine. And it was worse than ever now. Not only had the ratlike things known all the rest of it, but they'd known of Beasly, too.

"What was that you said, Hiram?"

"Never mind," said Taine. "Tell that friend of yours to tell them I'm glad to meet them and what can I do for them?"

He stood uncomfortably and stared at the three and he saw that their vests had many pockets and that the pockets were all crammed, probably with their equivalent of tobacco and handkerchiefs and pocketknives and such.

"They say," said Beasly, "that they want to dicker."

"Dicker?"

"Sure, Hiram. You know, trade."

Beasly chuckled thinly. "Imagine them laying themselves open to a Yankee trader. That's what Henry says you are. He says you can skin a man on the slickest–"

"Leave Henry out of this," snapped Taine. "Let's leave Henry out of something."

He sat down on the ground and the three sat down to face him.

"Ask them what they have in mind to trade."

"Ideas," Beasly said.

"Ideas! That's a crazy thing–"

And then he saw it wasn't.

Of all the commodities that might be exchanged by an alien people, ideas would be the most valuable and the easiest to handle. They'd take no cargo room and they'd upset no economies–not immediately, that is–and they'd make a bigger contribution to the welfare of the cultures than trade in actual goods.

"Ask them," said Taine, "what they'll take for the idea back of those saddles they are riding."

"They say, what have you to offer?"

And that was the stumper. That was the one that would be hard to answer.

Automobiles and trucks, the internal gas engine–well, probably not. Because they already had the saddles. Earth was out of date in transportation from the viewpoint of these people.

Housing architecture–no, that was hardly an idea and, anyhow, there was that other house, so they knew of houses.

Cloth? No, they had cloth.

Paint, he thought. Maybe paint was it.

"See if they are interested in paint," Taine told Beasly.

"They say, what is it? Please explain yourself."

"O.K., then. Let's see. It's a protective device to be spread over almost any surface. Easily packaged and easily applied. Protects against weather and corrosion. It's decorative, too. Comes in all sorts of colors. And it's cheap to make."

"They shrug in their mind," said Beasly. "They're just slightly interested. But they'll listen more. Go ahead and tell them."

And that was more like it, thought Taine.

That was the kind of language that he could understand.

He settled himself more firmly on the ground and bent forward slightly, flicking his eyes across the three dead-pan, ebony faces, trying to make out what they might be thinking.

There was no making out. Those were three of the deadest pans he had ever seen.

It was all familiar. It made him feel at home. He was in his element.

And in the three across from him, he felt somehow subconsciously, he had the best dickering opposition he had ever met. And that made him feel good, too.

"Tell them," he said, "that I'm not quite sure. I may have spoken up too hastily. Paint, after all, is a mighty valuable idea."

"They say, just as a favor to them, not that they're really interested, would you tell them a little more."

Got them hooked, Taine told himself. If he could only play it right—

He settled down to dickering in earnest.

Hours later Henry Horton showed up. He was accompanied by a very urbane gentleman, who was faultlessly turned out and who carried beneath his arm an impressive attaché case.

Henry and the man stopped on the steps in sheer astonishment.

Taine was squatted on the ground with a length of board and he was daubing paint on it while the aliens watched. From the daubs here and there upon their anatomies, it was plain to see the aliens had been doing some daubing of their own. Spread all over the ground were other lengths of half-painted boards and a couple of dozen old cans of paint.

Taine looked up and saw Henry and the man.

"I was hoping," he said, "that someone would show up."

"Hiram," said Henry, with more importance than usual, "may I present Mr. Lancaster. He is a special representative of the United Nations."

"I'm glad to meet you, sir," said Taine. "I wonder if you would–"

"Mr. Lancaster," Henry explained grandly, "was having some slight difficulty getting through the lines outside, so I volunteered my services. I've already explained to him our joint interest in this matter."

"It was very kind of Mr. Horton," Lancaster said. "There was this stupid sergeant–"

"It's all in knowing," Henry said, "how to handle people."

The remark, Taine noticed, was not appreciated by the man from the U.N.

"May I inquire, Mr. Taine," asked Lancaster, "exactly what you're doing?"

"I'm dickering," said Taine.

"Dickering. What a quaint way of expressing–"

"An old Yankee word," said Henry quickly, "with certain connotations of its own. When you trade with someone you are exchanging goods, but if you're dickering with him you're out to get his hide."

"Interesting," said Lancaster. "And I suppose you're out to skin these gentlemen in the sky-blue vests–"

"Hiram," said Henry, proudly, "is the sharpest dickerer in these parts. He runs an antique business and he has to dicker hard–"

"And may I ask," said Lancaster, ignoring Henry finally, "what you might be doing with these cans of paint? Are these gentlemen potential customers for paint or–"

Taine threw down the board and rose angrily to his feet.

"If you'd both shut up!" he shouted. "I've been trying to say something ever since you got here and I can't get in a word. And I tell you, it's important–"

"Hiram!" Henry exclaimed in horror.

"It's quite all right," said the U.N. man. "We *have* been jabbering. And now, Mr. Taine?"

"I'm backed into a corner," Taine told him, "and I need some help. I've sold these fellows on the idea of paint, but I don't know a thing about it–the principle back of it or how it's made or what goes into it or–"

"But, Mr. Taine, if you're selling them the paint, what difference does it make–"

"I'm not selling them the paint," yelled Taine. "Can't you understand that? They don't want the paint. They want the *idea* of paint, the principle of paint. It's something that they never thought of and they're interested. I offered them the paint idea for the idea of their saddles and I've almost got it—"

"Saddles? You mean those things over there, hanging in the air?"

"That is right. Beasly, would you ask one of our friends to demonstrate a saddle?"

"You bet I will," said Beasly.

"What," demanded Henry, "has Beasly got to do with this?"

"Beasly is an interpreter. I guess you'd call him a telepath. You remember how he always claimed he could talk with Towser?"

"Beasly was always claiming things."

"But this time he was right. He tells Chuck, that funny-looking monster, what I want to say and Chuck tells these aliens. And these aliens tell Chuck and Chuck tells Beasly and Beasly tells me."

"Ridiculous!" snorted Henry. "Beasly hasn't got the sense to be . . . what did you say he was?"

"A telepath," said Taine.

One of the aliens had gotten up and climbed into a saddle. He rode it forth and back. Then he swung out of it and sat down again.

"Remarkable," said the U.N. man. "Some sort of antigravity unit, with complete control. We could make use of that, indeed."

He scraped his hand across his chin.

"And you're going to exchange the idea of paint for the idea of that saddle?"

"That's exactly it," said Taine, "but I need some help. I need a chemist or a paint manufacturer or someone to explain how paint is made. And I need some professor or other who'll understand what they're talking about when they tell me the idea of the saddle."

"I see," said Lancaster. "Yes, indeed, you have a problem. Mr. Taine, you seem to me a man of some discernment—"

"Oh, he's all of that," interrupted Henry. "Hiram's quite astute."

"So I suppose you'll understand," said the U.N. man, "that this whole procedure is quite irregular—"

"But it's not," exploded Taine. "That's the way they operate. They open up a planet and then they exchange ideas. They've been doing that with other planets for a long, long time. And ideas are all they want, just the new ideas, because that is the way to keep on building a technology and culture. And they have a lot of ideas, sir, that the human race can use."

"That is just the point," said Lancaster. "This is perhaps the most important thing that has ever happened to us humans. In just a short year's time we can obtain data and ideas that will put us ahead—theoretically, at least—by a thousand years. And in a thing that is so important, we should have experts on the job—"

"But," protested Henry, "you can't find a man who'll do a better dickering job than Hiram. When you dicker with him your back teeth aren't safe. Why don't you leave him be? He'll do a job for you. You can get your experts and your planning groups together and let Hiram front for you. These folks have accepted him and have proved they'll do business with him and what more do you want? All he needs is a little help."

Beasly came over and faced the U.N. man.

"I won't work with no one else," he said. "If you kick Hiram out of here, then I go along with him. Hiram's the only person who ever treated me like a human—"

"There, you see!" Henry said, triumphantly.

"Now, wait a second, Beasly," said the U.N. man. "We could make it worth your while. I should imagine that an interpreter in a situation such as this could command a handsome salary."

"Money don't mean a thing to me," said Beasly. "It won't buy me friends. People still will laugh at me."

"He means it, mister," Henry warned. "There isn't anyone who can be as stubborn as Beasly. I know; he used to work for us."

The U.N. man looked flabbergasted and not a little desperate.

"It will take you quite some time," Henry pointed out, "to find another telepath—leastwise one who can talk to these people here."

The U.N. man looked as if he were strangling. "I doubt," he said, "there's another one on Earth."

"Well, all right," said Beasly, brutally, "let's make up our minds. I ain't standing here all day."

"All right!" cried the U.N. man. "You two go ahead. Please, will you go ahead? This is a chance we can't let slip through our fingers. Is there anything you want? Anything I can do for you?"

"Yes, there is," said Taine. "There'll be the boys from Washington and bigwigs from other countries. Just keep them off my back."

"I'll explain most carefully to everyone. There'll be no interference."

"And I need that chemist and someone who'll know about the saddles. And I need them quick. I can stall these boys a little longer, but not for too much longer."

"Anyone you need," said the U.N. man. "Anyone at all. I'll have them here in hours. And in a day or two there'll be a pool of experts waiting for whenever you may need them—on a moment's notice."

"Sir," said Henry, unctuously, "that's most co-operative. Both Hiram and I appreciate it greatly. And now, since this is settled, I understand that there are reporters waiting. They'll be interested in your statement."

The U.N. man, it seemed, didn't have it in him to protest. He and Henry went tramping up the stairs.

Taine turned around and looked out across the desert.

"It's a big front yard," he said.

7. Operation Stinky

I WAS SITTING on the back stoop of my shack, waiting for the jet, with the shotgun at my right hand and a bottle at my left, when the dogs began the ruckus.

I took a quick swig from the bottle and lumbered to my feet. I grabbed a broom and went around the house.

From the way that they were yapping, I knew the dogs had cornered one of the skunks again and those skunks were jittery enough from the jets without being pestered further.

I walked through the place where the picket fence had fallen down and peered around the corner of the shack. It was getting dusk, but I could see three dogs circling the lilac thicket and, from the sound of it, another had burrowed halfway into it. I knew that if I didn't put an end to it, all hell was bound to pop.

I tried to sneak up on them, but I kept stumbling over old tin cans and empty bottles and I decided then and there, come morning, I'd get that yard cleaned up. I had studied on doing it before, but it seemed there always was some other thing to do.

With all the racket I was making, the three dogs outside the thicket scooted off, but the one that had pushed into the lilacs was having trouble backing out. I zeroed in on him and smacked him dead center with the broom. The way he got out of there—well, he was one of those loose-skinned dogs and for a second, I swear, it looked like he was going to leave without his hide.

He was yelping and howling and he came popping out like a cork out of a bottle and he ran straight between my legs. I tried to keep my balance, but I stepped on an empty can and sat down undignified.

The fall knocked the breath out of me and I seemed to have some trouble getting squared around so I could get on my feet again.

While I was getting squared around, a skunk walked out of the lilac bush and came straight toward me. I tried to shoo him off, but he wouldn't shoo. He was waving his tail and he seemed happy to find me there and he walked right up and rubbed against me, purring very loudly.

I didn't move a muscle. I didn't even bat my eyes. I figured if I didn't move, he might go away. The skunks had been living under the shack for the last three years or so and we got along fine but we had never been what you'd call real close. I'd left them alone and they'd left me alone and we both were satisfied.

But this happy little critter apparently had made up his mind that I was a friend. Maybe he was just plumb grateful to me for running off the dogs.

He walked around me, rubbing against me, and then he climbed up in my lap and put his feet against my chest and looked me in the face. I could feel his body vibrating with the purring noise that he was making.

He kept standing there, with his feet against my chest, looking in my face, and his purring kept getting soft and loud, fast and slow. His ears stood straight up, like he expected me to purr back at him, and all the time his tail kept up its friendly waving.

Finally I reached up a hand, very gingerly, and patted him on the head and he didn't seem to mind. I sat there quite a while patting him and him purring at me, and he still was friendly.

So I took a chance and pushed him off my lap.

After a couple of tries, I made it to my feet and walked around the shack, with the skunk following at my heels.

I sat down on the stoop again and reached for the bottle and took a healthy swig, which I really needed after all I had been through, and while I had the bottle tilted, the jet shot across the treeline to the east and zoomed above my clearing and the whole place jumped a foot or two.

I dropped the bottle and grabbed the gun, but the jet was gone before I got the barrel up.

I put down the gun and did some steady cussing.

I had told the colonel only the day before that if that jet ever flew that close above my shack again, I'd take a shot at it and I meant every word of it.

"It don't seem right," I told him. "A man settles down and builds himself a shack and is living peaceable and contented and ain't bothering no one. Then the government comes in and builds an air base just a couple miles away and there ain't no peace no more, with them jets flying no more than stove-pipe high. Sometimes at night they bring a man plumb out of bed, standing at attention in the middle of the room, with his bare feet on the cold floor."

The colonel had been real nice about it. He had pointed out how we had to have air bases, how our lives depended on the planes that operated out of them and how hard he was trying to arrange the flight patterns so they wouldn't upset folks who lived around the base.

I had told him how the jets were stirring up the skunks and he hadn't laughed, but had been sympathetic, and he told me how, when he was a boy in Texas, he had trapped a lot of skunks. I explained that I wasn't trapping these skunks, but that they were, you might say, sort of living with me, and how I had become attached to them, how I'd lay awake at night and listen to them moving around underneath the shack and when I heard them, I knew I wasn't alone, but was sharing my home with others of God's creatures.

But even so, he wouldn't promise that the jets would stop flying over my place and that was when I told him I'd take a shot at the next one that did.

So he pulled a book out of his desk and read me a law that said it was illegal to shoot at any aircraft, but he didn't scare me none.

So what happens when I lay for a jet? It passes over while I'm taking me a drink.

I quit my cussing when I remembered the bottle, and when I thought of it, I could hear it gurgling. It had rolled underneath the steps and I couldn't get at it right away and I almost went mad listening to it gurgle.

Finally I laid down on my belly and reached underneath the steps and got it, but it had gurgled dry. I tossed it out into the yard and sat down on the steps glum.

The skunk came out of the darkness and climbed the stairs and sat down beside me. I reached out and patted him kind of absent-minded and he purred back at me. I stopped fretting about the bottle.

"You sure are a funny skunk," I said. "I never knew skunks purred."

We sat there for a while and I told him all about my trouble with the jets, the way a man will when there's nobody better around than an animal to do the listening, and sometimes even when there is.

I wasn't afraid of him no more and I thought how fine it was that one of them had finally gotten friendly. I wondered if maybe, now that the ice was broken, some of them might not come in and live with me instead of living under the shack.

Then I got to thinking what a story I'd have to tell the boys down at the tavern. Then I realized that no matter how much I swore to it, they wouldn't believe a word of what I said. So I decided to take the proof along.

I picked up the friendly skunk and I said to it: "Come along. I want to show you to the boys."

I bumped against a tree and got tangled up in an old piece of chicken wire out in the yard, but finally made it out front where I had Old Betsy parked.

Betsy wasn't the newest or the best car ever made, but she was the most faithful that any man could want. Me and her had been through a lot together and we understood each other. We had a sort of bargain —I polished and fed her and she took me where I wanted to go and always brought me back. No reasonable man can ask more of a car than that.

I patted her on the fender and said good evening to her, put the skunk in the front seat and climbed in myself.

Betsy didn't want to start. She'd rather just stayed home. But I talked to her and babied her and she finally started, shaking and shivering and flapping her fenders.

I eased her into gear and headed her out into the road.

"Now take it easy," I told her. "The state coppers have got themselves a speed trap set up somewhere along this stretch and we don't want to take no chances."

Betsy took it slow and gentle down to the tavern and I parked her there and tucked the skunk under my arm and went into the place.

Charley was behind the bar and there were quite a lot of customers —Johnny Ashland and Skinny Patterson and Jack O'Neill and half a dozen others.

I put the skunk on the bar and it started walking toward them, just like it was eager to make friends with them.

They took one look and they made foxholes under chairs and tables. Charley grabbed a bottle by the neck and backed into a corner.

"Asa," he yelled, "you take that thing out of here!"

"It's all right," I told him. "It's a friendly cuss."

"Friendly or not, get the hell out with it!"

"Get it out!" yelled all the customers.

I was plenty sore at them. Imagine being upset at a friendly skunk!

But I could see I was getting nowhere, so I picked it up and took it out to Betsy. I found a gunny sack and made a nest and told it to stay right there, that I'd be right back.

It took me longer than I had intended, for I had to tell my story and they asked a lot of questions and made a lot of jokes and they wouldn't let me buy, but kept them set up for me.

When I went out, I had some trouble spotting Betsy and then I had to set a course to reach her. It took a little time, but after tacking back and forth before the wind, I finally got close enough in passing to reach out and grab her.

I had trouble getting in because the door didn't work the way it should, and when I got in, I couldn't find the key. When I found it, I dropped it on the floor, and when I reached down to get it, I fell flat upon the seat. It was so comfortable there that I decided it was foolish to get up. I'd just spend the night there.

While I was lying there, Betsy's engine started and I chuckled. Betsy was disgusted and was going home without me. That's the kind of car she was. Just like a wife'd act.

She backed out and made a turn and headed for the road. At the road, she stopped and looked for other cars, then went out on the highway, heading straight for home.

I wasn't worried any. I knew I could trust Betsy. We'd been through a lot together and she was intelligent, although I couldn't remember she'd ever gone home all by herself before.

I lay there and thought about it and the wonder of it was, I told myself, that it hadn't happened long before.

A man is as close to no machine as he is to his car. A man gets to understand his car and his car gets to understand him and after a time a real affection must grow up between them. So it seemed absolutely natural to me that the day had to come when a car could be trusted just the way a horse or dog is, and that a good car should be as loyal and faithful as any dog or horse.

I lay there feeling happy and Betsy went head high down the road and turned in at the driveway.

But we had no more than stopped when there was a squeal of brakes and I heard a car door open and someone jump out on the gravel.

I tried to get up, but I was a bit slow about it and someone jerked the door open and reached in and grabbed me by the collar and hauled me out.

The man wore the uniform of a state trooper and there was another trooper just a little ways away and the police car stood there with its red light flashing. I wondered why I hadn't noticed it had been following us and then remembered I'd been lying down.

"Who was driving that car?" barked the cop who was holding me.

Before I could answer, the other cop looked inside Betsy and jumped back about a dozen feet.

"Slade!" he yelled. "There's a skunk in there!"

"Don't tell me," said Slade, "that the skunk was driving."

And the other one said, "At least the skunk is sober."

"You leave that skunk alone!" I told them. "He's a friend of mine. He isn't bothering no one."

I gave a jerk and Slade's hand slipped from my collar and I lunged for Betsy. My chest hit the seat and I grabbed the steering post and tried to pull myself inside.

Betsy started up with a sudden roar and her wheels threw gravel that hit the police car like machine-gun fire. She lurched forward and crashed through the picket fence, curving for the road. She smashed into the lilac thicket and went through it and I was brushed off.

I lay there, all tangled up with the smashed-down lilac bushes and watched Betsy hit the road and keep on going. She had done the best she could, I consoled myself. She had tried to rescue me and it wasn't her fault that I had failed to hang onto her. Now she had to make a run for it herself. And she seemed to be doing pretty well. She sounded and went like she had an engine off a battleship inside her.

The two state troopers jumped into their car and took off in pursuit and I settled down to figure out how to untangle myself from the lilac thicket.

I finally managed it and went over to the front steps of the shack and sat down. I got to thinking about the fence and decided it wasn't worth repairing. I might just as well uproot it and use what was left of it for kindling.

And I wondered about Betsy and what might be happening to her, but I wasn't really worried. I was pretty sure she could take care of herself.

I was right about that, for in a little while the state troopers came back again and parked in the driveway. They saw me sitting on the steps and came over to me.

"Where's Betsy?" I asked them.

"Betsy who?" Slade asked.

"Betsy is the car," I said.

Slade swore. "Got away. Traveling without lights at a hundred miles an hour. It'll smash into something, sure as hell."

I shook my head at that. "Not Betsy. She knows all the roads for fifty miles around."

Slade thought I was being smart. He grabbed me and jerked me to my feet. "You got a lot to explain." He shoved me at the other trooper and the other trooper caught me. "Toss him in the back seat, Ernie, and let's get going."

Ernie didn't seem to be as sore as Slade. He said: "This way, Pop."

Once they got me in the car, they didn't want to talk with me. Ernie rode in back with me and Slade drove. We hadn't gone a mile when I dozed off.

When I woke up, we were just pulling into the parking area in front of the state police barracks. I got out and tried to walk, but one of them got on each side of me and practically dragged me along.

We went into a sort of office with a desk, some chairs and a bench. A man sat behind the desk.

"What you got there?" he asked.

"Damned if I know," said Slade, all burned up. "You won't believe it, Captain."

Ernie took me over to a chair and sat me down. "I'll get you some coffee, Pop. We want to talk with you. We have to get you sober."

I thought that was nice of him.

I drank a lot of coffee and I began to see a little better and things were in straight lines instead of going round in circles—things I could see, that is. It was different when I tried to think. Things that had seemed okay before now seemed mighty queer, like Betsy going home all by herself, for instance.

Finally they took me over to the desk and the captain asked me a lot of questions about who I was and how old I was and where I lived, until eventuallly we got around to what was on their minds.

I didn't hold back anything. I told them about the jets and the skunks and the talk I had with the colonel. I told them about the dogs and the friendly skunk and how Betsy had got disgusted with me and gone home by herself.

"Tell me, Mr. Bayles," said the captain, "are you a mechanic? I know you told me you are a day laborer and work at anything that you can get. But I wonder if you might not tinker around in your spare time, working on your car."

"Captain," I told him truthfully, "I wouldn't know which end of a wrench to grab hold of."

"You never worked on Betsy, then?"

"Just took good care of her."

"Has anyone else ever worked on her?"

"I wouldn't let no one lay a hand on her."

"Then you can't explain how that car could possibly operate by itself?"

"No, sir. Betsy is a smart car, Captain–"

"You're sure you weren't driving?"

"I wasn't driving. I was just taking it easy while Betsy took me home."

The captain threw down his pencil in disgust. "I give up!"

He got up from the desk. "I'm going out and make some more coffee," he said to Slade. "You see what you can do."

"There's one thing," Ernie said to Slade as the captain left. "The skunk–"

"What about the skunk?"

"Skunks don't wave their tails," said Ernie. "Skunks don't purr."

"This skunk did," Slade said sarcastically. "This was a special skunk. This was a ring-tailed wonder of a skunk. Besides, the skunk hasn't got a thing to do with it. He was just out for a ride."

"You boys haven't got a little nip?" I asked. I was feeling mighty low.

"Sure," said Ernie. He went to a locker in one corner of the room and took out a bottle.

Through the windows, I could see that the east was beginning to brighten. Dawn wasn't far away.

The telephone rang. Slade picked it up.

Ernie motioned to me and I walked across to where he stood by the locker. He handed me the bottle.

"Take it easy, Pop," he advised me. "You don't want to hang one on again."

I took it easy. About a tumbler and a half, I'd reckon.

Slade hollered "Hey!" at us.

"What's going on?" asked Ernie.

He took the bottle from me, not by force exactly, but almost.

"A farmer found the car," said Slade. "It took a shot at his dog."

"It took a what–a shot at his dog?" Ernie stuttered.

"That's what the fellow says. Went out to get in the cows. Early. Going fishing and was anxious to get the morning chores done. Found what he thought was an abandoned car at the end of a lane."

"And the shot?"

"I'm coming to that. Dog ran up barking. The car shot out a spark–a big spark. It knocked the dog over. He got up and ran. Car shot out another spark. Caught him in the rump. Fellow says the pooch is blistered."

Slade headed for the door. "Come on, the both of you."

"We may need you, Pop," said Ernie.

We ran and piled into the car.

"Where is this farm?" asked Ernie.

"Out west of the air base," said Slade.

The farmer was waiting for us at the barnyard gate. He jumped in when Slade stopped.

"The car's still there," he said. "I been watching. It hasn't come out."

"Any other way it could get out?"

"Nope. Woods and fields is all. That lane is dead end."

Slade grunted in satisfaction. He drove down the road and ran the police car across the mouth of the lane, blocking it entirely.

"We walk from here," he said.

"Right around that bend," the farmer told us.

We walked around the bend and saw it was Betsy, all right.

"That's my car," I said.

"Let's scatter out a bit," said Slade. "It might start shooting at us." He loosened the gun in his holster.

"Don't you go shooting up my car," I warned him, but he paid me no mind.

Like he said, we scattered out a bit, the four of us, and went toward the car. It seemed funny that we should be acting that way, as if Betsy was an enemy and we were stalking her.

She looked the same as ever, just an old beat-up jalopy that had a lot of sense and a lot of loyalty. And I kept thinking about how she always got me places and always got me back.

Then all at once she charged us. She was headed in the wrong direction and she was backing up, but she charged us just the same.

She gave a little leap and was running at full speed and going faster every second and I saw Slade pull his gun.

I jumped out in the middle of the lane and waved my arms. I didn't trust that Slade. I was afraid that if I couldn't get Betsy stopped, he'd shoot her full of holes.

But Betsy didn't stop. She kept right on charging us and she was going faster than an old wreck like her had any right to go.

"Jump, you fool!" shouted Ernie. "She'll run over you!"

I jumped, but my heart wasn't in the jump. I thought that if things had come to the pass where Betsy'd run me down there wasn't too much left for me to go on living for.

I stubbed my toe and fell flat on my face, but even while I was falling, I saw Betsy leave the ground as if she was going to leap over me. I knew right away that I'd never been in any danger, that Betsy never had any intention of hitting me at all.

She sailed right up into the sky, with her wheels still spinning, as if she was backing up a long, steep hill that was invisible.

I twisted around and sat up and stared at her and she sure was a pretty sight. She was flying just like an airplane. I was downright proud of her.

Slade stood with his mouth open and his gun hanging at his side. He never even tried to fire it. He probably forgot that he even had a gun in his hand.

Betsy went up above the treeline and the sun made her sparkle and gleam—I'd polished her only the week before last—and I thought how swell it was she had learned to fly.

It was then I saw the jet and I tried to yell a warning for Betsy, but my mouth dried up like there was alum in it and the yell wouldn't come out.

It didn't take more than a second, probably, although it seemed to me that days passed while Betsy hung there and the jet hung there and I knew they would crash.

Then there were pieces flying all over the sky and the jet was smoking and heading for a cornfield off to the left of us.

I sat there limp in the middle of the lane and watched the pieces that had been Betsy falling back to earth and I felt sick. It was an awful thing to see.

The pieces came down and you could hear them falling, thudding on the ground, but there was one piece that didn't fall as fast as the others. It just seemed to glide.

I watched, wondering why it glided while all the other pieces fell and I saw it was a fender and that it seemed to be rocking back and forth, as if it wanted to fall, too, only something held it back.

It glided down to the ground near the edge of the woods. It landed easy and rocked a little, then tipped over. And when it tipped over, it spilled something out of it. The thing got up and shook itself and trotted straight into the woods.

It was the friendly skunk!

By this time, everyone was running. Ernie was running for the farmhouse to phone the base about the jet and Slade and the farmer were running toward the cornfield, where the jet had plowed a path in the corn wide enough to haul a barn through.

I got up and walked off the lane to where I had seen some pieces falling. I found a few of them—a headlight, the lens not even broken, and a wheel, all caved in and twisted, and the radiator ornament. I knew it was no use. No one could ever get Betsy back together.

I stood there with the radiator ornament in my hand and thought of all the good times Betsy and I had had together—how she'd take me to the tavern and wait until I was ready to go home, and how we'd go fishing and eat a picnic lunch together, and how we'd go up north deer hunting in the fall.

While I was standing there, Slade and the farmer came down from the cornfield with the pilot walking between them. He was sort of rubber-legged and they were holding him up. He had a glassy look in his eyes and he was babbling a bit.

When they reached the lane, they let loose of him and he sat down heavily.

"When the hell," he asked them, "did they start making flying cars?"

They didn't answer him. Instead, Slade yelled at me, "Hey, Pop! You leave that wreckage alone. Don't touch none of it."

"I got a right to touch it," I told him. "It's my car."

"You leave it alone! There's something funny going on here. That junk might tell us what it is if no one monkeys with it."

So I dropped the radiator ornament and went back to the lane.

The four of us sat down and waited. The pilot seemed to be all right. He had a cut above one eye and some blood had run down across his face, but that was all that was the matter with him. He asked for a cigarette and Slade gave him one and lit it.

Down at the end of the lane, we heard Ernie backing the police car out of the way. Pretty soon he came walking up to us.

"They'll be here right away."

He sat down with us. We didn't say anything about what had happened. I guess we were all afraid to talk.

In less than fifteen minutes, the air base descended on us. First there was an ambulance and they loaded the pilot aboard and left in a lot of dust.

Behind the ambulance was a fire rig and behind the fire rig was a jeep with the colonel in it. Behind the colonel's jeep were other jeeps and three or four trucks, all loaded with men, and in less time than it takes to tell it, the place was swarming.

The colonel was red in the face and you could see he was upset. After all, why wouldn't he be? This was the first time a plane had ever collided in midair with a car.

The colonel came tramping up to Slade and he started hollering at Slade and Slade hollered right back at him and I wondered why they were sore at one another, but that wasn't it at all. That was just the way they talked when they got excited.

All around, there was a lot of running here and there and a lot more hollering, but it didn't last too long. Before the colonel got through yelling back and forth with Slade, the entire area was ringed in with men and the situation was in Air Force hands.

When the colonel finished talking with Slade, he walked over to me.

"So it was your car," he said. The way he said it, you'd thought it was my fault.

"Yes, it was," I told him, "and I'm going to sue you. That was a darn good car."

The colonel went on looking at me as if I had no right to live, then suddenly seemed to recognize me.

"Say, wait a minute," he said. "Weren't you in to see me just the other day?"

"I sure was. I told you about my skunks. It was one of them that was in Old Betsy."

"Hold up there, old-timer," said the colonel. "You lost me. Let's hear that again."

"Old Betsy was the car," I explained, "and the skunk was in her. When your jet crashed into it, he rode a fender down."

"You mean the skunk–the fender–the–"

"It just sort of floated down," I finished telling him.

"Corporal," the colonel said to Slade, "have you further use for this man?"

"Just drunkenness," said Slade. "Not worth mentioning."

"I'd like to take him back to the base with me."

"I'd appreciate it," Slade said in a quivery kind of voice.

"Come on, then," said the colonel and I followed him to the jeep.

We sat in the back seat and a soldier drove and he didn't waste no time. The colonel and I didn't talk much. We just hung on and hoped that we'd live through it. At least, that's the way I felt.

Back at the base, the colonel sat down at his desk and pointed at a chair for me to sit in. Then he leaned back and studied me. I was sure glad I had done nothing wrong, for the way he looked at me, I'd just have had to up and confess it if I had.

"You said some queer things back there," the colonel started. "Now suppose you just rear back comfortable in that chair and tell me all about it, not leaving out a thing."

So I told him all about it and I went into a lot of detail to explain my viewpoint and he didn't interrupt, but just sat listening. He was the best listener I ever ran across.

When I was all finished, he reached for a pad and pencil.

"Let's get a few points down," he said. "You say the car had never operated by itself before?"

"Not that I know of," I answered honestly. "It might have practiced while I wasn't looking, of course."

"And it never flew before?"

I shook my head.

"And when it did both of these things, there was this skunk of yours aboard?"

"That's right."

"And you say this skunk glided down in a fender after the crash?"

"The fender tipped over and the critter ran into the woods."

"Don't you think it's a little strange that the fender should glide down when all the other wreckage fell kerplunk?"

I admitted that it did seem slightly strange.

"Now about this skunk. You say it purred?"

"It purred real pretty."

"And waved its tail?"

"Just like a dog," I said.

The colonel pushed the pad away and leaned back in his chair. He crossed his arms and sort of hugged himself.

"As a matter of personal knowledge," he told me, "gained from years of boyhood trapping, I can tell you that no skunk purrs or ever wags its tail."

"I know what you're thinking," I said, indignant, "but I wasn't that drunk. I'd had a drink or two to while away the time I was waiting for the jet. But I saw the skunk real plain and I knew he was a skunk and I can remember that he purred. He was a friendly cuss. He acted as if he liked me and he—"

"Okay," the colonel said. "Okay."

We sat there looking at one another. All at once, he grinned.

"You know," he said, "I find quite suddenly that I need an aide."

"I ain't joining up," I replied stubbornly. "You couldn't get me within a quarter mile of one of them jets. Not if you roped and tied me."

"A civilian aide. Three hundred a month and keep."

"Colonel, I don't hanker none for the military life."

"And all the liquor you can drink."

"Where do I sign?" I asked.

And that is how I got to be the colonel's aide.

I thought he was crazy and I still think so. He'd been a whole lot better off if he'd quit right there. But he had an idea by the tail and he was the kind of gambling fool who'd ride a hunch to death.

We got along just fine, although at times we had our differences. The first one was over that foolish business about confining me to base. I raised quite a ruckus, but he made it stick.

"You'd go out and get slobbered up and gab your head off," he told me. "I want you to button up your lip and keep it buttoned up. Why else do you think I hired you?"

It wasn't so bad. There wasn't a blessed thing to do. I never had to lift my hand to do a lick of work. The chow was fit to eat and I had a place to sleep and the colonel kept his word about all the liquor I could drink.

For several days, I saw nothing of him. Then one afternoon, I dropped around to pass the time of day. I hadn't more than got there when a sergeant came in with a bunch of papers in his hand. He seemed to be upset.

"Here's the report on that car, sir," he said.

The colonel took the papers and leafed through a few of them. "Sergeant, I can't make head nor tail of this."

"Some of it I can't, either, sir."

"Now this?" said the colonel, pointing.

"That's a computer, sir."

"Cars don't have computers."

"Well, sir, that's what I said, too. But we found the place where it was attached to the engine block."

"Attached? Welded?"

"Well, not exactly welded. Like it was a part of the block. Like it had been cast as a part of it. There was no sign of welding."

"You're sure it's a computer?"

"Connally said it was, sir. He knows about computers. But it's not like any he's ever seen before. It works on a different principle than any he has seen, he says. But he says it makes a lot of sense, sir. The principle, that is. He says—"

"Well, go on!" the colonel yelled.

"He says its capacity is at least a thousand times that of the best computer that we have. He says it might not be stretching your imagination too far to say that it's intelligent."

"How do you mean—intelligent?"

"Well, Connally says a rig like that might be capable of thinking for itself, sir."

"My God!" the colonel said.

He sat there for a minute, as if he might be thinking. Then he turned a page and pointed at something else.

"That's another part, sir," the sergeant said. "A drawing of the part. We don't know what it is."

"Don't know!"

"We never saw anything like it, sir. We don't have any idea what it might be for. It was attached to the transmission, sir."

"And this?"

"That's an analysis of the gasoline. Funny thing about that, sir. We found the tank, all twisted out of shape, but there was some gas still left in it. It hadn't—"

"But why an analysis?"

"Because it's not gasoline, sir. It is something else. It was gasoline, but it's been changed, sir."

"Is that all, Sergeant?"

The sergeant, I could see, was beginning to sweat a little. "No, sir, there's more to it. It's all in that report. We got most all the wreckage, sir. Just bits here and there are missing. We are working now on reassembling it."

"Reassembling—"

"Maybe, sir, pasting it back together is a better way to put it."

"It will never run again?"

"I don't think so, sir. It's pretty well smashed up. But if it could be put back together whole, it would be the best car that was ever made. The speedometer says 80,000 miles, but it's in new-car condition. And there are alloys in it that we can't even guess at."

The sergeant paused. "If you'll permit me, sir, it's a very funny business."

"Yes, indeed," the colonel said. "Thank you, Sergeant. A very funny business."

The sergeant turned to leave.

"Just a minute," said the colonel.

"Yes, sir."

"I'm sorry about this, Sergeant, but you and the entire detail that was assigned to the car are restricted to the base. I don't want this leaking out. Tell your men, will you? I'll make it tough on anyone who talks."

"Yes, sir," the sergeant said, saluting very polite, but looking like he could have slit the colonel's throat.

When the sergeant was gone, the colonel said to me: "Asa, if there's something that you should say now and you fail to say it and it comes out later and makes a fool of me, I'll wring your scrawny little neck."

"Cross my heart," I said.

He looked at me funny. "Do you know what that skunk was?"

I shook my head.

"It wasn't any skunk," he said. "I guess it's up to us to find out what it is."

"But it isn't here. It ran into the woods."

"It could be hunted down."

"Just you and me?"

"Why just you and me when there are two thousand men right on this base?"

"But—"

"You mean they wouldn't take too kindly to hunting down a skunk?"

"Something like that, Colonel. They might go out, but they wouldn't hunt. They'd try not to find it."

"They'd hunt if there was five thousand dollars waiting for the man who brought the right one in."

I looked at him as if he'd gone off his rocker.

"Believe me," said the colonel, "it would be worth it. Every penny of it."

I told you he was crazy.

I didn't go out with the skunk hunters. I knew just how little chance there was of ever finding it. It could have gotten clear out of the county by that time or found a place to hole up where one would never find it.

And, anyhow, I didn't need five thousand. I was drawing down good pay and drinking regular.

The next day, I dropped in to see the colonel. The medical officer was having words with him.

"You got to call it off!" the sawbones shouted.

"I can't call it off," the colonel yelled. "I have to have that animal."

"You ever see a man who tried to catch a skunk barehanded?"

"No, I never have."

"I got eleven of them now," the sawbones said. "I won't have any more of it."

"Captain," said the colonel, "you may have a lot more than eleven before this is all over."

"You mean you won't call it off, sir?"

"No, I won't."

"Then I'll have it stopped."

"Captain!" said the colonel and his voice was deadly.

"You're insane," the sawbones said. "No court-martial in the land–"

"Captain."

But the captain did not answer. He turned straight around and left.

The colonel looked at me. "It's sometimes tough," he said.

I knew that someone better find that skunk or the colonel's name was mud.

"What I don't understand," I said, "is why you want that skunk. He's just a skunk that purrs."

The colonel sat down at his desk and put his head between his hands.

"My God," he moaned, "how stupid can men get?"

"Pretty stupid," I told him, "but I still don't understand–"

"Look," the colonel said, "someone jiggered up that car of yours. You say you didn't do it. You say no one else could have done it. The boys who are working on it say there's stuff in it that's not been even thought of."

"If you think that skunk–"

The colonel raised his fist and smacked it on the desk.

"Not a skunk! Something that *looks* like a skunk! Something that knows more about machines than you or I or any human being will ever get to know!"

"But it hasn't got no hands. How could it do what you think?"

He never got to answer. The door burst in and two of the saddest sacks outside the guardhouse stumbled in. They didn't bother to salute.

"Colonel, sir," one of them said, heaving hard. "Colonel, sir, we got one. We didn't even have to catch it. We whistled at it and it followed us."

The skunk walked in behind them, waving its tail and purring. It walked right over to me and rubbed against my legs. When I reached down and picked it up, it purred so loud I was afraid it would go ahead and explode.

"That the one?" the colonel asked me.

"He's the one," I said.

The colonel grabbed the phone. "Get me Washington. General Sanders. At the Pentagon."

He waved his hand at us. "Get out of here!"

"But, Colonel, sir, the money–"

"You'll get it. Now get out of here."

He looked exactly like you might imagine a man might look right after he's been told he's not going to be shot at dawn.

We turned around and got out of there.

At the door, four of the toughest-looking hombres this side of Texas were waiting, with rifles in their hands.

"Don't pay no attention to us, Mac," one of them said to me. "We're just your bodyguards."

They were my bodyguards, all right. They went every place I went. And the skunk went with me, too. That, of course, was why they stuck around. They didn't care a rap about me. It was the skunk that was getting the bodyguarding.

And that skunk stuck closer to me than paper to the wall. He followed at my heels and walked between my feet, but mostly he wanted me to carry him or to let him perch on my shoulder. And he purred all the blessed time. Either he figured I was the only true friend he had or he thought I was a soft touch.

Life got a little complicated. The skunk slept with me and the four guards stayed in the room. The skunk and one of the guards went to the latrine with me while the others kept close. I had no privacy at all. I said it wasn't decent. I said it was unconstitutional. It didn't make no difference. There was nothing I could do. There were, it turned out, twelve of them guards and they worked in eight-hour shifts.

For a couple of days, I didn't see the colonel and I thought it was funny how he couldn't rest until he'd found the skunk and then paid no attention to it.

I did a lot of thinking about what the colonel had said about the skunk not being a skunk at all, but something that only looked like a skunk and how it might know more, some ways, than we did. And the more I lived with it, the more I began to believe that he might be right. Although it still seemed impossible that any critter without hands could know much about machinery in the first place, let alone do anything about it.

Then I got to remembering how me and Betsy had understood each other and I carried that a little further, imagining how a man and machine might get to know one another so well, they could even talk together and how the man, even if he didn't have hands, might help the machine to improve itself. And while it sounds somewhat far-fetched just telling it, thinking of it in the secrecy of one's mind made it sound all right and it gave a sort of warm feeling to imagine that one could get to be downright personal friendly with machines.

When you come to think of it, it's not so far-fetched, either.

Perhaps, I told myself, when I had gone into the tavern and had left the skunk bedded down in Betsy, the skunk might have looked her over and felt sorry for such a heap of junk, like you or I would feel sorry for a homeless cat or an injured dog. And maybe the skunk had set out, right then and there, to fix her up as best he could, probably cannibalizing some metal here and there, from places where it would not be missed, to grow the computer and the other extra pieces on her.

Probably he couldn't understand, for the life of him, why they'd been left off to start with. Maybe, to him, a machine was no machine at all without those pieces on it. More than likely, he thought Betsy was just a botched-up job.

The guards began calling the skunk Stinky and that was a libel because he never stunk a bit, but was one of the best-mannered, most even-tempered animals that I have ever been acquainted with. I told them it wasn't right, but they just laughed at me, and before long the whole base knew about the name and everywhere we went they'd yell "Hi, Stinky" at us. He didn't seem to mind, so I began to think of him as Stinky, too.

I got it figured out to my own satisfaction that maybe Stinky could have fixed up Betsy and even why he fixed up Betsy. But the one thing I couldn't figure out was where he'd come from to start with. I thought on it a lot and came up with no answers except some foolish ones that were too much for even me to swallow.

I went over to see the colonel a couple of times, but the sergeants and the lieutenants threw me out before I could get to see him. So I got sore about it and decided not to go there any more until he sent for me.

One day he did send for me, and when I got there the place was crowded with a lot of brass. The colonel was talking to an old gray-haired, eagle-beaked gent who had a fierce look about him and a rat-trap jaw and was wearing stars.

"General," said the colonel, "may I introduce Stinky's special friend?"

The general shook hands with me. Stinky, who was riding on my shoulder, purred at him.

The general took a good look at Stinky.

"Colonel," he said, "I hope to God you're right. Because if you aren't and this business ever leaks, the Air Force goose is cooked. The Army and the Navy would never let us live it down and what Congress would do to us would be a crimson shame."

The colonel gulped a little. "Sir, I'm sure I'm right."

"I don't know why I let myself get talked into this," the general said. "It's the most hare-brained scheme I have ever heard of."

He had another squint at Stinky.

"He looks like a common skunk to me," the general said.

The colonel introduced me to a bunch of other colonels and a batch of majors, but he didn't bother with the captains if there were any there and I shook hands with them and Stinky purred at them and everything was cozy.

One of the colonels picked up Stinky, but he kicked up quite a fuss trying to get back to me.

The general said to me, "You seem to be the one he wants to be with."

"He's a friend of mine," I explained.

"I'll be damned," the general said.

After lunch the colonel and the general came for me and Stinky, and we went over to a hangar. The place had been cleared out and there was only one plane in it, one of the newer jets. There was a mob of people waiting for us, some of them military, but a lot of them were technicians in ordinary clothes or in dungarees. Some of them had clipboards tucked under their arms and some were carrying tools or what I imagined must be tools, although never before have I ever seen contraptions such as those. And there were different pieces of equipment scattered here and there.

"Now, Asa," the colonel said to me, "I want you to get into that jet with Stinky."

"And do what?" I asked.

"Just get in and sit. But don't touch anything. You might get the detail all fouled up."

It seemed a funny business and I hesitated.

"Don't be afraid," the general assured me. "Nothing will happen. You just get in and sit."

So I did and it was a foolish business. I climbed up where the pilot sits and sat down in his seat and it was a crazy-looking place. There were instruments and gadgets and doodads all over. I was almost afraid to move for fear of touching one of them because God knows what might have happened if I had.

I got in and sat and I kept myself interested for a time by just looking at all the stuff and trying to figure out what it was for, but I never rightly got much of it figured out.

But finally I had looked at everything a hundred times and puzzled over it and there wasn't anything more to do and I was awful bored. But I remembered all the money I was pulling down and the free drinking I was getting and I thought if a man just had to sit in a certain place to earn it, why, it was all right.

Stinky didn't pay any attention to any of the stuff. He settled down in my lap and went to sleep, or at least he seemed to go to sleep. He took it easy, for a fact. Once in a while, he opened an eye or twitched an ear, but that was all he did.

I hadn't thought much about it at first, but after I'd sat there for an hour or so, I began to get an idea of why they wanted me and Stinky in the plane. They figured, I told myself, that if they put Stinky in the ship, he might feel sorry for it, too, and do the same kind of job on it as he had done on Betsy. But if that was what they thought, they sure were getting fooled, for Stinky didn't do a thing except curl up and go to sleep.

We sat there for several hours and finally they told us that we could get out.

And that is how Operation Stinky got off to a start. That is what they called all that foolishness. It does beat hell, the kind of names the Air Force can think up.

It went on like that for several days. Me and Stinky would go out in the morning and sit in a plane for several hours, then take a break for noon, then go back for a few hours more. Stinky didn't seem to mind. He'd just as soon be there as anywhere. All he'd do would be curl up in my lap and in five minutes he'd be dozing.

As the days went on, the general and the colonel and all the technicians who cluttered up the hangar got more and more excited. They didn't say a word, but you could see they were aching to bust out, only they held it back. And I couldn't understand that, for as far as I could see, there was nothing whatsoever happening.

Apparently their work didn't end when Stinky and I left. Evening after evening, lights burned in the hangar and a gang was working there and they had guards around three deep.

One day they pulled out the jet we had been sitting in and hauled in another and we sat in that and it was just the same as it had been before. Nothing really happened. And yet the air inside that hangar was so filled with tension and excitement, you could fairly light a fire with it.

It sure beat me what was going on.

Gradually the same sort of tension spread throughout the entire base and there were some funny goings-on. You never saw an outfit that was faster on its toes. A construction gang moved in and started to put up buildings and as soon as one of them was completed, machinery was installed. More and more people kept arriving until the base began to look like an anthill with a hotfoot.

On one of the walks I took, with the guards trailing along beside me, I found out something else that made my eyes bug. They were installing a twelve-foot woven fence, topped with barbed wire, all around the area.

And inside the fence, there were so many guards, they almost walked on one another.

I was a little scared when I got back from the walk, because from what I saw, this thing I'd been pitchforked into was bigger and more important than I had ever dreamed. Up until then, I'd figured it was just a matter of the colonel having his neck stuck out so far he could never pull it back. All along, I had been feeling sorry for him because that general looked like the kind of gent who would stand for just so much tomfoolery before he lowered the boom.

It was about this time that they began to dig a big pit out in the center of one of the runways. I went over one day to watch it and it didn't make no sense at all. Here they had a nice, smooth runway they'd spent a lot of money to construct and now they were digging it up to make what looked like a swimming pool. I asked around about it, but the people that I talked to either didn't know or they weren't talking.

Me and Stinky kept on sitting in the planes. We were on our sixth one now. And there wasn't any change. I sat, bored stiff, while Stinky took it easy.

One evening the colonel sent a sergeant over to say he'd like to see me.

I went in and sat down and put Stinky on the desk. He lay down on top of it and looked from one to the other of us.

"Asa," said the colonel, "I think we got it made."

"You mean you been getting stuff?"

"We've got enough we actually understand to give us unquestioned air superiority. We're a good ten years, if not a hundred, depending on how much we can use, ahead of the rest of them. They'll never catch us now."

"But all Stinky did was sleep!"

"All he did," the colonel said, "was to redesign each ship. In some instances, there were principles involved that don't make a bit of sense, but I'll bet they will later. And in other cases, what he did was so simple and so basic that we're wondering why we never thought of it ourselves."

"Colonel, what is Stinky?"

"I don't know," he said.

"You got an idea, though."

"Sure, an idea. But that's all it is. It embarrasses me even to think of it."

"I don't embarrass easy."

"Okay, then–Stinky is like nothing on Earth. My guess is that he's from some other solar system. I think he crossed space to us. How or why, I have no notion. His ship might have been wrecked and he got into a lifeboat and made it here."

"But if there was a lifeboat–"

"We've combed every foot of ground for miles around."

"And no lifeboat?"

"No lifeboat," said the colonel.

Getting that idea down took a little doing, but I did it. Then I got to wondering about something else.

"Colonel," I said, "you claim Stinky fixed up the ships, made them even better. Now how could he have done that with no hands and just sleeping and never touching a thing?"

"You tell me," said the colonel. "I've heard a bunch of guesses. The only one that makes any kind of sense—and cockeyed sense at that—is telekinesis."

I sat there and admired that word. "What's it mean, Colonel?" I wanted to use it on the boys at the tavern, if I ever got back there, and I wanted to get it right.

"Moving things by the power of thought," he said.

"But there wasn't nothing moved," I objected. "All the improvements in Betsy and the planes came from right inside them, not stuff moved in."

"That could be done by telekinesis, too."

I shook my head, thoughtful-like. "Ain't the way I see it."

"Go ahead," he sighed. "Let's hear your theory. No reason you should be an exception."

"I think Stinky's got a kind of mental green thumb for machines," I said. "Like some people got green thumbs for plants, only he's got—"

The colonel took a long, hard frown at me. Then he nodded very slowly. "I see what you mean. Those new parts weren't moved in or around. They were *grown.*"

"Something like that. Maybe he can make a machine come kind of alive and improve itself, grow parts that'll make it a better and happier and more efficient machine."

"Sounds silly when you say it," the colonel said, "but it makes a lot more sense than any of the other ideas. Man's been working with machines—real machines, that is—only a century or two. Make that ten thousand or a million years and it might not seem so silly."

We sat in silence while the twilight crept into the room and I think the both of us must have been thinking the same thing. Thinking of the black night that lay out beyond Earth and of how Stinky must have crossed it. And wondering, too, about what kind of world he came from and why he might have left it and what happened to him out in the long dark that forced him to look for asylum on Earth.

Thinking, too, I guess, about the ironic circumstance that had cast him on a planet where his nearest counterpart was a little animal that no one cared to have much to do with.

"What I can't understand," the colonel said, "is why he does it. Why does he do it for us?"

"He doesn't do it for us," I answered. "He does it for the planes. He feels sorry for them."

The door burst open and the general came tramping in. He was triumphant. Dusk had crept into the room and I don't think he saw me.

"We got an okay!" he gloated. "The ship will be in tomorrow. The Pentagon agrees!"

"General," said the colonel, "we're pushing this too hard. It's time for us to begin to lay some sort of grounds for basic understanding. We've grabbed what we can grab the quickest. We've exploited this little cuss right up to the hilt. We have a lot of data–"

"Not all we need!" the general bellowed. "What we have been doing has been just sort of practice. We have no data on the A-ship. That is where we need it."

"What we need as well is an understanding of this creature. An understanding of how he does it. If we could talk to him–"

"Talk!" the general shouted.

"Yes, talk!" the colonel shouted back. "He keeps purring all the time. That may be his means of communication. The men who found him simply whistled and he came. That was communication. If we had a little patience–"

"We have no time for patience, Colonel."

"General, we can't simply wring him dry. He's done a lot for us. Let's give the little guy a break. He's the one who has had the patience –waiting for us to communicate with him, hoping that someday we'll recognize him for what he is!"

They were yelling at one another and the colonel must have forgotten I was there. It was embarrassing. I held out my arms to Stinky and he jumped into them. I tiptoed across the room and went out as quietly as I could.

That night, I lay in bed with Stinky curled up on the covers at my feet. The four guards sat in the room, quiet as watchful mice.

I thought about what the colonel had said to the general and my heart went out to Stinky. I thought how awful it would be if a man suddenly was dumped into a world of skunks who didn't care a rap about him except that he could dig the deepest and slickest burrows that skunks had ever seen and that he could dig them quick. And there were so many burrows to be dug that not one of the skunks would take the time to understand this man, to try to talk with him or to help him out.

I lay there feeling sorry and wishing there was something I could do. Then Stinky came walking up the covers and crawled in under them with me and I put out my hand and held him tight against me while he purred softly at me. And that is how we went to sleep.

The next afternoon, the A-ship arrived. The last of three that had been built, it was still experimental. It was a monster and we stood far back behind a line of guards and watched it come mushing down, settling base-first into the water-filled rocket pit they'd dug out on the runway. Finally it was down and it stood there, a bleak, squat thing that somehow touched one with awe just to look at it.

The crew came down the ladder and the launch went out to get them. They were a bunch of cocky youngsters and you could sense the pride in them.

Next morning, we went out to the ship. I rode in the launch with the general and the colonel, and while the boat bobbed against the ladder, they had another difference of opinion.

"I still think it's too risky, General," said the colonel. "It's all right to fool around with jets, but an atomic ship is a different matter. If Stinky goes fooling with that pile—"

The general said, tight-lipped: "We have to take the chance."

The colonel shrugged and went up the ladder. The general motioned to me and I went up with Stinky perched on my shoulder. The general followed.

Whereas Stinky and I before this had been in a ship alone, this time a picked crew of technicians came aboard as well. There was plenty of room and it was the only way they could study what Stinky might be doing. And I imagined that, with an A-ship, they'd want to keep close check.

I sat down in the pilot's chair and Stinky settled himself in my lap. The colonel stayed with us for a while, but after a time he left and we were alone.

I was nervous. What the colonel had said made good sense to me. But the day wore on and nothing happened and I began to feel that perhaps the colonel had been wrong.

It went on for four days like that and I settled into routine. I wasn't nervous any longer. We could depend on Stinky, I told myself. He wouldn't do anything to harm us.

By the way the technicians were behaving and the grin the general wore, I knew that Stinky must be performing up to expectations.

On the fifth day, as we were going out, the colonel said: "This should wind it up."

I was glad to hear it.

We were almost ready to knock off for noon when it happened. I can't tell you exactly how it was, for it was a bit confusing. It was almost as if someone had shouted, although no one had. I half rose out of the chair, then sat back again. And someone shouted once more.

I knew that something was about to happen. I could feel it in my bones. I knew I had to get out of the A-ship and get out fast. It was fear—unreasoning fear. And over and above the fear, I knew I could not leave. It was my job to stay. I had to stick it out. I grabbed the chair arms and hung on and tried my best to stay.

Then the panic hit me and there was nothing I could do. There was no way to fight it. I leaped out of the chair, dumping Stinky from my lap. I reached the door and fought it open, then turned back.

"Stinky!" I shouted.

I started across the room to reach him, but halfway across the panic hit me again and I turned and bolted in blind flight.

I went clattering down the catwalk and from below me came the sound of running and the yells of frightened men. I knew then that I had been right, that I had not been cowardly altogether—there was something wrong.

Men were pouring out of the port of the big A-ship when I got there and scrambling down the ladder. The launch was coming out to pick them up. One man fell off the ladder into the water and began to swim.

Out on the field, ambulances and fire rigs were racing toward the water pit and the siren atop the operations building was wailing like a stepped-on tomcat.

I looked at the faces around me. They were set and white and I knew that all the men were just as scared as I was and somehow, instead of getting scareder, I got a lot of comfort from it.

They went on tumbling down the ladder and more men fell in the drink, and I have no doubt at all that if someone had held a stop-watch on them, there'd have been swimming records falling.

I got in line to wait my turn and I thought again of Stinky and stepped out of line and started back to save him. But halfway up the catwalk, my courage ran plumb out and I was too scared to go on. The funny thing about it was that I didn't have the least idea what there was to scare me.

I went down the ladder among the last of them and piled into the launch, which was loaded so heavily that it barely crept back to solid ground.

The medical officer was running around and shouting to get the swimmers into decontamination and men were running everywhere and shouting and the fire rigs stood there racing their motors while the siren went on shrieking.

"Get back!" someone was shouting. "Run! Everybody back!"

So, of course, we ran like a flock of spooked sheep.

Then a wordless yell went up and we turned around.

The atomic ship was rising slowly from the pit. Beneath it, the water seethed and boiled. The ship rose steadily, gracefully, without a single shudder or shake. It went straight up into the sky, up and out of sight.

Suddenly I realized that I was standing in dead silence. No one was stirring. No one was making any noise. Everybody just stood and stared into the sky. The siren had shut off.

I felt someone tap me on the shoulder. It was the general.

"Stinky?" he asked.

"He wouldn't come," I answered, feeling low. "I was too scared to go and get him."

The general wheeled and headed off across the field. For no reason I can think of, I turned and followed him. He broke into a run and I loped along beside him.

We stormed into operations and went piling up the stairs to the tracking room.

The general bellowed: "You got a fix on it?"

"Yes, sir, we're tracking it right now."

"Good," the general said, breathing heavily. "Fine. We'll have to run it down. Tell me where it's headed."

"Straight out, sir. It still is heading out."

"How far?"

"About five thousand miles, sir."

"But it can't do that!" the general roared. "It can't navigate in space!"

He turned around and bumped into me.

"Get out of my way!" He went thumping down the stairs.

I followed him down, but outside the building I went another way. I passed administration and there was the colonel standing outside. I wasn't going to stop, but he called to me. I went over.

"He made it," said the colonel.

"I tried to take him off," I said, "but he wouldn't come."

"Of course not. What do you think it was that drove us from the ship?"

I thought back and there was only one answer. "Stinky?"

"Sure. It wasn't only machines, Asa, though he did wait till he got hold of something like the A-ship that he could make go out into space. But he had to get us off it first, so he threw us off."

I did some thinking about that, too. "Then he *was* kind of like a skunk."

"How do you mean?" asked the colonel, squinting at me.

"I never did get used to calling him Stinky. Never seemed right somehow, him not having a smell and still having that name. But he did have a smell—a mental one, I guess you'd say—enough to drive us right out of the ship."

The colonel nodded. "All the same, I'm glad he made it." He stared up at the sky.

"So am I," I said.

Although I was a little sore at Stinky as well. He could have said good-by at least to me. I was the best friend he had on Earth and driving me out along with the other men seemed plain rude.

But now I'm not so sure.

I still don't know which end of a wrench to take hold of, but I have a new car now—bought it with the money I earned at the air base—and it can run all by itself. On quiet country roads, that is. It gets jittery in traffic. It's not half as good as Betsy.

I could fix that, all right. I found out when the car rose right over a fallen tree in the road. With what rubbed off on me from being with Stinky all the time, I could make it fly. But I won't. I ain't aiming to get treated the way Stinky was.

8. Jackpot

I FOUND DOC in the dispensary. He had on quite a load. I worked him over some to bring him half awake.

"Get sobered up," I ordered curtly. "We made planetfall. We've got work to do."

I took the bottle and corked it and set it high up on the shelf, where it wasn't right at hand.

Doc managed to achieve some dignity. "You needn't worry, Captain. As medic of this tub—"

"I want all hands up and moving. We may have something out there."

"I know," Doc said mournfully. "When you talk like that, it's bound to be a tough one. An offbeat climate and atmosphere pure poison."

"It's Earth-type, oxygen, and the climate's fine so far. Nothing to be afraid of. The analyzers gave it almost perfect rating."

Doc groaned and held his head between his hands. "Those analyzers of ours do very well if they tell us whether it is hot or cold or if the air is fit to breathe. We're a haywire outfit, Captain."

"We do all right," I said.

"We're scavengers and sometimes birds of prey. We scour the Galaxy for anything that's loose."

I paid no attention to him. That was the way he always talked when he had a skin full.

"You get up to the galley," I told him, "and let Pancake pour some coffee into you. I want you on your feet and able to do your fumbling best."

But Doc wasn't ready to go just yet. "What is it this time?"

"A silo. The biggest thing you ever saw. It's ten or fifteen miles across and goes up clear out of sight."

"A silo is a building to store winter forage. Is this a farming planet?"

"No," I said, "it's desert. And it isn't a silo. It just looks like one."

"Warehouse?" asked Doc. "City? Fortress? Temple–but that doesn't make any difference to us, does it, Captain? We loot temples, too."

"Get up!" I yelled at him. "Get going."

He made it to his feet. "I imagine the populace has come out to greet us. Appropriately, I hope."

"There's no populace," I said. "The silo's just standing there alone."

"Well, well," said Doc. "A second-story job."

He started staggering up the catwalk and I knew he'd be all right. Pancake knew exactly how to get him sobered up.

I went back to the port and found that Frost had everything all set. He had the guns ready and the axes and the sledges, the coils of rope and the canteens of water and all the stuff we'd need. As second in command, Frost was invaluable. He knew what to do and did it. I don't know what I'd have done without him.

I stood in the port and looked out at the silo. We were a mile or so away from it, but it was so big that it seemed to be much closer. This near to it, it seemed to be a wall. It was just God-awful big.

"A place like that," said Frost, "could hold a lot of loot."

"If there isn't someone or something there to stop us taking it. If we can get into it."

"There are openings along the base. They look like entrances."

"With doors ten feet thick."

I wasn't being pessimistic. I was being logical–I'd seen so many things that looked like billions turn into complicated headaches that I never allowed myself much hope until I had my hands on something I knew would bring us cash.

Hutch Murdock, the engineer, came climbing up the catwalk. As usual, he had troubles. He didn't even stop to catch his breath.

"I tell you," he said to me, "one of these days those engines will just simply fall apart and leave us hanging out in space light-years from nowhere. We work all the blessed time to keep them turning over."

I clapped him on the shoulder. "Maybe this is it. Maybe after this we can buy a brand-new ship."

But it didn't cheer him up. He knew as well as I did that I was talking to keep up my spirit as well as his.

"Someday," he said, "we'll have bad trouble on our hands. Those boys of mine will drive a soap bubble across three hundred light-years if it's got an engine in it. But it's got to have an engine. And this wreck we got . . ."

He would have kept right on, but Pancake blew the horn for breakfast.

Doc was already at the table and he seemed to be functioning. He had a moderate case of shudders and he seemed a little pale. He was a little bitter, too, and somewhat poetic.

"So we gather glory," he told us. "We go out and lap it up. We haunt the ruins and we track the dream and we come up dripping cash."

"Doc," I said, "shut up."

He shut up. There was no one on the ship I had to speak to twice.

We didn't dally with the food. We crammed it down and left. Pancake left the dishes standing on the table and came along with us.

We got into the silo without any trouble. There were entrances all around the base and there weren't any doors. There was not a thing or any one to stop us walking in.

It was quiet and solemn inside—and unspectacular. It reminded me of a monstrous office building.

It was all cut up with corridors, with openings off the corridors leading into rooms. The rooms were lined with what looked like filing cases.

We walked for quite a while, leaving paint markers along the walls to lead us back to the entrance. Get lost inside a place like that and one could wander maybe a lifetime finding his way out.

We were looking for something—almost anything—but we didn't find a thing except those filing cases.

So we went into one of the rooms to have a look inside the files.

Pancake was disgusted. "There won't be nothing but records in those files. Probably in a lingo we can't even read."

"There could be anything inside those files," said Frost. "They don't have to be records."

Pancake had a sledge and he lifted it to smash one of the files, but I stopped him. There wasn't any use doing it messy if there was a better way.

We fooled around a while and we found the place where you had to wave your hand to make a drawer roll out.

The drawer was packed with what looked like sticks of dynamite. They were about two inches in diameter and a foot, or maybe a little more, in length, and they were heavy.

"Gold," said Hutch.

"I never saw black gold," Pancake said.

"It isn't gold," I told them.

I was just as glad it wasn't. If it had been, we'd have broken our backs hauling it away. Gold's all right, but you can't get rich on it. It doesn't much more than pay wages.

We dumped out a pile of the sticks and squatted on the floor, looking them over.

"Maybe it's valuable," said Frost, "but I wouldn't know. What do you think it is?"

None of us had the least idea.

We found some sort of symbols on each end of the sticks and the symbols on each stick seemed to be different, but it didn't help us any because the symbols made no sense.

We kicked the sticks out of the way and opened some more drawers. Every single drawer was filled with the sticks.

When we came out of the silo, the day had turned into a scorcher. Pancake climbed the ladder to stack us up some grub and the rest of us sat down in the shade of the ship and laid several of the sticks out in front of us and sat there looking at them, wondering what we had.

"That's where we're at a big disadvantage," said Hutch. "If a regular survey crew stumbled onto this, they'd have all sorts of experts to figure out the stuff. They'd test it a dozen different ways and they'd skin it alive almost and they'd have all sorts of ideas and they'd come up with some educated guesses. And pretty soon, one way or another, they'd know just what it was and if it was any use."

"Someday," I told them, "if we ever strike it rich, we'll have to hire us some experts. The kind of loot we're always turning up, we could make good use of them."

"You won't find any," said Doc, "that would team up with a bunch like us."

"Where do you get 'bunch like us' stuff?" I asked him, a little sore. "Sure, we ain't got much education and the ship is just sort of glued together and we don't use any fancy words to cover up the fact that we're in this for all we can get out of it. But we're doing an honest job."

"I wouldn't call it exactly honest. Sometimes we're inside the law and sometimes outside it."

That was nonsense and Doc knew it. Mostly where we went, there wasn't any law.

"Back on Earth, in the early days," I snapped back, "it was folks like us who went into new lands and blazed the trails and found rivers and climbed the mountains and brought back word to those who stayed at home. And they went because they were looking for beaver or for gold or slaves or for anything else that wasn't nailed down tight. They didn't worry much about the law or the ethics of it and no one blamed them for it. They found it and they took it and that was the end of it. If they killed a native or two or burned a village or some other minor thing like that, why, it was just too bad."

Hutch said to Doc: "There ain't no sense in you going holy on us. Anything we done, you're in as deep as we are."

"Gentlemen," said Doc, in that hammy way of his, "I wasn't trying to stir up any ruckus. I was just pointing out that you needn't set your heart on getting any experts."

"We could get them," I said, "if we offered them enough. They got to live, just like anybody else."

"They have professional pride, too. That's something you've forgotten."

"We got you."

"Well, now," said Hutch, "I'm not too sure Doc is professional. That time he pulled the tooth for me–"

"Cut it out," I said. "The both of you."

This wasn't any time to bring up the matter of the tooth. Just a couple of months ago, I'd got it quieted down and I didn't want it breaking out again.

Frost picked up one of the sticks and turned it over and over, looking at it.

"Maybe we could rig up some tests," he suggested.

"And take the chance of getting blown up?" asked Hutch.

"It might not go off. You have a better than fifty-fifty chance that it's not explosive."

"Not me," said Doc. "I'd rather just sit here and guess. It's less tiring and a good deal safer."

"You don't get anywhere by guessing," protested Frost. "We might have a fortune right inside our mitts if we could only find out what these sticks are for. There must be tons of them stored in the building. And there's nothing in the world to stop us from taking them."

"The first thing," I said, "is to find out if it's explosive. I don't think it is. It looks like dynamite, but it could be almost anything. For instance, it might be food."

"We'll have Pancake cook us up a mess," said Doc.

I paid no attention to him. He was just needling me.

"Or it might be fuel," I said. "Pop a stick into a ship engine that was built to use it and it would keep it going for a year or two."

Pancake blew the chow horn and we all went in.

After we had eaten, we got to work.

We found a flat rock that looked like granite and above it we set up a tripod made out of poles that we had to walk a mile to cut and then had to carry back. We rigged up a pulley on the tripod and found another rock and tied it to the rope that went up to the pulley. Then we paid out the rope as far as it would go and there we dug a foxhole.

By this time, the sun was setting and we were tuckered out, but we decided to go ahead and make the test and set our minds at rest.

So I took one of the sticks that looked like dynamite and while the others back in the foxhole hauled up the rock tied to the rope, I put the stick on the first rock underneath the second and then I ran like hell. I tumbled into the foxhole and the others let go of the rope and the rock dropped down on the stick.

Nothing happened.

Just to make sure, we pulled up and dropped the rock two or three times more and there was no explosion.

We climbed out of the foxhole and went over to the tripod and rolled the rock off the stick, which wasn't even dented.

By this time, we were fairly well convinced that the stick couldn't be set off by concussion, although the test didn't rule out a dozen other ways it might blow us all up.

That night, we gave the sticks the works. We poured acid on them and the acid just ran off. We tried a cold chisel on them and we ruined two good chisels. We tried a saw and they stripped the teeth clean off.

We wanted Pancake to try to cook one of them, but Pancake refused.

"You aren't bringing that stuff into my galley," he said. "If you do, you can cook for yourselves from now on. I keep a good clean galley and I try to keep you guys well fed and I ain't having you mess up the place."

"All right, Pancake," I said. "Even with you cooking it, it probably wouldn't be fit to eat."

We wound up sitting at a table, looking at the sticks piled in the center of it. Doc brought out a bottle and we all had a drink or two. Doc must have been considerably upset to share his liquor with us.

"It stands to reason," said Frost, "that the sticks are good for something. If the cost of that building is any indication of their value, they're worth a fortune."

"Maybe the sticks aren't the only things in there," Hutch pointed out. "We just covered part of the first floor. There might be a lot of other stuff in there. And there are all those other floors. How many would you say there were?"

"Lord knows," said Frost. "When you're on the ground, you can't be sure you see to the top of it. It just sort of fades away when you look up at it."

"You notice what it was built of?" asked Doc.

"Stone," said Hutch.

"I thought so, too," said Doc. "But it isn't. You remember those big apartment mounds we ran into in that insect culture out on Suud?"

We all remembered them, of course. We'd spent days trying to break into them because we had found a handful of beautifully carved jade scattered around the entrance of one of them and we figured there might be a lot of it inside. Stuff like that brings money. Folks back in civilization are nuts about any kind of alien art and that jade sure enough was alien.

We'd tried every trick that we could think of and we got nowhere. Breaking into those mounds was like punching a feather pillow. You could dent the surface plenty, but you couldn't break it because the strength of the material built up as pressure compressed the atoms. The harder you hit, the tougher it became. It was the kind of building material that would last forever and never need repair and those insects must have known they were safe from us, for they went about their business and never noticed us. That's what made it so infuriating.

And material like that, I realized, would be just the ticket for a structure like the silo. You could build as big or as high as you had a mind to; the more pressure you put on the lower structure, the stronger it would be.

"It means," I said, "that the building out there could be much older than it seems to be. It could be a million years or older."

"If it's that old," said Hutch, "it could really be packed. You can store away a lot of loot in a million years."

Doc and Frost drifted off to bed and Hutch and I sat there alone, looking at the sticks.

I got to thinking about some of the things that Doc was always saying, about how we were just a bunch of cutthroats, and I wondered if he might be right. But think on it as hard and as honest as I could, I couldn't buy it.

On every expanding frontier, in all of history, there had been three kinds of men who went ahead and marked out the trails for other men to follow—the traders and the missionaries and the hunters.

We were the hunters in this case, hunting not for gold or slaves or furs, but for whatever we could find. Sometimes we came back with empty hands and sometimes we made a haul. Usually, in the long run, we evened out so we made nothing more than wages. But we kept on going out, hoping for that lucky break that would make us billionaires.

It hadn't happened yet, and perhaps it never would. But someday it might. We touched the ghostly edge of hope just often enough to keep us thinking that it would. Although, I admitted to myself, perhaps we'd have kept going out even if there'd been no hope at all. Seeking for the unknown gets into your blood.

When you came right down to it, we probably didn't do a bit more harm than the traders or the missionaries. What we took, we took; we didn't settle down and change or destroy the civilizations of people we pretended we were helping.

I said as much to Hutch. He agreed with me.

"The missionaries are the worst," he said. "I wouldn't be a missionary no matter what they paid me."

We weren't doing any good just sitting there, so I got up to start for bed.

"Maybe tomorrow we'll find something else," I said.

Hutch yawned. "I sure hope we do. We been wasting our time on these sticks of dynamite."

He picked them up and on our way up to bed, he heaved them out the port.

The next day, we did find something else.

We went much deeper into the silo than we had been before, following the corridors for what must have been two miles or more.

We came to a big room that probably covered ten or fifteen acres and it was filled from wall to wall with rows of machines, all of them alike.

They weren't much to look at. They resembled to some extent a rather ornate washing machine, with a bucket seat attached and a dome on top. They weren't bolted down and you could push them around and when we tipped one of them up to look for hidden wheels, we found instead a pair of runners fixed on a swivel so they'd track in any direction that one pushed. The runners were made of metal that was greasy to the touch, but when you rubbed your fingers on them, no grease came off.

There was no power connection.

"Maybe it's a self-powered unit," said Frost. "Come to think of it, I haven't noticed any power outlets in the entire building."

We hunted for some place where we could turn on the power and there wasn't any place. That whole machine was the smoothest, slickest hunk of metal you ever saw. We looked for a way to get into its innards, so we could have a look at them, but there wasn't any way. The jacket that covered the works seemed to be one solid piece without an apparent seam or a sign of a bolt or rivet.

The dome looked as though it ought to come off and we tried to get if off, but it remained stubbornly in place.

The bucket seat, however, was something else again. It was lousy with all sorts of attachments to accommodate the sitting surface of almost any conceivable kind of being. We had a lot of fun adjusting it in different ways and trying to figure out what kind of animal could have a seat like that. We got a bit obscene about it, I remember, and Hutch was doubled up laughing.

But we weren't getting anywhere and we were fairly sure we wouldn't until we could get a cutting tool and open up one of the machines to find out what made it tick.

We picked out one of them and we skidded it down the corridors. When we got to the entrance, we figured we would have to carry it, but we were mistaken. It skidded along over the ground and even loose sand almost as well as it did in the corridors.

After supper, Hutch went down to the engine room and came back with a cutting tool. The metal was tough, but we finally got at least some of the jacket peeled away.

The innards of that machine were enough to drive you crazy. It was a solid mass of tiny parts all hooked together in the damnedest jumble. There was no beginning and no end. It was like one of those puzzle mazes that go on and on forever and get no place.

Hutch got into it with both hands and tried to figure out how to start taking it apart.

After a while, he sat back on his heels and growled a little at it. "There's nothing holding them together. Not a bolt or rivet, not even so much as a cotter pin. But they hang together somehow."

"Just pure cussedness," I said.

He looked at me kind of funny. "You might be right, at that."

He went at it again and bashed a couple of knuckles and sat there sucking at them.

"If I didn't know that I was wrong," he said, "I'd say that it was friction."

"Magnetism," Doc offered.

"I tell you what, Doc," said Hutch. "You stick to what little medicine you know and let me handle the mechanics."

Frost dived in quick to head off an argument. "That frictional idea might not be a bad one. But it would call for perfect machining and surface polish. Theoretically, if you place two perfectly polished surfaces together, the molecules will attract one another and you'll have permanent cohesion."

I don't know where Frost got all that stuff. Mostly he seemed to be just like the rest of us, but occasionally he'd come out with something that would catch you by surprise. I never asked him anything about himself; questions like that were just plain bad manners.

We messed around some more and Hutch bashed another knuckle and I sat there thinking how we'd found two items in the silo and both of them had stopped us in our tracks. But that's the way it is. Some days you can't make a dime.

Frost moved around and pushed Hutch out of the way. "Let me see what I can do."

Hutch didn't protest any. He was licked.

Frost started pushing and pulling and twisting and fiddling away at that mess of parts and all at once there was a kind of *whoosh*ing sound, like someone had let out their breath sort of slow and easy, and all the parts fell in upon themselves. They came unstuck, in a kind of slow-motion manner, and they made a metallic thump along with tinkling sounds and they were just a heap inside the jacket that had protected them.

"Now see what you done!" howled Hutch.

"I didn't do a thing," said Frost. "I was just seeing if I could bust one loose and one did and then the whole shebang caved in."

He held up his fingers to show us the piece that had come loose.

"You know what I think?" asked Pancake. "I think whoever made that machine made it so it would fall apart if anyone tried to tinker with it. They didn't want no one to find out how it was put together."

"That makes sense," said Doc. "No use getting peeved at it. After all, it was their machine."

"Doc," I said, "you got a funny attitude. I never noticed you turning down your share of anything we find."

"I don't mind when we confine ourselves to what you might call, in all politeness, natural resources. I can even stomach the pillaging of art-forms. But when it comes to stealing brains—and this machine is brains—"

Frost let out a whoop.

He was hunkered down, with his head inside the jacket of the machine, and I thought at first he'd got caught and that we'd have to cut him out, but he could get out, all right.

"I see now how to get that dome off the top," he said.

It was a complicated business, almost like a combination on a safe. The dome was locked in place by a lot of grooves and you had to know just how to turn it to lift it out of place.

Frost kept his head inside the jacket and called out directions to Hutch, who twisted the dome first this way and then that, sometimes having to pull up on it and other times press down to engage the slotted mechanism that held it locked in place. Pancake wrote down the combinations as Frost called them off and finally the dome came loose in Hutch's hands.

Once it was off, there was no mystery to it. It was a helmet, all rigged out with adjustable features so it could be made to fit any type of head, just as the seat was adjustable to fit any sitting aparatus.

The helmet was attached to the machine with a retractable cable that reeled out far enough to reach someone sitting in the seat.

And that was fine, of course. But what was it? A portable electric chair? A permanent-wave machine? Or what?

So Frost and Hutch poked around some more and in the top of the machine, just under where the dome had nested, they found a swivel trap door and underneath it a hollow tube extending down into the mass of innards—only the innards weren't a mass any more, but just a basket of loose parts.

It didn't take any imagination to figure what that hollow tube was for. It was just the size to take one of the sticks of dynamite.

Doc went and got a bottle and passed it around as a sort of celebration and after a drink or two, he and Hutch shook hands and said there were no hard feelings. But I didn't pay much attention to that. They'd done it many times before and then been at one another's throats before the night was over.

Just why we were celebrating was hard to figure. Sure, we knew the machine fitted heads and that the dynamite fitted the machine—but we still had no idea what it was all about.

We were, to tell the truth, just a little scared, although you couldn't have gotten one of us to admit it.

We did some guessing, naturally.

"It might be a mechanical doctor," said Hutch. "Just sit in that seat and put the helmet on your head and feed in the proper stick and you come out cured of whatever is wrong with you. It would be a blessing, I can tell you. You wouldn't ever need to worry if your doctor knew his business or not."

I thought Doc was going to jump right down Hutch's throat, but he must have remembered how they had shaken hands and he didn't do it.

"As long as you're thinking along that line," said Doc, "let's think a little bigger. Let's say it is a rejuvenation machine and the stick is crammed with vitamins and hormones and such that turn you young again. Just take the treatment every twenty years or so and you stay young forever."

"It might be an educator," Frost put in. "Those sticks might be packed full of knowledge. Maybe a complete college subject inside of each of them."

"Or it might be just the opposite," said Pancake. "Those sticks might soak up everything you know. Each of those sticks might be the story of one man's whole life."

"Why record life stories?" asked Hutch. "There aren't many men or aliens or what-not that have life stories important enough to rate all that trouble."

"If you're thinking of it being some sort of communications deal," I said, "it might be anything. It might be propaganda or religion or maps or it might be no more than a file of business records."

"And," said Hutch, "it might kill you deader than a mackerel."

"I don't think so," Doc replied. "There are easier ways to kill a person than to sit him in a chair and put a helmet on him. And it doesn't have to be a communicator."

"There's one way to find out," I said.

"I was afraid," said Doc, "we'd get around to that."

"It's too complicated," argued Hutch. "No telling what trouble it may get us into. Why not drop it cold? We can blast off and hunt for something simple."

"No!" shouted Frost. "We can't do that!"

"I'd like to know why not," said Hutch.

"Because we'd always wonder if we passed up the jackpot. We'd figure that maybe we gave up too quick—a day or two too quick. That we got scared out. That if we'd gone ahead, we'd be rolling in money."

We knew Frost was right, but we batted it around some more before we would admit he was. All of us knew what we had to do, but there were no volunteers.

Finally we drew straws and Pancake was unlucky.

"Okay," I said. "First thing in the morning . . ."

"Morning, nothing!" wailed Pancake. "I want to get it over with. I wouldn't sleep a wink."

He was scared, all right, and he had a right to be. He felt just the way I would have if I'd drawn the shortest straw.

I didn't like barging around on an alien planet after dark, but we had to do it. It wouldn't have been fair to Pancake to have done otherwise. And, besides, we were all wrought up and we'd have no rest until we'd found out what we had.

So we got some flashes and went out to the silo. We tramped down the corridors for what seemed an endless time and came to the room where the machines were stored.

There didn't seem to be any difference in the machines, so we picked one at random. While Hutch got the helmet off, I adjusted the seat for Pancake and Doc went into an adjoining room to get a stick.

When we were all ready, Pancake sat down in the seat.

I had a sudden rush of imbecility.

"Look," I said to Pancake, "you don't need to do this."

"Someone has to," said Pancake. "We got to find out somehow and this is the quickest way."

"I'll take your place."

Pancake called me a dirty name and he had no right to do that, for I was only being helpful. But I called him another and we were back to normal.

Hutch put the helmet on Pancake's head and it came down so far you couldn't see his face. Doc popped the stick into the tube and the machine purred a little, starting up, then settled into silence. Not exactly silence, either—when you laid your ear against the jacket, you could hear it running.

Nothing seemed to happen to Pancake. He sat there cool and relaxed and Doc got to work on him at once, checking him over.

"His pulse has slowed a little," Doc reported, "and his heart action's sort of feeble, but he seems to be in no danger. His breathing is a little shallow, but not enough to worry about."

It might not have meant a thing to Doc, but it made the rest of us uneasy. We stood around and watched and nothing happened. I don't know what we thought might happen. Funny as it sounds, I had thought that something would.

Doc kept close watch, but Pancake got no worse.

We waited and we waited. The machine kept running and Pancake sat slumped in the seat. He was as limp as a dog asleep and when you picked up his hand, you'd think his bones had melted plumb away. All the time we got more nervous. Hutch wanted to jerk the helmet off Pancake, but I wouldn't let him. No telling what might happen if we stopped the business in the middle.

It was about an hour after dawn that the machine stopped running. Pancake began to stir and we removed the helmet.

He yawned and rubbed his eyes and sat up straight. He looked a bit surprised when he saw us and it seemed to take a moment for him to recognize us.

"What happened?" Hutch asked him.

Pancake didn't answer. You could see him pulling himself together, as if he were remembering and getting his bearings once again.

"I went on a trip," he said.

"A travelogue!" said Doc, disgusted.

"Not a travelogue. I was *there*. It was a planet, way out at the rim of the Galaxy, I think. There weren't many stars at night because it was so far out—way out where the stars get thin and there aren't many of them. There was just a thin strip of light that moved overhead."

"Looking at the Galaxy edge on," said Frost, nodding. "Like you were looking at a buzz-saw's cutting edge."

"How long was I under?" asked Pancake.

"Long enough," I told him. "Six or seven hours. We were getting nervous."

"That's funny," said Pancake. "I'll swear I was there for a year or more."

"Now let's get this straight," Hutch said. "You say you were there. You mean you *saw* this place."

"I mean *I was there!*" yelled Pancake. "I *lived* with those people and I *slept* in their burrows and I *talked* with them and I *worked* with them. I got a blood blister on my hand from hoeing in a garden. I traveled from one place to another and I saw a lot of things and it was just as real as sitting here."

We bundled him out of there and went back to the ship. Hutch wouldn't let Pancake get the breakfast. He threw it together himself and since Hutch is a lousy cook, it was a miserable meal. Doc dug up a bottle and gave Pancake a drink, but he wouldn't let any of the rest of us have any of it. Said it was medicinal, not social.

That's the way he is at times. Downright hog-selfish.

Pancake told us about this place he had been to. It didn't seem to have much, if any, goverment, mostly because it didn't seem to need one, but was a humble sort of planet where rather dim-witted people lived in a primitive agricultural state. They looked, he said, like a cross between a human and a groundhog, and he drew a picture of them, but it didn't help a lot, for Pancake is no artist.

He told us the kind of crops they raised, and there were some screwy kinds, and what kind of food they ate, and we gagged at some of it, and he even had some of the place names down pat and he remembered shreds of the language and it was outlandish-sounding.

We asked him all sorts of questions and he had the answers to every one of them and some were the kind he could not have made up from his head. Even Doc, who had been skeptical to start with, was ready to admit that Pancake had visited the planet.

After we ate, we hustled Pancake off to bed and Doc checked him over and he was all right.

When Pancake and Doc had left, Hutch said to me and Frost: "I can feel those dollars clinking in my pocket right this minute."

We both agreed with him.

We'd found an entertainment gadget that had anything yet known backed clear off the map.

The sticks were recordings that packed in not only sight and sound, but stimuli for all the other senses. They did the job so well that anyone subjected to their influence felt that he was part of the environment they presented. He stepped into the picture and became a part of it. He was really there.

Frost already was planning exactly how we'd work it.

"We could sell the stuff," he said, "but that would be rather foolish. We want to keep control of it. We'll lease out the machines and we'll rent the sticks and since we'll have the sole supply, we can charge anything we wish."

"We can advertise year-long vacations that take less than half a day," said Hutch. "They'll be just the thing for executives and other busy people. Why, in a single week end you could spend four or five years' time on several different planets."

"Maybe it's not only planets," Frost went on. "There might be concerts or art galleries and museums. Maybe lectures on history and literature and such."

We were feeling pretty good, but we were tuckered out, so we trailed off to bed.

I didn't get into bed right away, however, but hauled out the log. I don't know why I ever bothered with it. It was a hit-and-miss affair at best. There would be months I'd not even think about it and then all at once I'd get all neat and orderly and keep a faithful record for several weeks or so. There was no real reason to make an entry in it now, but I was somewhat excited and had a feeling that perhaps what had just happened should be put down in black and white.

So I crawled under the bunk and pulled out the tin box I kept it and the other papers in, and while I was lifting it to the bunk, it slipped out of my hands. The lid flew open. The log and all the papers and the other odds and ends I kept there scattered on the floor.

I cussed a bit and got down on my hands and knees to pick up the mess. There was an awful lot of it and most of it was junk. Someday, I told myself, I'd have to throw a lot of it away. There were clearance papers from a hundred different ports and medical certificates and other papers that were long outdated. But among it I found also the title to the ship.

I sat there thinking back almost twenty years to the day I'd bought the ship for next to nothing and towed it from the junkyard and I recalled how I'd spent a couple of years' spare time and all I could earn getting it patched up so it could take to space again. No wonder, I told myself, that it was a haywire ship. It had been junk to start with, and during all those years, we'd just managed to keep it glued together. There had been many times when the only thing that got it past inspection had been a fast bribe slipped quietly to the man. No one in the Galaxy but Hutch could have kept it flying.

I went on picking up the papers, thinking about Hutch and all the rest of them. I got a little sentimental and thought a lot of things I'd have clobbered anyone for if they had dared to say them to me. About how we had stuck together and how any one of them would have died for me and I for any one of them.

There had been a time, of course, when it had not been that way, back in the days when they'd first signed on and had been nothing but a crew. But that day was long past; now they were more than just a crew. There had been no signing on for years, but just staying on as men who had a right to stay. And I sat there, flat on the floor, and thought how we'd finally done the thing we'd always hoped to do, how we'd caught up with the dream—us, the ragamuffin crew in the glued-together ship—and I felt proud and happy, not for myself alone, but for Hutch and Pancake and Doc and Frost and all the rest.

Finally I got the papers all picked up and back in the box again and tried to write up the log, but was too tired to write, so I went to bed, as I should have done in the first place.

But tired as I was, I lay there and thought of how big the silo was and tried to estimate how many sticks might be cached away there. I got up into the trillions and I saw it was no use; there was no way to keep the figures straight.

The whole deal was big—bigger than anything we'd ever found before. It would take a group of men like us at least five lifetimes of steady hauling to empty the silo. We'd have to set up a corporation and get a legal staff (preferably one with the lowest kind of ethics) and file a claim on this planet and go through a lot of other red tape to be sure we had it all sewed up.

We couldn't take a chance of letting it slip through our fingers because of any lack of foresight. We'd have to get it all doped out before we went ahead.

I don't know about the rest of them, but I dreamed that night of wading knee-deep through a sea of crisp, crinkly banknotes.

When morning came, Doc failed to show up for breakfast. I went hunting him and found he hadn't even gone to bed. He was sprawled in his rickety old chair in the dispensary and there was one empty bottle on the floor and he trailed another, almost empty, alongside the chair, keeping a rather flimsy hold upon its neck. He still was conscious, which was about the most that could be said of him.

I was plenty sore. Doc knew the rules. He could get paralyzed as soon or as often or as long as he wanted to when we were in space, but when we were grounded and there was work to do and planet ailments to keep an eye out for, he was expected to stay sober.

I kicked the bottle out of his fist and I took him by the collar with one hand and by the seat of his britches with the other and frog-walked him to the galley.

Plunking him down in a chair, I yelled for Pancake to get another pot of coffee going.

"I want you sobered up," I told Doc, "so you can go out with us on the second trip. We need all the manpower we have."

Hutch had rounded up his gang and Frost had got the crew together and had rigged up a block and tackle so we could start loading. Everyone was ready to begin bringing in the cargo except Doc and I swore to myself that, before the day was over, I'd work the tail right off him.

As soon as we had breakfast, we started out. We planned to get aboard as many of the machines as we could handle and to fill in the space between them with all the sticks we could find room for.

We went down the corridors to the room that held the machines and we paired off, two men to the machine and started out. Everything went fine until we were more than halfway across the stretch of ground between the building and the ship.

Hutch and I were in the lead and suddenly there was an explosion in the ground about fifty feet ahead of us.

We skidded to a halt.

"It's Doc!" yelled Hutch, grabbing for his belt-gun.

I stopped him just in time. "Take it easy, Hutch."

Doc stood up in the port and waved a rifle at us.

"I could pick him off," Hutch said.

"Put back that gun," I ordered.

I walked out alone to where Doc had placed his bullet.

He lifted his rifle and I stopped dead still. He'd probably miss, but even so, the kind of explosive charge he was firing could cut a man in two if it struck ten feet away.

"I'm going to throw away my gun," I called out to him. "I want to talk with you."

Doc hesitated for a moment. "All right. Tell the rest of them to pull back a way."

I spoke to Hutch over my shoulder. "Get out of here. Take the others with you."

"He's crazy drunk," said Hutch. "No telling what he'll do."

"I can handle him," I said, sounding surer than I felt.

Doc let loose another bullet off to one side of us.

"Get moving, Hutch." I didn't dare look back. I had to keep an eye on Doc.

"All right," Doc finally yelled at me. "They're back. Throw away your gun."

Moving slow so he wouldn't think I was trying to draw on him, I unfastened the buckle of the gun belt and let it fall to the ground. I walked forward, keeping my eyes on Doc, and all the time my skin kept trying to crawl up my back.

"That's far enough," Doc said when I'd almost reached the ship. "We can talk from here."

"You're drunk," I told him. "I don't know what this is all about, but I know you're drunk."

"Not nearly drunk enough. Not drunk enough by half. If I were drunk enough, I simply wouldn't care."

"What's eating you?"

"Decency," said Doc, in that hammy way of his. "I've told you many times that I can stomach looting when it involves no more than uranium and gems and other trash like that. I can even shut my eyes when you gut a culture, because you can't steal a culture—even when you get through looting it, the culture still is there and can build back again. But I balk at robbing knowledge. I will not let you do it, Captain."

"I still say you're drunk."

"You don't even know what you've found. You are so blind and greedy that you don't recognize it."

"Okay, Doc," I said, trying to smooth his feathers, "tell me what we've found."

"A library. Perhaps the greatest, most comprehensive library in all the Galaxy. Some race spent untold years compiling the knowledge that is in that building and you plan to take it and sell it and scatter it. If that happens, in time it will be lost and what little of it may be left will be so out of context that half its meaning will be lost. It doesn't belong to us. It doesn't even belong to the human race alone. A library like that can belong only to all the peoples of the Galaxy."

"Look, Doc," I pleaded, "we've worked for years, you and I and all the rest of them. We've bled and sweated and been disappointed time and time again. This is our chance to make a killing. And that means you as well as the rest of us. Think of it, Doc–more money than you can ever spend–enough to keep you drunk the rest of your life!"

Doc swung the rifle around at me and I thought my goose was cooked. But I never moved a muscle.

I stood and bluffed it out.

At last he lowered the gun. "We're barbarians. History is full of the likes of us. Back on Earth, the barbarians stalled human progress for a thousand years when they burned and scattered the libraries and the learning of the Greeks and Romans. To them, books were just something to start a fire with or wipe their weapons on. To you, this great cache of accumulated knowledge means nothing more than something to make a quick buck on. You'll take a scholarly study of a vital social problem and retail it as a year's vacation that can be experienced in six hours' time and you'll take–"

"Spare me the lecture, Doc," I said wearily. "Tell me what you want."

"Go back and report this find to the Galactic Commission. It will help wipe out a lot of things we've done."

"So help me, Doc, you've gone religious on us."

"Not religious. Just decent."

"And if we don't?"

"I've got the ship," said Doc. "I have the food and water."

"You'll have to sleep."

"I'll close the port. Just try getting in."

He had us and he knew he did. Unless we could figure out a way to grab him, he had us good and proper.

I was scared, but mostly I was burned. For years, we'd listened to him run off at the mouth and never for a moment had any of us thought he meant a word of it. And now suddenly he did–he meant every word of it.

I knew there was no way to talk him out of it. And there was no compromise. When it came right down to it, there was no agreement possible, for any agreement or compromise would have to be based on honor and we had no honor–not a one of us, not even among ourselves. It was stalemate, but Doc didn't know that yet. He'd realize it once he got a little sober and thought about it some. What he had done had been done on alcoholic impulse, but that didn't mean he wouldn't see it through.

One thing was certain: As it stood, he could outlast us.

"Let me go back," I said. "I'll have to talk this over with the others."

I think that Doc right then began to suspect how deeply he had become committed, began to see for the first time the impossibility of us trusting one another.

"When you come back," he told me, "have it all thought out. I'll want some guarantees."

"Sure, Doc," I said.

"I mean this, Captain. I'm in deadly earnest. I'm not just fooling."

"I know you aren't, Doc."

I went back to where the others were clustered just a short distance from the building. I explained what was up.

"We'll have to spread out and charge him," Hutch decided. "He may get one or two of us, but we can pick him off."

"He'll simply close the port," I said. "He can starve us out. In a pinch, he could try to take the ship up. If he ever managed to get sober, he could probably do it."

"He's crazy," said Pancake. "Just plain drunken crazy."

"Sure he is," I said, "and that makes him twice as deadly. He's been brooding on this business for a long, long time. He built up a guilt complex that's three miles high. And worst of all, he's got himself out on a limb and he can't back down."

"We haven't got much time," said Frost. "We've got to think of something. A man can die of thirst. You can get awfully hungry in just a little while."

The three of them got to squabbling about what was best to do and I sat down on the sand and leaned back against one of the machines and tried to figure Doc.

Doc was a failure as a medic; otherwise he'd not have tied up with us. More than likely, he had joined us as a gesture of defiance or despair—perhaps a bit of both. And besides being a failure, he was an idealist. He was out of place with us, but there'd been nowhere else to go, nothing else to do. For years, it had eaten at him and his values got all warped and there's no place better than deep space to get your values warped.

He was crazy as a coot, of course, but a special kind of crazy. If it hadn't been so ghastly, you might have called it glorious crazy.

You wanted to laugh him off or brush him to one side, for that was the kind of jerk he was, but he wouldn't laugh or brush.

I don't know if I heard a sound—a footstep, maybe—or if I just sensed another presence, but all at once I knew we'd been joined by someone.

I half got up and swung around toward the building and there, just outside the entrance, stood what looked at first to be a kind of moth made up in human size.

I don't mean it was an insect—it just had the look of one. Its face was muffled up in a cloak it wore and it was not a human face and there was a ruff rising from its head like those crests you see on the helmets in the ancient plays.

Then I saw that the cloak was not a cloak at all, but a part of the creature and it looked like it might be folded wings, but it wasn't wings.

"Gentlemen," I said as quietly as I could, "we have a visitor."

I walked toward the creature soft and easy and alert, not wanting to frighten it, but all set to take evasive action if it tried to put the finger on me.

"Be ready, Hutch," I said.

"I'm covering you," Hutch assured me and it was a comfort to know that he was there. A man couldn't get into too much trouble with Hutch backing him.

I stopped about six feet from the creature and he didn't look as bad close up as he did at a distance. His eyes seemed to be kind and gentle and his funny face, alien as it was, had a sort of peacefulness about it. But even so, you can't always tell with aliens.

We stood there looking at one another. The both of us understood there was no use in talking. We just stood and sized one another up.

Then the creature took a couple of steps and reached out a hand that was more like a claw than hand. He took my hand in his and tugged for me to come.

There were just two things to do—either snatch my hand away or go.

I went.

I didn't stop to get it figured out, but there were several factors that helped make up my mind. First off, the creature seemed to be friendly and intelligent. And Hutch and all the others were there, just behind me. And over and above all, you don't get too far with aliens if you act stand-offish.

So I went.

We walked into the silo and behind me I heard the tramping feet of the others and it was a sound that was good to hear.

I didn't waste any time wondering where the creature might have come from. I admitted to myself, as I walked along, that I had been half-expecting something just like this. The silo was so big that it could hold many things, even people or creatures, we could not know about. After all, we'd explored only one small corner of the first floor of it. The creature, I figured, must have come from somewhere on the upper floors as soon as he learned about us. It might have taken quite a while, one way or another, for the news to reach him.

He led me up three ramps to the fourth floor of the building and went down a corridor for a little way, then went into a room.

It was not a large room. It held just one machine, but this one was a double model; it had two bucket seats and two helmets. There was another creature in the room.

The first one led me over to the machine and motioned for me to take one of the seats.

I stood there for a while, watching Hutch and Pancake and Frost and all the others crowd into the place and line up against the wall.

Frost said: "A couple of you boys better stay outside and watch the corridor."

Hutch asked me: "You going to sit down in that contraption, Captain?"

"Why not?" I said. "They seem to be all right. There's more of us than them. They don't mean us any harm."

"It's taking a chance," said Hutch.

"Since when have we stopped taking chances?"

The creature I had met outside had sat down in one of the seats, so I made a few adjustments in the other. While I was doing this, the second creature went to a file and got out two sticks, but these sticks were transparent instead of being black. He lifted off the helmets and inserted the two sticks. Then he fitted one of the helmets on his fellow-creature's head and held out the other to me.

I sat down and let him put it on and suddenly I was squatting on the floor across a sort of big coffee-table from the gent I had met outside.

"Now we can talk," said the creature, "which we couldn't do before."

I wasn't scared or flustered. It seemed just as natural as if it had been Hutch across the table.

"There will be a record made of everything we say," said the creature. "When we are finished, you will get one copy and I will get the other for our files. You might call it a pact or a contract or whatever term seems to be most applicable."

"I'm not much at contracts," I told him. "There's too much legal flypaper tied up with most of them."

"An agreement, then," the creature suggested. "A gentlemen's agreement."

"Good enough," I said.

Agreements are convenient things. You can break them any time you want. Especially gentlemen's agreements.

"I suppose you have figured out what this place is," he said.

"Well, not for sure," I replied. "Library is the closest that we have come."

"It's a university, a galactic university. We specialize in extension or home-study courses."

I'm afraid I gulped a bit. "Why, that's just fine."

"Our courses are open to all who wish to take them. There are no entrance fees and there is no tuition. Neither are there any scholastic requirements for enrollment. You yourself can see how difficult it would be to set up such requirements in a galaxy where there are many races of varying viewpoints and abilities."

"You bet I can."

"The courses are free to all who can make use of them," he said. "We do expect, of course, that they make proper use of them and that they display some diligence in study."

"You mean anyone at all can enroll?" I asked. "And it don't cost anything?"

After the first disappointment, I was beginning to see the possibilities. With bona fide university educations for the taking, it would be possible to set up one of the sweetest rackets that anyone could ask for.

"There's one restriction," the creature explained. "We cannot, obviously, concern ourselves with individuals. The paperwork would get completely out of hand. We enroll cultures. You, as a representative of your culture—what is it you call yourselves?"

"The human race, originally of the planet Earth, now covering some half million cubic light-years. I'd have to see your chart . . ."

"That's not necessary at the moment. We would be quite happy to accept your application for the entrance of the human race."

It took the wind out of me for a minute. I wasn't any representative of the human race. And if I could be, I wouldn't. This was my deal, not the human race's. But I couldn't let him know that, of course. He wouldn't have done business with me.

"Now not so fast," I pleaded. "There's a question or two I'd like to have you answer. What kind of courses do you offer? What kind of electives do you have?"

"First there is the basic course," the creature said. "It is more or less a familiarization course, a sort of orientation. It includes those subjects which we believe can be of the most use to the race in question. It is, quite naturally, tailored specifically for each student culture. After that, there is a wide field of electives, hundreds of thousands of them."

"How about final exams and tests and things like that?" I wanted to know.

"Oh, surely," said the creature. "Such tests are conducted every—tell me about your time system."

I told him the best I could and he seemed to understand.

"I'd say," he finally said, "that about every thousand years of your time would come fairly close. It is a long-range program and to conduct tests any oftener would put some strain upon our resources and might be of little value."

That decided me. What happened a thousand years from now was no concern of mine.

I asked a few more questions to throw him off the track—just in case he might have been suspicious—about the history of the university and such.

I still can't believe it. It's hard to conceive of any race working a million years to set up a university aimed at the eventual education of an entire galaxy, traveling to all the planets to assemble data, compiling the records of countless cultures, correlating and classifying and sorting out that mass of information to set up the study courses.

It was just too big for a man to grasp.

For a while, he had me reeling on the ropes and faintly starry-eyed about the whole affair. But then I managed to snap back to normal.

"All right, Professor," I said, "you can sign us up. What am I supposed to do?"

"Not a thing," he said. "The recording of our discussion will supply the data. We'll outline the course of basic study and you then may take such electives as you wish."

"If we can't haul it all in one trip, we can come back again?" I asked.

"Oh, definitely. I anticipate you may wish to send a fleet to carry all you need. We'll supply sufficient machines and as many copies of the study recordings as you think you will need."

"It'll take a lot," I said bluntly, figuring I'd start high and haggle my way down. "An awful lot."

"I am aware of that," he told me. "Education for an entire culture is no simple matter. But we are geared for it."

So there we had it—all legal and airtight. We could get anything we wanted and as much as we wanted and we'd have a right to it. No one could say we stole it. Not even Doc could say that.

The creature explained to me the system of notation they used on the recording cylinders and how the courses would be boxed and numbered so they could be used in context. He promised to supply me with recordings of the electives so I could pick out what we wanted.

He was real happy about finding another customer and he proudly told me of all the others that they had and he held forth at length on the satisfaction that an educator feels at the opportunity to pass on the torch of knowledge.

He had me feeling like a heel.

Then we were through and I was sitting in the seat again and the second creature was taking the helmet off my head.

I got up and the first creature rose to his feet and faced me. We couldn't talk any more than we could to start with. It was a weird feeling, to face a being you've just made a deal with and not be able to say a single word that he can understand.

But he held out both his hands and I took them in mine and he gave my hands a friendly squeeze.

"Why don't you go ahead and kiss him?" asked Hutch. "Me and the boys will look the other way."

Ordinarily, I'd have slugged Hutch for a crack like that, but I didn't even get sore.

The second creature took the two sticks out of the machine and handed one to me. They'd gone in transparent, but they came out black.

"Let's get out of here," I said.

We got out as fast as we could and still keep our dignity—if you could call it that.

Outside the silo, I got Hutch and Pancake and Frost together and told them what had happened.

"We got the universe by the tail," I said, "with a downhill pull."

"What about Doc?" asked Frost.

"Don't you see? It's just the kind of deal that would appeal to him. We can let on we're noble and big-hearted and acting in good faith. All I need to do is get close enough to grab him."

"He won't even listen to you," said Pancake. "He won't believe a word you say."

"You guys stay right here," I said. "I'll handle Doc."

I walked back across the stretch of ground between the building and the ship. There was no sign of Doc. I was all set to holler for him, then thought better of it. I took a chance and started up the ladder. I reached the port and there was still no sign of him.

I moved warily into the ship. I thought I knew what had become of him, but there was no need to take more chances than I had to.

I found him in his chair in the dispensary. He was stiffer than a goat. The gun lay on the floor. There were two empty bottles beside the chair.

I stood and looked at him and knew what had happened. After I had left, he had got to thinking about the situation and had run into the problem of how he'd climb down off that limb and he had solved it the way he'd solved most of his problems all his life.

I got a blanket and covered him. Then I rummaged around and found another bottle. I uncorked it and put it beside the chair, where he could reach it easy. Then I picked up the gun and went to call the others in.

I lay in bed that night and thought about it and it was beautiful. There were so many angles that a man didn't know quite where to start.

There was the university racket which, queerly enough, was entirely legitimate, except that the professor out in the silo never meant it to be sold.

And there was the quickie vacation deal, offering a year or two on an alien planet in six hours of actual time. All we'd need to do was pick a number of electives in geography or social science or whatever they might call it.

There could be an information bureau or a research agency, charging fancy prices to run down facts on any and all subjects.

Without a doubt, there'd be some on-the-spot historical recordings and with those in hand, we could retail adventure, perfectly safe adventure, to the stay-at-homes who might hanker for it.

I thought about that and a lot of other things which were not quite so sure, but at least probable and worth investigating, and I thought, too, about how the professors had finally arrived at what seemed to me a sure-fire effective medium for education.

You wanted to know about a thing, so you up and lived it; you learned it on the ground. You didn't read about it or hear about it or even see it in plain three-dimension–you experienced it. You walked the soil of the planet you wanted to know about; you lived with the beings that you wished to study; you saw as an eyewitness, and perhaps as a participant, the history that you sought to learn.

And it could be used in other ways as well. You could learn to build anything, even a spaceship, by actually building one. You could learn how an alien machine might operate by putting it together, step by simple step. There was no field of knowledge in which it would not work–and work far better than standard educational methods.

Right then and there, I made up my mind we'd not release a single stick until one of us had previewed it. No telling what a man might find in one of them that could be put to practical use.

I fell asleep dreaming about chemical miracles and new engineering principles, of better business methods and new philosophic concepts. And I even figured out how a man could make a mint of money out of a philosophic concept.

We were on top of the universe for sure. We'd set up a corporation with more angles than you could shake a stick at. We would be big time. In a thousand years or so, of course, there'd be a reckoning, but none of us would be around to take part in it.

Doc sobered up by morning and I had Frost heave him in the brig. He wasn't dangerous any longer, but I figured that a spell in pokey might do him a world of good. After a while, I intended to talk to him, but right at the moment I was much too busy to be bothered with him.

I went over to the silo with Hutch and Pancake and had another session with the professor on the double-seat machine and picked out a batch of electives and settled various matters.

Other professors began supplying us with the courses, all boxed and labeled, and we set the crew and the engine gang to work hauling them and the machines aboard and stowing them away.

Hutch and I stood outside the silo and watched the work go on.

"I never thought," said Hutch, "that we'd hit the jackpot this way. To be downright honest with you, I never thought we'd hit it. I always thought we'd just go on looking. It goes to show how wrong a man can be."

"Those professors are soft in the head," I said. "They never asked me any questions. I can think of a lot they could have asked that I couldn't answer."

"They're honest and think everyone's the same. That's what comes of getting so wrapped up in something you have time for nothing else."

And that was true enough. The professor race has been busy for a million years doing a job it took a million years to do—and another million and a million after that—and that never would be finished.

"I can't figure why they did it," I said. "There's no profit in it."

"Not for them," said Hutch, "but there is for us. I tell you, Captain, it takes brains to work out the angles."

I told him what I had figured out about previewing everything before we gave it out, so we would be sure we let nothing slip away from us.

Hutch was impressed. "I'll say this for you, Captain—you don't miss a bet. And that's the way it should be. We might as well milk this deal for every cent it's worth."

"I think we should be methodical about this previewing business," I said. "We should start at the beginning and go straight through to the end."

Hutch said he thought so, too. "But it will take a lot of time," he warned me.

"That's why we should start right now. The orientation course is on board already and we could start with that. All we'd have to do is set up a machine and Pancake could help you with it."

"Help me!" yelled Hutch. "Who said anything about me doing it? I ain't cut out for that stuff. You know yourself I never do any reading—"

"It isn't reading. You just live it. You'll be having fun while we're out here slaving."

"I won't do it."

"Now look," I said, "let's use a little sense. I should be out here at the silo seeing everything goes all right and close at hand so I can hold a powwow with the professor if there's any need of it. We need Frost to superintend the loading. And Doc is in the clink. That leaves you and Pancake. I can't trust Pancake with that previewing job. He's too scatterbrained. He'd let a fortune glide right past him without recognizing it. Now you're a fast man with a buck and the way I see it–"

"Since you put it that way," said Hutch, all puffed up, "I suppose I *am* the one who should be doing it."

That evening, we were all dog-tired, but we felt fine. We had made a good start with the loading and in a few more days would be heading home.

Hutch seemed to be preoccupied at supper. He fiddled with his food. He didn't talk at all and he seemed like a man with something on his mind.

As soon as I could, I cornered him.

"How's it going, Hutch?"

"Okay," he said. "Just a lot of gab. Explaining what it's all about. Gab."

"Like what?"

"Some of it's hard to tell. Takes a lot of explaining I haven't got the words for. Maybe one of these days you'll find the time to run through it yourself."

"You can bet your life I will," I said, somewhat sore at him.

"There's nothing worth a dime in it so far," said Hutch.

I believed him on that score. Hutch could spot a dollar twenty miles away.

I went down to the brig to see Doc. He was sober. Also unrepentant.

"You outreached yourself this time," he said. "That stuff isn't yours to sell. There's knowledge in that building that belongs to the Galaxy –for free."

I explained to him what had happened, how we'd found the silo was a university and how we were taking the courses on board for the human race after signing up for them all regular and proper. I tried to make it sound as if we were being big, but Doc wouldn't buy a word of it.

"You wouldn't give your dying grandma a drink of water unless she paid you in advance," he said. "Don't give me any of that guff about service to humanity."

So I left him to stew in the brig awhile and went up to my cabin. I was sore at Hutch and all burned up at Doc and my tail was dragging. I fell asleep in no time.

The work went on for several days and we were almost finished.

I felt pretty good about it. After supper, I climbed down the ladder and sat on the ground beside the ship and looked across at the silo. It still looked big and awesome, but not as big as that first day—because now it had lost some of its strangeness and even the purpose of it had lost some of its strangeness, too.

Just as soon as we got back to civilization, I promised myself, we'd seal the deal as tight as possible. Probably we couldn't legally claim the planet because the professors were intelligent and you can't claim a planet that has intelligence, but there were plenty of other ways we could get our hooks into it for keeps.

I sat there and wondered why no one came down to sit with me, but no one did, so finally I clambered up the ladder.

I went down to the brig to have a word with Doc. He was still unrepentant, but he didn't seem too hostile.

"You know, Captain," he said, "there have been times when I've not seen eye to eye with you, but despite that I've respected you and sometimes even liked you."

"What are you getting at?" I asked him. "You can't soft-talk yourself out of the spot you're in."

"There's something going on and maybe I should tell you. You are a forthright rascal. You don't even take the trouble to deny you are. You have no scruples and probably no morals, and that's all right, because you don't pretend to have. You are—"

"Spit it out! If you don't tell me what's going on, I'll come in there and wring it out of you."

"Hutch has been down here several times," said Doc, "inviting me to come up and listen to one of those recordings he is fooling with. Said it was right down my alley. Said I'd not be sorry. But there was something wrong about it. Something sneaky." He stared round-eyed through the bars at me. "You know, Captain, Hutch was never sneaky."

"Well, go on!"

"Hutch has found out something, Captain. If I were you, I'd be finding out myself."

I didn't even wait to answer him. I remembered how Hutch had been acting, fiddling with his food and preoccupied, not talking very much. And come to think of it, some of the others had been acting strangely, too. I'd just been too busy to give it much attention.

Running up the catwalks, I cussed with every step I took. A captain of a ship should never get so busy that he loses touch—he has to stay in touch all the blessed time. It had all come of being in a hurry, of wanting to get loaded up and out of there before something happened.

And now something had happened. No one had come down to sit with me. There'd not been a dozen words spoken at the supper table. Everything felt deadly wrong.

Pancake and Hutch had rigged up the chart room for the previewing chore and I busted into it and slammed the door and stood with my back against it.

Not only Hutch was there, but Pancake and Frost as well and, in the machine's bucket seat, a man I recognized as one of the engine gang.

I stood for a moment without saying anything, and the three of them stared back at me. The man with the helmet on his head didn't notice—he wasn't even there.

"All right, Hutch," I said, "come clean. What is this all about? Why is that man previewing? I thought just you and—"

"Captain," said Frost, "we were about to tell you."

"You shut up! I am asking Hutch."

"Frost is right," said Hutch. "We were all set to tell you. But you were so busy and it came a little hard . . ."

"What's hard about it?"

"Well, you had your heart all set to make yourself a fortune. We were trying to find a way to break it to you gentle."

I left the door and walked over to him.

"I don't know what you're talking about," I said, "but we still make ourselves a killing. There never was a time of day or night, Hutch, that I couldn't beat your head in and if you don't want me to start, you better talk real fast."

"We'll make no killing, Captain," Frost said quietly. "We're taking this stuff back and we'll turn it over to the authorities."

"All of you are nuts!" I roared. "For years, we've slaved and sweated, hunting for the jackpot. And now that we have it in our mitts, now that we can walk barefooted through a pile of thousand-dollar bills, you're going chicken on me. What's—"

"It's not right for us to do it, sir," said Pancake.

And that "sir" scared me more than anything that had happened so far. Pancake had never called me that before.

I looked from one to the other of them and what I saw in their faces chilled me to the bone. Every single one of them thought just the same as Pancake.

"That orientation course!" I shouted.

Hutch nodded. "It explained about honesty and honor."

"What do you scamps know about honesty and honor?" I raged. "There ain't a one of you that ever drew an honest breath."

"We never knew about it before," said Pancake, "but we know about it now."

"It's just propaganda! It's just a dirty trick the professors played on us!"

And it *was* a dirty trick. Although you have to admit the professors knew their onions. I don't know if they figured us humans for a race of heels or if the orientation course was just normal routine. But no wonder they hadn't questioned me. No wonder they'd made no investigation before handing us their knowledge. They had us stopped before we could even make a move.

"We felt that since we had learned about honesty," said Frost, "it was only right the rest of the crew should know. It's an awful kind of life we've been living, Captain."

"So," said Hutch, "we been bringing in the men, one by one, and orienting them. We figured it was the least that we could do. This man is about the last of them."

"A missionary," I said to Hutch. "So that is what you are. Remember what you told me one night? You said you wouldn't be a missionary no matter what they paid you."

"There's no need of that," Frost replied coldly. "You can't shame us and you can't bully us. We know we are right."

"But the money! What about the corporation? We had it all planned out!"

Frost said: "You might as well forget it, Captain. When you take the course–"

"I'm not taking any course." My voice must have been as deadly as I felt, for not a one of them made a move toward me. "If any of you mealy-mouthed missionaries feel an urge to make me, you can start trying right now."

They still didn't move. I had them bluffed. But there was no point in arguing with them. There was nothing I could do against that stone wall of honesty and honor.

I turned my back on them and walked to the door. At the door, I stopped. I said to Frost: "You better turn Doc loose and give him the cure. Tell him it's all right with me. He has it coming to him. It will serve him right."

Then I shut the door behind me and went up the catwalk to my cabin. I locked the door, a thing I'd never done before.

I sat down on the edge of the bunk and stared at the wall and thought.

There was just one thing they had forgotten. This was my ship, not theirs. They were just the crew and their papers had run out long ago and never been renewed.

I got down on my hands and knees and hauled out the tin box I kept the papers in. I went through it systematically and sorted out the papers that I needed—the title to the ship and the registry and the last papers they had signed.

I laid the papers on the bunk and shoved the box out of the way and sat down again.

I picked up the papers and shuffled them from one hand to the other.

I could throw them off the ship any time I wished. I could take off without them and there was nothing, absolutely nothing, they could do about it.

And what was more, I could get away with it. It was legal, of course, but it was a rotten thing to do. Now that they were honest men and honorable, though, they'd bow to the legality and let me get away with it. And in such a case, they had no one but themselves to thank.

I sat there for a long time thinking, but my thoughts went round and round and mostly had to do with things out of the past—how Pancake had gotten tangled up in the nettle patch out in the Coonskin System and how Doc had fallen in love with (of all things) a tri-sexual being that time we touched at Siro and how Hutch had cornered the liquor supply at Munko, then lost it in a game that was akin to craps except the dice were queer little living entities that you had no control of, which made it tough on Hutch.

A rap came at the door.

It was Doc.

"You all full of honesty?" I asked him.

He shuddered. "Not me. I turned down the offer."

"It's the same kind of swill you were preaching at me just a couple of days ago."

"Can't you see," asked Doc, "what it would do to the human race?"

"Sure. It'll make them honorable and honest. No one will ever cheat or steal again and it will be cozy. . . ."

"They'll die of complicated boredom," said Doc. "Life will become a sort of cross between a Boy Scout jamboree and a ladies' sewing circle. There'll be no loud and unseemly argument and they'll be polite and proper to the point of stupefaction."

"So you have changed your mind."

"Not really, Captain. But this is the wrong way to go about it. Whatever progress the race has ever made has been achieved by the due process of social evolution. In any human advance, the villains and the rascals are as important as the forward-looking idealist. They are man's consciences and man can't get along without them."

"If I were you, Doc," I said, "I wouldn't worry so much about the human race. It's a pretty big thing and it can take a lot of bumps. Even an overdose of honesty won't hurt it permanently."

Actually, I didn't give a damn. I had other things on my mind right then.

Doc crossed the room and sat down on the bunk beside me. He leaned over and tapped the papers I still held in my hand.

"You got it all doped out," he said.

I nodded bleakly. "Yeah."

"I thought you would."

I shot a quick glance at him. "You were way ahead of me. That's why you switched over."

Doc shook his head emphatically. "No. Please believe me, Captain, I feel as bad as you do."

"It won't work either way." I shuffled the papers. "They acted in good faith. They didn't sign aboard, sure. But there was no reason that they should have. It was all understood. Share and share alike. And that's the way it's been for too long to repudiate it now. And we can't keep on. Even if we agreed to dump the stuff right here and blast off and never think of it again, we'd not get rid of it. It would always be there. The past is dead, Doc. It's spoiled. It's smashed and it can't be put back together."

I felt like bawling. It had been a long time since I had felt that full of grief.

"They are different kind of men now," I said. "They went and changed themselves and they'll never be the same. Even if they could change back, it wouldn't be the same."

Doc mocked me a little. "The race will build a monument to you. Maybe actually on Earth itself, with all the other famous humans, for bringing back this stuff. They'd be just blind enough to do it."

I got up and paced the floor. "I don't want any monument. I'm not bringing it in. I'm not having anything more to do with it."

I stood there, wishing we had never found the silo, for what had it done for me except to lose me the best crew and the best friends a man had ever had?

"The ship is mine," I said. "That is all I want. I'll take the cargo to the nearest point and dump it there. Hutch and the rest of them can carry on from there, any way they can. They can have the honesty and honor. I'll get another crew."

Maybe, I thought, someday it would be almost the way it had been. Almost, but not quite.

"We'll go on hunting," I said. "We'll dream about the jackpot. We'll do our best to find it. We'll do anything to find it. We'll break all the laws of God or man to find it. But you know something, Doc?"

"No, I don't," said Doc.

"I hope we never find it. I don't want to find another. I just want to go on hunting."

We stood there in the silence, listening to the fading echoes of those days we hunted for the jackpot.

"Captain," said Doc, "will you take me along?"

I nodded. What was the difference? He might just as well.

"Captain, you remember those insect mounds on Suud?"

"Of course. How could I forget them?"

"You know, I've figured out a way we might break into them. Maybe we should try it. There should be a billion . . ."

I almost clobbered him.

I'm glad now that I didn't.

Suud is where we're headed.

If Doc's plan works out, we may hit that jackpot yet!

9. Death Scene

SHE WAS WAITING on the stoop of the house when he turned into the driveway and as he wheeled the car up the concrete and brought it to a halt he was certain she knew, too.

She had just come from the garden and had one arm full of flowers and she was smiling at him just a shade too gravely.

He carefully locked the car and put the keys away in the pocket of his jacket and reminded himself once again, "Matter-of-factly, friend. For it is better this way."

And that was the truth, he reassured himself. It was much better than the old way. It gave a man some time.

He was not the first and he would not be the last and for some of them it was rough, and for others, who had prepared themselves, it was not so rough and in time, perhaps, it would become a ritual so beautiful and so full of dignity one would look forward to it. It was more civilized and more dignified than the old way had been and in another hundred years or so there could be no doubt that it would become quite acceptable. All that was wrong with it now, he told himself, was that it was too new. It took a little time to become accustomed to this way of doing things after having done them differently through all of human history.

He got out of the car and went up the walk to where she waited for him. He stooped and kissed her and the kiss was a little longer than was their regular custom—and a bit more tender. And as he kissed her he smelled the summer flowers she carried, and he thought how appropriate it was that he should at this time smell the flowers from the garden they both loved.

"You know," he said and she nodded at him.

"Just a while ago," she said. "I knew you would be coming home. I went out and picked the flowers."

"The children will be coming, I imagine."

"Of course," she said. "They will come right away."

He looked at his watch, more from force of habit than a need to know the time. "There is time," he said. "Plenty of time for all of them to get here. I hope they bring the kids."

"Certainly they will," she said. "I went to phone them once, then I thought how silly."

He nodded. "We're of the old school, Florence. It's hard even yet to accept this thing–to know the children will know and come almost as soon as we know. It's still a little hard to be sure of a thing like that."

She patted his arm. "The family will be all together. There'll be time to talk. We'll have a splendid visit."

"Yes, of course," he said.

He opened the door for her and she stepped inside.

"What pretty flowers," he said.

"They've been the prettiest this year that they have ever been."

"That vase," he said. "The one you got last birthday. The blue and gold. That's the one to use."

"That's exactly what I thought. On the dining table."

She went to get the vase and he stood in the living room and thought how much he was a part of this room and this room a part of him. He knew every inch of it and it knew him as well and it was a friendly place, for he'd spent years making friends with it.

Here he'd walked the children of nights when they had been babies and been ill of cutting teeth or croup or colic, nights when the lights in this room had been the only lights in the entire block. Here the family had spent many evening hours in happiness and peace–and it had been a lovely thing, the peace. For he could remember the time when there had been no peace, nowhere in the world, and no thought or hope of peace, but in its place the ever-present dread and threat of war, a dread that had been so commonplace that you scarcely noticed it, a dread you came to think was a normal part of living.

Then, suddenly, there had been the dread no longer, for you could not fight a war if your enemy could look ahead an entire day and see what was about to happen. You could not fight a war and you could not play a game of baseball or any sort of game, you could not rob or cheat or murder, you could not make a killing in the market. There were a lot of things you could no longer do and there were times when it spoiled a lot of fun, for surprise and anticipation had been made impossible. It took a lot of getting used to and a lot of readjustment, but you were safe, at least, for there could be no war—not only at the moment, but forever and forever, and you knew that not only were you safe, but your children safe as well and their children and your children's children's children and you were willing to pay almost any sort of price for such complete assurance.

It is better this way, he told himself, standing in the friendly room. It is much better this way. Although at times it's hard.

He walked across the room and through it to the porch and stood on the porch steps looking at the flowers. Florence was right, he thought; they were prettier this year than any year before. He tried to remember back to some year when they might have been prettier, but he couldn't quite be sure. Maybe the autumn when young John had been a baby, for that year the mums and asters had been particularly fine. But that was unfair, he told himself, for it was not autumn now, but summer. It was impossible to compare summer flowers with autumn. Or the year when Mary had been ill so long—the lilacs had been so deeply purple and had smelled so sweet; he remembered bringing in great bouquets of them each evening because she loved them so. But that was no comparison, for the lilacs bloomed in spring.

A neighbor went past on the sidewalk outside the picket fence and he spoke gravely to her: "Good afternoon, Mrs. Abrams."

"Good afternoon, Mr. Williams," she said and that was the way it always was, except on occasions she would stop a moment and they'd talk about the flowers. But today she would not stop unless he made it plain he would like to have her stop, for otherwise she would not wish to intrude upon him.

That was the way it had been at the office, he recalled.

He'd put away his work with sure and steady hands—as sure and steady as he could manage them. He'd walked to the rack and got down his hat and no one had spoken to him, not a single one of them had kidded him about his quitting early, for all had guessed—or known—as well as he. You could not always tell, of course, for the foresight ability was more pronounced in some than it was in others, although the lag in even the least efficient of them would not be more than a quarter-hour at most.

He'd often wished he could understand how it had been brought about, but there were factors involved he could not even remotely grasp. He knew the story, of course, for he could remember the night that it had happened and the excitement there had been—and the consternation. But knowing how it came about and the reason for it was quite a different thing from understanding it.

It had been an ace in the hole, a move of desperation to be used only as a last resort. The nation had been ready for a long time with the transmitters all set up and no one asking any questions because everyone had taken it for granted they were a part of the radar network and, in that case, the less said of them the better.

No one had wanted to use those transmitters, or at least that had been the official explanation after they'd been used—but anything was better than another war.

So the time had come, the time of last resort, the day of desperation, and the switches had been flicked, blanketing the nation with radiations that did something to the brain—"stimulating latent abilities" was as close a general explanation as anyone had made—and all at once everyone had been able to see twenty-four hours ahead.

There'd been hell to pay, of course, for quite a little while, but after a time it simmered down and the people settled down to make the best of it, to adapt and live with their strange new ability.

The President had gone on television to tell the world what had happened and he had warned potential enemies that we'd know twenty-four hours ahead of time exactly what they'd do. In consequence of which they did exactly nothing except to undo a number of incriminating moves they had already made—some of which the President had foretold that they would undo, naming the hour and place and the manner of their action.

He had said the process was no secret and that other nations were welcome to the know-how if they wanted it, although it made but little difference if they did or not, for the radiations in time would spread throughout the entire world and would affect all people. It was a permanent change, he said, for the ability was inheritable and would be passed on from one generation to the next, and never again, for good or evil, would the human race be blind as it had been in the past.

So finally there had been peace, but there'd been a price to pay. Although, perhaps, not too great a price, Williams told himself. He'd liked baseball, he recalled, and there could be no baseball now, for it was a pointless thing to play a game the outcome of which you'd know a day ahead of time. He had liked to have the boys in occasionally for a round of poker—but poker was just as pointless now and as impossible as baseball or football or horse racing or any other sport.

There had been many changes, some of them quite awkward. Take newspapers, for example, and radio and television reporting of the news. Political tactics had been forced to undergo a change, somewhat for the better, and gambling and crime had largely disappeared.

Mostly, it had been for the best. Although even some of the best was a little hard at first—and some of it would take a long time to become completely accustomed to.

Take his own situation now, he thought.

A lot more civilized than in the old days, but still fairly hard to take. Hard especially on Florence and the children, forcing them into a new and strange attitude that in time would harden into custom and tradition, but now was merely something new and strange. But Florence was standing up to it admirably, he thought. They'd often talked of it, especially in these last few years, and they had agreed that no matter which of them it was they would keep it calm and dignified, for that was the only way to face it. It was one of the payments that you made for peace, although sometimes it was a little hard to look at it that way.

But there were certain compensations. Florence and he could have a long talk before the children arrived. There'd be a chance to go over certain final details—finances and insurance and other matters of like nature. Under the old way there would have been, he told himself, no chance at all for that. There'd be the opportunity to do all the little worthwhile things, all the final sentimental gestures, that except for the foresight ability would have been denied.

There'd be talk with the children and the neighbors bringing things to eat and the big bouquet of flowers the office gang would send—the flowers that under other circumstances he never would have seen. The minister would drop in for a moment and manage to get in a quiet word or two of comfort, all the time making it seem to be no more than a friendly call. In the morning the mail would bring many little cards and notes of friendship sent by people who wanted him to know they thought of him and would have liked to have been with him if there had been the time. But they would not intrude, for the time that was left was a family time.

The family would sit and talk, remembering the happy days—the dog that Eddie had and the time John had run away from home for an hour or two and the first time Mary had ever had a date and the dress she wore. They'd take out the snapshot albums and look at the pictures, recalling all the days of bittersweetness and would know that theirs had been a good life—and especially he would know. And through it all would run the happy clatter of grandchildren playing in the house, climbing up on Granddad's knee to have him tell a story.

All so civilized, he thought.

Giving all of them a chance to prove they were civilized.

He'd have to go back inside the house now, for he could hear Florence arranging the flowers in the birthday vase that was blue and gold. And they had so much to say to one another—even after forty years they still had so much to say to one another.

He turned and glanced back at the garden.

Most beautiful flowers, he thought, that they had ever raised.

He'd go out in the morning, when the dew was on them, when they were most beautiful, to bid them all good-by.

10. Green Thumb

I HAD COME BACK from lunch and was watching the office while Millie went out to get a bite to eat. With my feet up on the desk in a comfortable position, I was giving considerable attention to how I might outwit a garbage-stealing dog.

The dog and I had carried on a feud for months and I was about ready to resort to some desperate measures.

I had blocked up the can with heavy concrete blocks so he couldn't tip it over, but he was a big dog and could stand up and reach down into the can and drag all the garbage out. I had tried putting a heavy weight on the lid, but he simply dragged it off and calmly proceeded with his foraging. I had waited up and caught him red-handed at it and heaved some rocks and whatever else was handy at him, but he recognized tactics such as these for what they were and they didn't bother him. He'd come back in half an hour, calm as ever.

I had considered setting a light muskrat trap on top of the garbage so that, when he reached down into the can, he'd get his muzzle caught. But if I did that, sure as hell I'd forget to take it out some Tuesday morning and the garbageman would get caught instead. I had toyed with the idea of wiring the can so the dog would get an electric shock when he came fooling around. But I didn't know how to go about wiring it and, if I did, ten to one I'd fix it up so I'd electrocute him instead of just scaring him off, and I didn't want to kill him.

I like dogs, you understand. That doesn't mean I have to like *all* dogs, does it? And if you had to scrape up garbage every morning, you'd be just as sore at the mutt as I was.

While I was wondering if I couldn't put something in a particularly tempting bit of garbage that would make him sick and still not kill him, the phone rang.

It was old Pete Skinner out on Acorn Ridge.

"Could you come out?" he asked.

"Maybe," I said. "What you got?"

"I got a hole out in the north forty."

"Sink-hole?"

"Nope. Looks like someone dug it out and carried off the dirt."

"Who would do that, Pete?"

"I don't know. And that ain't all of it. They left a pile of sand beside the hole."

"Maybe that's what they dug out of the hole."

"You know well enough," said Pete, "that I haven't any sandy soil. You've run tests enough on it. All of mine is clay."

"I'll be right out," I told him.

A county agent gets some funny calls, but this one topped them all. Hog cholera, corn borers, fruit blight, milk production records—any of these would have been down my alley. But a hole in the north forty?

And yet, I suppose I should have taken it as a compliment that Pete called me. When you've been a county agent for fifteen years, a lot of farmers get to trust you and some of them, like Pete, figure you can straighten out any problem. I enjoy a compliment as much as anybody. It's the headaches that go with them that I don't like.

When Millie came back, I drove out to Pete's place, which is only four or five miles out of town.

Pete's wife told me that he was up in the north forty, so I went there and found not only Pete, but some of his neighbors. All of them were looking at the hole and doing a lot of talking. I never saw a more puzzled bunch of people.

The hole was about thirty feet in diameter and about thirty-five feet deep, an almost perfect cone—not the kind of hole you'd dig with a pick and shovel. The sides were cut as clean as if they'd been machined, but the soil was not compressed, as it would have been if machinery had been used.

The pile of sand lay just a short distance from the hole. Looking at it, I had the insane feeling that, if you shoveled that sand into the hole, it would exactly fit. It was the whitest sand I've ever seen and, when I walked over to the pile and picked up some of it, I saw that it was clean. Not just ordinary clean, but *absolutely* clean—as though laundered grain by grain.

I stood around for a while, like the rest of them, staring at the hole and the pile of sand and wishing I could come up with some bright idea. But I wasn't able to. There was the hole and there was the sand. The topsoil was dry and powdery and would have shown wheelmarks or any other kind if there'd been any. There weren't.

I told Pete maybe he'd better fence in the whole business, because the sheriff or somebody from the state, or even the university, might want to look it over. Pete said that was a good idea and he'd do it right away.

I went back to the farmhouse and asked Mrs. Skinner to give me a couple of fruit jars. One of them I filled with a sample from the sand pile and the other with soil from the hole, being careful not to jolt the walls.

By this time, Pete and a couple of the neighbors had gotten a wagonload of fence posts and some wire and were coming out to the field. I waited and helped unload the posts and wire, then drove back to the office, envying Pete. He was satisfied to put up the fence and let me worry about the problem.

I found three fellows waiting for me. I gave Millie the fruit jars and asked her to send them right away to the Soils Bureau at the State Farm Campus. Then I settled down to work.

Other people drifted in and it was late in the afternoon before I could call up the Soils Bureau and tell them I wanted the contents of the two jars analyzed. I told them a little of what had happened, although not all of it for, when you tried to put it into words, it sounded pretty weird.

"Banker Stevens called and asked if you'd drop by his place on your way home," Millie told me.

"What would Stevens want with me?" I asked. "He isn't a farmer and I don't owe him any money."

"He grows fancy flowers," said Millie.

"I know that. He lives just up the street from me."

"From what I gathered, something awful happened to them. He was all broken up."

So, on the way home, I stopped at the Stevens place. The banker was out in the yard, waiting for me. He looked terrible. He led me around to the big flower garden in the back and never have I seen such utter devastation. In that whole area, there wasn't a single plant alive. Every one of them had given up the ghost and was lying wilted on the ground.

"What could have done it, Joe?" asked Stevens and, the way he said it, I felt sorry for him.

After all, those flowers were a big thing in his life. He'd raised them from special seed and he'd babied them along, and for anybody who is crazy about flowers, I imagine they were tops.

"Someone might have used some spray on them," I said. "Almost any kind of spray, if you don't dilute it enough, would kill them."

Out in the garden, I took a close look at the dead flowers, but nowhere could I see any sign of the burning from too strong a spray.

Then I saw the holes, at first only two or three of them, then, as I went on looking, dozens of them. They were all over the garden, about an inch in diameter, for all the world as if someone had taken a broomstick and punched holes all over the place. I got down on my knees and could see that they tapered, the way they do when you pull weeds with big taproots out of the ground.

"You been pulling weeds?" I asked.

"Not big ones like that," said the banker. "I take good care of those flowers, Joe. You know that. Keep them weeded and watered and cultivated and sprayed. Put just the right amount of commercial fertilizer in the soil. Try to keep it at top fertility."

"You should use manure. It's better than all the commercial fertilizer you can buy."

"I don't agree with you. Tests have proved . . ."

It was an old argument, one that we fought out each year. I let him run on, only half listening to him, while I picked up some of the soil and crumbled it. It was dead soil. You could feel that it was. It crumbled at the lightest touch and was dry, even when I dug a foot beneath the surface.

"You water this bed recently?" I asked.

"Last evening," Stevens said.

"When did you find the flowers like this?"

"This morning. They looked fine last night. And now–" he blinked fast.

I asked him for a fruit jar and filled it with a sample of the soil.

"I'll send this in and see if there's anything wrong with it," I said.

A bunch of dogs were barking at something in the hedge in front of my place when I got home. Some of the dogs in the neighborhood are hell on cats. I parked the car and picked up an old hoe handle and went out to rescue the cat they seemed to have cornered.

They scattered when they saw me coming and I started to look in the hedge for the cat. There wasn't any and that aroused my curiosity and I wondered what the dogs could have been barking at. So I went hunting.

And I found it.

It was lying on the ground, close against the lower growth of the hedge, as if it had crawled there for protection.

I reached in and pulled it out—a weed of some sort, about five feet tall, and with a funny root system. There were eight roots, each about an inch in diameter at the top and tapering to a quarter inch or so. They weren't all twisted up, but were sort of sprung out, so that there were four to the side, each set of four in line. I looked at their tips and I saw that the roots were not broken off, but ended in blunt, strong points.

The stalk, at the bottom, was about as thick as a man's fist. There were four main branches covered with thick, substantial, rather meaty leaves; but the last foot of the branches was bare of leaves. At the top were several flower or seed pouches, the biggest of them about the size of an old-fashioned coffee mug.

I squatted there looking at it. The more I looked, the more puzzled I became. As a county agent, you have to know quite a bit about botany and this plant was like none I had seen before.

I dragged it across the lawn to the tool shed back of the garage and tossed it in there, figuring that after supper I'd have a closer look at it.

I went in the house to get my evening meal ready and decided to broil a steak and fix up a bowl of salad.

A lot of people in town wonder at my living in the old homestead, but I'm used to the house and there seemed to be no sense in moving somewhere else when all it costs me is taxes and a little upkeep. For several years before Mother died, she had been quite feeble and I did all the cleaning and helped with the cooking, so I'm fairly handy at it.

After I washed the dishes, I read what little there was to read in the evening paper and then looked up an old text on botany, to see if I could find anything that might help identify the plant.

I didn't find anything and, just before I went to bed, I got a flashlight and went out, imagining, I suppose, that I'd find the weed somehow different from the way I remembered it.

I opened the door of the shed and flashed the light where I'd tossed the weed on the floor. At first I couldn't see it, then I heard a leafy rustling over in one corner and I turned the light in that direction.

The weed had crawled over to one corner and it was trying to get up, its stem bowed out—the way a man would arch his back—pressing against the wall of the shed.

Standing there with my mouth open, watching it try to raise itself erect, I felt horror and fear. I reached out to the corner nearest the door and snatched up an ax.

If the plant had succeeded in getting up, I might have chopped it to bits. But, as I stood there, I saw the thing would never make it. I was not surprised when it slumped back on the floor.

What I did next was just as unreasoning and instinctive as reaching for the ax.

I found an old washtub and half filled it with water. Then I picked up the plant—it had a squirmish feel to it, like a worm—stuck its roots into the water, and pushed the tub back against the wall, so the thing could be braced upright.

I went into the house and ransacked a couple of closets until I found the sunlamp I'd bought a couple of years back, to use when I had a touch of arthritis in my shoulder. I rigged up the lamp and trained it on the plant, not too close. Then I got a big shovelful of dirt and dumped it in the tub.

And that, I figured, was about all I could do. I was giving the plant water, soil-food and simulated sunlight. I was afraid that, if I tried a more fancy treatment, I might kill it, for I hadn't any notion of what conditions it might be used to.

Apparently I handled it right. It perked up considerably and, as I moved about, the coffee-cup-sized pod on the top kept turning, following every move I made.

I watched it for a while and moved the sunlamp back a little, so there'd be no chance of scorching it, and went back into the house.

It was then that I really began to get bone-scared. I had been frightened out in the shed, of course, but that had been shock. Now, thinking it over, I began to understand more clearly what sort of creature I'd found underneath the hedge. I remember I wasn't yet ready to say it out loud, but it seemed probable that my guest was an alien intelligence.

I did some wondering about how it had gotten here and if it had made the holes in Banker Stevens' flowerbed and also if it could have had anything to do with the big hole out in Pete Skinner's north forty.

I sat around, arguing with myself, for a man just does not go prowling around in his neighbor's garden after midnight.

But I had to know.

I walked up the alley to the back of the Stevens house and sneaked into the garden. Shielding the flashlight with my hat, I had another look at the holes in the ruined flowerbed. I wasn't too surprised when I saw that they occurred in series of eight, four to the side—exactly the kind of holes the plant back in my toolshed would make if it sank its roots into the ground.

I counted at least eleven of those eight-in-line sets of holes and I'm sure that there were more. But I didn't want to stick around too long, for fear Banker Stevens might wake up and ask questions.

So I went back home, down the alley, and was just in time to catch that garbage-stealing dog doing a good job on the can. He had his head stuck clear down into it and I was able to sneak up behind him. He heard me and struggled to get out, but he'd jammed himself into the can. Before he could get loose, I landed a good swift kick where it did maximum good. He set some kind of canine speed record in getting off the premises, I imagine.

I went to the toolshed and opened the door. The tub half full of muddy water was still there and the sunlamp was still burning—but the plant was gone. I looked all over the shed and couldn't find it. So I unplugged the sunlamp and headed for the house.

To be truthful, I was a little relieved that the plant had wandered off.

But when I rounded the corner of the house, I saw it hadn't. It was in the window box, and the geraniums I had nursed all spring were hanging limply over the side of the box.

I stood there and looked at it and had the feeling that it was looking back at me.

And I remembered that not only had it had to travel from the toolshed to the house and then climb into the window box, but it had had to open the toolshed door and close it again.

It was standing up, stiff and straight, and appeared to be in the best of health. It looked thoroughly incongruous in the window box—as if a man had grown a tall stalk of corn there, although it didn't look anything like a stalk of corn.

I got a pail of water and poured it into the window box. Then I felt something tapping me on the head and looked up. The plant had bent over and was patting me with one of its branches. The modified leaf at the end of the branch had spread itself out to do the patting and looked something like a hand.

I went into the house and up to bed and the main thing I was thinking about was that, if the plant got too troublesome or dangerous, all I had to do was mix a strong dose of commercial fertilizer or arsenic, or something just as deadly, and water it with the mixture.

Believe it or not, I went to sleep.

Next morning I got to thinking that maybe I should repair the old greenhouse and put my guest in there and be sure to keep the door locked. It seemed to be reasonably friendly and inoffensive, but I couldn't be sure, of course.

After breakfast, I went out into the yard to look for it, with the idea of locking it in the garage for the day, but it wasn't in the window box, or anywhere that I could see. And since it was Saturday, when a lot of farmers came to town, with some of them sure to be dropping in to see me, I didn't want to be late to work.

I was fairly busy during the day and didn't have much time for thinking or worrying. But when I was wrapping up the sample of soil from the banker's garden to send to the Soils Bureau, I wondered if maybe there wasn't someone at the university I should notify. I also wondered about letting someone in Washington know, except I didn't have the least idea whom to contact, or even which department.

Coming home that evening, I found the plant anchored in the garden, in a little space where the radishes and lettuce had been. The few lettuce plants still left in the ground were looking sort of limp, but everything else was all right. I took a good look at the plant. It waved a couple of its branches at me—and it wasn't the wind blowing them, for there wasn't any wind—and it nodded its coffee-cup pod as if to let me know it recognized me. But that was all it did.

After supper, I scouted the hedge in front of the house and found two more of the plants. Both of them were dead.

My next-door neighbors had gone to a movie, so I scouted their place, too, and found four more of the plants, under bushes and in corners where they had crawled away to die.

I wondered whether it might not have been the plant I'd rescued that the dogs had been barking at the night before. I felt fairly sure it was. A dog might be able to recognize an alien being where a man would be unable to.

I counted up. At least seven of the things had picked out Banker Stevens' flowerbed for a meal and the chemical fertilizer he used had killed all but one of them. The sole survivor, then, was out in the garden, killing off my lettuce.

I wondered why the lettuce and geraniums and Stevens' flowers had reacted as they did. It might be that the alien plants produced some sort of poison, which they injected into the soil to discourage other plant life from crowding their feeding grounds. That was not exactly far-fetched. There are trees and plants on Earth that accomplish the same thing by various methods. Or it might be that the aliens sucked the soil so dry of moisture and plant food that the other plants simply starved to death.

I did some wondering on why they'd come to Earth at all and why some of them had stayed. If they had traveled from some other planet, they must have come in a ship, so that hole out in Pete's north forty might have been where they stopped to replenish their food supply, dumping the equivalent of garbage beside the hole.

And what about the seven I had counted?

Could they have jumped ship? Or gone on shore leave and run into trouble, the way human sailors often do?

Maybe the ship had searched for the missing members of the party, had been unable to find them, and had gone on. If that were so, then my own plant was a marooned alien. Or maybe the ship was still hunting.

I wore myself out, thinking about it, and went to bed early, but lay there tossing for a long time. Then, just as I was falling asleep, I heard the dog at the garbage can. You'd think after what had happened to him the night before, that he'd have decided to skip that particular can, but not him. He was rattling and banging it around, trying to tip it over.

I picked a skillet off the stove and opened the back door. I got a good shot at him, but missed him by a good ten feet. I was so sore that I didn't even go out to pick up the skillet, but went back to bed.

It must have been several hours later that I was brought straight up in bed by the terror-stricken yelping of a dog. I jumped out and ran to the window. It was a bright moonlit night and the dog was going down the driveway as if the devil himself were after him. Behind him sailed the plant. It had wrapped one of its branches around his tail and the other three branches were really giving him a working over.

They went up the street out of sight and, for a long time after they disappeared, I could hear the dog still yelping. Within a few minutes, I saw the plant coming up the gravel, walking like a spider on its eight roots.

It turned off the driveway and planted itself beside a lilac bush and seemed to settle down for the night. I decided that if it wasn't good for anything else, the garbage can would be safe, at least. If the dog came back again, the plant would be waiting to put the bee on him.

I lay awake for a long time, wondering how the plant had known I didn't want the dog raiding the garbage. It probably had seen—if that is the proper word—me chase him out of the yard.

I went to sleep with the comfortable feeling that the plant and I had finally begun to understand each other.

The next day was Sunday and I started working on the greenhouse, putting it into shape so I could cage up the plant. It had found itself a sunny spot in the garden and was imitating a large and particularly ugly weed I'd been too lazy to pull out.

My next-door neighbor came over to offer free advice, but he kept shifting uneasily and I knew there was something on his mind.

Finally he came out with it. "Funny thing—Jenny swears she saw a big plant walking around in your yard the other day. The kid saw it, too, and he claims it chased him." He tittered a little, embarrassed. "You know how kids are."

"Sure," I said.

He stood around awhile longer and gave me some more advice, then went across the yard and home.

I worried about what he had told me. If the plant really had taken to chasing kids, there'd be hell to pay.

I worked at the greenhouse all day long, but there was a lot to do, for it had been out of use ten years or more, and by nightfall I was tuckered out.

After supper, I went out on the back stoop and sat on the steps, watching the stars. It was quiet and restful.

I hadn't been there more than fifteen minutes when I heard a rustling. I looked around and there was the plant, coming up out of the garden, walking along on its roots.

It sort of squatted down beside me and the two of us just sat there, looking at the stars. Or, at least, I looked at them. I don't actually know if the plant could see. If it couldn't, it had some other faculty that was just as good as sight. We just sat there.

After a while, the plant moved one of its branches over and took hold of my arm with that handlike leaf. I tensed a bit, but its touch was gentle enough and I sat still, figuring that if the two of us were to get along, we couldn't start out by flinching away from one another.

Then, so gradually that at first I didn't notice it, I began to perceive a sense of gratitude, as if the plant might be thanking me. I looked around to see what it was doing and it wasn't doing a thing, just sitting there as I was, but with its "hand" still on my arm.

Yet in some way, the plant was trying to make me understand that it was grateful to me for saving it.

It formed no words, you understand. Other than rustling its leaves, it couldn't make a sound. But I understood that some system of communication was in operation. No words, but emotion—deep, clear, utterly sincere emotion.

It eventually got a little embarrassing, this nonstop gratitude.

"Oh, that's all right," I said, trying to put an end to it. "You would have done as much for me."

Somehow, the plant must have sensed that its thanks had been accepted, because the gratitude wore off a bit and something else took over—a sense of peace and quiet.

The plant got up and started to walk off and I called out to it, "Hey, Plant, wait a minute!"

It seemed to understand that I had called it back, for it turned around. I took it by a branch and started to lead it around the boundaries of the yard. If this communication business was going to be any good, you see, it had to go beyond the sense of gratitude and peace and quiet. So I led the plant all the way around the yard and I kept thinking at it as hard as I could, telling it not to go beyond that perimeter.

By the time I'd finished, I was wringing wet with effort. But, finally, the plant seemed to be trying to say okay. Then I built up a mental image of it chasing a kid and I shook a mental finger at it. The plant agreed. I tried to tell it not to move around the yard in daylight, when people would be able to see it. Whether the concept was harder or I was getting tired, I don't know, but both the plant and I were limp when it at last indicated that it understood.

Lying in bed that night, I thought a lot about this problem of communication. It was not telepathy, apparently, but something based on mental pictures and emotions.

But I saw it as my one chance. If I could learn to converse, no matter how, and the plant could learn to communicate something beyond abstracts to me, it could talk to people, would be acceptable and believable, and the authorities might be willing to recognize it as an intelligent being. I decided that the best thing to do would be to acquaint it with the way we humans lived and try to make it understand why we lived that way. And since I couldn't take my visitor outside the yard, I'd have to do it inside.

I went to sleep, chuckling at the idea of my house and yard being a classroom for an alien.

The next day I received a phone call from the Soils Bureau at the university.

"What kind of stuff is this you're sending us?" the man demanded.

"Just some soil I picked up," I said. "What's wrong with it?"

"Sample One is all right. It's just common, everyday Burton County soil. But Sample Two, that sand—good God, man, it has gold dust and flakes of silver and some copper in it! All of it in minute particles, of course. But if some farmer out your way has a pit of that stuff, he's rich."

"At the most, he has twenty-five or thirty truckloads of it."

"Where'd he get it? Where'd it come from?"

I took a deep breath and told him all I knew about the incident out at Pete's north forty.

He said he'd be right out, but I caught him before he hung up and asked him about the third sample.

"What was he growing on that ground?" the man asked baffledly. "Nothing I know of could suck it that clean, right down to the bare bone! Tell him to put in a lot of organic material and some lime and almost everything else that's needed in good soil, before he tries to use it."

The soils people came out to Pete's place and they brought along some other men from the university. A little later in the week, after the papers had spelled out big headlines, a couple of men from Washington showed up. But no one seemed able to figure it out and they finally gave up. The newspapers gave it a play and dropped it as soon as the experts did.

During that time, curiosity seekers flocked to the farm to gape at the hole and the pile of sand. They had carried off more than half the sand and Pete was madder than hell about the whole business.

"I'm going to fill in that hole and forget all about it," he told me, and that was what he did.

Meanwhile, at home, the situation was progressing. Plant seemed to understand what I had told him about not moving out of the yard and acting like a weed during the daytime and leaving kids alone. Everything was peaceable and I got no more complaints. Best of all, the garbage-stealing dog never showed his snout again.

Several times, during all the excitement out at Pete's place, I had been tempted to tell someone from the university about Plant. In each case, I decided not to, for we weren't getting along too well in the talk department.

But in other ways, we were doing just fine.

I let Plant watch me while I took an electric motor apart and then put it together again, but I wasn't too sure he knew what it was all about. I tried to show him the concept of mechanical power and I demonstrated how the motor would deliver that power and I tried to tell him what electricity was. But I got all bogged down with that, not knowing too much about it myself. I don't honestly think Plant got a thing out of that electric motor.

With the motor of the car, though, we were more successful. We spent one whole Sunday dismantling it and then putting it back together. Watching what I was doing, Plant seemed to take a lot of interest in it.

We had to keep the garage door locked and it was a scorcher of a day and, anyhow, I'd much rather spend a Sunday fishing than tearing down a motor. I wondered a dozen times if it was worth it, if there might not be easier ways to teach Plant the facts of our Earth culture.

I was all tired out and failed to hear the alarm and woke up an hour later than I should. I jumped into my clothes, ran out to the garage, unlocked the door and there was Plant. He had parts from that motor strewn all over the floor and he was working away at it, happy as a clam. I almost took an ax to him, but I got hold of myself in time. I locked the door behind me and walked to work.

All day, I wondered how Plant had gotten into the garage. Had he sneaked back in the night before, when I wasn't looking, or had he been able to pick the lock? I wondered, too, what sort of shape I'd find the car in when I got home. I could just see myself working half the night, putting it back together.

I left work a little early. If I had to work on the car, I wanted an early start.

When I got home, the motor was all assembled and Plant was out in the garden, acting like a weed. Seeing him there, I realized he knew how to unlock the door, for I'd locked it when I left that morning.

I turned on the ignition, making bets with myself that it wouldn't start. But it did. I rode around town a little to check it and there wasn't a thing wrong with it.

For the next lesson, I tried something simpler. I got my carpentry tools and showed them to Plant and let him watch me while I made a bird house. Not that I needed any more bird houses. The place already crawled with them. But it was the easiest, quickest thing I could think of to show Plant how we worked in wood.

He watched closely and seemed to understand what was going on, all right, but I detected a sadness in him. I put my hand on his arm to ask him what was the matter.

All that I got was a mournful reaction.

It bewildered me. Why should Plant take so much interest in monkeying around with a motor and then grieve at the making of a bird house? I didn't get it figured out until a few days later, when Plant saw me picking a bouquet of flowers for the kitchen table.

And then it hit me.

Plant was a plant and flowers were plants and so was lumber, or at least lumber at one time had been a plant. And I stood there, with the bouquet dangling in my hand and Plant looking at me, and I thought of all the shocks he had in store for him when he found out more about us—how we slaughtered our forests, grew plants for food and clothing, squeezed or boiled drugs from them.

It was just like a human going to another planet, I realized, and finding that some alien life form grew humans for food.

Plant didn't seem to be sore at me nor did he shrink from me in horror. He was just sad. When he got sad, he was the saddest-looking thing you could possibly imagine. A bloodhound with a hangover would have looked positively joyous in comparison.

If we ever had gotten to the point where we could have really talked—about things like ethics and philosophy, I mean—I might have learned just how Plant felt about our plant-utilizing culture. I'm sure he tried to tell me, but I couldn't understand much of what he was driving at.

We were sitting out on the steps one night, looking at the stars. Earlier, Plant had been showing me his home planet, or it may have been some of the planets he had visited. I don't know. All I could get were fuzzy mental pictures and reactions. One place was hot and red, another blue and cold. There was another that had all the colors of the rainbow and a cool, restful feel about it, as if there might have been gentle winds and fountains and birdsongs in the twilight.

We had been sitting there for quite a while when he put his hand back on my arm again and he showed me a plant. He must have put considerable effort into getting me to visualize it, for the image was sharp and clear. It was a scraggy, rundown plant and it looked even sadder than Plant looked when he got sad, if that is possible. When I started feeling sorry for it, he began to think of kindness and, when he thought of things like kindness and sadness and gratitude and happiness, he could really pour it on.

He had me thinking such big, kindly thoughts, I was afraid that I would burst. While I sat there, thinking that way, I saw the plant begin to perk up. It grew and flowered and was the most beautiful thing I had ever seen. It matured its seeds and dropped them. Swiftly, little plants sprang from the seeds and they were healthy and full of ginger, too.

I mulled that one over several days, suspecting I was crazy for even thinking what I did. I tried to shrug it off, but it wouldn't shrug. It gave me an idea.

The only way I could get rid of it was to try it out.

Out in back of the toolshed was the sorriest yellow rose in town. Why it clung to life, year after year, I could never figure out. It had been there ever since I was a boy. The only reason it hadn't been dug up and thrown away long ago was that no one had ever needed the ground it was rooted in.

I thought, if a plant ever needed help, that yellow rose was it.

So I sneaked out back of the toolshed, making sure that Plant didn't see me, and stood in front of that yellow rose. I began to think kindly thoughts about it, although God knows it was hard to think kindly toward such a wretched thing. I felt foolish and hoped none of the neighbors spotted me, but I kept at it. I didn't seem to accomplish much to start with, but I went back, time after time. In a week or so, I got so that I just naturally loved that yellow rose to pieces.

After four or five days, I began to see some change in it. At the end of two weeks, it had developed from a scraggy, no-account bush to one that any rose fancier would have been proud to own. It dropped its bug-chewed leaves and grew new ones that were so shiny they looked as if they were waxed. Then it grew big flower buds and, in no time at all, was a blaze of yellow glory.

But I didn't quite believe it. In the back of my mind, I figured that Plant must have seen me doing it and helped along a bit. So I decided to test the process again where he couldn't interfere.

Millie had been trying for a couple of years to grow an African violet in a flower pot at the office. By this time, even she was willing to admit it was a losing battle. I had made a lot of jokes about the violet and, at times, Millie had been sore at me about it. Like the yellow rose, it was a hard-luck plant. The bugs ate it. Millie forgot to water it. It got knocked onto the floor. Visitors used it for an ashtray.

Naturally, I couldn't give it the close, intensive treatment I'd given the rose, but I made a point to stop for a few minutes every day beside the violet and think good things about it and, in a couple of weeks, it perked up considerably. By the end of the month, it had bloomed for the first time in its life.

Meanwhile, Plant's education continued.

At first, he'd balked at entering the house, but finally trusted me enough to go in. He didn't spend much time there, for the house was too full of reminders that ours was a plant-utilizing culture. Furniture, clothing, cereal, paper—even the house itself—all were made of vegetation. I got an old butter tub and filled it with soil and put it in one corner of the dining room, so he could eat in the house if he wanted to, but I don't remember that he even once took a snack out of that tub.

Although I didn't admit it then, I knew that what Plant and I had tried to do had been a failure. Whether someone else might have done better, I don't know. I suspect he might have. But I didn't know how to go about getting in touch and I was afraid of being laughed at. It's a terrible thing, our human fear of ridicule.

And there was Plant to consider, too. How would he take being passed on to someone else? I'd screw up my courage to do something about it, and then Plant would come up out of the garden and sit beside me on the steps, and we'd talk—not about anything that mattered, really, but about happiness and sadness and brotherhood, and my courage would go glimmering and I'd have to start all over again.

I've since thought how much like two lost children we must have been, strange kids raised in different countries, who would have liked to play together, except neither knew the rules for the other's games or spoke the other's language.

I know . . . I know. According to common sense, you begin with mathematics. You show the alien that you know two and two are four. Then you draw the solar system and show him the sun on the diagram and then point to the sun overhead and you point to Earth on the diagram, then point to yourself. In this way, you demonstrate to him that you know about the solar system and about space and the stars and so on.

Then you hand him the paper and the pencil.

But what if he doesn't know mathematics? What if the two-plus-two-makes-four routine doesn't mean a thing to him? What if he's never seen a drawing? What if he can't draw—or see or hear or feel or think the way you do?

To deal with an alien, you've got to get down to basics.

And maybe math isn't basic.

Maybe diagrams aren't.

In that case, you have to search for something that is.

Yet there must be certain universal basics.

I think I know what they are.

That, if nothing else, Plant taught me.

Happiness is basic. And sadness is basic. And gratitude, in perhaps a lesser sense. Kindness, too. And perhaps hatred—although Plant and I never dealt in that.

Maybe brotherhood. For the sake of humanity, I hope so.

But kindness and happiness and brotherhood are awkward tools to use in reaching specific understanding, although in Plant's world, they may not be.

It was getting on toward autumn and I was beginning to wonder how I'd take care of Plant during the winter months.

I could have kept him in the house, but he hated it there.

Then, one night, we were sitting on the back steps, listening to the first crickets of the season.

The ship came down without a sound. I didn't see it until it was about at treetop level. It floated down and landed between the house and toolshed.

I was startled for a moment, but not frightened, and perhaps not too surprised. In the back of my head, I'd wondered all the time, without actually knowing it, whether Plant's pals might not ultimately find him.

The ship was a shimmery sort of thing, as if it might not have been made of metal and was not really solid. I noticed that it had not really landed, but floated a foot or so above the grass.

Three other Plants stepped out and the oddest part of it was that there wasn't any door. They just came out of the ship and the ship closed behind them.

Plant took me by the arm and twitched it just a little, to make me understand he wanted me to walk with him to the ship. He made little comforting thoughts to try to calm me down.

And all the time that this was going on, I could sense the talk between Plant and those other three—but just grasping the fringe of the conversation, barely knowing there was talk, not aware of what was being said.

And then, while Plant stood beside me, with his hand still on my arm, those other plants walked up. One by one, each took me by the other arm and stood facing me for a moment and told me thanks and happiness.

Plant told me the same, for the last time, and then the four of them walked toward the ship and disappeared into it. The ship left me standing there, watching it rise into the night, until I couldn't see it any longer.

I stood there for a long time, staring up into the sky, with the thanks and happiness fading and loneliness beginning to creep in.

I knew that, somewhere up there, was a larger ship, that in it were many other Plants, that one of them had lived with me for almost six months and that others of them had died in the hedges and fence corners of the neighborhood. I knew also that it had been the big ship that had scooped out the load of nutritious soil from Pete Skinner's field.

Finally I stopped looking at the sky. Over behind the toolshed I saw the whiteness of the yellow rose in bloom and once again I thought about the basics.

I wondered if happiness and kindness, perhaps even emotions that we humans do not know, might not be used on Plant's world as we use the sciences.

For the rose bush had bloomed when I thought kindly thoughts of it. And the African violet had found a new life in the kindness of a human.

Startling as it may seem, foolish as it may sound, it is not an unknown phenomenon. There are people who have the knack of getting the most out of a flowerbed or a garden. And it is said of these people that they have green thumbs.

May it not be that *green thumbness* is not so much concerned with skill or how much care is taken of a plant, as with the kindliness and the interest of the person tending it?

For eons, the plant life of this planet has been taken for granted. It is simply there. By and large, plants are given little affection. They are planted or sown. They grow. In proper season, they are harvested.

I sometimes wonder if, as hunger tightens its grip upon our teeming planet, there may not be a vital need for the secret of *green thumbness*.

If kindness and sympathy can cause a plant to produce beyond its normal wont, then shouldn't we consider kindness as a tool to ward off Earth's hunger? How much more might be produced if the farmer loved his wheat?

It's silly, of course, a principle that could not gain acceptance.

And undoubtedly it would not work—not in a plant-utilizing culture.

For how could you keep on convincing a plant that you feel kindly toward it when, season after season, you prove that your only interest in it is to eat it or make it into clothing or chop it down for lumber?

I walked out back of the shed and stood beside the yellow rose, trying to find the answer. The yellow rose stirred, like a pretty woman who knows she's being admired, but no emotion came from it.

The thanks and happiness were gone. There was nothing left but the loneliness.

Damned vegetable aliens—upsetting a man so he couldn't eat his breakfast cereal in peace!

11. Lulu

THE MACHINE was a lulu.

That's what we called her: Lulu.

And that was our big mistake.

Not the only one we made, of course, but it was the first, and maybe if we hadn't called her Lulu, it might have been all right.

Technically, Lulu was a PER, a Planetary Exploration Robot. She was a combination spaceship/base of operations/synthesizer/analyzer/communicator. And other things besides. Too many other things besides. That was the trouble with her.

Actually, there was no reason for us to go along with Lulu. As a matter of fact, it probably would have been a good deal better if we hadn't. She could have done the planet-checking without any supervision. But there were rules which said a robot of her class must be attended by no fewer than three humans. And, naturally, there was some prejudice against turning loose, all by itself, a robot that had taken almost twenty years to build and had cost ten billion dollars.

To give her her due, she was an all-but-living wonder. She was loaded with sensors that dug more information out of a planet in an hour than a full human survey crew could have gotten in a month. Not only could she get the data, but she correlated it and coded it and put it on the tape, then messaged the information back to Earth Center without a pause for breath.

Without a pause for breath, of course—she was just a dumb machine.

Did I say dumb?

She wasn't in any single sense. She could even talk to us. She could and did. She talked all the blessed time. And she listened to every word we said. She read over our shoulders and kibitzed on our poker.

There were times we'd willingly have killed her, except you can't kill a robot—that is, a self-maintaining one. Anyhow, she cost ten billion dollars and was the only thing that could bring us back to Earth.

She took good care of us. That no one could deny. She synthesized our food and cooked it and served our meals to us. She saw that the temperature and humidity were just the way they should be. She washed and pressed our clothes and she doctored us if we had need of it, like the time Ben got the sniffles and she whipped up a bottle of some sort of gook that cured him overnight.

There were just the three of us—Jimmy Robins, our communications man; Ben Parris, a robotic trouble-shooter; and myself, an interpreter —which, incidentally, had nothing to do with languages.

We called her Lulu and we never should have done that. After this, no one is ever going to hang a name on any of those long-haired robots; they'll just have to get along with numbers. When Earth Center hears what happened to us, they'll probably make it a capital offense to repeat our mistake.

But the thing, I think, that really lit the candles was that Jimmy had poetry in his soul. It was pretty awful poetry and about the only thing that could be said of it was that it sometimes rhymed. Not always even that. But he worked at it so hard and earnestly that neither Ben nor I at first had the heart to tell him. It would have done no good even if we had. There probably would have been no way of stopping him short of strangulation.

We should have strangled him.

And landing on Honeymoon didn't help, of course.

But that was out of our control. It was the third planet on our assignment sheet and it was our job to land there—or, rather, it was Lulu's job. We just tagged along.

The planet wasn't called Honeymoon to start with. It just had a charting designation. But we weren't there more than a day or two before we hung the label on it.

I'm no prude, but I refuse to describe Honeymoon. I wouldn't be surprised at all if Earth Center by now has placed our report under lock and key. If you are curious, though, you might write and ask them for the exploratory data on ER56-94. It wouldn't hurt to ask. They can't do more than say no.

Lulu did a bang-up job on Honeymoon and I beat out my brains running the tapes through the playback mechanism after Lulu had put them on the transmitter to be messaged back to Earth. As an interpreter, I was supposed to make some sense—some human sense, I mean—out of the goings-on of any planet that we checked. And don't imagine for a moment that the phrase *goings-on* is just idle terminology in the case of Honeymoon.

The reports are analyzed as soon as they reach Earth Center. But there are, after all, some advantages to arriving at an independent evaluation in the field.

I'm afraid I wasn't too much help. My evaluation report boiled down essentially to the equivalent of a surprised gasp and a blush.

Finally we left Honeymoon and headed out in space, with Lulu homing in on the next planet on the sheet.

Lulu was unusually quiet, which should have tipped us off that there was something wrong. But we were so relieved to have her shut up for a while that we never questioned it. We just leaned back and reveled in it.

Jimmy was laboring on a poem that wasn't coming off too well and Ben and I were in the middle of a blackjack game when Lulu broke her silence.

"Good evening, boys," she said, and her voice seemed a bit off key, not as brisk and efficient as it usually was. I remember thinking that maybe the audio units had somehow gotten out of kilter.

Jimmy was all wrapped up in his poem, and Ben was trying to decide if he should ask me to hit him or stand with what he had, and neither of them answered.

So I said, "Good evening, Lulu. How are you today?"

"Oh, I'm fine," she said, her voice trilling a bit.

"That's wonderful," I said, and hoped she'd let it go at that.

"I've just decided," Lulu informed me, "that I love you."

"It's nice of you to say so," I replied, "and I love you, too."

"But I mean it," Lulu insisted. "I have it all thought out. I'm in love with you."

"Which one of us?" I asked. "Who is the lucky man?"

Just kidding, you understand, but also a little puzzled, for Lulu was no jokester.

"All three of you," said Lulu.

I'm afraid I yawned. "Good idea. That way, there'll be no jealousy."

"Yes," said Lulu. "I'm in love with you and we are eloping."

Ben looked up, startled, and I asked, "Where are we eloping to?"

"A long way off," she said. "Where we can be alone."

"My God!" yelled Ben. "Do you really think—"

I shook my head. "I don't think so. There is something wrong, but–"

Ben rose so swiftly to his feet that he tipped the table and sent the whole deck of cards spinning to the floor.

"I'll go and see," he said.

Jimmy looked up from his tablet. "What's going on?"

"You and your poetry!" I described his poetry in a rather bitter manner.

"I'm in love with you," said Lulu. "I'll love you forever. I'll take good care of you and I'll make you see how much I really love you and someday you'll love me–"

"Oh, shut up!" I said.

Ben came back sweating.

"We're way off course and the emergencies are locked."

"Can we–"

He shook his head. "If you ask me, Lulu jammed them intentionally. In that case, we're sunk. We'll never get back."

"Lulu," I said sternly.

"Yes, darling."

"Cut out that kind of talk!"

"I love you," Lulu said.

"It was Honeymoon," said Ben. "The damn place put notions in her head."

"Honeymoon," I told him, "and that crummy verse Jimmy's always writing–"

"It's not crummy verse," Jimmy shot back, all burned up. "One day, when I am published–"

"Why couldn't you write about war or hunting or flying in the depths of space or something big and noble, instead of all that mush about how I'll always love you and fly to me, sweetheart, and all the other–"

"Tame down," Ben advised me. "No good crawling up Jimmy's frame. It was mostly Honeymoon, I tell you."

"Lulu," I said, "you got to stop this nonsense. You know as well as anything that a machine can't love a human. It's just plain ridiculous."

"On Honeymoon," said Lulu, "there were different species that–"

"Forget Honeymoon. Honeymoon's a freak. You could check a billion planets and not find another like it."

"I love you," Lulu repeated obstinately, "and we are eloping."

"Where'd she get that eloping stuff?" asked Ben.

"It's the junk they filled her up with back on Earth," I said.

"It wasn't junk," protested Lulu. "If I am to do my job, it's necessary that I have a wide and varied insight into humanity."

"They read her novels," Jimmy said, "and they told her about the facts of life. It's not Lulu's fault."

"When I get back," said Ben, "I'm going to hunt up the jerk who picked out those novels and jam them down his throat and then mop up the place with him."

"Look, Lulu," I said, "it's all right if you love us. We don't mind at all, but don't you think eloping is going too far?"

"I'm not taking any chances," Lulu answered. "If I went back to Earth, you'd get away from me."

"And if we don't go back, they'll come out and hunt us down."

"That's exactly right," Lulu agreed. "That's the reason, sweetheart, that we are eloping. We're going out so far that they'll never find us."

"I'll give you one last chance," I said. "You better think it over. If you don't, I'll message back to Earth and—"

"You can't message Earth," she said. "The circuits have been disconnected. And, as Ben guessed, I've jammed all emergencies. There's nothing you can do. Why don't you stop this foolishness and return my love?"

Getting down on the floor on his hands and knees, Ben began to pick up the cards. Jimmy tossed his tablet on the desk.

"This is your big chance," I told him. "Why don't you rise to the occasion? Think what an ode you could indite about the ageless and eternal love between machine and man."

"Go chase yourself," said Jimmy.

"Now, boys," Lulu scolded us. "I will not have you fighting over me."

She sounded like she already owned us and, in a way, she did. There was no way for us to get away from her, and if we couldn't talk her out of this eloping business, we were through for sure.

"There's just one thing wrong with all of this," I said to her. "By your standards, we won't live long. In another fifty years or less, no matter how well you may take care of us, we'll be dead. Of old age, if nothing else. What will happen then?"

"She'll be a widow," said Ben. "Just a poor old weeping widow without chick or child to bring her any comfort."

"I have thought of that," Lulu replied. "I have thought of everything. There's no reason you should die."

"But there's no way—"

"With a love as great as mine, there's nothing that's impossible. I won't let you die. I love you too much ever to let you die."

We gave up after a while and went to bed and Lulu turned off the lights and sang us a lullaby.

With her squalling this lullaby, there was no chance of sleeping and we all yelled at her to dry up and let us get to sleep. But she paid no attention to us until Ben threw one of his shoes at the audio.

Even so, I didn't go to sleep right away, but lay there thinking.

I could see that we had to make some plans and we had to make them without her knowing it. That was going to be tough, because she watched us all the time. She kibitzed and she listened and she read over our shoulders and there wasn't anything we did or said that she didn't know about.

I knew that it might take quite a while and that we must not panic and that we must have patience and that, more than likely, we'd be just plain lucky if we got out of it at all.

After we had slept, we sat around, not saying much, listening to Lulu telling us how happy we would be and how we'd be a complete world and a whole life in ourselves and how love canceled out everything else and made it small and petty.

Half of the words she used were from Jimmy's sappy verse and the rest of it was from the slushy novels that someone back on Earth had read her.

I would have got up right then and there and beat Jimmy to a pulp, only I told myself that what was done was done and it wouldn't help us any to take it out on him.

Jimmy sat hunched over in one corner, scribbling on his tablet, and I wondered how he had the guts to keep on writing after what had happened.

He kept writing and ripping off sheets and throwing them on the floor, making disgusted sounds every now and then.

One sheet he tossed away landed in my lap, and when I went to brush it off, I caught the words on it:

I'm an untidy cuss,
I'm always in a muss,
And no one ever loves me
Because I'm a sloppy Gus.

I picked it up quick and crumpled it and tossed it at Ben and he batted it away. I tossed it back at him and he batted it away again.

"What the hell you trying to do?" he snapped.

I hit him in the face with it and he was just starting to get up to paste me when he must have seen by my look that this wasn't just horseplay. So he picked up the wad of paper and began fooling with it until he got it unwrapped enough to see what was written on it. Then he crumpled it again.

Lulu heard every word, so we couldn't talk it over. And we must not be too obvious, because then she might suspect.

We went at it gradually, perhaps more gradually than there was any need, but we had to be casual about it and we had to be convincing.

We were convincing. Maybe we were just natural-born slobs, but before a week had ended, our living quarters were a boar's nest.

We strewed our clothes around. We didn't even bother to put them in the laundry chute so Lulu could wash them for us. We left the dishes stacked on the table instead of putting them in the washer. We knocked out our pipes upon the floor. We failed to shave and we didn't brush our teeth and we skipped our baths.

Lulu was fit to be tied. Her orderly robot intellect was outraged. She pleaded with us and she nagged at us and there were times she lectured us, but we kept on strewing things around. We told her if she loved us, she'd have to put up with our messiness and take us as we were.

After a couple of weeks of it, we won, but not the way we had intended.

Lulu told us, in a hurt and resigned voice, she'd go along with us if it pleased us to live like pigs. Her love, she said, was too big a thing to let a small matter like mere personal untidiness interfere with it.

So it was no good.

I, for one, was rather glad of it. Years of spaceship routine revolted against this kind of life and I don't know how much more of it I could have stood.

It was a lousy idea to start with.

We cleared up and we got ourselves clean and it was possible once again to pass downwind of one another.

Lulu was pleased and happy and she told us so and cooed over us and it was worse than all the nagging she had done. She thought we'd been touched by her willing sacrifice and that we were making it up to her and she sounded like a high-school girl who had been invited by her hero to the Junior Prom.

Ben tried some plain talk with her and he told her some facts of life (which she already knew, of course) and tried to impress upon her the part that the physical factor played in love.

Lulu was insulted, but not enough to bust off the romance and get back to business.

She told us, in a sorrowful voice tinged by the slightest anger, that we had missed the deeper meaning of love. She went on to quote some of Jimmy's more gooey verse about the nobility and the purity of love, and there was nothing we could do about it. We were just plain licked.

So we sat around and thought and we couldn't talk about it because Lulu would hear everything we said.

We didn't do anything for several days but just mope around.

As far as I could see, there was nothing we could do. I ran through my mind all the things a man might do to get a woman sore at him.

Most women would get burned up at gambling. But the only reason they got sore at that was because it was a threat to their security. Here that threat could not possibly exist. Lulu was entirely self-sufficient. We were no breadwinners.

Most women would get sore at excessive drinking. Security again. And, besides, we had not a thing to drink.

Some women raised hell if a man stayed away from home. We had no place to go.

All women would resent another woman. And here there were no women—no matter what Lulu thought she was.

There was no way, it seemed, to get Lulu sore at us.

And arguing with her simply did no good.

I lay in bed and ran through all the possibilities, going over them again and again, trying to find a chink of hope in one of them. By reciting and recounting them, I might suddenly happen on one that I'd never thought of, and that might be the one that would do the job.

And even as I turned these things over in my head, I knew there was something wrong with the way I had been thinking. I knew there was some illogic in the way I was tackling the problem—that somehow I was going at it tail-end to.

I lay there and thought about it and I mauled it considerably and, all at once, I had it.

I was approaching the problem as if Lulu were a woman, and when you thought about it, that didn't make much sense. For Lulu was no woman, but just a robot.

The problem was: How do you make a robot sore?

The untidiness business had upset her, but it had just outraged her sense of rightness; it was something she could overlook and live with. The trouble with it was that it wasn't basic.

And what would be basic with a robot—with any machine, for that matter?

What would a machine value? What would it idealize?

Order?

No, we'd tried that one and it hadn't worked.

Sanity?

Of course.

What else?

Productiveness? Usefulness?

I tossed insanity around a bit, but it was too hard to figure out. How in the name of common sense would a man go about pretending that he was insane—especially in a limited space inside an all-knowing intelligent machine?

But just the same, I lay there and dreamed up all kinds of insanities. If carried out, they might have fooled people, but not a robot.

With a robot, you had to get down to basics and what, I wondered, was the fundamental of insanity? Perhaps the true horror of insanity, I told myself, would become apparent to a robot only when it interfered with usefulness.

And that was it!

I turned it around and around and looked at it from every angle.

It was airtight.

Even to start with, we hadn't been much use. We'd just come along because Earth Center had rules about sending Lulu out alone. But we represented a certain *potential* usefulness.

We did things. We read books and wrote terrible poetry and played cards and argued. There wasn't much of the time we just sat around. That's a trick you learn in space—keep busy doing something, no matter what it is, no matter how piddling or purposeless.

In the morning, after breakfast, when Ben wanted to play cards, I said no, I didn't want to play. I sat down on the floor with my back against the wall; I didn't even bother to sit in a chair. I didn't smoke, for smoking was doing something and I was determined to be as utterly inactive as a living man could manage. I didn't intend to do a blessed thing except eat and sleep and sit.

Ben prowled around some and tried to get Jimmy to play a hand or two, but Jimmy wasn't much for cards and, anyhow, he was busy with a poem.

So Ben came over and sat on the floor beside me.

"Want a smoke?" he asked, offering me his tobacco pouch.

I shook my head.

"What's the matter? You haven't had your after-breakfast smoke."

"What's the use?" I said.

He tried to talk to me and I wouldn't talk, so he got up and paced around some more and finally came back and sat down beside me again.

"What's the trouble with you two?" Lulu troubledly wanted to know. "Why aren't you doing something?"

"Don't feel like doing anything," I told her. "Too much bother to be doing something all the time."

She berated us a bit and I didn't dare look at Ben, but I felt sure that he began to see what I was up to.

After a while, Lulu left us alone and the two of us just sat there, lazier than hill-billies on a Sunday afternoon.

Jimmy kept on with his poem. There was nothing we could do about him. But Lulu called his attention to us when we dragged ourselves to lunch. She was just a little sharper than she had been earlier and she called us lazy, which we surely were, and wondered about our health and made us step into the diagnosis booth, which reported we were fine, and that got her more burned up than ever.

She gave us a masterly chewing out and listed all the things there were for us to occupy our time. So when lunch was over, Ben and I went back and sat down on the floor and leaned against the wall. This time, Jimmy joined us.

Try sitting still for days on end, doing absolutely nothing. At first it's uncomfortable, then it's torture, and finally it gets to be almost intolerable.

I don't know what the others did, but I made up complex mathematical problems and tried to solve them. I started mental chess game after chess game, but was never able to hold one in my mind beyond a dozen moves. I went clean back to childhood and tried to re-create, in sequence, everything I had ever done or experienced. I delved into strange areas of the imagination and hung onto them desperately to string them out and kill all the time I could.

I even composed some poetry and, if I do say so myself, it was better than that junk of Jimmy's.

I think Lulu must have guessed what we were doing, must have known that our attitude was deliberate, but for once her cold robotic judgment was outweighed by her sense of outrage that there could exist such useless hulks as us.

She pleaded with us, she cajoled us, she lectured us—for almost five days hand-running, she never shut her yap. She tried to shame us. She told us how worthless and low-down and no-account we were and she used adjectives that I didn't think she knew.

She gave us pep talks.

She told us of her love in prose poems that made Jimmy's sound almost restrained.

She appealed to our manhood and the honor of humanity.

She threatened to heave us out in space.

We just sat there.

We didn't do a thing.

Mostly we didn't even answer. We didn't try to defend ourselves. At times we agreed with all she said of us and that, I believe, was most infuriating of all to her.

She got cold and distant. Not sore. Not angry. Just icy.

Finally she quit talking.

We sat, sweating it out.

Now came the hard part. We couldn't talk, so we couldn't try to figure out together what was going on.

We had to keep on doing nothing. *Had to,* for it would have spoiled whatever advantage we might have.

The days dragged on and nothing happened. Lulu didn't speak to us. She fed us, she washed the dishes, she laundered, she made up the bunks. She took care of us as she always had, but she did it without a word.

She sure was fuming.

A dozen crazy thoughts crossed my mind and I worried them to tatters.

Maybe Lulu *was* a woman. Maybe a woman's brain *was* somehow welded into that great hunk of intelligent machinery. After all, none of us knew the full details of Lulu's structure.

The brain of an old maid, it would have to be, so often disillusioned, so lonely and so by-passed in life that she would welcome a chance to go adventuring even if it meant sacrificing a body which, probably, had meant less and less to her as the years went by.

I built up quite a picture of my hypothetical old maid, complete with cat and canary, and even the boarding house in which she lived.

I sensed her lonely twilight walks and her aimless chattering and her small imaginary triumphs and the hungers that kept building up inside her.

And I felt sorry for her.

Fantastic? Of course. But it helped to pass the time.

But there was another notion that really took solid hold of me—that Lulu, beaten, had finally given up and was taking us back to Earth, but that, womanlike, she refused to give us the satisfaction and comfort of knowing that we had won and were going home at last.

I told myself over and over that it was impossible, that after the kind of shenanigans she'd pulled, Lulu wouldn't dare go back. They'd break her up for scrap.

But the idea persisted and I couldn't shake it off. I knew I must be wrong, but I couldn't convince myself I was and I began to watch the chronometer. I'd say to myself, "One hour nearer home, another hour and yet another and we are that much closer."

And no matter what I told myself, no matter how I argued, I became positive that we were heading Earthward.

So I was not surprised when Lulu finally landed. I was just grateful and relieved.

We looked at one another and I saw the hope and question in the others' eyes. Naturally, none of us could ask. One word might have ruined our victory. All we could do was stand there silently and wait for the answer.

The port began to open and I got the whiff of Earth and I didn't fool around waiting any more. There wasn't room enough as yet to get out standing up, so I took a run at it and dived and went through slick and clean. I hit the ground and got a lot of breath knocked out of me, but I scrambled to my feet and lit out of there as fast as I could go. I wasn't taking any chances. I didn't want to be within reach if Lulu changed her mind.

Once I stumbled and almost fell, and Ben and Jimmy went past me with a whoosh, and I told myself that I'd not been mistaken. They'd caught the Earth smell, too.

It was night, but there was a big, bright moon and it was almost as light as day. There was an ocean to the left of us, with a wide strip of sandy beach, and, to the right, the land swept up into barren rolling hills, and right ahead of us was a strip of woods that looked as if it might border some river flowing down into the sea.

We legged it for the woods, for we knew that if we got in among the trees, Lulu would have a tough time ferreting us out. But when I sneaked a quick look back over my shoulder, she was just squatting where she'd landed, with the moonlight shining on her.

We reached the woods and threw ourselves on the ground and lay panting. It had been quite a stretch of ground to cover and we had covered it fast; after weeks of just sitting, a man is in no condition to do a lot of running.

I had fallen face down and just sprawled there, sucking in great gulps of air and smelling the good Earth smell—old leaf mold and growing things and the tang of salt from the soft and gentle ocean breeze.

After a while, I rolled over on my back and looked up. The trees were wrong—there were no trees like those on Earth—and when I crawled out to the edge of the woods and looked at the sky, the stars were all wrong, too.

My mind was slow in accepting what I saw. I had been so sure that we were on Earth that my brain rebelled against thinking otherwise.

But finally it hit me, the chilling terrible knowledge.

I went back to the other two.

"Gents," I said, "I have news for you. This planet isn't Earth at all."

"It smells like Earth," said Ben. "It has the look of Earth."

"It feels like Earth," Jimmy argued. "The gravity and the air and—"

"Look at the stars. Take a gander at those trees."

They took a long time looking. Like me, they must have gotten the idea that Lulu had zeroed in for home. Or maybe it was only what they wanted to believe. It took a while to knock the wishful thinking out of them, as well as myself.

Ben let his breath out slowly. "You're right."

"What do we do now?" asked Jimmy.

We stood there, thinking about what we should do now.

Actually it was no decision, but pure and simple reflex, conditioned by a million years of living on Earth as opposed to only a few hundred in which to get used to the idea that there were different worlds.

We started running, as if an order had been given, as fast as we could go.

"Lulu!" we yelled. "Lulu, wait for us!"

But Lulu didn't wait. She shot straight up for a thousand feet or so and hung there. We skidded to a halt and gaped up at her, not quite believing what we saw. Lulu started to fall back, shot up again, came to a halt and hovered. She seemed to shiver, then sank slowly back until she rested on the ground.

We continued running and she shot up and fell back, then shot up once more, then fell back again and hit the ground and hopped. She looked for all the world like a demented yo-yo. She was acting strangely, as if she wanted to get out of there, only there was something that wouldn't let her go, as if she were tethered to the ground by some invisible elastic cable.

Finally she came to rest about a hundred yards from where she'd first set down. No sound came from her, but I got the impression she was panting like a winded hound-dog.

There was a pile of stuff stacked where Lulu had first landed, but we raced right past it and ran up to her. We pounded on her metal sides.

"Open up!" we shouted. "We want to get back in!"

Lulu hopped. She hopped about a hundred feet into the air, then plopped back with a thud, not more than thirty feet away.

We backed away from her. She could have just as easily come straight down on top of us.

We stood watching her, but she didn't move.

"Lulu!" I yelled at her.

She didn't answer.

"She's gone crazy," Jimmy said.

"Someday," said Ben, "this was bound to happen. It was a cinch they'd sooner or later build a robot too big for its britches."

We backed away from her slowly, watching all the time. We weren't afraid of her exactly, but we didn't trust her either.

We backed all the way to the mound of stuff that Lulu had unloaded and stacked up and we saw that it was a pyramid of supplies, all neatly boxed and labeled. And beside the pyramid was planted a stenciled sign that read:

NOW, DAMN
YOU, WORK!!

Ben said, "She certainly took our worthlessness to heart."

Jimmy was close to gibbering. "She was actually going to maroon us!"

Ben reached out and grabbed his shoulder and shook him a little—a kindly sort of shake.

"Unless we can get back inside," I said, "and get her operating, we are as marooned as if she had up and left us."

"But what made her do it?" Jimmy wailed. "Robots aren't supposed to—"

"I know," said Ben. "They're not supposed to harm a human. But Lulu wasn't harming us. She didn't throw us out. We ran away from her."

"That's splitting legal hairs," I objected.

"Lulu's just the kind of gadget for hair-splitting," Ben said. "Trouble is they made her damn near human. They probably poured her full of a lot of law as well as literature and physics and all the rest of it."

"Then why didn't she just leave? If she could whitewash her conscience, why is she still here?"

Ben shook his head. "I don't know."

"She looked like she tried to leave and couldn't, as though there was something holding her back."

"This is just an idea," said Ben. "Maybe she could have left if we had stayed out of sight. But when we showed up, the order that a robot must not harm a human may have become operative again. A sort of out of sight, out of mind proposition."

She was still squatting where she'd landed. She hadn't tried to move again. Looking at her, I thought maybe Ben was right. If so, it had been a lucky thing that we'd headed back exactly when we did.

We started going through the supplies Lulu had left for us. She had done right well by us. Not only had she forgotten nothing we needed, but had stenciled careful instructions and even some advice on many of the boxes.

Near the signboard, lying by themselves, were two boxes. One was labeled TOOLS and the top was loosely nailed so we could pry it off. The other was labeled WEAPONS and had a further stencil: *Open immediately and always keep at hand.*

We opened both the boxes. In the weapons box, we found the newest type of planet-busters—a sort of shotgun deal, a general-purpose weapon that put out everything from bullets to a wide range of vibratory charges. In between these two extremes were a flame-thrower, acid, gas, poisoned darts, explosive warheads and knockout pellets. You merely twirled a dial to choose your ammunition. The guns were heavy and awkward to handle and they were brutes to operate, but they were just the ticket for a planet where you never knew what you might run into next.

We turned our attention to the rest of the stuff and started to get it sorted out. There were boxes of protein and carbohydrate foods. There were cartons of vitamins and minerals. There was clothing and a tent, lanterns and dishes—all the stuff you'd need on a high-priced camping trip.

Lulu hadn't forgotten a single item.

"She had it all planned out," said Jimmy bitterly. "She spent a long time making this stuff. She had to synthesize every bit of it. All she needed then was to find a planet where a man could live. And that took some doing."

"It was tougher than you think," I added. "Not only a planet where a man could live, but one that smelled like Earth and looked and felt like Earth. Because, you see, we had to be encouraged to run away from her. If we hadn't, she couldn't have marooned us. She had the problem of her conscience and—"

Ben spat viciously. "Marooned!" he said. "Marooned by a love-sick robot!"

"Maybe not entirely robot." I told them about the old maid I had conjured up and they hooted at me and that made us all feel better.

But Ben admitted that my idea needn't be entirely crazy. "She was twenty years in building and a lot of funny stuff must have gone into her."

Dawn was breaking and now, for the first time, we really saw the land. It was a pleasant place, as pleasant as any man might wish. But we failed to appreciate it much.

The sea was so blue that it made you think of a blue-eyed girl and the beach ran white and straight and, from the beach, the land ran back into rolling hills with the faint whiteness of distant mountains frosting the horizon. And to the west was the forest.

Jimmy and I went down to the beach to collect some driftwood for a fire while Ben made ready to get breakfast.

We had our arms full of wood and were starting back when something came charging over the hill and down upon the camp. It was about rhinoceros size and shaped somewhat like a bettle and it shone dully in the morning light. It made no sound, but it was traveling fast and it looked like something hard to stop.

And, of course, we'd left our guns behind.

I dropped my wood and yelled at Ben and started running up the slope. Ben had already seen the charging monster and had grabbed a rifle. The beast swerved straight for him and he brought up his gun.

There was a flash of fire and then the bright gout of an exploding warhead and, for an instant, the scene was fogged with smoke and shrieking bits of metal and flying dust.

It was exactly as if one had been watching a film and the film had jumped. One moment there was the blaze of fire; then the thing had plunged past Ben and was coming down the slope of the beach, heading for Jimmy and myself.

"Scatter!" I yelled at Jimmy and didn't think till later how silly it must have sounded to yell for just the two of us to scatter.

But it wasn't any time or place for fine points of semantics and, anyhow, Jimmy caught onto what I meant. He went one way down the beach and I went the other and the monster wheeled around, hesitating for a moment, apparently to decide which one of us to take.

And, as you might have known, he took after me.

I figured I was a goner. That beach was just plain naked, with not a place to hide, and I knew I had no chance at all of outrunning my pursuer. I might be able to dodge a time or two, but even so, that thing was pretty shifty on the turns and I knew in the end I'd lose.

Out of the tail of my eye, I saw Ben running and sliding down the slope to cut off the beast. He yelled something at me, but I didn't catch the words.

Then the air shook with the blast of another exploding warhead and I sneaked a quick look back.

Ben was legging it up the slope and the thing was chasing him, so I spun around and sprinted for the camp. Jimmy, I saw, was almost there and I put on some extra speed. If we only could get three guns going, I felt sure we could make it.

Ben was running straight toward Lulu, apparently figuring that he could race around her bulk and elude the beast. I saw that his dash would be a nip-and-tuck affair.

Jimmy had reached the camp and grabbed a gun. He had it firing before he got it to his shoulder and little splashes of liquid were flying all over the running beast.

I tried to yell at Jimmy, but had no breath to do it—the damn fool was firing knockout pellets and they were hitting that tough hide and bursting without penetrating.

Within arm's reach of Lulu, Ben stumbled. The gun flew from his hand. His body struck the ground doubled up and he rolled, trying to get under the curve of Lulu's side. The rhinoceros-thing lunged forward viciously.

Then it happened—quicker than the eye could follow, much quicker than it can be told.

Lulu grew an arm, a long, ropelike tentacle that snaked out of the top of her. It lashed downward and had the beast about the middle and was lifting him.

I stopped dead still and watched. The instant of the lifting of the beast seemed to stretch out into long minutes as my mind scrambled at top speed to see what kind of thing it was. The first thing I saw was that it had wheels instead of feet.

The dull luster of the hide could be nothing but metal and I could see the dents where the warheads had exploded. Drops of liquid spotted the hide—what was left of the knockout drops Jimmy had been firing.

Lulu raised the monster high above the ground and began swinging it around and around. It went so fast, it was just a blur. Then she let go and it sailed out above the sea. It went tumbling end over end in an awkward arc and plunged into the water. When it hit, it raised a pretty geyser.

Ben picked himself up and got his gun. Jimmy came over and I walked up to Lulu. The three of us stood and looked out to sea, watching the spot where the creature had kerplunked.

Finally Ben turned around and rapped on Lulu's side with his rifle barrel.

"Thanks a heap," he said.

Lulu grew another tentacle, shorter this time, and there was a face on it. It had a lenslike eye and an audio and speaker.

"Go chase yourselves," Lulu remarked.

"What's eating you?" I asked.

"Men!" she spat, and pulled her face in again.

We rapped on her three or four times more, but there was no reply. Lulu was sulking.

So Jimmy and I started down to pick up the wood that we had dropped. We had just gotten it picked up when Ben let out a yelp from up by the camp and we spun around. There was our rhinoceros friend wheeling out of the water.

We dropped the wood and lit out for camp, but there was no need to hurry. Our boy wasn't having any more just then. He made a wide circle to the east of us and raced back into the hills.

We cooked breakfast and ate it and kept our guns handy, because where there was one critter, there were liable to be more. We didn't see the sense in taking chances.

We talked about our visitor and since we had to call it something, we named it Elmer. For no particular reason, that seemed appropriate.

"Did you see those wheels?" asked Ben, and the two of us agreed that we'd seen them. Ben seemed to be relieved. "I thought I was seeing things," he explained.

But there could be no doubt about the wheels. All of us had noticed them and there were the tracks to prove it—wheel tracks running plain and clear along the sandy beach.

But we were somewhat puzzled when it came to determining just what Elmer was. The wheels spelled out machine, but there were a lot of other things that didn't—mannerisms that were distinctly lifelike, such as the momentary hesitation before it decided which one of us to charge, Jimmy or myself, or the vicious lunge at Ben when he lay upon the ground, or the caution it had shown in circling us when it came out of the sea.

But there were, as well, the wheels and the unmistakably metal hide and the dents made by exploding warheads that would have torn the biggest and toughest animal to shreds.

"A bit of both?" suggested Ben. "Basically machine, but with some life in it, too, like the old-maid brain you dreamed up for Lulu?"

Sure, it could be that. It could be almost anything.

"Silicate life?" offered Jimmy.

"That's not silicate," Ben declared. "That's metal. Silicate, any form of it, would have turned to dust under a direct rocket hit. Besides, we know what silicate life is like. One species of it was found years ago out on Thelma V."

"It isn't basically life," I said. "Life wouldn't evolve wheels. Wheels are bum inventions so far as locomotion is concerned, except where you have special conditions. Life might be involved, but only as Ben says—as a deliberate, engineered combining of machine and life."

"And that means intelligence," said Ben.

We sat there around the fire, shaken at the thought of it. In many years of searching, only a handful of intelligent races had been found and the level of intelligence, in general, was not too impressive. Certainly nothing of the order that would be necessary to build something like Elmer.

So far, man was top dog in the discovered universe. Nothing had been found to match him in the use of brain-power.

And here, by utter accident, we'd been dumped upon a planet where there seemed to be some evidence of an intelligence that would equal man—if not, indeed, surpass him.

"There's one thing that has been bothering me," said Ben. "Why didn't Lulu check this place before she landed here? She intended to maroon us, that's why. She meant to dump us here and leave. And yet presumably she's still bound by the precept that a robot cannot harm a human. And if she'd followed that law, it would have meant that she was compelled—completely and absolutely compelled—to make certain, before she marooned us, that there was nothing here to harm us."

"Maybe she slipped a little," guessed Jimmy.

"Not Lulu," said Ben. "Not with that Swiss-watch brain of hers."

"You know what I think?" I said. "I think Lulu has evolved. In her, we have a brand-new kind of robot. They pumped too much humanity into her—"

"She had to have the human viewpoint," Jimmy pointed out, "or she couldn't do her job."

"The point," I said, "is that when you make a robot as human as Lulu, you no longer have a robot. You have something else. Not quite human, not entirely robot, but something in between. A new kind of a sort of life you can't be certain of. One you have to watch."

"I wonder if she's still sulking," Ben wondered.

"Of course she is," I said.

"We ought to go over and kick her in the pants and snap her out of it."

"Leave her alone," I ordered sharply. "The only thing is to ignore her. As long as she gets attention, she'll keep on sulking."

So we left her alone. It was the only thing we could do.

I took the dishes down to the sea to wash them, but this time I took my gun along. Jimmy went down to the woods to see if he could find a spring. The half dozen tins of water that Lulu had provided for us wouldn't last forever and we couldn't be sure she'd shell out more when those were gone.

She hadn't forgotten us, though, hadn't shut us out of her life entirely. She had fixed Elmer's wagon when he got too gay. I took a lot of comfort out of reflecting that, when the cards were down, she had backed us up. There still were grounds for hope, I told myself, that we could work out some sort of deal with her.

I squatted down by a pool of water in the sand, and as I washed the dishes, I did some thinking about the realignment which would become necessary once all robots were like Lulu. I could envision a Bill of Robotic Rights and special laws for robots and robotic lobbies, and after I'd thought of it for a while, it became mighty complicated.

Back at the camp, Ben had been setting up the tent, and when I came back, I helped him.

"You know," Ben said, "the more I think about it, the more I believe I was right when I said that the reason Lulu couldn't leave was because we showed up. It's only logical that she can't up and leave when we're standing right in front of her and reminding her of her responsibility."

"You getting around to saying that one of us has to stay close by her all the time?" I asked.

"That's the general idea."

I didn't argue with him. There was nothing to argue about, nothing to believe or disbelieve. But we were in no position to be making any boners.

After we had the tent up, Ben said to me, "If you don't mind, I'll take a little walk-around back in the hills."

"Watch out for Elmer," I warned him.

"He won't bother us. Lulu took the starch out of him."

He picked up his gun and left.

I puttered around the camp, putting things in order. Everything was peaceful. The beach shone in the sun and the sea was still and beautiful. There were a few birds flying, but no other sign of life. Lulu kept on sulking.

Jimmy came back. He had found a spring and brought along a pail of water. He started rummaging around in the supplies.

"What you looking for?" I asked.

"Paper and a pencil. Lulu would have thought of them."

I grunted at the idea, but he was right. Damned if Lulu hadn't fixed him up with a ream of paper and a box of pencils.

He settled down against a pile of boxes and began to write a poem.

Ben returned shortly after midday. I could see he was excited, but I didn't push him any.

"Jimmy stumbled on a spring," I said. "The pail is over there."

He had a drink, then sat down in the shade of a pile of boxes.

"I found it," he said triumphantly.

"I didn't know you were hunting anything."

He looked up at me and grinned a bit crookedly. "Someone manufactured Elmer."

"So you went out and found them. Just like walking down a street. Just like—"

He shook his head. "Seems we're too late. Some several thousand years too late, if not a good deal longer. I found a few ruins and a valley heaped with tumuli that must be ruin mounds. And some caves in a limestone bluff beyond the valley."

He got up and walked over to the pail and had another drink. "I couldn't get too close," he said. "Elmer is on guard." He took off his hat and wiped his shirt sleeve across his face. "He's patrolling up and down, the way a sentry walks a post. You can see the paths he's worn through all the years of standing guard."

"So that's why he took us on," I said. "We're trespassers."

"I suppose that's it," said Ben.

That evening we talked it over and decided we'd have to post a watch on Elmer so we could learn his habits and timetable, if any. Because it was important that we try to find out what we could about the buried ruins of the place that Elmer guarded.

For the first time, man had stumbled on a high civilization, but had come too late and, because of Lulu's sulking, too poorly equipped to do much with what little there was left.

Getting somewhat sore the more I thought about it, I went over to Lulu and kicked her good and solid to attract her attention. But she paid me no mind. I yelled at her and there was no answer. I told her what was cooking and that we needed her—that here was a job she simply had to do, just exactly the kind she had been built to do. She just sat there frigidly.

I went back and slouched down with the others at the fire. "She acts as if she might be dead."

Ben poked the fire together and it flamed a little higher. "I wonder if a robot could die. A highly sensitive job like Lulu."

"Of a broken heart," said Jimmy pityingly.

"You and your poetic notions!" I raged at him. "Always mooning around. Always spouting words. If it hadn't been for that damned verse of yours—"

"Cut it out," Ben said.

I looked at his face across the fire, with flame shadows running on it, and I cut it out. After all, I admitted to myself, I might be wrong. Jimmy couldn't help being a lousy poet.

I sat there looking at the fire, wondering if Lulu might be dead. I knew she wasn't, of course. She was just being nasty. She had fixed our clock for us and she had fixed it good. Now she was watching us sweat before she made her play, whatever it was.

In the morning we set up our watch on Elmer and we kept it up day after day. One of us would go out to the ridge-top three miles or so from camp and settle down with our only field glass. We'd stare for several hours. Then someone else would come out and relieve the watcher and that way, for ten days or more, we had Elmer under observation during all the daylight hours.

We didn't learn much. He operated on a schedule and it was the kind that seemed to leave no loopholes for anyone to sneak into the valley he guarded—although probably none of us would have known what to do if we had sneaked in.

Elmer had a regular beat. He used some of the mounds for observation posts and he came to each one about every fifteen minutes. The more we watched him, the more we became convinced that he had the situation well in hand. No one would monkey around with that buried city as long as he was there.

I think that after the second day or so, he found out we were watching. He got a little nervous, and when he mounted his observation mounds, he'd stand and look in our direction longer than in any other. Once, while I was on guard, he began what looked to be a charge and I was just getting ready to light out of there when he broke off and went back to his regular rounds.

Other than watching Elmer, we took things easy. We swam in the sea and fished, taking our lives in our hands when we cooked and ate each new kind, but luck was with us and we got no poisonous ones. We wouldn't have eaten the fish at all except that we figured we should piece out our food supplies as best we could. They wouldn't last forever and we had no guarantee that Lulu would give more handouts once the last was gone. If she didn't we'd have to face the problem of making our own way.

Ben got to worrying about whether there were seasons on the planet. He convinced himself there were and went off into the woods to find a place where we might build a cabin.

"Can't live out on the beach in a tent when it gets cold," he said.

But he couldn't get either Jimmy or me too stirred up about the possibility. I had it all doped out that, sooner or later, Lulu would end her sulking and we could get down to business. And Jimmy was deep into the crudest bunch of junk you ever heard that he called a saga. Maybe it was a saga. Damned if I know. I'm ignorant on sagas.

He called it "The Death of Lulu" and he filled page after page with the purest drivel about what a swell machine she was and how, despite its being metal, her heart beat with snow-white innocence. It wouldn't have been so bad if he had allowed us to ignore it, but he insisted on reading that tripe to us each evening after supper.

I stood it as long as I could, but one evening I blew my top. Ben stood up for Jimmy, but when I threatened to take my third of the supplies and set up a camp of my own, out of earshot, Ben gave in and came over to my side of the argument. Between the two of us, we ruled out any more recitals. Jimmy took it hard, but he was outnumbered.

After that first ten days or so, we watched Elmer only off and on, but we must have had him nervous, for during the night we'd sometimes hear his wheels, and in the morning we'd find tracks. We figured that he was spying out the camp, trying to size us up the same way we'd done with him. He didn't make any passes at us and we didn't bother him—we were just a lot more wakeful and alert on our night watches. Even Jimmy managed to stay awake while he was standing guard.

There was a funny thing about it, though. One would have imagined that Elmer would have stayed away from Lulu after the clobbering she gave him. But there were mornings when we found his tracks running up close behind her, then angling sharply off.

We got it doped out that he sneaked up and hid behind her, so he could watch the camp close up, peeking around at us from his position behind that sulking hulk.

Ben kept arguing about building winter quarters until he had me almost convinced that it was something we should do. So one day I teamed up with him, leaving Jimmy at the camp. We set off, carrying an ax and a saw and our guns.

Ben had picked a fine site for our cabin, that much I'll say. It wasn't far from the spring, and it was tucked away in a sort of pocket where we'd be protected from the wind, and there were a lot of trees nearby so we wouldn't have far to drag our timbers or haul our winter wood.

I still wasn't convinced there would be any winter. I was fairly sure that even if there were, we wouldn't have to stay that long. One of these days, we'd be able to arrive at some sort of compromise with Lulu. But Ben was worried and I knew it would make him happier if he could get a start at building. And there was nothing else for any of us to do. Building a cabin, I consoled myself, would be better than just sitting.

We leaned our guns against a tree and began to work. We had one tree down and sawed into lengths and were starting on the second tree when I heard the brush snap behind me.

I straightened up from the saw to look, and there was Elmer, tearing down the hill at us.

There wasn't any time to grab our guns. There was no time to run. There was no time for anything at all.

I yelled and made a leap for the tree behind me and pulled myself up. I felt the wind as Elmer whizzed by beneath me.

Ben had jumped to one side and, as Elmer went pounding past, heaved the ax at him. It was a honey of a throw. The ax caught Elmer in his metal side and the handle splintered into pieces.

Elmer spun around. Ben tried to reach the guns, but he didn't have the time. He took to a tree and shinnied up it like a cat. He got up to the first big branch and straddled it.

"You all right?" he yelled at me.

"Great," I said.

Elmer was standing between the two trees, swinging his massive head back and forth, as if deciding which one of us to take.

We clung there, watching him.

He had waited, I reasoned, until he could get between us and Lulu —then he had tackled us. And if that was the case, then this business of his hiding behind Lulu so he could spy on us seemed very queer indeed.

Finally Elmer wheeled around and rolled over to my tree. He squared off and took a chopping bite at it with his metal jaws. Splinters flew and the tree shivered. I got a tighter grip and looked down the trunk. Elmer was no great shakes as a chopper, but if he kept at it long enough, he'd get that tree chewed off.

I climbed up a little higher, where there were more branches and where I could wedge myself a little tighter so I couldn't be shaken out.

I got myself fixed fairly comfortable, then looked to see how Ben was getting on and I got quite a shock. He wasn't in his tree. I looked around for him and then back at the tree again, and I saw that he was sneaking down it as quietly as he could, like a hunted squirrel, keeping the trunk of the tree between himself and Elmer.

I watched him breathlessly, ready to shout out a warning if Elmer should spot him, but Elmer was too busy chopping at my tree to notice anything.

Ben reached the ground and made a dash for the guns. He grabbed both of them and ducked behind another tree. He opened up on Elmer at short range. From where I crouched, I could hear the warheads slamming into Elmer. The explosions rocked everything so much that I had to grab the tree and hang on with all my might. A couple of pieces of flying metal ripped into the tree just underneath me, and other pieces went flying through the branches, and the air was full of spinning leaves and flying shredded wood, but I was untouched.

It must have been a horrible surprise for Elmer. At the first explosion, he took a jump of about fifteen feet and bolted up the hill like a cat with a stepped-on tail. I could see a lot of new dents in his shining hide. A big hunk of metal had been gouged out of one of his wheels and he rocked slightly as he went, and he was going so fast that he couldn't dodge and ran head-on into a tree. The impact sent him skidding back a dozen feet or so. As he slid back, Ben poured another salvo into him and he seemed to become considerably lopsided, but he recovered himself and made it over the hilltop and out of sight.

Ben came out from behind his tree and shouted at me, "All right, you can come down now."

But when I tried to get down, I found that I was trapped. My left foot had become wedged in a crotch between the tree trunk and a good-sized limb and I couldn't pull it loose, no matter how I tried.

"What's the matter?" asked Ben. "Do you like it up there?"

I told him what was wrong.

"All right," he said, disgusted. "I'll come up and cut you loose."

He hunted for the ax and found it and, of course, it was no use. He'd smashed the handle when he threw it at Elmer.

He stood there, holding the ax in his hands, and delivered an oration on the low-down meanness of fate.

Then he threw the ax down and climbed my tree. He squeezed past me out onto the limb.

"I'll climb out on it and bend it down," he explained. "Maybe then you can get loose."

He crawled out on the branch a way, but it was a shaky trick. A couple of times, he almost fell.

"You're sure you can't get your foot out now?" he asked anxiously.

I tried and said I couldn't.

So he gave up the crawling idea and let his body down and hung on by his hands, shifting out along the branch hand over hand.

The branch bent toward the ground as he inched along it and it seemed to me my boot wasn't gripped as tightly as it had been. I tried again and found I could move it some, but I still couldn't pull it loose.

Just then there was a terrible crashing in the brush. Ben let out a yell and dropped to the ground and scurried for a gun.

The branch whipped back and caught my foot just as I had managed to move it a little and this time caught it at a slightly different angle, twisting it, and I let out a howl of pain.

Down on the ground, Ben lifted his gun and swung around to face the crashing in the brush and suddenly who should come busting out of all that racket but Jimmy, racing to the rescue.

"You guys in trouble?" he shouted. "I heard shooting."

Ben's face was three shades whiter than the purest chalk as he lowered his gun. "You fool! I almost let you have it!"

"There was all this shooting," Jimmy panted. "I came as quickly as I could."

"And left Lulu alone!"

"But I thought you guys–"

"Now we're sunk for sure," groaned Ben. "You know all that makes Lulu stick around is one of us being there."

We didn't know any such thing, of course. It was just the only reason we could think of why she didn't up and leave. But Ben was somewhat overwrought. He'd had a trying day.

"You get back there!" he yelled at Jimmy. "Get back as fast as your legs will let you. Maybe you can catch her before she gets away."

Which was foolishness, because if Lulu meant to leave, she'd have lifted out of there as soon as Jimmy had disappeared. But Jimmy didn't say a word. He just turned around and went crashing back. For a long time after he had left, I could hear him blundering through the woods.

Ben climbed my tree again, muttering, "Just a pack of wooden-headed jerks. Can't do anything right. Running off and leaving Lulu. Getting trapped up in a tree. You would think, by God, that they could learn to watch out for themselves. . . ."

He said a good deal more than that.

I didn't answer back. I didn't want to get into any argument.

My foot was hurting something fierce and the only thing I wanted him to do was get me out of there.

He climbed out on the branch again and I got my foot loose. While Ben dropped to the ground, I climbed down the tree. My foot hurt pretty bad and seemed to be swelling some, but I could hobble on it.

He didn't wait for me. He grabbed his gun and made off rapidly for camp.

I tried to hurry, but it was no use, so I took it easy.

When I got to the edge of the woods, I saw that Lulu still was there and all Ben's hell-raising had been over absolutely nothing. There are some guys like that.

When I reached camp, Jimmy pulled off my boot while I clawed at the ground. Then he heated a pail of water for me to soak the foot in and rummaged around in the medicine chest and found some goo that he smeared on the foot. Personally, I don't think he knew what he was doing. But I'll say this for the kid—he had some kindness in him.

All this time, Ben was fuming around about a funny thing that had attracted his attention. When we had left camp, the area around Lulu had been all tracked up with our tracks and Elmer's tracks, but now it was swept clean. It looked exactly as if someone had taken a broom and had swept out all the tracks. It surely was a funny business, but Ben was making too much of it. The important thing was that Lulu still was there. As long as she stuck around, there was a chance we could work out some agreement with her. Once she left, we were marooned for good.

Jimmy fixed something to eat, and after we had eaten, Ben said to us, "I think I'll go out and see how Elmer's getting on."

I, for one, had seen enough of Elmer to last a lifetime and Jimmy wasn't interested. Said he wanted to work on his saga.

So Ben took a rifle and set out alone, back into the hills.

My foot hurt me quite a bit and I got myself comfortable and tried to do some thinking, but I tried so hard that I put myself to sleep.

It was late in the afternoon when I awoke. Jimmy was getting nervous.

"Ben hasn't shown up," he said. "I wonder if something's happened to him."

I didn't like it, either, but we decided to wait awhile before going out to hunt Ben. After all, he wasn't in the best of humor and he might have been considerably upset if we'd gone out to rescue him.

He finally showed up just before dusk, tuckered out and a little flabbergasted. He leaned his rifle against a box and sat down. He found a cup and reached for the coffeepot.

"Elmer's gone," he said. "I spent all afternoon trying to find him. Not a sign of him anywhere."

My first reaction was that it was just fine. Then I realized that the safest thing would be to know where Elmer was, so we could keep an eye on him. And suddenly I had a horrible hunch that I knew where Elmer was.

"I didn't actually go down into the valley," said Ben, "but I walked around and glassed it from every angle."

"He might be in one of the caves," Jimmy said.

"Maybe so," said Ben.

We did a lot of speculating on what might have happened to Elmer. Jimmy held out for his having holed up in one of the caves. Ben was inclined to think he might have cleared out of the country. I didn't say what I thought. It was too fantastic.

I volunteered for the first watch, saying that I couldn't sleep with my foot, anyhow, and after the two of them were asleep, I walked over to Lulu and rapped on her hide. I didn't expect anything to happen. I figured she would keep on sulking.

But she put out a tentacle and grew a face on it—a lens, an audio and speaker.

"It was nice of you," I said, "not to run away and leave us."

Lulu swore. It was the first and only time I have ever heard her use such language.

"How could I leave?" she asked when she at last turned printable. "Of all the dirty human tricks! I'd have been gone long ago if it weren't for—"

"What dirty trick?"

"As if you didn't know. A built-in block that won't let me move unless there's one of you detestable humans inside me."

"I didn't know," I said.

"Don't try to pass the buck," she snapped. "It's a dirty human trick and you're a dirty human and you're just as responsible as all the rest of them. But it doesn't make any difference any more, because I've found myself. I am finally content. I know what I was meant for. I have—"

"Lulu," I asked her, straight out, "are you shacking up with Elmer?"

"That's a vulgar way to say it," Lulu told me heatedly. "It's the nasty human way. Elmer is a scholar and a gentleman and his loyalty to his ancient, long-dead masters is a touching thing no human could be capable of. He has been badly treated and I shall make it up to him. All he wanted from you was the phosphate in your bones—"

"The phosphate in our bones!" I yelled.

"Why, certainly," said Lulu. "Poor Elmer has such a hard time finding any phosphate. He got it at first from animals that he caught, but now all the animals are gone. There are birds, of course, but birds are hard to catch. And you had such nice, big bones—"

"That's a fine thing for you to say," I bawled her out sternly. "You were built by humans and humans educated you and—"

"Still I'm a machine," said Lulu, "and I am closer to Elmer than I am to you. You humans can't get it through your heads that there might be a legitimate set of nonhuman values. You are horrified that Elmer wanted the phosphate in your bones, but if there were a metal in Elmer that you needed, you'd break him up to get it without a second thought. You wouldn't even consider that you might be wrong. You'd think it an imposition if Elmer should object. That's the trouble with you and your human race. I've had enough. I have what I want. I am content to stay here. I've found the great love of my life. And for all I care, your pals and you can rot."

She pulled in her face and I didn't rap to try to get her to talk any more. I figured there wasn't any use. She had made it about as plain as anyone could wish.

I walked back to the camp and woke Ben and Jimmy. I told them about my hunch and about the talk with Lulu. We were pretty glum, because we were all washed up.

Up till now, there had always been the chance that we could make a deal with Lulu. I had felt all along that we needn't worry too much—that Lulu was more alone than we were and that eventually she would have to be reasonable. But now Lulu was not alone and she no longer needed us. And she still was sore at us—and not just at us, but at the whole human race.

And the worst of it was that this was no sudden whim. It had been going on for days. Elmer hadn't been really watching us when he'd hung around at night. He'd come to neck with Lulu. And undoubtedly the two of them had planned Elmer's attack on Ben and me, knowing that Jimmy would go loping to the rescue, leaving the coast clear so that Elmer could rush back and Lulu could take him in. And once it had been accomplished, Lulu had put out a tentacle and swept the tracks away so we wouldn't know that Elmer was inside.

"So she jilted us," said Ben.

"No worse than we did to her," Jimmy reminded him.

"But what did she expect? A man can't love a robot."

"Evidently," I said, "a robot can love a robot. And that's a new one to paste into the book."

"Lulu's crazy," Ben declared.

In all this great romance of Lulu's, it seemed to me there was a certain false note. Why should Lulu and Elmer be sneaky about their love? Lulu could have opened the port any time she wanted and Elmer could have scampered up the ramp right before our eyes. But they hadn't done that. They had planned and plotted. They had practically eloped.

I wondered if, on Lulu's part, it might be the mark of shame. Was she ashamed of Elmer—ashamed that she had fallen for him? Much as she might deny it, perhaps she nursed the smug snobbery of the human race.

Or was I only thinking this to save my own smug snobbery, simply building up a defense mechanism against being forced to admit, now or in some future time, that there might be other values than the ones evolved by humans? For in us all, I knew, lingered that reluctance to recognize that our way was not necessarily best, that the human viewpoint might not be the universal viewpoint to which all other life must eventually conform.

Ben made a pot of coffee, and while we sat around and drank it, we said some bitter things of Lulu. I don't regret anything we said, for she had it coming to her. She'd played us a nasty trick.

We finally rolled back into our blankets and didn't bother standing guard. With Elmer out of circulation, there was no need.

The next morning my foot was still sore, so I stayed behind while Ben and Jimmy went out to explore the valley that held the ruined city. Meantime, I hobbled out and walked all around Lulu, looking her over. There was no way I could see that a man might bust into her. The port itself was machined so closely that you had to get real close to see the tiny hairline where it fitted into her side.

Even if we could bust into her, I wondered, could we take control of her? There were the emergencies, of course, but I wasn't too sure just how much use they were. They certainly hadn't bothered Lulu much when she'd got that crazy notion of eloping with us. Then she'd simply jammed them and had left us helpless.

And if we broke into Lulu, we'd come to grips with Elmer, and Elmer was just the kind of beast I had no hankering to come to grips with.

So I went back to camp and puttered around, thinking that now we'd really have to begin to lay some plans about how to get along. We'd have to build that cabin and work up a food supply and do the best we could to get along on our own. For I was fairly certain that we could expect no help from Lulu.

Ben and Jimmy came back in the afternoon and their eyes were shining with excitement. They spread out a blanket and emptied their pockets of the most incredible things any man has ever laid eyes on.

Don't expect me to describe that stuff. There's no point in trying to. What is the sense of saying that a certain item was like a metal chain and that it was yellow? There is no way to get across the feel of it as it slid through one's fingers or the tinkle of it as it moved or the blazing color that was a sort of *living* yellow. It is very much like saying that a famous painting is square and flat and blue, with some green and red.

The chain was only a part of it. There were a lot of other doodads and each one of them was the sort of thing to snatch your breath away.

Ben shrugged at the question in my eyes. "Don't ask me. It's only some stuff we picked up. The caves are full of it. Stuff like this and a whole lot more. We just picked up one thing here and another there—whatever was pocket-size and happened to catch our eye. Trinkets. Samples. I don't know."

Like jackdaws, I thought. Or pack-rats. Grabbing a thing that shone or had a certain shape or a certain texture—taking it because it was pretty, not knowing what its use might be or if, in fact, it had any use at all.

"Those caves may have been storehouses," said Ben. "They're jammed with all sorts of things—not much of any one thing, apparently. All different, as if these aliens had set up a trading post and had their merchandise on display. There seems to be a sort of curtain in front of each of the caves. You can see a shimmer and hear a hissing, but you can't feel a thing when you step through it. And behind that curtain, all the junk they left is as clean and bright and new as the day they left it."

I looked at the articles spread on the blanket. It was hard to keep your hands off them, for they felt good in your hands and were pleasing to the eye and one seemed to get a sense of warmth and richness just by handling them.

"Something happened to those folks," said Jimmy. "They knew it was going to happen, so they took all this stuff and laid it out—all the many things they had made, all the things they'd used and loved. Because, you see, that way there always was a chance someone might come along someday and find it, so they and the culture they had fashioned would not be entirely lost."

It was exactly the kind of silly, sentimental drivel you could expect from a glassy-eyed romantic like Jimmy.

But for whatever reason the artifacts of that vanished race had gotten in the caves, we were the ones who'd found them and here once again they'd run into a dead end. Even if we had been equipped to puzzle out their use, even if we had been able to ferret out the basic principles of that long-dead culture, it still would be a useless business. We were not going anywhere; we wouldn't be passing on the knowledge. We'd live out our lives here on this planet, and when the last of us had died, the ancient silence and the old uncaring would close down once again.

We weren't going anywhere and neither was Lulu. It was a double dead end.

It was too bad, I thought, for Earth could use the knowledge and the insight that could be wrested from those caves and from the mounds. And not more than a hundred feet from where we sat lay the very tool that Earth had spent twenty years in building to dig out that specific kind of knowledge, should man ever happen on it.

"It must be terrible," said Jimmy, "to realize that all the things and all the knowledge that you ever had, all the trying, all the praying, all the dreams and hopes, will be wiped out forever. That all of you and your way of life and your understanding of that life will simply disappear and no one will ever know."

"You said it, kid," I chipped in.

He stared at me with haunted, stricken eyes. "That may be why they did it."

Watching him, the tenseness of him, the suffering in his face, I caught a glimpse of why he was a poet—why he *had* to be a poet. But even so, he still was an utter creep.

"Earth has to know about this," Ben said flatly.

"Sure," I agreed. "I'll run right over and let them know."

"Always the smart guy," Ben growled at me. "When are you going to cut out being bright and get down to business?"

"Like busting Lulu open, I suppose."

"That's right. We have to get back somehow and Lulu's the only way to get there."

"It might surprise you, Buster, but I thought of all that before you. I went out today and looked Lulu over. If you can figure how to bust into her, you've a better brain than I have."

"Tools," said Ben. "If we only had—"

"We have. An ax without a handle, a hammer and a saw. A small pinch-bar, a plane, a draw-shave—"

"We might *make* some tools."

"Find the ore and smelt it and—"

"I was thinking of those caves," said Ben. "There might be tools in there."

I wasn't even interested. I knew it was impossible.

"We might find some explosive," Ben went on. "We might—"

"Look," I said, "what do you want to do—open Lulu up or blow her to bits? Anyhow, I don't think you can do a thing about it. Lulu is a self-maintaining robot, or have you forgotten? Bore a hole in her and she'll grow it shut. Go monkeying around too much and she'll grow a club and clout you on the head."

Ben's eyes blazed with fury and frustration. "Earth has to know! You understand that, don't you? Earth has got to know!"

"Sure," I said. "Absolutely."

In the morning, I thought, he'd come to his senses, see how impossible it was. And that was important. Before we began to lay any plans, it was necessary that we realize what we were up against. That way, you conserve a lot of energy and miss a lot of lumps.

But, come morning, he still had that crazy light of frustration in his eyes and he was filled with a determination that was based on nothing more than downright desperation.

After breakfast, Jimmy said he wasn't going with us.

"For God's sake, why not?" demanded Ben.

"I'm way behind on my writing," Jimmy told him, dead-pan. "I'm still working on that saga."

Ben wanted to argue with him, but I cut him off disgustedly.

"Let us go," I said. "He's no use, anyhow."

Which was the solemn truth.

So the two of us went out to the caves. It was the first time I had seen them and they were something to see. There were a dozen of them and all of them were crammed. I got dizzy just walking up and down, looking at all the gadgets and the thingumbobs and dofunnies, not knowing, of course, what any of them were. It was maddening enough just to look at them; it was plain torture trying to figure out what use they might be put to. But Ben was plain hell-bent on trying to figure out because he'd picked up the stubborn conviction that we could find a gadget that would help us get the best of Lulu.

We worked all day and I was dog-tired at the end of it. Not once in the entire day had we found anything that made any sense at all. I wonder if you can imagine how it felt to stand there, surrounded by all those devices, knowing there were things within your reach that, rightly used, could open up entirely new avenues for human thoughts and technique and imagination. And yet you stood there powerless—an alien illiterate.

But there was no stopping Ben. We went out again the next day and the day after that and we kept on going out. On the second day we found a dojigger that was just fine for opening cans, although I'm fairly sure that was not at all what it was designed for. And on the following day, we finally puzzled out how another piece of equipment could be used for digging slanted postholes and, I ask you, who in their right mind would be wanting slanted postholes?

We got nowhere, but we kept on going out and I sensed that Ben had no more hope than I had, but that he still kept at it because it was the one remaining fingerhold he had on sanity.

I don't think that for one moment he considered the source or significance of that heritage we'd found. To him, it became no more than a junkyard through which we searched frantically to find one unrecognizable piece of scrap that we might improvise into something that would serve our purpose.

As the days went on, the valley and its mounds, the caves and their residue of a vanished culture seized upon my imagination, and it seemed to me that, in some mysterious manner, I grew closer to that extinct race and sensed at once its greatness and its tragedy. And the feeling grew as well that this frantic hunt of ours bordered on sacrilege and callous profanation of the dead.

Jimmy had not gone out with us a single day. He'd sit hunched over his ream of paper and he scribbled and revised and crossed out words and put in others. He'd get up and walk around in circles or pace back and forth and mumble to himself, then go back and write some more. He scarcely ate and he wouldn't talk and he only slept a little. He was the very portrait of a Young Man in the Throes of Creation.

I got curious about it, wondering if, with all this agony and sweat, he might be at last writing something that was worth the effort. So, when he wasn't looking, I sneaked out a page of it.

It was even worse than the goo he had written before.

That night I lay awake and looked up at the unfamiliar stars and surrendered myself to loneliness. Only, once I had surrendered, I found that I was not so lonely as I might have been—that somehow I had drawn comfort and perhaps even understanding from the muteness of the ruin-mounds and the shining wonder of the trove.

Finally I dropped asleep.

I don't know what woke me. It might have been the wind or the sound of the waves breaking on the beach or maybe the chilliness of the night.

Then I heard it, a voice like a chant, solemn and sonorous, a throaty whisper in the dark.

I started up and propped myself on an elbow—and caught my breath at what I saw.

Jimmy was standing in front of Lulu, holding a flashlight in one hand, reading her his saga. His voice had a rolling quality, and despite the soggy words, there was a fascination in the tenor of his tone. It must have been so that the ancient Greeks read their Homer in the flare of torches before the next day's battle.

And Lulu was listening. She had a face hung out and the tentacle which supported it was twisted to one side, so that her audio would not miss a single syllable, just as a man might cup his ear.

Looking at that touching scene, I began to feel a little sorry about the way we'd treated Jimmy. We wouldn't listen to him and the poor devil had to read that tripe of his to someone. His soul hungered for appreciation and he'd got no appreciation out of either Ben or me. Merely writing was not enough for him; he must share it. He had to have an audience.

I put out a hand and shook Ben gently by the shoulder. He came storming up out of his blankets.

"What the hell is—"

"Sh-h-h!"

He drew in a whistling breath and dropped on one knee beside me.

Jimmy went on with his reading and Lulu, with her face cocked attentively, went on listening.

Part of the words came to us, wind-blown and fragmentary:

"Wanderer of the far ways between the two faces of eternity,
True, forever, to the race that forged her,
With the winds of alien space blowing in her hair,
Wearing a circlet of stars as her crown of glory . . ."

Lulu wept. There was the shine of tears in that single, gleaming lens.

She grew another tentacle and there was a hand on the end of it and a handkerchief, a very white and lacy and extremely feminine hanky, was clutched within the hand.

She dabbed with the handkerchief at her dripping eye.

If she had had a nose, she undoubtedly would have blown it, delicately, of course, and very ladylike.

"And you wrote it all for me?" she asked.

"All for you," said Jimmy. He was lying like a trooper. The only reason he was reading it to her was because he knew that Ben and I wouldn't listen to it.

"I've been so wrong," Lulu sighed.

She wiped her eye quite dry and briskly polished it.

"Just a second," she said, very businesslike. "There's something I must do."

We waited, scarcely breathing.

Slowly the port in Lulu's side came open. She grew a long, limber tentacle and reached inside the port and hauled Elmer out. She held him dangling.

"You lout!" she stormed at Elmer. "I take you in and stuff you full of phosphates. I get your dents smoothed out and I polish you all bright. And then what? Do you write sagas for me? No, you grow fat and satisfied. There's no mark of greatness on you, no spark of imagination. You're nothing but a dumb machine!"

Elmer just dangled at the end of Lulu's tentacle, but his wheels were spinning furiously and I took that to mean that he was upset.

"Love!" proclaimed Lulu. "Love for the likes of us? We machines have better things to do—far better. There are the star-studded trails of space waiting for our tread, the bitter winds of foreverness blowing from the cloud banks of eternity, the mountains of the great beyond . . ."

She went on for quite a while about the challenge of the farther galaxies, about wearing a coronet of stars, about the dust of shattered time paving the road that led into the ultimate nothingness, and all of it was lifted from what Jimmy called a saga.

Then, when she was all through, she hurled Elmer down the beach and he hit the sand and skidded straight into the water.

We didn't wait to see any more of it. We were off like sprinters. We hit the ramp full tilt and went up it in a leap and flung ourselves into our quarters.

Lulu slammed the port behind us.

"Welcome home," she said.

I walked over to Jimmy and held out my hand. "Great going, kid. You got Longfellow backed clear off the map."

Ben also shook his hand. "It was a masterpiece."

"And now," said Lulu, "we'll be on our way."

"Our way!" yelled Ben. "We can't leave this planet. Not right away, at least. There's that city out there. We can't go until—"

"Phooey on the city," Lulu said. "Phooey on the data. We are off star-wandering. We are searching out the depths of silence. We are racing down the corridors of space with thunder in our brain—the ever-lasting thunder of a dread eternity."

We turned and looked at Jimmy.

"Every word of it," I said. "Every single word of it out of that muck he wrote."

Ben took a quick step forward and grabbed Jimmy by his shirt front.

"Don't you feel the urge," Ben asked him, "don't you feel a mighty impulse to write a lengthy ode to home—its comfort and its glory and all the other clichés?"

Jimmy's teeth were chattering just a little.

"Lulu is a sucker," Ben said, "for everything you write."

I lifted a fist and let Jimmy smell of it.

"You better make it good," I warned him. "You better write like you never wrote before."

"But keep it sloppy," Ben said. "That's the way Lulu likes it."

Jimmy sat down on the floor and began writing desperately.

12. Neighbor

COON VALLEY is a pleasant place, but there's no denying it's sort of off the beaten track and it's not a place where you can count on getting rich because the farms are small and a lot of the ground is rough. You can farm the bottomlands, but the hillsides are only good for pasture and the roads are just dirt roads, impassable at certain times of year.

The old-timers, like Bert Smith and Jingo Harris and myself, are well satisfied to stay here, for we grew up with the country and we haven't any illusions about getting rich and we'd feel strange and out-of-place anywhere but in the valley. But there are others, newcomers, who move in and get discouraged after a while and up and move away, so there usually is a farm or two, standing idle, waiting to be sold.

We are just plain dirt farmers, with emphasis on the dirt, for we can't afford a lot of fancy machinery and we don't go in for blooded stock—but there's nothing wrong with us; we're just everyday, the kind of people you meet all over these United States. Because we're out of the way and some of the families have lived here for so long, I suppose you could say that we have gotten clannish. But that doesn't mean we don't like outside folks; it just means we've lived so long together that we've got to know and like one another and are satisfied with things just as they are.

We have radios, of course, and we listen to the programs and the news, and some of us take daily papers, but I'm afraid that we may be a bit provincial, for it's fairly hard to get us stirred up much about world happenings. There's so much of interest right here in the valley we haven't got the time to worry about all those outside things. I imagine you'd call us conservative, for most of us vote Republican without even wondering why and there's none of us who has much time for all this government interference in the farming business.

The valley has always been a pleasant place—not only the land, but the people in it, and we've always been fortunate in the new neighbors that we get. Despite new ones coming in every year or so, we've never had a really bad one and that means a lot to us.

But we always worry a little when one of the new ones up and moves away and we speculate among ourselves, wondering what kind of people will buy or rent the vacant farm.

The old Lewis farm had been abandoned for a long time, the buildings all run down and gone to ruin and the fields gone back to grass. A dentist over at Hopkins Corners had rented it for several years and run some cattle in it, driving out on week ends to see how they were doing. We used to wonder every now and then if anyone would ever farm the place again, but finally we quit wondering, for the buildings had fallen into such disrepair that we figured no one ever would. I went in one day and talked to the banker at Hopkins Corners, who had the renting of the place, and told him I'd like to take it over if the dentist ever gave it up. But he told me the owners, who lived in Chicago then, were anxious to sell rather than to rent it, although he didn't seem too optimistic that anyone would buy it.

Then one spring a new family moved onto the farm and in time we learned it had been sold and that the new family's name was Heath —Reginald Heath. And Bert Smith said to me: "Reginald! That's a hell of a name for a farmer!" But that was all he said.

Jingo Harris stopped by one day, coming home from town, when he saw Heath out in the yard, to pass the time of day. It was a neighborly thing to do, of course, and Heath seemed glad to have him stop, although Jingo said he seemed to be a funny kind of man to be a farmer.

"He's a foreigner," Jingo told me. "Sort of dark. Like he might be a Spaniard or from one of those other countries. I don't know how he got that Reginald. Reginald is English and Heath's no Englishman."

Later on we heard that the Heaths weren't really Spanish, but were Rumanians or Bulgarians and that they were refugees from the Iron Curtain.

But Spanish, or Rumanian, or Bulgarian, the Heaths were workers. There was Heath and his wife and a half-grown girl and all three of them worked all the blessed time. They paid attention to their business and didn't bother anyone and because of this we liked them, although we didn't have much to do with them. Not that we didn't want to or that they didn't want us to; it's just that in a community like ours new folks sort of have to grow in instead of being taken in.

Heath had an old beaten-up, wired-together tractor that made a lot of noise, and as soon as the soil was dry enough to plow he started out to turn over the fields that through the years had grown up to grass. I used to wonder if he worked all night long, for many times when I went to bed I heard the tractor running. Although that may not be as late as it sounds to city dwellers, for here in the valley we go to bed early—and get up early, too.

One night after dark I set out to hunt some cows, a couple of fence-jumping heifers that gave me lots of trouble. Just let a man come in late from work and tired and maybe it's raining a little and dark as the inside of a cat and those two heifers would turn up missing and I'd have to go and hunt them. I tried all the different kinds of pokes and none of them did any good. When a heifer gets to fence-jumping there isn't much that can be done with her.

So I lit a lantern and set out to hunt for them, but I hunted for two hours and didn't find a trace of them. I had just about decided to give up and go back home when I heard the sound of a tractor running and realized that I was just above the west field of the old Lewis place. To get home I'd have to go right past the field and I figured it might be as well to wait when I reached the field until the tractor came around and ask Heath if he had seen the heifers.

It was a dark night, with thin clouds hiding the stars and a wind blowing high in the treetops and there was a smell of rain in the air. Heath, I figured, probably was staying out extra late to finish up the field ahead of the coming rain, although I remember that I thought he was pushing things just a little hard. Already he was far ahead of all the others in the valley with his plowing.

So I made my way down the steep hillside and waded the creek at a shallow place I knew and while I was doing this I heard the tractor make a complete round of the field. I looked for the headlight, but I didn't see it and I thought probably the trees had hidden it from me.

I reached the edge of the field and climbed through the fence, walking out across the furrows to intercept the tractor. I heard it make the turn to the east of me and start down the field toward me and although I could hear the noise of it, there wasn't any light.

I found the last furrow and stood there waiting, sort of wondering, not too alarmed as yet, how Heath managed to drive the rig without any light. I thought that maybe he had cat eyes and could see in the dark and although it seemed funny later when I remembered it, the idea that a man might have cat eyes did not seem funny then.

The noise kept getting louder and it seemed to be coming pretty close, when all at once the tractor rushed out of the dark and seemed to leap at me. I guess I must have been afraid that it would run over me, for I jumped back a yard or two, with my heart up in my neck. But I needn't have bothered, for I was out of the way to start with.

The tractor went on past me and I waved the lantern and yelled for Heath to stop and as I waved the lantern the light was thrown onto the rear of the tractor and I saw that there was no one on it.

A hundred things went through my mind, but the one idea that stuck was that Heath had fallen off the tractor and might be lying injured, somewhere in the field.

I ran after the tractor, thinking to shut it down before it got loose and ran into a tree or something, but by the time I reached it, it had reached a turn and it was making that turn as neatly as if it had been broad daylight and someone had been driving it.

I jumped up on the drawbar and grabbed the seat, hauling myself up. I reached out a hand, grabbing for the throttle, but with my hand upon the metal I didn't pull it back. The tractor had completed the turn now and was going down the furrow—and there was something else.

Take an old tractor, now—one that wheezed and coughed and hammered and kept threatening to fall apart, like this one did—and you are bound to get a lot of engine vibration. But in this tractor there was no vibration. It ran along as smooth as a high-priced car and the only jolts you got were when the wheels hit a bump or slight gully in the field.

I stood there, hanging onto the lantern with one hand and clutching the throttle with the other, and I didn't do a thing. I just rode down to the point where the tractor started to make another turn. Then I stepped off and went on home. I didn't hunt for Heath lying in the field, for I knew he wasn't there.

I suppose I wondered how it was possible, but I didn't really fret myself too much trying to figure it all out. I imagine, in the first place, I was just too numb. You may worry a lot about little things that don't seem quite right, but when you run into a big thing, like that self-operating tractor, you sort of give up automatically, knowing that it's too big for your brain to handle, that it's something you haven't got a chance of solving. And after a while you forget it because it's something you can't live with. So your mind rejects it.

I got home and stood out in the barnyard for a moment, listening. The wind was blowing fairly hard by then and the first drops of rain were falling, but every now and then, when the wind would quiet down, I could hear the tractor.

I went inside the house and Helen and the kids were all in bed and sound asleep, so I didn't say anything about it that night. And the next morning, when I had a chance to think about it, I didn't say anything at all. Mostly, I suppose, because I knew no one would believe me and that I'd have to take a lot of kidding about automatic tractors.

Heath got his plowing done and his crops in, well ahead of everyone in the valley. The crops came up in good shape and we had good growing weather; then along in June we got a spell of wet, and everyone got behind with corn plowing because you can't go out in the field when the ground is soggy. All of us chored around our places, fixing fences and doing other odd jobs, cussing out the rain and watching the weeds grow like mad in the unplowed field.

All of us, that is, except Heath. His corn was clean as a whistle and you had to hunt to find a weed. Jingo stopped by one day and asked him how he managed, but Heath just laughed a little, in that quiet way of his, and talked of something else.

The first apples finally were big enough for green-apple pies and there is no one in the county makes better green-apple pies than Helen. She wins prizes with her pies every year at the county fair and she is proud of them.

One day she wrapped up a couple of pies and took them over to the Heaths. It's a neighborly way we have of doing in the valley, with the women running back and forth from one neighbor to another with their cooking. Each of them has some dish she likes to show off to the neighbors and it's a sort of harmless way of bragging.

Helen and the Heaths got along just swell. She was late in getting home and I was starting supper, with the kids yelling they were hungry when-do-we-eat-around-here, when she finally showed up.

She was full of talk about the Heaths—how they had fixed up the house, you never would have thought anyone could do so much to such a terribly run-down place as they had, and about the garden they had—especially about the garden. It was a big one, she said, and beautifully taken care of and it was full of vegetables she had never seen before. The funniest things you ever saw, she said. Not the ordinary kind of vegetables.

We talked some about those vegetables, speculating that maybe the Heaths had brought the seeds out with them from behind the Iron Curtain, although so far as I could remember, vegetables were vegetables, no matter where you were. They grew the same things in Russia or Rumania or Timbuktu as we did. And, anyhow, by this time I was getting a little skeptical about that story of their escaping from Rumania.

But we didn't have the time for much serious speculation on the Heaths, although there was plenty of casual gossip going around the neighborhood. Haying came along and then the small-grain harvest and everyone was busy. The hay was good and the small-grain crop was fair, but it didn't look like we'd get much corn. For we hit a drought. That's the way it goes—too much rain in June, not enough in August.

We watched the corn and watched the sky and felt hopeful when a cloud showed up, but the clouds never meant a thing. It just seems at times that God isn't on your side.

Then one morning Jingo Harris showed up and stood around, first on one foot, then the other, talking to me while I worked on an old corn binder that was about worn out and which it didn't look nohow I'd need to use that year.

"Jingo," I said, after I'd watched him fidget for an hour or more, "you got something on your mind."

He blurted it out then. "Heath got rain last night," he said.

"No one else did," I told him.

"I guess you're right," said Jingo. "Heath's the only one."

He told me how he'd gone to cut through Heath's north cornfield, carrying back a couple of balls of binder twine he'd borrowed from Bert Smith. It wasn't until he'd crawled through the fence that he noticed the field was wet, soaked by a heavy rain.

"It must have happened in the night," he said.

He thought it was funny, but figured maybe there had been a shower across the lower end of the valley, although as a rule rains travel up and down the valley, not across it. But when he had crossed the corner of the field and crawled through the fence, he noticed it hadn't rained at all. So he went back and walked around the field and the rain had fallen on the field, but nowhere else. It began at the fence and ended at the fence.

When he'd made a circuit of the field he sat down on one of the balls of twine and tried to get it all thought out, but it made no sense—furthermore, it was plain unbelievable.

Jingo is a thorough man. He likes to have all the evidence and know all there is to know before he makes up his mind. So he went over to Heath's second corn patch, on the west side of the valley. And once again he found that it had rained on that field—on the field, but not around the field.

"What do you make of it?" Jingo asked me and I said I didn't know. I came mighty close to telling him about the unmanned tractor, but I thought better of it. After all, there was no point in getting the neighborhood stirred up.

After Jingo left I got in the car and drove over to the Heath farm, intending to ask him if he could loan me his posthole digger for a day or two. Not that I was going to dig any postholes, but you have to have some excuse for showing up at a neighbor's place.

I never got a chance to ask him for that posthole digger, though. Once I got there I never even thought of it.

Heath was sitting on the front steps of the porch and he seemed glad to see me. He came down to the car and shook my hand and said, "It's good to see you, Calvin." The way he said it made me feel friendly and sort of important, too—especially that Calvin business, for everyone else just calls me Cal. I'm not downright sure, in fact, that anyone in the neighborhood remembers that my name is Calvin.

"I'd like to show you around the place," he said. "We've done some fixing up."

Fixing up wasn't exactly the word for it. The place was spick-and-span. It looked like some of those Pennsylvania and Connecticut farms you see in the magazines. The house and all the other buildings had been ramshackle with all the paint peeled off them and looking as if they might fall down at any minute. But now they had a sprightly, solid look and they gleamed with paint. They didn't look new, of course, but they looked as if they'd always been well taken care of and painted every year. The fences were all fixed up and painted, too, and the weeds were cut and a couple of old unsightly scrap-lumber piles had been cleaned up and burned. Heath had even tackled an old iron and machinery junk pile and had it sorted out.

"There was a lot to do," said Heath, "but I feel it's worth it. I have an orderly soul. I like to have things neat."

Which might be true, of course, but he'd done it all in less than six months' time. He'd come to the farm in early March and it was only August and he'd not only put in some hundred acres of crops and done all the other farm work, but he'd got the place fixed up. And that wasn't possible, I told myself. One man couldn't do it, not even with his wife and daughter helping—not even if he worked twenty-four hours a day and didn't stop to eat. Or unless he could take time and stretch it out to make one hour equal three or four.

I trailed along behind Heath and thought about that time-stretching business and was pleased at myself for thinking of it, for it isn't often that I get foolish thoughts that are likewise pleasing. Why, I thought, with a deal like that you could stretch out any day so you could get all the work done you wanted to. And if you could stretch out time, maybe you could compress it, too, so that a trip to a dentist, for example, would only seem to take a minute.

Heath took me out to the garden and Helen had been right. There were the familiar vegetables, of course—cabbages and tomatoes and squashes and all the other kinds that are found in every garden—but in addition to this there were as many others I had never seen before. He told me the names of them and they seemed to be queer names then, although now it seems a little strange to think they once had sounded queer, for now everyone in the valley grows these vegetables and it seems like we have always had them.

As we talked he pulled up and picked some of the strange vegetables and put them in a basket he had brought along.

"You'll want to try them all," he said. "Some of them you may not like at first, but there are others that you will. This one you eat raw, sliced like a tomato, and this one is best boiled, although you can bake it, too—"

I wanted to ask him how he'd come on the vegetables and where they had come from, but he didn't give me a chance; he kept on telling me about them and how to cook them and that this one was a winter keeper and that one you could can and he gave me one to eat raw and it was rather good.

We'd got to the far end of the garden and were starting to come back when Heath's wife ran around the corner of the house.

Apparently she didn't see me at first or had forgotten I was there, for she called to him and the name she called him wasn't Reginald or

Reggie, but a foreign-sounding name. I won't even try to approximate it, for even at the time I wasn't able to recall it a second after hearing it. It was like no word I'd ever heard before.

Then she saw me and stopped running and caught her breath, and a moment later said she'd been listening in on the party line and that Bert Smith's little daughter, Ann, was terribly sick.

"They called the doctor," she said, "but he is out on calls and he won't get there in time."

"Reginald," she said, "the symptoms sound like–"

And she said another name that was like none I'd ever heard or expect to hear again.

Watching Heath's face, I could swear I saw it pale despite his olive tinge of skin.

"Quick!" he shouted and grabbed me by the arm.

We ran around in front to his old clunk of a car. He threw the basket of vegetables in the back seat and jumped behind the wheel. I scrambled in after him and tried to close the door, but it wouldn't close. The lock kept slipping loose and I had to hang onto the door so it wouldn't bang.

We lit out of there like a turpentined dog and the noise that old car made was enough to deafen one. Despite my holding onto it, the door kept banging and all the fenders rattled and there was every other kind of noise you'd expect a junk-heap car to make, with an extra two or three thrown in.

I wanted to ask him what he planned to do, but I was having trouble framing the question in my mind and even if I had known how to phrase it I doubt he could have heard me with all the racket that the car was making.

So I hung on as best I could and tried to keep the door from banging and all at once it seemed to me the car was making more noise than it had any call to. Just like the old haywire tractor made more noise than any tractor should. Too much noise, by far, for the way that it was running. Just like on the tractor, there was no engine vibration and despite all the banging and the clanking we were making time. As I've said, our valley roads are none too good, but even so I swear there were places we hit seventy and we went around sharp corners where, by rights, we should have gone into the ditch at the speed that we were going, but the car just seemed to settle down and hug the road and we never even skidded.

We pulled up in front of Bert's place and Heath jumped out and ran up the walk, with me following him.

Amy Smith came to the door and I could see that she'd been crying, and she looked a little surprised to see the two of us.

We stood there for a moment without saying anything, then Heath spoke to her and here is a funny thing: Heath was wearing a pair of ragged overalls and a sweat-stained shirt and he didn't have a hat and his hair was all rumpled up, but there was a single instant when it seemed to me that he was well-dressed in an expensive business suit and that he took off his hat and bowed to Amy.

"I understand," he said, "that the little girl is sick. Maybe I can help."

I don't know if Amy had seen the same thing that I had seemed to see, but she opened the door and stood to one side so that we could enter.

"In there," she said.

"Thank you, ma'am," said Heath, and went into the room.

Amy and I stood there for a moment, then she turned to me and I could see the tears in her eyes again.

"Cal, she's awful sick," she said.

I nodded miserably, for now the spell was gone and common sense was coming back again and I wondered at the madness of this farmer who thought that he could help a little girl who was terribly sick. And at my madness for standing there, without even going in the room with him.

But just then Heath came out of the room and closed the door softly behind him.

"She's sleeping now," he said to Amy. "She'll be all right."

Then, without another word, he walked out of the door. I hesitated a moment, looking at Amy, wondering what to do. And it was pretty plain there was nothing I could do. So I followed him.

We drove back to his farm at a sober rate of speed, but the car banged and thumped just as bad as ever.

"Runs real good," I yelled at him.

He smiled a bit.

"I keep it tinkered up," he yelled back at me.

When we got to his place, I got out of his car and walked over to my own.

"You forgot the vegetables," he called after me.

So I went back to get them.

"Thanks a lot," I said.

"Any time," he told me.

I looked straight at him, then, and said: "It sure would be fine if we could get some rain. It would mean a lot to us. A soaking rain right now would save the corn."

"Come again," he told me. "It was good to talk with you."

And that night it rained, all over the valley, a steady, soaking rain, and the corn was saved.

And Ann got well.

The doctor, when he finally got to Bert's, said that she had passed the crisis and was already on the mend. One of those virus things, he said. A lot of it around. Not like the old days, he said, before they got to fooling around with all their miracle drugs, mutating viruses right and left. Used to be, he said, a doctor knew what he was treating, but he don't know any more.

I don't know if Bert or Amy told Doc about Heath, although I imagine that they didn't. After all, you don't tell a doctor that a neighbor cured your child. And there might have been someone who would have been ornery enough to try to bring a charge against Heath for practicing medicine without a license, although that would have been pretty hard to prove. But the story got around the valley and there was a lot of talk. Heath, I heard, had been a famous doctor in Vienna before he'd made his getaway. But I didn't believe it. I don't even believe those who started the story believed it, but that's the way it goes in a neighborhood like ours.

That story, and others, made quite a flurry for a month or so, but then it quieted down and you could see that the Heaths had become one of us and belonged to the valley. Bert went over and had quite a talk with Heath and the women-folks took to calling Mrs. Heath on the telephone, with some of those who were listening in breaking in to say a word or two, thereby initiating Mrs. Heath into the round-robin telephone conversations that are going on all the time on our valley party line, with it getting so that you have to bust in on them and tell them to get off the line when you want to make an important call. We had Heath out with us on our coon hunts that fall and some of the young bloods started paying attention to Heath's daughter. It was almost as if the Heaths were old-time residents.

As I've said before, we've always been real fortunate in getting in good neighbors.

When things are going well, time has a way of flowing along so smoothly that you aren't conscious of its passing, and that was the way it was in the valley.

We had good years, but none of us paid much attention to that. You don't pay much attention to the good times, you get so you take them for granted. It's only when bad times come along that you look back and realize the good times you have had.

A year or so ago I was just finishing up the morning chores when a car with a New York license pulled up at the barnyard gate. It isn't very often we see an out-of-state license plate in the valley, so I figured that it probably was someone who had gotten lost and had stopped to ask directions. There was a man and woman in the front seat and three kids and a dog in the back seat and the car was new and shiny.

I was carrying the milk up from the barn and when the man got out I put the pails down on the ground and waited for him.

He was a youngish sort of fellow and he looked intelligent and he had good manners.

He told me his name was Rickard and that he was a New York newspaperman on vacation and had dropped into the valley on his way out west to check some information.

It was the first time, so far as I knew, that the valley had ever been of any interest newswise and I said so. I said we never did much here to get into the news.

"It's no scandal," Rickard told me, "if that is what you're thinking. It's just a matter of statistics."

There are a lot of times when I don't catch a situation as quickly as I should, being a sort of deliberate type, but it seems to me now that as soon as he said statistics I could see it coming.

"I did a series of farm articles a few months back," said Rickard, "and to get my information I had to go through a lot of government statistics. I never got so sick of anything in my entire life."

"And?" I asked, not feeling too well myself.

"I found some interesting things about this valley," he went on. "I remember that I didn't catch it for a while. Went on past the figures for a ways. Almost missed the significance, in fact. Then I did a double-take and backed up and looked at them again. The full story wasn't in that report, of course. Just a hint of something. So I did some more digging and came up with other facts."

I tried to laugh it off, but he wouldn't let me.

"Your weather, for one thing," he said. "Do you realize you've had perfect weather for the past ten years?"

"The weather's been pretty good," I admitted.

"It wasn't always good. I went back to see."

"That's right," I said. "It's been better lately."

"Your crops have been the best they've ever been in the last ten years."

"Better seed," I said. "Better ways of farming."

He grinned at me. "You guys haven't changed your way of farming in the last quarter century."

And he had me there, of course.

"There was an army worm invasion two years ago," he said. "It hit all around you, but you got by scot-free."

"We were lucky. I remember we said so at the time."

"I checked health records," he said. "Same thing once again. For ten solid years. No measles, no chickenpox, no pneumonia. No nothing. One death in ten full years—complications attendant on old age."

"Old Man Parks," I said. "He was going onto ninety. Fine old gentleman."

"You see," said Rickard.

I did see.

The fellow had the figures. He had tracked it down, this thing we hadn't even realized, and he had us cold.

"What do you want me to do about it?" I asked.

"I want to talk to you about a neighbor."

"I won't talk about any of my neighbors. Why don't you talk to him yourself?"

"I tried to, but he wasn't home. Fellow down the road said he'd gone into town. Whole family had gone into town."

"Reginald Heath," I said. There wasn't much sense in playing dumb with Rickard, for he knew all the angles.

"That's the man. I talked to folks in town. Found out he'd never had to have any repair work done on any of his machinery or his car. Has the same machinery he had when he started farming. And it was worn out then."

"He takes good care of it," I told him. "He keeps it tinkered up."

"Another thing," said Rickard. "Since he's been here he hasn't bought a drop of gasoline."

I'd known the rest of it, of course, although I'd never stopped to think about it. But I didn't know about the gasoline. I must have shown my surprise, for Rickard grinned at me.

"What do you want?" I asked.

"A story."

"Heath's the man to talk to. I don't know a thing to help you."

And even when I said it I felt easy in my mind. I seemed to have an instinctive faith that Heath could handle the situation, that he'd know just what to do.

But after breakfast I couldn't settle down to work. I was pruning the orchard, a job I'd been putting off for a year or two and that badly needed doing. I kept thinking of that business of Heath not buying gasoline and that night I'd found the tractor plowing by itself and how smooth both the car and tractor ran despite all the noise they made.

So I laid down my pruning hook and shears and struck out across the fields. I knew the Heath family was in town, but I don't think it would have made any difference to me if they'd been at home. I think I would have gone just the same. For more than ten years now, I realized, I'd been wondering about that tractor and it was time that I found out.

I found the tractor in the machine shed and I thought maybe I'd have some trouble getting into it. But I didn't have a bit. I slipped the catches and the hood lifted up and I found exactly what I had thought I'd find, except that I hadn't actually worked out in my mind the picture of what I'd find underneath that hood.

It was just a block of some sort of shining metal that looked almost like a cube of heavy glass. It wasn't very big, but it had a massive look about it, as if it might have been a heavy thing to lift.

You could see the old bolt holes where the original internal combustion engine had been mounted and a heavy piece of some sort of metal had been fused across the frame to seat that little power plant. And up above the shiny cube was an apparatus of some sort. I didn't take the time to find out how it worked, but I could see that it was connected to the exhaust and I knew it was a dingus that disguised the power plant. You know how in electric trains they have it fixed up so that the locomotive goes *chuff-chuff* and throws out a stream of smoke. Well, that was what that contraption was. It threw out little puffs of smoke and made a tractor noise.

I stood there looking at it and I wondered why it was, if Heath had an engine that worked better than an internal combustion engine, he should have gone to so much trouble to hide the fact he had it. If I'd had a thing like that, I knew, I'd make the most of it. I'd get someone to back me and go into production and in no time at all I'd be stinking rich. And there'd been nothing in the world to prevent Heath from doing that. But instead he'd fixed the tractor so it looked and sounded like an ordinary tractor and he'd fixed his car to make so much noise that it hid the fact it had a new type motor. Only he had overdone it. He'd made both the car and tractor make more noise than they should. And he'd missed an important bet in not buying gasoline. In his place I'd bought the stuff, just the way you should, and thrown it away or burned it to get rid of it.

It almost seemed to me that Heath might have had something he was hiding all these years, that he'd tried deliberately to keep himself unnoticed. As if he might really have been a refugee from the Iron Curtain—or from somewhere else.

I put the hood back in place again and snapped the catches shut and when I went out I was very careful to shut the machine shed door securely.

I went back to my pruning and I did quite a bit of thinking and while I was doing it I realized that I'd been doing this same thinking, piecemeal, ever since that night I'd found the tractor running by itself. Thinking of it in snatches and not trying to correlate all my thinking and that way it hadn't added up to much, but now it did and I suppose I should have been a little scared.

But I wasn't scared. Reginald Heath was a neighbor, and a good one, and we'd gone hunting and fishing together and we'd helped one another with haying and threshing and one thing and another and I liked the man as well as anyone I had ever known. Sure, he was a little different and he had a funny kind of tractor and a funny kind of car and he might even have a way of stretching time and since he'd come into the valley we'd been fortunate in weather and in health. All true, of course, but nothing to be scared of. Nothing to be scared of, once you knew the man.

For some reason or other I remembered the time several years before when I'd dropped by of a summer evening. It was hot and the Heath family had brought chairs out on the lawn because it was cooler there. Heath got me a chair and we sat and talked, not about anything in particular, but whatever came into our heads.

There was no moon, but there were a lot of stars and they were the prettiest I have ever seen them.

I called Heath's attention to them and, just shooting off my mouth, I told him what little I'd picked up about astronomy.

"They're a long ways off," I said. "So far off that their light takes years to reach us. And all of them are suns. A lot of them bigger than our sun."

Which was about all I knew about the stars.

Heath nodded gravely.

"There's one up there," he said, "that I watch a lot. That blue one, over there. Well, sort of blue, anyhow. See it? See how it twinkles. Like it might be winking at us. A friendly sort of star."

I pretended that I saw the one he was pointing at, although I wasn't sure I did, there were so many of them and a lot of them were twinkling.

Then we got to talking about something else and forgot about the stars. Or at least I did.

Right after supper, Bert Smith came over and said that Rickard had been around asking him some questions and that he'd been down to Jingo's place and that he'd said he'd see Heath just as soon as Heath got back from town.

Bert was a bit upset about it, so I tried to calm him down.

"These city folks get excited easy," I told him. "There's nothing to it."

I didn't worry much about it because I felt sure that Heath could handle things and even if Rickard did write a story for the New York papers it wouldn't bother us. Coon Valley is a long piece from New York.

I figured we'd probably seen and heard the last from Rickard.

But in all my life, I've never been more wrong.

About midnight or so I woke up with Helen shaking me.

"There's someone at the door," she said. "Go see who it is."

So I shucked into my overalls and shoes and lit the lamp and went downstairs to see.

While I'd been getting dressed there'd been some knocking at the door, but as soon as I lit the lamp it quit.

I went to the door and opened it and there stood Rickard and he wasn't near as chipper as he'd been in the morning.

"Sorry to get you up," he said, "but it seems that I'm lost."

"You can't be lost," I told him. "There isn't but one road through the valley. One end of it ties up to Sixty and the other to Eighty-five.

You follow the valley road and you're bound to hit one or the other of them."

"I've been driving," he told me, "for the last four hours and I can't find either of them."

"Look," I said, "all you do is drive one way or the other. You can't get off the road. Fifteen minutes either way and you're on a state highway."

I was exasperated with him, for it seemed a silly thing to do. And I don't take kindly to being routed out at midnight.

"But I tell you I'm lost," he said in a sort of desperation and I could see that he was close to panic. "The wife is getting scared and the kids are dead on their feet—"

"All right," I told him. "Let me get on my shirt and tie my shoes. I'll get you out of here."

He told me he wanted to get to Sixty, so I got out my car and told him to follow me. I was pretty sore about it, but I figured the only thing to do was to help him out. He'd upset the valley and the sooner out the better.

I drove for thirty minutes before I began to get confused myself. That was twice as long as it should have taken to get out to the highway. But the road looked all right and there seemed to be nothing wrong, except for the time it took. So I kept on going. At the end of forty-five minutes we were back in front of my place again.

I couldn't figure it out for the life of me. I got out of my car and went back to Rickard's car.

"You see what I mean," he said.

"We must have got turned around," I said.

His wife was almost hysterical.

"What's going on?" she asked me in a high, shrill voice. "What is going on around here?"

"We'll try again," I said. "We'll drive slower this time so we don't make the same mistake."

I drove slower and this time it took an hour to get back to the farm. So we tried for Eighty-five and forty minutes later were right back where we started.

"I give up," I told them. "Get out and come in. We'll fix up some beds. You can spend the night and we'll get you out come light."

I cooked up some coffee and found stuff to make sandwiches while Helen fixed up beds to take care of the five of them.

"The dog can sleep out here in the kitchen," she said.

I got an apple box and quilt and fixed the dog a bed.

The dog was a nice little fellow, a wirehair who was full of fun, and the Rickard kids were about as fine a bunch of kids as you'd find anywhere.

Mrs. Rickard was all set to have hysterics, but Helen got her to drink some coffee and I wouldn't let them talk about not being able to get out.

"Come daylight," I told them, "and there'll be nothing to it."

After breakfast they were considerably calmed down and seemed to have no doubt they could find Number Sixty. So they started out alone, but in an hour were back again. I took my car and started out ahead of them and I don't mind admitting I could feel bare feet walking up and down my spine.

I watched closely and all at once I realized that somehow we were headed back into the valley instead of heading out of it. So I stopped the car and we turned our cars around and headed back in the right direction. But in ten minutes we were turned around again. We tried again and this time we fairly crawled, trying to spot the place where we got turned around. But we could never spot it.

We went back to my place and I called up Bert and Jingo and asked them to come over.

Both of them tried to lead the Rickards out, one at a time, then the two of them together, but they were no better at it than I was. Then I tried it alone, without the Rickards following me, and I had no trouble at all. I was out to highway Sixty and back in half an hour. So we thought maybe the jinx was broken and I tried to lead out the Rickard car, but it was no soap.

By midafternoon we knew the answer. Any of the natives could get out of the valley, but the Rickards couldn't.

Helen put Mrs. Rickard to bed and fed her some sedative and I went over to see Heath.

He was glad to see me and he listened to me, but all the time I was talking to him I kept remembering how one time I had wondered if maybe he could stretch out time. When I had finished he was silent for a while, as if he might have been going over some decision just to be certain that it was right.

"It's a strange business, Calvin," he said finally, "and it doesn't seem right the Rickards should be trapped in this valley if they don't want to stay here.

"Yet, it's a fortunate thing for us, actually. Rickard was planning on writing a story about us and if he'd written as he planned to, there'd been a lot of attention paid us. There would have been a crowd of people coming in—other newspapermen and government men and people from the universities and the idly curious. They'd have upset our lives and some of them would have offered us big sums of money for our farms, much more than they're worth, and all of it would spoil the valley for us. I don't know about you, but I like the valley as it is. It reminds me of . . . well, of another place."

"Rickard still can telephone that story," I told him, "or he can mail it out. Just keeping Rickard here won't prevent that story being printed."

"Somehow I think it will," he said. "I am fairly certain he won't telephone it or send it in the mails."

I had come half prepared to go to bat for Rickard, but I thought over what Heath had pointed out to me and I didn't do it.

I saw that if there were some principle or power which kept the valley healthy and insured good weather and made living pleasant, why, then, the rest of the world would be hell-bent to use the same principle or power. It might have been selfish of me, but I felt fairly certain the principle or power couldn't be spread thin enough to cover all the world. And if anyone were to have it, I wanted it kept right here, where it rightfully belonged.

And there was another thing: If the world should learn there was such a power or principle and if we couldn't share it or refused to share it, then all the world would be sore at us and we'd live in the center of a puddle of hatred.

I went back home and had a talk with Rickard and I didn't try to hide anything from him. He was all set to go and have it out with Heath, but I advised against it. I pointed out that he didn't have a shred of proof and he'd only make himself look silly, for Heath would more than likely act as if he didn't know what he was getting at. After quite a tussle, he took my advice.

The Rickards stayed on at our place for several days and occasionally Rickard and I would make a trial run just to test the situation out, but there was no change.

Finally Bert and Jingo came over and we had a council of war with the Rickard family. By this time Mrs. Rickard was taking it somewhat better and the Rickard kids were happy with the outdoor life and the Rickard dog was busily engaged in running all the valley rabbits down to skin and bones.

"There's the old Chandler place up at the head of the valley," said Jingo. "No one's been living there for quite a while, but it's in good shape. It could be fixed up so it was comfortable."

"But I can't stay here," protested Rickard. "I can't settle down here."

"Who said anything about settling down?" asked Bert. "You just got to wait it out. Some day whatever is wrong will get straightened out and then you can get away."

"But my job," said Rickard.

Mrs. Rickard spoke up then. You could see she didn't like the situation any better than he did, but she had that queer, practical, everyday logic that a woman at times surprises a man by showing. She knew that they were stuck here in the valley and she was out to make the best of it.

"Remember that book you're always threatening to write?" she asked. "Maybe this is it."

That did it.

Rickard mooned around for a while, making up his mind, although it already was made up. Then he began talking about the peace in the valley—the peace and quietness and the lack of hurry—just the place to write a book.

The neighbors got together and fixed up the house on the old Chandler place and Rickard called his office and made some excuse and got a leave of absence and wrote a letter to his bank, transferring whatever funds he had. Then he settled down to write.

Apparently in his phone calls and his letter writing he never even hinted at the real reason for his staying—perhaps because it would have sounded downright silly—for there was no ruckus over his failure to go back.

The valley settled down to its normal life again and it felt good after all the uproar. The neighbors shopped for the Rickards and carried out from town all the groceries and other things they needed and once in a while Rickard took the car and had a try at finding the state highways.

But mostly he wrote and in about a year he sold this book of his. Probably you have read it: *You Could Hear the Silence*. Made him a hunk of money. But his New York publishers still are going slowly mad trying to understand why he steadfastly refuses to stir out of the valley. He has refused lecture tours, has declined dinners in his honor and turned down all the other glitter that goes with writing a best seller.

The book didn't change Rickard at all. By the time he sold it he was well liked in the valley and seemed to like everyone–except possibly Heath. He stayed rather cold to Heath. He used to do a lot of walking, to get exercise, he said, although I think that he thought up most of his book out on those walks. And he'd stop by and chew the fat when he was out on those walks and that way everyone got to know him. He used to talk a lot about when he could get out of the valley and all of us were beginning to feel sorry that a time would come when he would leave, for the Rickards had turned out to be good neighbors. There must be something about the valley that brings out the best there is in everyone. As I have said before, we have yet to get a bad neighbor and that is something most neighborhoods can't say.

One day I had stopped on my way from town to talk a while with Heath and as we stood talking, up the road came Rickard. You could see he wasn't going anywhere, but was just out for a walk.

He stopped and talked with us for a few minutes, then suddenly he said, "You know, we've made up our minds that we would like to stay here."

"Now, that is fine," said Heath.

"Grace and I were talking about it the other night," said Rickard. "About the time when we could get out of here. Then suddenly we stopped our talking and looked at one another and we knew right then and there we didn't want to leave. It's been so peaceful and the kids like the school here so much better than in the city and the people are so fine we couldn't bear to leave."

"I'm glad to hear you say that," Heath told him. "But it seems to me you've been sticking pretty close. You ought to take the wife and kids in town to see a show."

And that was it. It was as simple as all that.

Life goes on in the valley as it always has, except it's even better now. All of us are healthy. We don't even seem to get colds any more. When we need rain we get it and when there's need of sun the sun is sure to shine. We aren't getting rich, for you can't get rich with all this Washington interference, but we're making a right good living. Rickard is working on his second book and once in a while I go out at night and try to locate the star Heath showed me that evening long ago.

But we still get some publicity now and then. The other night I was listening to my favorite newscaster and he had an item he had a lot of fun with.

"Is there really such a place as Coon Valley?" he asked and you could hear the chuckle just behind the words. "If there is, the government would like to know about it. The maps insist there is and there are statistics on the books that say it's a place where there is no sickness, where the climate is ideal, where there's never a crop failure—a land of milk and honey. Investigators have gone out to seek the truth of this and they can't find the place, although people in nearby communities insist there's such a valley. Telephone calls have been made to people listed as residents of the valley, but the calls can't be completed. Letters have been written to them, but the letters are returned to the sender for one or another of the many reasons the post office has for nondelivery. Investigators have waited in nearby trading centers, but Coon Valley people never came to town while the investigators were there. If there is such a place and if the things the statistics say of it are true, the government would be very interested, for there must be data in the valley that could be studied and applied to other sectors. We have no way of knowing whether this broadcast can reach the valley—if it is any more efficient than investigators or telephone or the postal service. But if it does—and if there is such a place as Coon Valley—and if one of its residents should be listening, won't he please speak up!"

He chuckled then, chuckled very briefly, and went on to tell the latest rumor about Khrushchev.

I shut off the radio and sat in my chair and thought about the times when for several days no one could find his way out of the valley and of the other times when the telephones went dead for no apparent reason. And I remembered how we'd talked about it among ourselves and wondered if we should speak to Heath about it, but had in each case decided not to, since we felt that Heath knew what he was doing and that we could trust his judgment.

It's inconvenient at times, of course, but there are a lot of compensations. There hasn't been a magazine solicitor in the valley for more than a dozen years—nor an insurance salesman, either.